Decaying Days: Evolve

Decaying Days, Volume 2

Rachael Boucker

Published by Scratcher Publications, 2020.

This is a work of fiction. Similarities to real people, places, or events are entirely coincidental.

DECAYING DAYS: EVOLVE

First edition. January 12, 2020.

Copyright © 2020 Rachael Boucker.

ISBN: 978-1916306523

Written by Rachael Boucker.

As this monstrous story has grown, so has the support for its upbringing.

I would like to dedicate this book to Asiza, Becky, Laura, Richard, Rosie, and Zavier. Without you, I would have put this untamed monster into a cage and thrown away the key.

Anika West
31 years ago

... I write to you in desperation. Earlier today, Dr Davidson suggested the key to control may be found by testing on a live human. These past two years underground have warped him. I am afraid for myself and my colleagues, and urge you to send help.

Another distant cheer came from somewhere in the complex. Anika laid her weary head on her arms and groaned. "The resurrection of two corpses is nothing to celebrate," Anika mumbled. "Edgar lies in the infirmary while they raise their glasses." Delivery confirmations continued to pop up on the computer screen as Anika slipped into slumber.

Anika's email would pass unread, from Inbox to Inbox, before eventually finding an administrator who would act upon it. She was two weeks away from rescue and about to see the full depth of Davidson's ambition.

***

Dr Tobias Davidson uncorked the champagne and generously filled the glasses. They would drink to their success, not merely toast it. Irene Grey, Anne Meyers, Albert Tanner, Christian Forde, and Thomas Jonstone, his entire team was present, except for Edgar Trist. Davidson had noticed that his beloved Anika West was also missing. He presumed that she would blame her absence on the hormones. No matter, enough of the staff was present to start the celebrations.

"To us," Irene said with a smile and raised her glass. "I know I speak for everyone, when I say that the struggle has been worth it. Anything we did before, and anything we achieve in the future, will pale in comparison to what we have accomplished here today."

"Here, here," chimed the room. They all took a large swig of the champagne.

Davidson stood up and cleared his throat. "I want to thank you all for your substantial contributions to this formula. What happens next would not be possible without your continued involvement." He raised his glass once more. "To project Re-gen!"

"To project Re-gen!" They cheered, and gulped down more of the bubbly delight.

A smile spread across Davidson's lips as the realisation rippled through his colleagues. They dropped to the floor, slumped over tables, all of them succumbing to a sleep that would seal their fate.

"I will need you all for the next phase." Davidson's thin lips spread wider with maniacal joy. "I am so grateful for your contribution."

***

Anika spent the night in front of the computer, occasionally refreshing the screen in between snoozes. When morning came, she carried her heels and tiptoed through the structure in her stockings. The lights in the corridors were dimmed. *'That's strange,'* Anika thought. Regardless of the hour there was usually somebody working somewhere. Day and night lost all meaning in an underground bunker. *'They must have partied harder than I thought.'* That explanation was weak. Anika had heard a chorus of laughter and cheering early in the evening. The night had been silent after that.

Her padded footsteps, her breath, the swish of her skirt fabric, all of these sounds were uncontested in the silent corridors. The utility hatch was just ahead. She was the only one to venture out. Everyone else seemed to thrive in the clinical and sterile environment of the lab. Anika needed to feel the sun on her face and sift dirt through her fingers, needed a reminder of a world that existed outside of project Re-gen.

She climbed the metal rungs inside of the vertical shaft and opened the hatch. There was nothing clinical or sterile about the tropical forest that greeted her. Life flourished all around her, unrestrained, growing wild and diverse.

Anika found the pair of flats she had stashed near the hatch, slipped them on, and trekked through the wilderness to her favourite thinking spot. The leaves slid through her dancing fingers. Botany was her first love, and while she had an adept knowledge of human genetics, it was the anatomy of plants which had first quenched her scientific thirst.

She peeled a little bark off of a tree and rubbed its oozing milky sap into her face. It revitalised her skin and lightened the bags under her eyes.

She sat under that tree for some time feeling refreshed but troubled. *'Has the work I have done on Re-gen undone all the good I brought into the world? Can such an evil ever be quantified or counteracted?'*

Anika West had been the youngest member of the Scientific Initiative Alliance, before she met Tobias Davidson. It was her impetus that led to a breakthrough in fungus colonisation. The fungus strain she developed was edible, nutritionally complete, self multiplying, and could grow in the harshest of environments. *'The world may never go hungry again, but what use is that if Tobias's monsters are set free to devour it?'*

Anika crushed some vibrant flower petals, mixed the red colouring with the milky sap to make a lip stain, and dabbed it onto her pout.

She inhaled deeply, enjoying the fragrance and freshness of the air. The long grass blew around her. The trees grew tall and were filled with bird song, bright flowers and insects painted her jungle surroundings with colour, and the faint smell of salt on the breeze reminded her that the beach and the ocean were a short walk away.

'I could stay here forever, in ignorance and bliss.' She should have done just that. When she heard the wailing scream coming from the complex, she should have ran into the overgrowth, and lived off the land until help arrived, but she didn't. Anika picked up her heels and raced towards the unfamiliar wailing sound.

***

He floated somewhere between dazed and unconscious.

"Edgar, please, you need to wake up!"

"My, love," Edgar Trist mumbled. He reached out for his wife's honey coloured curls but found only air.

"Trist, we are in danger!" Anika tapped his left cheek. The yellow seepage pooling through the bandage on the right side of his face, told her everything she needed to know about his bite wound; it was badly infected.

There had been no question he would take part in project Re-gen, his wife had insisted that he go. "Dr Davidson, your idol, you must go." He remembered her beaming smile stretching her lips, plumping her cheeks, and brightening her eyes.

"But it will mean months if not years away from you," Edgar Trist said out loud. "I couldn't bear it."

"Your dream world must be lovely, Lord knows that it can't be worse than reality, but I need you to wake up. I can't survive this on my own." Anika slumped at his bedside. *'Why am I even trying? He's injured, septic, what use can this man be?'* Trist was still human, and she so badly needed another soul to fight in humanity's corner.

***

Three days earlier, Anika had run back from the jungle, through the utility hatch, into this maze of horror and madness.

She found Irene first, locked away in an observation room with the animated dead. They didn't attack Irene. They treated her as one of their own. The dead clawed and groaned against the window when they saw Anika, and Irene stood right beside them wailing and clawing. Anika stepped closer. Irene's breath misted on the glass, a pulse visibly thumped in her neck, and yet her living body was desperate to claw through the glass and kill Anika.

Irene was smarter than the dead. She tried the door handle, and even punched a code into the PIN pad. The door remained locked. Anika hoped that the code continued to elude her.

'An accident, a horrible accident,' that's what she thought at first, but then why were the lights still dimmed? Where was everyone else?

She found them one by one.

Albert was in one of the testing rooms with soundproof glass. There was no need to subtitle the silent violence he acted out in response to Anika's presence.

She found Thomas in the testing room next to Albert, alive, human, and frantically miming for her help from behind the window. Anika unlocked the door and set him free.

"My wrists, they're bound. You need to untie them."

Monstrous cries rang out and vibrated through Anika's skin. She dropped the scalpel twice before steadying her hands enough to cut through Thomas's ropes.

"Which is the quickest way out?" Thomas rubbed his wrists. His eyes darted from left to right. The corridor beyond the glass was so poorly lit they could make just about anything come to life in the shadows.

"Not everyone is accounted for, there could still be survivors."

"No, it's just us. We need to go now."

"We can't—"

"Help. Please, oh please. Lord of all, help me!" The screams devolved into sobs.

"Someone is still alive." Anika pushed passed Thomas.

"This is suicide." Despite his grumbling, Irene's echoing shrieks kept Thomas bound to her side.

"Help, they're eating my brain, in the name of the Lord, HELP ME!" Christian was in the office trying to scratch out the bugs he envisioned burrowing into his head. His skin was stretching and contorting. He morphed into something new, something with horns, tusks, and hooves. In shock and ignorance, Anika and Thomas ran, leaving Christian to mutate alone.

Christian's agonised yowls drowned out Anne's muffled cries for help, but Anika spotted her as they ran past.

"Leave her," Thomas said pulling on Anika's sleeve. "We don't have time."

Anika took back her arm and rammed the door. "It won't budge. We must smash the glass."

Thomas looked nervously around. He caught sight of Anne's pleading eyes, but they were not as swaying as the exit. "We should just go," he whispered.

"Help me get to Anne, and we'll all leave." Together they broke through the glass, and pulled Anne out, but if Thomas had helped from the start they would already have been on their way to the hatch when something else broke free.

Down the hall came the sound of more shattering glass, and Irene's monstrous wail. Anika and Thomas ran, dragging a whimpering Anne down the corridors. They ducked into the refectory, where there was food and water, but no escape.

They heard Christian barrel past. His heavy footfalls clubbed the floor and his gruff cries still mimicked calls for help.

"Davidson drugged us," Thomas whispered. "He put something in the champagne and used the formula on the others." A piercing wail rang out in the distance. "He must have meant it for us too."

They were immobile for a long time in the kitchen storeroom, huddled, and listening. The champagne glasses and uneaten snacks from last night's festivities still sat on the tables.

The refectory door slammed on the wall. Anika cracked the kitchen door and watched three figures prowling around tables and overturned chairs. Edgar Trist's browning blood stained the dead child. Irene was more thorough in her search, than her undead companions. Her eyes had become white. A shiver ran through Anika, it tried to emerge as a squeak, but she repressed it. This glimpse of Irene and her two zombie companions was enough to keep the survivors in hiding for hours. The fiends had searched and moved on, long before Anika checked and confirmed their absence.

Anika took Thomas and Anne by the hand, and as a hunched chain, they scuttled to the corridor.

"You can't hide." Davidson's voice echoed through many speakers, giving the impression that it was coming from multiple directions. *"I will find you."* His hubris was just what they needed.

"Quick," hissed Anika. "His voice will draw the monsters."

The darkened halls were enclosing. With no light at all on this side of the complex, the company's steps were slow and considered in the darkness.

Davidson's demonic calls echoed behind them, heavy footfalls thundered in front. Anika pulled the others into the nearest room and pushed the door to, not daring to click it shut. They were in Davidson's office. It was sterile and white like the rest of the complex. Everything in here was pristine and organised by an obsessive mind. That mind had now snapped. "Where are you, my dear?" Davidson continued to call. His voice didn't come through the speakers this time. He sounded close.

"There must be something in here to help us," Thomas said. He rummaged through files and drawers.

"Thomas, stop it, they'll hear you," Anne hissed.

"There's... No, it can't be. Communications have been down for months." Thomas threw the report. "Your boyfriend is a liar and a madman."

"He's not—" Anika started.

"The satellite phone!" Thomas pushed past and picked it up. "It's dead, there's not even a dial tone."

"I've already sent a message for help, it got through. We just have to wait."

"Tsk, all of this is giving me a damn headache. Are there any pills in here?" Thomas rummaged through more of Davidson's drawers.

"No, just stay calm."

"Ah, it hurts so much."

"Shut up, just shut up," Anne squeaked, hugging her knees and rocking. "The monsters will hear you."

They all hushed and listened to the steps rampaging down nearby corridors.

Again they remained hidden and cowering for longer than they needed to. Thomas's headache got worse as the endless hours drew on.

"You don't need to hide, my love," Davidson shouted on the second morning. "The injection I have here is for your child. Aren't you curious how a developing foetus will translate the formula in its DNA? You and I shall raise a miracle, Anika, together, just like you wanted."

Thomas's headache became so bad that Anika and Anne made him bite down on a ruler, to stop him from screaming out and giving away their location. Davidson's voice became distant once more. Anika and Anne cautiously ventured out, and half carried Thomas toward the infirmary, and the painkillers he needed.

"I can't go on," said Thomas. "Just leave me behind... hind... be... leave... behind."

Anika saw little in the perpetual darkness, but one of her senses alerted her to something just out of sight.

Thomas's shoulders relaxed, and he collapsed onto all fours. The headache had subsided and his body washed with relief.

Anika continued on towards the smell in the darkness. Her foot sloshed in something sticky and viscous.

"Thomas, are you all right?" Anne crouched down. She placed her hand under Thomas's chin and tilted his head forward.

Anika dared to explore the heap before her with her fingertips. There was fur, and horns, and blood. Entrails — that's what she could smell, that's what she now stood in. In front of her, hidden in the dark, lay the mutilated corpse of Christian Forde.

There was something wrong with Thomas's eyes, they were pale and inhuman. Anne stepped back. "Anika," she called. "I need help there is something wrong with—"

Thomas bit down hard into Anne's throat. Blood gushed from the lethal wound and Thomas feasted on it. Anika watched Anne die in slow motion, although in actuality it was over quickly.

A survival instinct kicked in and she ran, leaving Thomas to scream a wail that gargled with Anne's blood.

***

"That's how I ended up here. I ran, and the only route in my mind led to the infirmary, our destination before..." Anika wiped fresh tears from her cheeks. "I'm sorry, Edgar, to have forgotten about you. It wasn't intentional. How could it have been? You're the only one who treated me as an equal here, treated me like a friend."

She had been hiding out in the infirmary for a day. When she first found Trist, his saline bag was empty and fever was sweating out of him. She injected antibiotics and painkillers into his cannula and put up more saline, but her efforts came too late. His bandaged wound oozed with pus. All she could do now was pray (to a god she struggled to believe in) that he would wake up.

They were still out there. Thomas skulked down the corridors, making his whereabouts known with a wail, and Anne was out there too. Anika pushed aside the blind to look through the window in the door. There she was, dead, soaked in her own blood and yet she shuffled around. She was pitiful, not like the raging dead Anika had seen before. Anne was quiet and meek, slowly wandering without purpose. Occasionally, she would pause and sway on the spot. Anika wanted to call out to her, to offer her sanctuary, but the memory of that sweet child and how it turned on Edgar, stopped her from making such a foolish mistake.

She went back to Trist's side, shook his shoulders, and tapped his clammy left cheek for the hundredth time. "Please, Edgar, I don't want to die alone." His mumbles continued to be incoherent and unresponsive to her words.

Edgar Trist was septic, delirious, and edging closer to certain death. Anika West hid in an isolated complex, with a mad man and his abominations. It would be eleven days before someone rescued her, and she had locked herself in a room with no food, and a man who would soon be dead, and potentially ravenous.

Chapter 1: Tyde

Where are you? God damn it, I'm looking
for you, but you're just not fucking
here. Are you coming or not?
I'm alone with your dog on a yacht

Tyde said goodbye to Kronic and lumbered through the tree line with Cleaver towards his boat. Her belongings weighed him down. '*How much can one dog possibly need?*' he thought. Kronic's motorbike roared to life in the distance. Tyde turned and squinted through the trees, but he couldn't see his friend or the two wheeled beast that bore his tremendous weight.

He was alone, save for the furry companion who desperately pulled on her lead, trying to make her way back to Kronic. This was not a safe place to be alone anymore. Greenshore used to be an idyllic little seaside town. Ice cream had been sold on the pebbled beach to laughing children. People strolled, drinking in the scenery and ocean air. It was a place to de-stress and unwind.

Today, wails filled the air. The townspeople locked themselves in buildings, surviving on what meagre supplies they had squirrelled away. Few had anticipated the apocalypse. They should have done. A little over a year ago when the dead rose and living Wailers flaunted their cannibalistic tastes, a few people suspected that the world would be lost to rowed teeth and clawed hands, but the majority wholeheartedly believed in a cure. Dr Loralias Adder devised a serum, a miracle cure. It was too good to be true. The serum immunised the living, the dead stayed dead, and Wailers wore collars that fed the serum into their brain, keeping them docile and compliant. It kept the illusion of control in place long enough for any real hope of control to be swept away.

The serum failed. One cold but bright autumn day six weeks ago, hundreds of thousands of humans became ravenous Wailers, hunting their human prey to near extinction, and the dead were free to rise unchecked. The short journey Tyde just made from Kronic's maisonette to the beach had been teaming with both. Kronic was the powerhouse that had kept the fiends at bay. Now that Tyde and Cleaver were alone, they were vulnerable.

Tyde slid down the hill, surfing between the trees on their many shed leaves, until he reached the concealed bay. Cleaver boarded first. Tyde threw Cleaver's bags on board his boat, ran up the plank onto the deck, and then he kicked the plank away. He pushed the button on the winch and the chain that held the anchor began to wind.

They were coming. Wails rang out as a pack of ravenous soulless humanoids sprinted through the trees toward the boat. Tyde willed the crank to wind faster, but it could not oblige.

He dipped his right hand into a barrel full of water and opened the valve in his palm. He sucked the cool sea water through the opening and it flowed through a series of tubes and valves that ran up his arm and across his pecks. The water travelled into his left arm and filled it. Sagging skin on his forearm plumped and stretched as the pressure built up.

When he opened the hole in his palm water shot out at great velocity.

The Wailers had reached the bottom of the hill that surrounded the horseshoe bay. They jumped at the boat, most falling into the water, but a few managed to grasp the side and pull themselves up.

Tyde's pressurised jet stream tore at their flesh, but did little damage. Their lack of pain receptors meant that his attacks were no deterrent. If he could get a little closer, spurt a concentrated stream through an eye, he would end the walking nightmares, but he was tethered to the middle of the deck by the barrel that supplied his water.

CLUNK. The anchor was up. Tyde made a run for the control room and started his baby up. Lola had always been a reliable starter and burst to life with the turn of a key and the flick of a lever. Within seconds he was too far from the shore for the Wailers to jump on board. Cleaver saw to the four that had already made it onto Lola's deck.

She was a feisty staffy, a terrier widely built with stumpy legs. She barked ferociously at her would be attackers. The four surrounded her and closed ranks. Cleaver jumped at the smallest of them and went for its throat. She allowed her teeth and powerful jaws to set the equation, four became three, but those three had her pinned. One knelt on her neck, weighing her head down. Cleaver wriggled with all her might, her barks and growls pitched with fear as this brindle beauty realised that she couldn't move.

"Over here!" Tyde yelled. His body separated the salt from the sea water as he sprayed it at the Wailers. Now he sucked air into his arm flaps pumping them up like giant balloons and raising the psi. One of his rock salt cylinders slipped out of its fleshy compartment and plugged the hole in his palm. The compressed salt shot out of him like a bullet. The Wailer man kneeling on Cleaver's neck dropped, and the dog wriggled free. Three enemies became two. Tyde had one more salt cylinder. He jettisoned it into his arm tube and built up the pressure again. He aimed at the Wailer's head and the target dropped.

Cleaver barked and leapt at the final Wailer. This woman was stouter than the first that Cleaver had dealt with, and refused to topple over. Cleaver edged the Wailer back, and when the Wailer woman tumbled over the side of the boat, Cleaver nearly followed. Tyde grabbed her collar, pulled her back, and collapsed with her on top of him. Cleaver snapped round to face him with her teeth still bared, then her face softened and her tail wagged. Tyde patted her and breathed a heavy sigh of relief, before reclaiming his feet and hauling the Wailer bodies overboard.

Tyde dug through the bags that Kronic had given him. He laid Cleaver's blanket on the floor of his control room, and settled her on it with a bone. "You earned it, baby girl," he said, tousling her ears. He stroked her from head to tail, checking for any sore spots. "Good girl, Cleaver, you're ok." Cleaver ignored him and gnawed on her bone.

They were not in the greatest of situations. Tyde was a wanted smuggler hunted by foreign Authority officers. He had spent the last six weeks either locked up on Conclee's shore, or running from his captors after his escape. As far as he knew, they were still pursuing him. Venturing into deeper waters was risky.

Hugging the shore line came with its own dangers. Wailers and desperate civilians might swim for the boat, and the water-logged dead clogged up the machinery with the decomposing lumps that slithered off their bones.

Tyde had a hidey hole nearby, a cave inside of the chalk cliffs. He was the only seaman reckless and skilled enough to pilot into that cave.

Tyde angled his boat toward the opening without a second thought. Lola had a narrow aft, but even with Tyde at the helm the walls of the cave tickled her sides. Safety was elusive even when docked. The cave was made from such soft rock that it was liable to subsidence. The waves licking at Lola's hull were a chalky stew. Tyde added his own ingredients to the mix as he washed soluble Wailer debris off the deck.

Tyde waited out the day in the cave and made his move that night. Aided by night vision headgear, he kept Lola dark and edged out of the cave and back into the deep blue. He stayed a steady and slow course around the coast. Lola's engine gurgled and the boat stealthily made it to the river mouth. He could breathe a little now, the Conclee Authority were less likely to track him down the river, but the risk of alerting survivors or Wailers to his presence increased. Wails rang out through the night. As he travelled further inland, they got quieter. By the time he sailed into the Forest of Eaves, there was hardly any noise at all.

Mallard Hill was close. Tyde chugged along, looking for somewhere to hide Lola. He spotted a disused boathouse big enough to conceal Lola from view. It was in poor condition and seemed to sway on the water. Tyde turned the engine off, drifted in, and closed up the shed's water gates.

He shone a torch around the boathouse. The white wash on the wood had worn away leaving only flakes and painted nooks. The wood submerged in the water was green with algae and rotting away. It looked abandoned, but Tyde never took chances with his boat. Lola was belled up, if anyone tried to board her, an alarm would be transmitted to a receiver on his belt.

Tyde got a few hours of shut eye and let the sun rise before leaving Lola. He widened two small holes at the bottom of the shed's door and wall, threaded a chain through, padlocked it, and then piled handfuls of mud on top of the lock, hiding it from view. A shiny padlock only said one thing to Tyde, *I hide something worth taking*. He didn't want his lock to speak the same words to others.

Tyde walked up the jetty with Cleaver at his heels. The path into the Forest of Eaves was so overgrown it was barely visible. Cleaver froze and pricked her ears at the sound of a distant wail. The forest was sparsely populated. A single wail was a refreshing change to the chorus that greeted her every morning in Greenshore. Tyde tugged on the lead and they pressed on into the forest.

The Forest of Eaves was a place so vast, that a dead thing could wander until it withered and rotted without ever finding a meal. Zombies wandered deep into the woodland — away from the isolated villages — drawn by animal or bird calls, and stumbled aimlessly until they dropped. Decaying leaves littered the ground, hiding these toothy landmines. They were little more than snapping teeth, though some of them still had the strength to drag themselves forward on gnarled hands.

Even stripped bare for winter the canopy darkened the forest. The dense cragged trees had scores of twigged branches that knitted together above Tyde's head. The Eaves were carpeted with the dead and dying foliage, the decay was just what the forest needed to be reborn in the spring.

Tyde and Cleaver met no Wailers or dead on their way to Mallard Hill. The reason for this became apparent as they neared the village. Encompassed by a twelve ft high wall, nothing could have wandered out of there into the woodland, and the next village over was many miles away. The wall was a work of art, a sculpture which mirrored the lines and forms of the forest, trees wrought in metal and wood. Tyde saw no opening or gate.

He approached and made his presence known. "Hello, anyone in there?"

"Friend or foe?" yelled the responder behind the wall.

"We've yet to meet, we might be soul mates for all I know," Tyde shouted.

"Leave, outsiders aren't welcome here."

"Someone called Leo invited my friend Kronic. Kronic told me to come ahead of him and wait."

"Damn it, where's Leo? ... Well go get him."

An opening appeared not far from Tyde. It had been well camouflaged as part of the wall. A stern looking man in Authority uniform stepped through. Tyde backed away. "Look,

I don't want any trouble. I can camp out in the woods. If you would direct my friend to me when he arrives that would be swell, then we can leave together."

"No, I think you would be more comfortable waiting inside, don't you?" The man angled his weapon and gestured to the opening. Tyde reluctantly followed the officer inside and got his first glance of Mallard Hill.

The road filled with villagers eager to get a look at the newcomer. Tens quickly became hundreds. There was something off about these people. Tyde might have put his finger on it sooner had he not been distracted by the sheer number of them. All of them were un-afflicted with no visible mutations.

"Is this a designated safe zone?"

"No," the Authority officer replied. "Everyone who is here now was a resident before the Calamity." He opened the door to the police station and nudged Tyde with his gun. "After you." Cleaver barked and glowered at the gun. "You too, mutt."

They walked through the silent station until they reached an office. The name on the door was Lieutenant Doven Spear. Tyde pointed to it. "This you?"

The officer nodded and waved him through the door. "You can call me Spear. Please sit."

Now they were alone together, Tyde noticed that the oddness of the villagers extended to Spear. His blue irises were large, magnified by contact lenses, but any visual impairment would have excluded Spear from the Authority's military during his screening process. His face was hauntingly pale and

Spear's straw blond hair had visible black roots — Black roots. No matter the hair colour most of the villagers had black roots.

"You're all Marazsian aren't you?"

Tyde's question put Spear on edge. Marazsha had been the host country for the rebellion war against the Authority. Minister Plack had blown the once proud and strong nation off the map thirty years before, as the rebel war reached its conclusion. Marazsian refugees were scattered all over the globe, but they were treated like second-class citizens. Their physical attributes were distinctive: Black hair, black eyes, and pale sometimes even greyish skin.

"Not all of us, some are known rebel affiliates. How did you know?"

"My friend Kronic, the one who I'm supposed to meet here, he's Marazsian on his dad's side. He's grown a tough skin over the years to combat the crap he gets because of it."

Spear rubbed his temples and mulled over his limited options. Tyde stayed silent as his fate was debated inside of the other man's head.

"You'll stay with me," Spear said finally. "Not just at my house, everywhere I go, so will you. You'll be my shadow until this friend of yours arrives. Then I'll decide what to do with you."

Chapter 2: Claire

The door caved in. Somewhere out of view Shadow yowled and hissed. Claire lay on the floor. She hadn't the strength to open her eyes. If she could speak, she would have begged for death. The sickness had done more than dehydrate her, and zap her strength, it had broken her.

An unknown voice yelled, "All clear." With Wailers and the dead her death would be assured, but her intruders were neither. Death was still an option with other survivor groups and the one she favoured. Claire reached out for her puppy, Lucky, and found empty rags.

The memory stung her. Lucky had died.

"Not uncommon I'm afraid, for a hand-reared pup with no milk from mum," Leighton had said when she found him.

"But he is strong, he is a fighter," she had insisted.

"I'm sorry, Claire, nature is just cruel like that sometimes."

Nature was not the one to steal the pup's life, but Brutus would never reveal the truth to her.

Claire heard the unpeeling of Velcro and felt a cuff being tightened around her bicep. There was scratching and jabbing in the crease of her other arm, then in the back of her hand.

"It's no good, she's too dehydrated, I can't get a line in," said a man.

"Let me try," said a soft female voice. The woman flicked the back of Claire's wrist until a vein plumped enough to see and puncture. She threaded the cannula in and taped it in place. "There. Pass the saline please."

Claire's eyelids were peeled back one at a time and someone shone a bright light into her hazel eyes. She could not will her eyes to open of her own accord, and once the lids had fallen, they stayed shut.

"Can you hear me? We're here to help."

'Doctors, damn it, I want it all to end, I can't live like this,' Claire thought. Her eyes were sunken and her face was gaunt and pale. Vomit had discoloured her blonde hair and dried in it. Her stomach was raw from retching and acid had burnt all along her throat. "Please." Claire croaked out her words. "Help me, to die. I don't want to live, as a Wailer."

"Are these symptoms of Wailer regression?" the woman asked her colleague.

"Highly unlikely," said the man. "Sickness is reportedly an early symptom, but never to this extreme. We'll take precautions just in case, and run tests to make sure she's not contagious."

The woman rolled Claire onto her side and pulled her trousers down a little. "Anti-sickness meds," she said, thrusting a large needle into Claire's upper butt-cheek. "You will feel better soon."

"Kill me, please," Claire whimpered. Though she was only nineteen years old, Claire was ready for her life to be over.

The man moved to the doorway and talked to someone, their voices were muffled. Claire got the sense there were a lot more people intruding in the Moorland school, than the two doctors and the person in the doorway.

"Good," the man said returning to Claire and his colleague. "They've loaded up all the guns and food. Time to go."

Claire felt strong arms lift her high off of the floor. It wasn't one of the doctors, she could hear them talking to one another. Their voices grew quieter. The strong-armed man carried her out of the art block and placed her on the back seat of a car. The engine started, and they pulled away.

Though she had hunted and scavenged on the Moorland estate with Brutus in those early days, she still didn't know it well enough to figure out where she was being taken. The car jostled her as it bumped down the road. When it careened over a speed bump, Claire slipped from the seat and crumpled in the footwell. Those same strong arms picked her up again and lay her back on the seat. Claire saw this monstrously large figure through blurred eyes. He was holding the saline up high so gravity could do its work. There seemed to be an orange glow around him.

Her car was part of a convoy, Claire gathered, from the noise of other engines close by. They all came to a halt. A car door slammed and a large gate creaked open. Then they crawled forward and parked up.

"Take her to a room for some rest. She can have clean clothes and a shower when she's feeling up to it. Keep someone posted on her door as she may be at risk of turning Wailer."

Claire was lifted once more and carried, a seemingly endless distance, to her new room. The feel of a real bed and clean bedding was euphoric. She had thought nothing in life could give her pleasure again, but this soft, fresh bed did. Claire buried her face into the pillow. The floral scent coming from the fabric masked the smell of her soiled hair and clothes. Soon she was sleeping deeply and drooling into the pillow.

After a sleep, Claire felt more like herself than she had in weeks. More importantly the sickness had gone. She was famished. Her hunger was so strong it felt like her stomach would dissolve itself.

"Excuse me," she called, rapping her knuckles against the locked door. "I require food now. And I believe I was promised a shower and a change of clothes?"

"Ok," said a booming voice. The man shuffled off.

Claire had expected that food would materialise instantly, but it appeared it needed retrieving. She passed the time by searching her small room. Her near empty saline bag was up on an IV pole. She wheeled it around the room with her. There was a television with a built-in movie memory box mounted on to the wall. The remote sat on top of the bedside table. She turned the TV on and flicked through the thousands of saved films and series.

Knock, knock. "Claire, I'm one of the people who found you at the school. I've brought you some food, may I come in?"

Claire recognised the woman's voice. "You may." The woman walked in and set the tray down on the bed. "That injection you gave me is marvellous. I don't feel sick at all." Claire dragged her drip stand over to the bed and sat next to the tray.

The woman sat down on one of two small chairs. She was about a decade older than Claire, but she looked better than she did today. The woman's mousey brown hair had chocolate lowlights, plaited into a beautiful and complex up-do. She wore makeup and sparkly piercings. "Do you know what a warrant card is, Claire?"

Claire nodded and swallowed a large mouthful. "It's an Authority devise that holds information and images of all citizens. It has built-in facial recognition software so it can scan a suspect and confirm their identity."

"We took a warrant card with us to the school. We believe one or more of your group is already known to the Authority. You were flagged up on its database, Miss Ivanthor, but not because you are a criminal. You and your brother Terrence are VIP missing persons."

"Terry," Claire whispered, feeling intense guilt for forgetting his demise even for a moment. "My brother became Wailer and was killed." Claire was no longer grateful for the food. Grief robbed her of her newly found appetite. "Do you have a point to make? I would sooner eat my meal in peace than listen to you waffle on."

"I do, and I am sorry to bring up such sad memories for you, Claire. You need to know that we will look after you here. Anything you need or want, you only have to ask." She stood and showed Claire around the rest of the apartment. "You will not be locked in the bedroom again. All these rooms are yours. If you want to go for a walk all you have to do is ask, and you will have your own personal chaperone."

Claire followed her. There was an abundance of toiletries and makeup in the bathroom and food in the kitchen. When she opened up the fridge, the light came on. Nowhere else in the Moorland estate had power.

A strut returned to her step. She was Claire Gabriela Ivanthor, Countess of Soarken and sole heir to the vast Ivanthor estate.

"I want Ethan brought here," Claire said taking a few more treats out of the fridge and tucking into them. "I want you to treat him as well as me. He can have the other bed. I want Shadow brought here for him too. Do you have more apartments, like this one? Brutus can sleep in with me but the others will need their own space. You have electricity, they could even bring their console with them, right?"

"I'm not sure who all those people are, perhaps we should sit down and you can tell me a little more about your group. I need to know who I'm looking for and where to look, if I'm to bring them here."

Chapter 3: The Lost Diner

Kronic was sick of this argument and struggling to remain diplomatic. "I am invited, Felicity can stay camouflaged. The two of us will meet Tyde, make nice with the locals, and then we'll come back for you. There's no point going in as a big group and scaring them."

"But Paul is badly injured, they could have medical supplies to help him," said Sadie.

"For fuck sake, Sade, how many more fucking times," Kronic groaned "It's a village in the middle of fucking nowhere. There is no hospital, just a small doctor's surgery that some guy runs out of his house. There is nothing they have for Paul that we haven't already got stored in the van."

"You said they have a doctor, we don't have one of those stored in the van do we?"

Kronic sucked in a deep breath and held it for the count of five. "I've had no contact with Leo in weeks, for all we know the whole village could be a Wailer nest. The Forest of Eaves is massive. If we get chased and separated you'd be stuck, lost in the trees for weeks. I'm going to check it out first. End of."

"We are in the forest now." Sadie glared at him. "This diner is in the middle of the Forest of Eaves so your argument is crap. I am sick of getting separated, we need to stay together."

Kronic brought his fist down on the table. It split in half and the room went silent. He stared at the damage he had once again unintentionally caused. "I'm going outside for a smoke." He passed close to Luke on his way out. "Sort your missus out while I'm gone."

The atmosphere in the diner was thick and tense. Sadie knew that she had caused it. It wasn't even as though she was that against Kronic's plan. It was a good plan, and it was the most cautious route to take. But after everything they had been through in the last few days, Sadie had all these intense emotions and no clear place to vent them.

Luke walked behind Sadie and put his wing across her chest. He pulled her close and nuzzled into her. "Sadie—"

"I concede, we'll do what Kronic says." Sadie sulked. Luke came close to stealing all of her tension with a kiss, but the actions of her youngest kept her uptight and rigid. "Verity-Elise, get down from the ceiling. I mean it, Madam, down now!"

It rained dust and cobwebs and crumbling plaster. Madam was filthy, and having the time of her life. She raced along the ceiling on all fours squealing with laughter. "Can't catch Madmam," she yelled.

> *'She's right,' shrugged the Broken Child, the depressive and self-destructive third of Sadie's shattered psyche. 'You can't catch her. The ceiling is too high in here.'*
>
> *'She wants to play,' said the Brain. 'She's two. It's not like she's using her ability to be a pain. Play with her and lead the game in a way that brings her down by choice.'*

Both Brain and Child were putting their views over to the Bitch, who was currently the dominant self in Sadie's mind. The Bitch's first instinct had been to shout at the toddler for adding to her stress and threaten to knock her down with a broom.

"Catch you?" said Sadie smiling. "But you're it, you have to catch *me*." She ran and hid under a large food trolley and listened to Madam giggling.

"Me too," said Kyan rushing to find his own hiding spot. Luke also joined in the game, wriggling his awkward winged shape out of sight.

Madam's giggles didn't stop as she crept down the wall and tiptoed over to where her family hid. Sadie yelled, "BOO," grabbed her tiny ringlet topped daughter, and tickled her.

Serenity, Rapz, and Felicity hung back and watched. Sadie succeeded in more than getting her toddler down to safety; she had defused the atmosphere and tension between the Odd Blockers.

Kronic walked back through the door. "Any further objections to me and Fliss scouting ahead? ... Good." He laid out a tourist map of the hiking trails on the table where Felicity sat. "We're here, and Mallard Hill is here. None of the trails go to the village, it's tucked right out of the way, but this one will get us close, then we will come off the track and compass it from there."

"We're going by foot?"

"It's only five, maybe six miles. We can't take the van, aside from being full of food and an unconscious twat, it won't take my weight. And if we take the patrol car, we'll be putting Paul in danger, 'cause I ain't moving the poor fucker, he's lost a fair bit of blood from those bites."

"By foot it is." Felicity would return to Soarken after seeing the group safely to Mallard Hill. She had unfinished business there.

Felicity gave Luke a curious glance. During her days as an infection control officer, a vigilante group who fixed Wailer and undead problems for a price had plagued her. A man known as Guy ran it. Luke already admitted that he had worked for Guy, but was he her nemesis? Was Luke the masked cleanup expert known as the Silver Dragon?

She almost caught the Dragon once. He had hidden in a freezer under a semi-defrosted zombie. She'd been called away just before finding him. Now that Luke had transformed, it was hard for Felicity to ignore his silver lizard like wings and tail. He looked like a dragon. The shape of the wings and the tail even resembled the dragon motif on the Silver Dragon's balaclava. Was Luke emulating his own hidden persona, or was he merely a fan of the Dragon's work? Felicity's investigative nature had not ended with her job.

"Earth to, Fliss, you coming or what?" Kronic waved his hands in front of her vacant eyes.

"Sorry, I got lost in thought, let's go."

The Odd Blockers had been so flustered when they arrived that no one could sleep. They ate, planned, and argued. The diner had been abandoned for years, and being isolated, it was the perfect place to regroup. They were forced to come here when Wailers overran their flats.

Kronic was banking on them remaining isolated. With him and Felicity gone, their two most effective survivors were Serenity, a woman who emitted something unknown, a pheromone they suspected, that repelled the Wailers and dead. Its range was small. She could only keep one or two safe in her personal space. The other was eight-year-old Kyan, whose electrical surges had taken down a large zombie group the night before, but he had little control over his ability.

Luke, unfortunately, had been much more effective as a human. His mutated body was so alien to him, that his once formidable fighting and parkour skills were now non-existent.

Rapz felt the pressure. If a fight came to their door, he would step up. He had no fancy mutation, but he could wield a knife and swing a bat. Their group had three children (including Serenity's baby), an injured man, and Chris, whose actions had endangered the group, and left them no choice but to tie him up. They were not an effective fighting force.

"Luke, do you wanna head out front and practice some of those fighting moves you were showing me?"

Luke's eyes brightened. He needed to learn how to use his new body. "Sure, go easy on me though, I'm learning."

"I think I said something to that effect the first time you trained me," Rapz laughed.

***

"It's still freezing," Kronic noted as they strolled along the trail. He pulled a pair of gloves out of his inside pocket and put them on. He tried to zip up his motorbike jacket, but his widened torso wouldn't fit inside anymore. "How can you walk around like that in this weather?"

"Clothes feel unnatural, and I don't seem to have a temperature gauge anymore. I'm not feeling the cold." Felicity was the most visually mutated of the Odd Blockers. Her body was hairless and covered in scales. The pigment and texture of these scales were fluid, allowing her to mimic and camouflage into her surroundings.

The mud path through the woods was frozen solid. This made the journey a little easier for Kronic, as his colossal weight forced his feet to sink in softer earth.

"Have you ever been here before?"

"Nope," said Kronic through chattering teeth.

"Not even when you met up with Leo?"

"Technically, we've never met. We both have gaming channels and often team up online. I've researched Mallard Hill on the net, but it's just a middle of nowhere village with not much going on."

"Do you realise how ridiculous that sounds?"

"It's a meeting point, a grid reference. If Tyde isn't at the village, he'll be on the river close by."

They walked in silence after that until they needed to leave the trail. The path offered them no more safety than a route of their own design, yet they felt exposed in the thick trees.

"Hold up," Felicity hissed, putting a hand on Kronic's chest. She shimmered out of view, but Kronic could still feel the press of her hand.

A frost covered zombie dragged itself through the trees. It stumbled and tripped over the tree roots. Every time it fell, it picked itself back up and continued.

"Fliss, leave it, there's no point," Kronic whispered, but her hand had already left his chest. She did not re-materialise, but now and then Kronic glimpsed a shift in the scenery, as her camouflage failed to keep up with her movement.

Felicity snuck between the trunks and boughs. The zombie was ambiguous. Even up close, Felicity couldn't connect it to a gender. It must have been wandering for days in the cold. Frostbite had blackened its fingers, and its nose had crumbled away, as had some of its bare toes.

Its red flannel pyjamas were white and crisp with frost. The tangled eaves above blocked out much of the light. Brightened chinks shone through, and as the ghoul passed under them they danced light upon it, causing the frost covered flesh to glisten. Mother Nature had sprinkled its gore and decay with glitter.

Felicity positioned herself in front of it. Black tendrils of death spread out from its gaping nasal cavity, across its cheeks, and around the curve of its eye socket. One eye was twisted and fixed to the side looking out into the forest. The other flickered in its socket. It looked right through the spot that Felicity occupied.

'I doubt it has any functioning senses.' Felicity picked up a twig and snapped it in front of its face. *'Didn't think so.'*

"Seriously, Fliss, we don't have time for this." The zombie didn't react to the floating, snapping twig, or Kronic's voice, and continued to stumble forward.

Felicity retreated to Kronic and reappeared as her scaly self.

"Before you ask, no you can't keep it. I don't give a shit if they make good pets, Fliss, not happening."

The zombie, still oblivious to everything going on around, walked into a tree, collapsed and felt around for leverage.

"Let's go." Felicity left the zombie alone. It was a pitiful thing, existing on borrowed time.

They followed the compass north-east through the trees until they reached the foot of a large hill with a concave top.

"Do we go up and over?" asked Felicity.

"Nah, that's Mallard Hill, the hill. On top is a duck filled lake, hence the name. Mallard Hill the village is on the other side. Be quicker to go around than over."

After a short trek, they arrived at the village wall. "Ok, who put a giant fucking wall here?" Kronic lifted his voice to the sky, as expected, he received no divine reply. "I think it's time you did your disappearing trick, but walk real slow. You're not as invisible when you move quickly."

"I'll always be close. Let me know if you need me." Felicity shimmered out of view and Kronic strolled up to the wall.

"Hey," Kronic yelled, "any fucker alive in there?"

Silence was all that greeted him.

"Leo, it's Kronic." He waited, but no response came. "Tyde, are you in there?"

He ran his hands along the walls perimeter as he circled it, looking for a gate or a door, but he found nothing. This sculpted masterpiece represented the trees and the flow of the forest, though all its nooks and crags were decorative, no foot or hand holds were functional.

"TYDE!" Kronic bellowed. He was about to write the village off as abandoned and head towards the river, when he heard something within the wall. It was a familiar bark and its owner was bounding towards him.

"Cleaver, come on girl!"

She was close. Kronic punched a hole in the wall and curled a metal panel back on itself. Cleaver hadn't the patience to wait for him to widen it. Her head was through and her shoulders were stuck, but her stumpy legs still bounded, wedging her through further. Her rapid pants were wheezy with excitement. Kronic forced the metal a little more, and she was through. Her still bounding legs sprinted forward. She rounded in a wide circle, jumping up at Kronic, bounding off a short distance, then coming back to claw and lick at him, before repeating.

"I missed you too. Ok, calm down."

But Cleaver was incapable of calming down. She hadn't seen Kronic in days, which was clearly a lifetime in dog years. She threatened to lick and claw her way through his middle with her unyielding affections.

"Ah, mate, look what you did to the wall. Spear is gonna be pissed, I mean he's already pissed that I invited strangers, but this will make him proper wig out." Leo clicked his tongue on the roof of his mouth. He inhaled a drawn out whistle as he examined the damage in more detail.

"I called, no one answered." Kronic studied Leo as he stepped through the hole in the wall. His voice had the same deep and masculine tone he was used to hearing over the headset, but Leo looked nothing like he had expected. "You're a kid, jeez, I must be old enough to be your dad!"

"I'm sixteen," groaned Leo.

"Prove I couldn't be a father at eleven," scoffed Kronic.

"I'm a little scrawny, I know laugh it up, but you!" Leo whistled again and beamed. "You're massive, I mean I've seen profile pics, but I never imagined you were so large." He sighed and looked back through the gap. "We best go through, your welcoming committee awaits."

Inside the wall, outside the wall, Cleaver didn't care which so long as she was at Kronic's side.

There was a gathering inside the perimeter. Like they had for Tyde, most of the residents poured out of their homes to inspect the new arrival.

"Are you alone?" Spear asked as he patted Kronic down for weapons.

"You see anyone with me?"

"And you don't carry weapons?"

"Don't need them." Kronic looked at Tyde who stood silently at Spear's side, but he did not return the glance.

Spear glared. "Come with me."

Kronic noticed it sooner than Tyde had. He'd never seen so many Marazsians gathered in one place. "You're all Marazsian? Like me?"

"Mostly, yes." Spear paused in speech for a moment but continued to march him forward. "Do you know much about your heritage?"

"No. Any man over a certain age could be my dad. Never met him, and on paper he doesn't exist. Mum never told me his name."

"She didn't want you to learn where you came from?"

"Nah," laughed Kronic. "She just didn't know it. It was a tossup between two one-night stands as to who fathered me. If my mum had thought the dates fit for me to be Marazsian, she would have aborted me."

"That's nice. Classy lady," Spear scoffed.

"Don't judge. My mum's an honest woman. Never once lied to me. I can't fault her for that. It's one of the reasons I love her."

"Where is she now?" Spear opened the door to the police station. Tyde led the way with Cleaver and Kronic close behind.

"We lost contact a while back, she didn't approve of my ex. When shit hit the fan, I tried ringing her, but none of the numbers I have for her worked."

"That's harsh, bud," said Tyde. "I didn't know that."

"Take a seat," said Spear closing the door to his office, "You too." He pointed to a folded blanket in the corner of the stark room. Cleaver's ears dropped and her tail stopped wagging. She sulked to her makeshift bed as commanded.

Kronic sat on the floor too. None of the seats would survive an encounter with him.

"Time to cut the crap. You're not alone. We have surveillance in Ellie's Diner. We've been using that place as an outpost for years. So how about you tell me who you are and why you're here."

Chapter 4: Lara

Her Wailer brethren walked at her flank. Originally human, they were all afflicted with the same brain masses as the dead, which bypassed human consciousness and remade them as something else. Survival was at the forefront of their agenda. The zombies that shared their land were an annoyance, and would lead to disease, but the humans caused the greatest threat to their species. They had collared them, drugged them, and forced them to exist in a way that suited their needs. Worse than that, they hunted them the second the serum's control failed.

The group followed Lara down the Odd Block stairs. She knew how deep each step would be without looking. As a newly regressed Wailer, Lara still held residual memories. She focused on a memory of a living survivor, and was taking the hunt to his most likely location.

The dead milled around. Lara nudged and pushed through them. They had no interest in her or the other Wailers. She sensed a symbiotic relationship between them, the plague of dead helped them to exterminate humankind, but once they reached that goal they would readdress their symbiosis.

The word 'Chris,' reverberated in her head, and linked to a clear image of him in her mind's eye. Her physical eyes were still large and oval, but their warm brown colouring had drained and been replaced with a milky hue. She continued to push her way through the grimy, putrid dead. Ever the clean freak, the Lara that existed in human form yesterday, would not have suffered such filth.

They exited the Odd Block and skulked down the road. The frigid wind was still brutal, and a layer of frost and ice covered the pavements. Though Wailer nerves were no longer capable of transmitting pain, their living organs still needed warmth. They knew this and ducked into a house searching for clothing and footwear.

A thick, warm, and hooded coat hung in the entrance hall. Lara pulled it from the hook and clumsily zipped herself into it. She measured potential shoes by lining up her feet against them. There were hiking boots that matched. If any of the Wailers could have tied laces, it would have been Lara, with her residual memories guiding her hands, but alas, that skill was already beyond her grasp. She slipped her damp socked feet into the boots and tucked the laces in with them.

A clatter came from upstairs. Lara cocked her head at the sound. She climbed the staircase with care, intently listening, not allowing her own movements to drown out the subtle sounds. The thick carpet muffled the floorboard creaking underfoot, but the sound repeated with every Wailer that passed over it.

"Shh, stay quiet and they'll go away," someone whispered, in response to a whimper.

Lara placed her ear against the door. Taking deep breaths, she filtered the air through her nose. Her sense of smell was incredible. She detected three distinct aromas. They were close. She breathed deeply again. The human smell sent her into a frenzy. The need to destroy and devour was overwhelming. Rage and endorphins flooded her body. She had never experienced pure and relentless elation like this in her human form.

The Wailer group was made up of two adult males and four adult females including Lara. They stepped over the threshold, and bunched together in the bedroom. The Wailer to Lara's left let out a shriek. A muffled squeal pinpointed their prey. They flipped the bed across the room. Two adult humans and a whimpering child cowered on the floor. The female released her cupped hand from her son's mouth and shielded him with her body.

The sight of them huddled, along with their enticing scent, pushed Lara's elation into climax. She viewed the world anew. A glow emanated from these people, not like Innocence's mutation, more like she could perceive their heat through sight. Lara lunged at the nearest human, tearing at the man with her hands and teeth. It was about more than sustenance. The need to be top of the food chain drove the ferocity of the attacks.

The meat was sweet and succulent, best served raw and still pulsating. Lara ripped mouthful after mouthful from her victim. Only when the body succumbed to death did her intense desires recede.

They rolled the dead parents off the child. Lara lunged forward, but one of her kin placed a hand on the boy.

"It hurts, Mummy, it hurts," said the child holding his head. "Hurt... Mummy... it."

Lara leaned in more slowly and sniffed at the child. His parents' warm blood drenched him, their screams had been piercing, yet the boy focused solely on the pain tearing through his brain, burning behind his eyes.

Lara raided the drawers for warm, dry clothes to dress the boy in. His rebirth was swift. Lara had him redressed before his human life ended. His residual memories would not be useful for the hunt (the only survivors he'd known, had just died on top of him), but they did give him a sharpened mind.

The Wailer group, now seven strong, took back to the streets. They followed Lara and her image of Chris, out of Soarken and toward the Forest of Eaves.

Chapter 5: The Brutes

The adrenaline finally wore off and the Brutes succumbed to exhaustion. Events from the night filtered into their dreams: Rounding up the dead, baiting the Wailers, pedalling for their lives from the swelling horde of their creation.

Ethan's dream caused the lad to sweat and fidget in his sleeping bag. *He stood on the porch of the Odd Block with a candle in his hand. The wind blew out the flame. Ethan stared into the night, squinting, and straining his ears. He pulled out a lighter and clicked the ignition again and again. He stared back out of the door. The street had vanished, a sheet of blackness stood in its place. The wind had disappeared too. Ethan clicked the lighter again. It lit this time, revealing a decomposing face inches from his own.*

Soundless screams poured out of Ethan. He spun around to find the back door bricked up, and made for the stairs. He wanted to sprint with all his might, but it felt like he was wading through treacle. He opened his mouth to scream, but again no sound came out. On all fours he dragged himself up the stairs. When he reached the first landing, he tried to hammer the door, but his fist moved so slow with no force at all. There was no sound to his knock, no sound to his voice. No one could hear his pleas as he was buried beneath the horde.

"Ethan, wake up." George shook him by the shoulders. "It's just a dream."

Ethan lurched away from George. Cocooned in the sleeping bag, he smacked his head on the wall.

"It's ok, mate, just a dream." George unzipped him and helped him up.

The door to their communal sleeping room opened and Brutus strolled in. "Good, you're all awake. I want to get back to that block of flats before the Authority picks it clean. Get dressed."

"I'll stay here with Claire," said Ethan. Sweat soaked through his t-shirt.

"Don't be daft," said Leighton, grinning and ruffling the boy's damp hair. "You opened the door, you led them in. You had a greater hand in this than any of us."

Ethan felt nauseated. "I'm still tired, I just want to sleep." He did. He wanted to sleep, and cry, inside of his sleeping bag.

"This isn't up for discussion, Ethan," Brutus barked. "You're coming. Get up. We need to comb through that block for useable supplies."

"You said one of the group was Authority, do you reckon her gear would have some kind of override code for our guns?" asked Joel.

"Could be, but we have to get there before the Authority clears it." Brutus and his gang scored several guns after attacking an Authority patrol car in the Spokes. They were fingerprint encrypted and all had the safety on.

Brutus checked in on Claire. She was passed out under the table near her sick bucket. Brutus lifted her onto the homemade floor-bed, tucked her in, and kissed her cheek. "I'll be back soon, babe." She didn't stir. Her condition was worsening. The sickness drained her of fluids and nutrients leaving her weak. At the rate she was deteriorating she would lose her life to dehydration, long before changing into a Wailer.

Brutus locked Claire in their room. It was hard to watch her suffer. Much easier to go back to the block and distract himself, revel even, in the destruction he had wrought. He needed to see the blood, needed to confirm their deaths. They all did, except for Ethan. He was hoping for evidence of escape, though that would put him in danger. His task had been to lead the dead into the block and into the garden, destroying all hope of escape. He had not led them into the garden. He'd kept the back door shut.

"Move out." Brutus's minions filed out with him. They pushed an industrial dumpster in front of the art block's damaged outer door.

Ethan pulled his hood up over his bowed head, dug his hands deep into his pocket, and plodded along the icy streets. Brutus and Joel set the pace ahead, while George, Leighton, and Caleb raced back and forth, scooping up glovefuls of settled ice, and trying to hit each other with it.

"All right, you've had your fun," called Brutus. "We're getting close. Expect trouble, they can't have all wandered off, there'll be a lot of dead trapped inside."

Light and dark tracks shaded the frosty ground, marked by the extensive footfall since it settled. There were vehicle skid marks too, old and faded almost as white as the untouched frost. Someone had escaped. Brutus frowned. Ethan's eyes trailed the ground, and he noticed it too. He was both relieved and filled with dread.

The block no longer writhed with beasts. The Wailers had gone, but some dead lingered in bumbling pockets throughout the structure. Most had stopped travelling and stood swaying instead.

"Here's what we're going to do," said Brutus. The others huddled in to hear his hushed instructions. "We go in quiet, shut the back door and kill them as they come down the stairs." Ethan paled at the words *back door*.

When they got in there the back door was already closed. "I left in a hurry," Ethan spluttered, his defence now well rehearsed in his head. "The rock must have slipped and let the door close behind me."

"Don't worry about it," said Brutus, draping his arm over the lad. "You did so well, you led them all in here. This win is on you more than anyone else."

Their faint voices caught the attention of the walking rots. Slow and unsteady steps carried the ravenous corpses down through the Odd Block.

The brothers, Leighton and Joel, howled with joy and jumped straight into the fray. Brutus was slow, deliberate, and devastating. Overkill every time. George and Caleb wielded knives. George used quick and considered strikes. Caleb jumped around, flailing and dancing, his wide swings sliced at the targets, but Ethan struggled to see the plan or intent in his chaos.

A bloated and blackened corpse stumbled past Brutus, Ethan felt sure he had allowed it to slip by. He stood ready though, and lunged at the man,, toppling him over. His knee landed hard into the bloat's belly and forced rancid air out of multiple orifices. Ethan didn't remember making the head wound that quieted that zombie. He just remembered the goose flesh that raced throughout his body, as his instincts turned him to face another danger.

How he knew that she was slinking up behind him, was one of those unfathomable mysteries. She slipped through the fray unharmed, winding through the stamping feet, before finding her way to Ethan. Her moan wasn't hoarse or menacing; it still held the same angelic tone of the toddler it once belonged to. Unlike the others, she looked human. Her neck had a fatal bite wound, but her pretty face and perfect pigtails were clean and crisp. She was barely dead, no blackness or bloating.

She instantly reminded Ethan of the little girl he saw on the top-floor windowsill, when they scoped the block out. Was this her? Was he staring into the fluffy lashed eyes of his murder victim? The twin corkscrews of hair on the top of her head swayed as she edged closer. *'I'm sorry,'* Ethan screamed in his head. Her little red shoes clipped and clopped across the concrete, all other sounds dropped away. *'Forgive me, I didn't want to.'* She couldn't forgive him, this little girl who looked loved. Her clothes were neat and coordinated; someone had invested time in her appearance.

The claw of Brutus's hammer curled through the air and shattered the little zombie girl's face. "Open your eyes, Ethan, do you want teeth marks?"

The stairs became a mound of silenced bodies. Standing on the pile, the Brutes leered down at Ethan. He was slow to regain control of his hyperventilation.

"She, she," Ethan panted.

"Lived here? Yeah, I'm pretty sure she did." Brutus wiped a splattering of blood from his face. "None of these others were fresh, let's keep moving."

Brutus dragged Ethan up. The carpet of flesh on the stairs squished and shifted under his feet. He clung to the banister and teetered till he reached the top.

"Think we should shift the bodies first, Brutus?" Joel suggested. "Won't be able to make a quick getaway down here."

"We are a reckoning. We run from nothing." Brutus pushed a shaky Ethan up the last step.

There were two doors on the middle floor. Number seven was still closed and seemed untouched, and number five to their right had its door smashed open. They walked into Lara and Chris's flat. Muddy and blood speckled footprints encircled the living room. The carpet at the centre remained clean.

Brutus knew that there wasn't enough blood in the room to have come from an injury. He was disappointed and walked into the hall, continuing to look for clues to tell him the inhabitants' fate. He stopped dead in the kitchen doorway. "You remember I said not to worry about the stone and the back door?" Brutus asked. Ethan nodded. "Maybe you should."

A bed sheet rope was wrapped around the kitchen taps and pulled through several cupboard door handles.

"Check the cupboards for food," Brutus growled and walked back into the long hallway.

Ethan did as he was told, but once he knew the pantry was bare, he couldn't help but lean over the sink to see the sheet rope swaying all the way to the ground. He could see over the garages from up here too. Faded tyre marks, from at least two vehicles, led away. Ethan beamed from ear to ear, but he washed his smile away, before rejoining the group.

"Hey, guys check this out," yelled Leighton from the back bedroom.

He picked up a crumpled sheet of lined paper and started to read aloud to his gathering audience. "This world of grey, ain't black or white, it's filled with dead and gruesome fights, I spit, I sing, I rap, I rhyme, but I'll never find that perfect line, 'cause I've got numbered days, it's a matter of time, until I pay the muncher's fine... It goes on," said Leighton. Rapz's notes peppered the floor and walls. "Joel, Joel." Leighton grabbed at his brother excitedly. "You remember that rapper you liked, who performed at Shot-Glass-Harry's club? This is his shit, right?"

"Yeah, Laurence Tanshaw, aka Rapz, I never pictured him living in the Moorland though." Joel sighed. He grabbed handfuls of balled paper and plumped his pockets with them for nostalgia.

"Move out," Brutus called. "We still have the rest of the block to search."

They kicked in the door of number seven to be thorough, but found it to be bare.

Number nine, on the top-floor was much more inviting. What was left of the devastated door, flopped on its hinges. Brutus's spirits lifted, until he saw the overturned chair under the open loft hatch.

Brutus threw himself up into the loft. Joel, Leighton, and George followed him up, and between them, they kicked and smashed their way through all of Sadie's stored belongings. Poorly wrapped fragiles smashed, as their boxes crumpled and compressed. There was squeaking from baby toys, and once triggered, a lullaby recording persisted through the commotion.

"Over here," called George.

Brutus pushed past him. The beams creaked as he thundered through the hole in the wall. The next loft was bare, making it much easier to see the next hole.

"Leighton," said Brutus pointing to the next hatch without stopping.

"On it." Leighton dropped down to search the flat below.

They went through the next wall and were in the adjoining block. Boxes cluttered this loft to the rafters. "I got this one," yelled Joel, digging his way through to the hatch.

In the final space cool light poured through the large hole in the roof and the hatch to the flat below lay wide open.

"Damn it!"

***

Caleb, back in Luke and Sadie's flat, was in his element rummaging through all their stuff. He flung hats, scarves and children's shoes out of the small cupboard between the kitchen and bathroom.

Even when a shoe hit him in the shin, Ethan remained stationary. He didn't dare venture in further than the door. That little zombie girl might have died anywhere, but the second he found the blood, he would have to own the responsibility of her death. He felt certain she died in here and stared at the living room windowsill, the one she had sat on.

Ethan simultaneously imagined the smiling, curly haired tot and the stumbling zombie child. The images over lapped, and when the claw of Brutus's hammer came down, it shattered them both. Ethan hung his head, the pile of shoes and winter wear that had built up at his feet blurred through his gathering tears.

"Get the fuck in!" shouted Caleb, dragging out a pair of Luke's boots. "Got me a pair of proper stompers now."

Ethan blinked away the tears and willed away the flush from his face. As his vision cleared, he felt compelled to pick up something from the pile. At first glance he wasn't sure what the garment in his hand was. He unscrewed it and manipulated it back into shape. It was a black balaclava with a silver dragon curled around the eye. He caught the breath in his throat before it turned into a gasp, and found himself flung back into that terrible moment when his whole life changed.

Ethan sat in twenty-three Ballmont road, his home. His mother Lynne cried and told the Authority officers she had locked his dad away, to await intervention after his collar failed. She explained that she took refuge with her son at her sister's house. The officers believed her. Neighbours had been fighting in the street over collar rights when they'd arrived at the call. The man who strung Ethan's father from the tree was described as wearing a black balaclava with a silver dragon printed around the eye.

One of Guy's vigilantes for hire had done this, the notorious Silver Dragon. The Authority thought a neighbour hired him. Lynne stayed quiet. She was the one who had made the call, and after that day she was so guilt ridden and bereft she couldn't feel any other emotions. She never recovered and killed herself.

These memories were linked to the sight of this balaclava. With shaking hands, Ethan wanted to fling this thing away, hard, with all the revulsion that now filled his soul. But he couldn't part with it.

"So how many of them actually died in here?" snarled Brutus, as he dropped back down into Luke and Sadie's flat. "How many?" Brutus raged. Leighton, Joel, and George dropped down too.

"Just that one little girl," said Joel, "although others might have been killed on the road."

"She didn't die here," said George. The others glowered at him. "There is no blood pool or arterial spray in this block consistent with her wound. Didn't you see what she was wearing? Who has time to dress their child and do their hair, in the middle of the night when monsters are banging down their door? She's fresh and from the area, but she's not from this block. I'd put money on it."

"All of 'em got away?" Caleb soaked up the disappointment and anger that rippled through the group. "Your fault, ain't it?" He yelled, grabbing hold of Ethan and dragging the boy into the living room. "You was 'sposed to leave the door open, fill up the garden with biters." He tried to open the window, but it was locked. He held Ethan against the wall with his knee and jabbed his knife into the keyhole, forcing the window's handle. Ethan squirmed. Caleb heaved him up and tilted him out of the window.

"Whoa, Caleb, don't," yelled Leighton.

Ethan dangled upside down, Caleb held him by the ankles. As Ethan swayed in the frigid air, a perplexed zombie watched with confusion and interest from the ground.

"It wasn't his fault," screamed George trying desperately to put his own grip on Ethan. "They had an escape route running through the roof, none of us could have known about that."

"Still left out back though didn' they?" Caleb said. He knew who the alpha dog was and if Brutus had an issue, he would have spoken up.

"They left out the front," yelled Ethan. "Look!" He pointed at a black car shaped void in the frost further down the road, and the tyre tracks it had left.

"Pull him up," said Brutus flatly. Once they moved away from the window, he hung his head out to confirm what Ethan said. "A car left that spot recently."

Ethan's heart raced, his half-truth had saved his life. He just hoped the others didn't spot the tyre marks out back by the garages. After all that, Luke's balaclava was still clutched between fingers and thumb. He stuffed it into a pocket in his body warmer. It was a prop that would help him retell his story, old and fresh, to Claire when he saw her later.

Discovering the stash of food, which the Odd Blockers had left behind, refreshed their spirits and lightened their moods a little. The tins smelled faintly of disinfectant and they were hand labelled, even colour coordinated by what they contained. The Brutes didn't take the food because they needed to, they'd amassed a huge collection of supplies back at the school, they took it because it was their right. They had fought and deserved the spoils.

Brutus pulled Ethan to one side. "I'm sorry Caleb got carried away, he's a... a—"

"A nut job, a crazy person, an insane liability," Ethan said.

"I was going to say character." Brutus smiled. "I do care about you, Ethan, I wouldn't push you so hard if I didn't, but you're not reaching your potential yet. You got scared, but the back door was an oversight, and it can't happen again. Who knows how many of them we would have got, if the garden was filled. Some of them went out via that rope. Now they're out there, and if they figure out it was us that attacked them, we could be in real shit."

'And whose fault is that,' thought Ethan. *'You were the one who insisted on attacking innocent people. You started it!'* He wished he had the courage to say that out loud, but he would find himself head first out of a window again if he did.

George had been right. There was no evidence of death in this flat, but it had been flooded with feet and jostling bodies. Furniture had hit the deck hard and possessions lay strewn and trampled.

Ethan brought up the rear as they all left with full packs. He picked up a few photographs that had been re-homed on the floor. Though dog-ended and crumpled, between the three photographs he had a clear picture of all four family members. He focussed on Madam first, she was the toddler he had seen alive and well before the attack. With an image of the zombie girl in his mind, he was certain it was not the same child. His eye's burrowed into the image of Luke. The Silver Dragon. He loosened his grip and watched the photos float down to the floor.

"We couldn't have known about the escape through the lofts," George reassured Ethan on the way back.

"Yeah," said Leighton putting an arm round the teen. "I saw the big guy and the funky looking lady use the front door of this block, never the other."

Brutus lagged behind, having his own heart to heart with Caleb. "I'm not saying don't scare the boy, just don't do anything life altering."

"Life alterin'?" said Caleb, looking perplexed.

"Don't break a leg. That will put him out of action for ages. A broken jaw will stop him eating, make him even weaker." Caleb still looked unsure. "Scare the crap out of him as much as you like, if he fucks up, but don't hurt him too badly. I have to be his friend, I need him to look up to me, but that boy needs a bully to toughen up. I think you're the right man for the task."

Joel had gone on ahead to the school, but now he was pelting it back to the group for all he was worth.

"School, compromised." He wheezed and gasped between words. "Claire's, gone, food's, gone, guns, gone." He clasped his knees and drew his breaths deeply, while his news sank in.

Chapter 6: Mallard Hill

"Tyde told you this place was just a pit stop? A meeting place? The whole point was to gather my friends, regroup with him and Cleaver, and move on."

Spear stared at Kronic. "That is indeed the story he gave."

"Then what's your fucking problem?" Kronic snapped. "Leo invited me, he said this place was safe—"

"It is, for *our* kind. You have brought a group of non-Marazsians into our home, and in Authority vehicles no less—"

"YOU'RE Authority!"

"Yes, some of us are, how else do you think we kept this oasis for our people safe? The war all those years ago was about independence, self-sufficiency, away from the Authority. We lost on a grand scale, but here, in this middle of nowhere village we can live the way we want. So long as the Authority thinks it controls this part of the forest, they don't look too closely."

"I get it, by some of you being Authority, you can give false reports and raise the alarm if an inspection is coming."

"Exactly!"

"Sorry, did some fucker forget to tell you the world has gone to shit? There will be no inspections, no paperwork. You're officially out of a job, as well as being out of your minds. So can I take my dog and my friend, and go?"

"The Authority is not gone. I intercepted communications from the higher ups, hidden away in bunkers. They believe this village has been destroyed. Leaving us free to live our lives."

"Huh, strange that. An entire village being immune and also being invisible to the enemy. If I gave enough of a crap, I'd ask you how you ended the world, but I don't, so bye." Kronic rose and gestured for Tyde to follow.

"Sit down!" Spear bellowed. He gripped his solid handmade desk and rose from his seat. "We didn't do this and we're not immune, just cautious. When Adder's serum was shipped here, our doctor switched it all out for placebos. I'm glad he did, because those inoculations were slow burners. Everyone who had one becomes either Wailer or mutant. Like I said, we've been intercepting comms from what remains of the Authority. Now stay here. I'll be back."

"You know I'm only sitting here out of courtesy, I can leave whenever I want."

"Impervious to bullets are we?" Spear asked, tapping his holstered gun as he walked past.

"Pretty thick skinned, so yeah, I reckon so."

"Cleaver's not though is she?" he said as he headed out of the door.

"Did that cunt-bag just threaten my dog?" Kronic, brimming with fire, shot up from the floor and turned to follow Spear. He stopped when he felt an invisible hand on his shoulder.

"Where have you been?" Tyde said launching himself and landing a bear-hug on Kronic. He was grateful to have some time alone with his friend. "The last few days I've been followed everywhere. I couldn't even take a piss in private.

Which, yes I know my man-ware is impressive, but I don't need a quad-daily jaw-drop to remind me of that."

"Impressive?" Kronic laughed, carefully nudging Tyde out of the hug. "They were probably trying to figure out why it's green."

"Now come on, you know a sea-weed wrap does wonders for a man's girth."

"So, what's the plan?" a voice hissed loudly through their chuckles.

"Are we... are we alone?" Tyde said nervously.

"Tyde Fliss, Fliss Tyde," Kronic said.

Tyde still looked confused and was horrified when an invisible hand grasped his and started to shake it. "Nice to meet you," Felicity whispered. The speed of the shaking hand revealed hints of form and shape.

"So, where have I been? Long story short, I wrecked my bike, met a frogman who knocked me out, borrowed a tractor, got to Soarken, met a chameleon." Kronic pointed to the seemingly empty space at his side. "Then I got to Luke's flat, Madam wouldn't stop climbing on the ceiling and Luke went missing. Some twat filled the flats with Wailers and dead, but we escaped through the secret roof passage. Kyan nearly electrocuted us all, Luke found us and now he has wings, and here we are."

"I'm sorry, what? That sounds like an amazing trip, do you have any left?"

"He's not on drugs. That's more or less what happened," said Felicity.

"It would require the longer version to understand I expect," said Tyde still feeling bemused.

"Do we even have a plan?" Felicity sighed.

The door swung open and Spear returned.

"Ok, I've discussed it with the council, and they decided that you can see out the winter here."

"What do you mean, winter here? We're not on fucking holiday," Kronic snapped.

"That's the thing, winter has set in early and foreign Authority officers may still await me on the waves. I've asked, no let's be honest." Tyde sheepishly met Kronic's stare. "I've begged and grovelled, and Spear has kindly considered allowing us to stay until the waters are fairer."

"There is one further matter of security." Spear was less reluctant to meet Kronic's death stare. "Did anyone you know turn Wailer recently?"

"No," said Kronic.

"Are you sure? There is a large Wailer sect heading down the road into the forest. We have only known Wailers to migrate territories when they're hunting someone specific, usually a loved one."

"Nothing comes to mind."

"Ok." Spear groaned feeling as though Kronic was being less than forthcoming. "Tyde has water guns, one of your group has wings, I need a list of all mutations."

"Luke has wings, Kyan, the boy, has electric discharge, the little girl can climb and I can punch through walls, wanna see?" he said, sticking his thumb towards the wall behind him.

"No, that won't be necessary, we saw you snap a table in two, on the diner surveillance footage. What about the scaly one?"

"Oh, that's just Felicity, she has real bad dry skin." Kronic jolted as Felicity jabbed him with her elbow. "You two can talk ointments, when you see her at the diner."

"So she has no special ability with her mutation?"

Kronic shrugged. "I dunno does dandruff rain or using your skin as sandpaper count?" Felicity kicked him this time. "You would need, to, ask, her, at, the, diner," Kronic repeated more slowly for Felicity's benefit.

"Don't patronise me, I can understand you," snapped Spear. He was already regretting extending hospitality to them.

"Sorry," said Kronic. "May I have the tour now?" He pulled the door open wide.

"Not yet, the un-mutated in your group are potential Wailers I'll need details on them too." Spear jumped as Felicity slammed the door behind her.

Kronic stood rigid. "Sorry," he said, "I was a little heavy handed." He then shouted, "Perhaps it's my time of the month!" Another door slammed further down the hall. Kronic shrugged and smiled. "I have that effect on doors."

Chapter 7: The Lost Diner

Chris thrashed about and smacked his bound feet against the van door. Rapz and Luke put down the long sticks they had been duelling with and went to investigate.

Luke flung open the rear doors. "Damn it, Chris, you've smashed jars, wrecked food!"

Chris glared at them as Rapz pulled his gag off. "Untie me now!"

"You almost killed Rapz. What assurances do we have that all the crazy is out of your system?"

"I don't have to give you assurances. I don't owe you anything. Release me, give me a bag of food and directions back to Soarken, then I'm gone."

"Why should we spare food on you? You tried to steal all of our supplies."

"You weren't there," Chris snapped. He looked at Luke's mutated form with revile. "You were off nesting or whatever it is you bats do. I had to take the supplies to Prospect Heath, to barter help for Lara who was too sick to escape. No one else was coming out of that block, it was overrun. No one would miss it." It was painful for Rapz to listen to. He wanted to believe that Chris had acted out of more than cowardice. "Besides, I helped haul this over from Crazy-cat-lady's place, so I've got more of a right to this food than most."

"Fine," said Luke. He undid the restraints. "We'll give you food and point you in the right direction. You're on foot though. You've got no claim to any of our vehicles."

Chris flung himself out of the van. "I'd best use the restroom while I'm here."

He stormed into the café hoping to find weapons. If he would have asked for them, Luke would have obliged. Despite his tumultuous time with the Odd Blockers, Luke wouldn't have sent an unarmed man into Wailer territory. Chris wanted to take, not ask for things he was already entitled to.

Sadie and her children were still using the diner as their own personal playground. Chris headed toward the sign for toilets, he had no intention of interacting with them, but Madam kept jumping in front of him and stunting his progress. "Damn it, kid, move!" He picked her up by her armpit and swung her out of the way.

"Let go of my sister!" screeched Kyan, he lunged at Chris and pushed him. It wasn't big or life threatening, but Kyan sent an electric jolt into Chris.

Chris pushed Kyan back hard, sending the boy flying into chairs.

Sadie was on him in a flash, she checked that both of her children were ok, and then unleashed a *Bitch* fuelled rant on him. "You vile and pathetic creature. You are the runt of a demonic litter. If the devil hadn't enjoyed bestiality so much, you would have been just another half-baked load, ejaculated onto your mother's udders!"

"What gives you the right to speak to me like that?"

"You just THREW my children. What gives you the right to continue breathing?"

Chris looked away from her manic gaze and retreated to the restroom.

Hearing the shouting, Rapz and Luke rushed toward the café.

"Wait," said Rapz, "look over there."

Luke skidded to a halt just short of the diner's door. He squinted at the fast paced shimmer, moving through the trees. Felicity's scaly form took shape as her feet hit the gravel car park. They were not expecting her back yet.

"Go inside, I have news." Felicity fetched Serenity from the patrol car where she had been re-dressing Paul's wounds.

The Odd Blockers gathered around her. Even after a ten mile round trip, Felicity got straight to it without pausing for rest. "The Marazsians will be here soon." She continued, having already briefed them on her experiences within the village. "Kronic and Tyde seem willing to see through the winter with them, but I'm not so sure we can trust them. It's not safe to stay here either. Spear said there is a group of Wailers heading up the forest road. On my way out of the village, I heard scouts giving an update. They've turned off the main road and are heading here, to the diner. The group is large and has been recruiting all the way from Soarken. You can either go to the village or come back to Soarken with me, but you need to leave now."

"Wait, you're not coming?" This shocked Rapz, but he got the sense that the others had expected it.

"I have to go back. I have something to do in Soarken." There was a suspect that had gotten away and a new lead she wanted to follow. She couldn't call herself Authority anymore, but she needed closure before she could identify herself as something else.

"What about Kronic?" Luke asked. "I know he considers you a friend. Did you even say goodbye?"

"No, you'll have to do that for me. Tell him I'll be back before winter is out. Then I'll be ready to take that boat ride with him."

"I cannot speak for all," said Serenity, "but I believe that the village is the safer option for me and Innocence, and so I shall miss you, Felicity. I hope our paths cross again soon."

"Chris wants to go back to Soarken," said Rapz pointing at the bathroom sign, "Perhaps you could travel together."

Felicity stared at him, trying to figure out if he was being serious. "I would just as soon not."

Sadie was happy to see Felicity go.

After a brief exchange of farewells they prepared to leave, which for Sadie meant trying to talk her suctioned toddler back into the car. Once she had managed that, she turned her mothering on Kyan.

"I want you to go over there." Sadie pointed to the empty side of the gravel car park. "And vent some electricity before we go."

"Mum, I'm fine, I don't need to," Kyan assured her.

"Just go and have a try. Point your hands at the ground and see if you can get a few sparks out, so you're empty for the road."

"Muuum," Kyan groaned, "I've already been. I'm fine."

"You're not fine, Kyan." Sadie put her hands on her hips. "You're starting to hum."

"Well I am *now*, you keep telling me I need to go, when I don't."

Sadie tilted her head, glared, and pointed once more.

"OK," Kyan sighed, "I'll go try. Again."

"Thank you, sweetie," Sadie said with a smile.

Kyan stomped over to the bit of gravel that his mother had been pointing at. He forced a little electricity out. The hum persisted though, every time he purged it, his current started to build up again.

The gravel crunched softly as someone walked up behind him.

"It's not working." Kyan was starting to worry. Five minutes ago, he felt like he was in control, that he could build and vent his electricity at will, now he wasn't so sure. His hum started to grow louder with fizzles and pops.

"It'll be fine." Rapz was at his side.

"Is Mum still watching?"

"Nah, Madam got back out of the car. The little minx is on the roof, so your mum and Luke have their hands full."

"I can't make it stop, it just keeps coming back."

"When I did my first set, I was so nervous my hands were shaking, even on stage. The more I tried to get them to stop, the more they shook. I bet that's your problem, you need to be calm to be electric free, but the humming makes you tense and builds up the current."

"Well, yeah, but what can I do about that?"

"Stop trying, just chat with me and it'll sort itself. Ask me anything."

"Are we really going on a boat to a whole other country?"

"Yeah, Kronic said it's surrounded by sea mines and has loads of indigenous plants and animals so we can live there without worries."

"But there will be no consoles or TV, it'll be boring."

"Boring? No way, you will learn to hunt and fish and arrange wildflowers—"

"Flower arranging? Really?" Kyan sighed.

"You'll need something to brighten up the wood cabins we're going to build."

"Build our own houses, now that sounds cool."

"It's cooler than cool, my man, it's awesome, and do you know what else is?"

"What?"

"You've stopped humming."

"I have?" Kyan smiled and tried to shoot the earth. He was once again spark free.

A growing rumble and bird calls, coming from the forest to their right, caught their attention.

"Get to the cars!" Luke screamed. He tucked Madam under his winged arm and spread the other like a parachute to slow his fall. He corkscrewed down from the roof and hurried to the car. From the roof he had seen something hurtling through the forest. Rapz and Kyan couldn't see it, but they heard it. Whatever it was, it was almost upon them.

"RUN!"

***

Lara had led her small Wailer group out of Soarken. Her memories were still sharp and honed on Chris and the diner.

On each new street, the veteran Wailers in her company let out a call to arms. They travelled and recruited at an alarming pace, only stopping once to snack on a stray human that ran into their stampeding herd. By the time Lara and her friends had reached the forest road, their numbers exceeded forty. All of them were following Lara's lead. Ignorant to blisters and exhaustion, they ran to Ellie's Diner.

***

"Sir, the Wailer group has picked up its pace. They will reach the caf within half an hour."

"Are you ready to mobilise?" asked Spear.

"Yes, sir."

"Then move out. Digger is in command."

***

"I can't spark, I'm all out."

"Forget it." Rapz grabbed Kyan's wrist and pulled him away from the trees. "Just run." A wail, forty strong, rippled through the forest. "Run faster!"

***

Chris turned the taps. No water came out. He picked up an abandoned water bottle from the sink's edge, splashed some on his face, dribbled the last of it on the mirror and smeared away years of grime with his sleeve. His hands rested either side of his head, which flopped on to its own reflection. The glass was cold against his skin. He allowed time to slip by while maintaining this lean.

It was quiet. At some point the diner had become empty. He listened hard and heard giggling and footfalls on the roof. *'They've lost that mutant toddler again. Why are they even bothering? She doesn't want to live. If she did, she would behave.'* Chris pictured each of the Odd Blocker's faces. *'And they call me a liability? I'm better off without them.'* The last image he drew from his memory was of Rapz. *'I'm better off on my own, as soon as they go, I'll take my own route.'* The mirror under his reddening head shuddered as if a large vehicle was passing nearby, but the shrieks were not mechanical. *'Here we go again. Maybe no one compromised the block; maybe Wailers just have a sixth sense and taste for stupid people.'*

There was hollering and wailing, car doors slamming, thumping fists on metal and glass. Chris slowly rose and slid the bolt across the bathroom door. He slunk back into a stall and bolted that too. The toilet was full of grime and backwashed sewage. Chris dipped both hands in and slathered it onto his coat to mask his smell.

***

Road, was a generous description of the single lane mud trail that led out of Mallard Hill. The villagers had two Authority patrol cars which belonged to their military personnel. These heavy all-terrain vehicles snapped and crushed their way through the deliberately unkempt track. It was almost indiscernible from the forest floor as they got closer to Ellie's Diner. The people inside of the cars knew this part of the Eaves well. They could see their route through the forest as clearly as any road could mark it.

The car park at Ellie's Diner was squirming with Wailers.

"Drive-by formation," Digger ordered through his helmet comms.

Both patrol cars came to a stop with the passenger doors facing the mob.

"Set to single shot, avoid shooting the cars, and only hit clear targets."

"You mean like the white-eyed fella, whose trying to stomp a hole through that windshield?"

"Yes, Elaine, I do."

Bullets tore at the swarm, slow and considered, almost every shot hit its mark. The two passengers shot out of their windows. The drivers, Digger and Mal, had access hatches above their heads, they stood on their seats and, resting their rifles on the roof, they took aim.

"On foot now, keep a tight line and push them back." Digger, Mal, Tori, and Elaine advanced, continuing to fire with deliberation.

To begin with, the foes were too frenzied to abandon the hunt, but after half of them had dropped, self preservation kicked in. The Wailers retreated into the diner. Luke, Serenity, Madam, and Innocence strapped into Luke's dented and battered car.

Digger rapped on the window. With shaking hands Serenity wound it down. The swinging wing mirror tapped out its dying beats on the side of the car. "She's seen better days," said Digger. "Gather what you need and ride in that car with Mal." Mal waved over to them as a way of introduction.

Rapz was in the driver's seat of the patrol car. Digger motioned for him to wind down his window. Tori and Elaine took a knee in front of the diner and aimed their guns inside. They would unload their ammo only if the Wailers became hostile again. The Wailers taking refuge in there stayed tucked out of sight.

"Here is how this will work, occupants of the red car will ride in the lead car with Mal, followed by the van Tori will drive, followed by your patrol car, with mine bringing up the rear. You will drive at our speed and not break formation. Questions? Good, move out." There was no pause long enough for anyone to voice their questions even if they'd had them.

Luke forced the bent door open. He caressed the dents in the car's bonnet as he walked past. His elongated hand dropped to his side when his fingers found air.

"You will need to remove the child from your neck before you belt up," Mal said as they all walked over to his car.

"Yeah?" Luke said, feeling Madam tightening her grip around his neck. "Good luck with that."

The four vehicles filed out, following Mal's lead. They left the grit of the gravel car park and headed into the Eaves.

"I'm having real trouble shifting this van through this debris, sir," Tori's voice crackled through the headset. *"Permission to park the van and return with a winch."*

"Permission denied, just stick her in a lower gear and try to drive on the flattened — What's this joker doing? Tori, Mal, stop and hold your positions."

Digger got out of the car and marched toward the Odd Block's patrol car. It had come to an abrupt halt. The side door swung up and Kyan and Sadie shot out and raced into the forest.

"What are you doing? We're minutes away from base." Digger called, tearing after them.

"Stay back," said Sadie. "He got frustrated with the Wailers attacking and the uncertainty of where we're going, just give him some space and a few minutes."

"We don't have time—"

Kyan cried out as the bright surge poured out of him, scorching the forest floor.

"It's ok, baby," Sadie said from a safe distance. Her hand instinctively reached in his direction. She wanted so badly to hold him and make it all better. "Take your time, we're not going anywhere without you."

Digger walked a little closer. He was in awe of the power flowing out of the boy. He stopped when he reached Sadie and saw the tear pricked eyes behind her smile.

"You're going to be just fine, it's ok," she called. She did her best to hide it, but Digger could hear her voice starting to crack.

"What can I do to help?" Digger said.

"There's a fire extinguisher in the car, he's not hit any trees, but some leaves are smoking. We'll want to put those out before we go."

Digger patted her shoulder and walked back to the car.

"You're doing great, sweetie, nearly over."

"Everyone's looking at me," Kyan whinged.

"No one is looking at you, I promise. Look how small those sparks are getting, you're almost there."

Kyan started to cry. He'd lost his home, his sense of self, and he had no idea what to expect in his future. Sadie could resist her child's pain no longer. She ran and put her arm around him and kissed the top of his head. That last little jolt struck her touch, but she kept her grip and led him back.

Digger passed her with the extinguisher. Sadie reached for it. "No, let me, you two just get back in the car." He looked at Kyan's puffy, tear streaked face. "You were brave. You made your mum proud." Kyan smiled at him and snuggled against Sadie.

Chapter 8: Claire

Claire's initial gorge and self-indulgence was waning. The sickness had returned. It was still much less intense than it had been without the medication, but she wanted to know how much time she had left. She was also missing Brutus and Ethan. Her cage might be gilded, but a cage it remained.

Knock, knock, knock. "Claire?" That was her warning. Claire knew to be in her bedroom if anyone came calling. The door opened and the pierced and beautified woman called through. "I have your anti-sickness meds."

She wasn't alone this time, a stern-looking woman in a lab coat walked in. Her honey coloured hair was pulled into a functional bun and her cold eyes seemed to stare through Claire.

"My name is Dr Loralias Adder and I am in charge of this facility."

Adder was blocking the doorway so Jenna put her hand on Adder's shoulder and glided past. She sat on the bed next to Claire, took her hand and placed a pill on her palm. She smiled at her and mimed, "It'll be ok," then got up to pour Claire some water.

"We have determined the cause of your sickness. You will need antiemetic drugs three times a day for the foreseeable future," Adder said.

"Is it Wailerism? Am I changing?" Claire asked.

"There's good news and bad news I'm afraid." Jenna handed over a cup of water and sat next to Claire again. "The good news is that you have not started to change just yet, but the bad news is that you will."

"You are genetically predisposed for a Wailer mutation. That is inevitable." Adder's words offered no comfort. They were matter of fact and matched her deadpan face.

"Why have I not changed yet? Are you sure it's not happening now? Can you stop it?" Claire addressed her questions to Jenna, but it was Adder who answered them.

"You have delayed the onset of your symptoms by conceiving."

"Conceiving? I'm pregnant? Are you sure?"

"If all your questions pertain to the accuracy of my tests, then this will be a pointless conversation. I do not make mistakes in my lab."

Claire's inner princess was preparing to war with Adder's superiority complex.

Jenna read the room and stepped in. "You are absolutely right, your time is best spent in the lab. Might I take it from here?"

Adder nodded and left without saying goodbye.

"I am so sorry, Claire. Dr Adder is a brilliant scientist, but has no real people skills." Jenna took the water from Claire's trembling hand and placed it on the bedside table. "The pregnancy is what's made you so sick. You have Hyperemesis Gravidarum, a brutal form of morning sickness. Some women report it eases off at about five to six months, but for others it lasts for the whole pregnancy."

"How far along am I?"

"About six weeks."

Claire thought about eight more months of dehydration and vomiting. She thought about bringing an unplanned child into this wasteland of a world. "Can you terminate it?"

"I wouldn't advise it. As far as we can tell, it's the pregnancy that has stopped you from mutating. The baby is keeping you human. We're not sure if that is down to hormones, chemical changes, or something about the foetus itself. Dr Adder will want to run more tests and keep you close as the baby grows."

"A baby born with my genes, what chance will it have to be human?"

"A good one. It's had no direct exposure to the mutating formula, and with eight months for Adder to complete a cure, I'd say that little one has a better shot than most of us. When you're further along, we could do an amniocentesis and check out the baby's DNA profile." Jenna pulled out a pack of cards from her back pocket. "Want to play a few hands and help me procrastinate?"

"You won't be missed?" Claire would be glad for the company and subject change.

"Dr Adder and Graham can fetch their own stuff in my absence."

"I think you're a lot smarter than people give you credit for."

Jenna laughed. "Try telling that to the guys I work with."

Claire took the cards and started to shuffle. "Aces are high, and I want to stretch my legs when we're done."

"Now that we're sure you're a Wailer in waiting, we will need added security measures. I can't walk you myself, but two of our army personnel could escort you."

"I don't care who walks me, I just need to clear my head."

Jenna and Claire played a few hands before Adrienne Reese's stop-start voice came over the intercom.

"Dr Adder, say, return, to the lab."

Jenna rolled her eyes. "Duty calls. They probably need a coffee refill."

"Why do you put up with it? Surely you're not being paid anymore?"

"No, that's true, but I like to be close to Adder, she needs me. I've been with her throughout her career. We even went to school together."

"Was she this cold as a child?"

"Not always." Jenna smiled. Her eyes went vacant as she contemplated her earliest memory of Loralias. "I will be down to see you later, stay strong."

"Thank you, and the escort?"

"I'll arrange that for you now."

Raymond Saxon, a seven ft blonde, and a uniformed woman named Delilah, gave Claire a restricted tour of Prospect Heath. Orange mushrooms that re-programmed their minds infected them both. Their walk was robotic and their speech was limited and stuttered.

The icy grounds were beautiful. Cobbled paths wound from the four entry points around the garden. They all came to dead ends as they met the new high fence erected when the flats had been converted into Adder's lab.

Claire appreciated the aesthetics of the paths, but she didn't follow them. She made her own course over the frozen grass and leaves, weaving around the willows and shrubs.

'Will Brutus want the baby? Can we last as a couple? I'm not mum material, and after I've ejected the thing, how long till I turn? What if I eat it?' Claire's steps were heavy, she was stomping, trying to kick out her uncertainties. They had given her extra socks, gloves, hat, all the winter wear she could need. She wanted to stay out as long as she could, even with her two disproportioned shadows.

"Claire. Over here, Claire!"

The Brutes gathered at the fence staring through the bars. Saxon and Delilah quickly put themselves between Claire and her friends.

"It's ok, I know them." Claire tried to push past but they wouldn't budge.

"Stay," Saxon said.

Eager to reaffirm his position in the group Caleb scaled the fence and darted towards them. He juggled his knife between his hands and danced in front of the Mushroom-men. "Give 'er over, or get sliced."

Saxon caught one of Caleb's wrists. He squeezed, not with all his might, just enough to bring the bones to breaking point. Caleb squawked and shrilled. He dropped the knife and fell to his knees. The rest of the Brutes scrambled over the fence.

"Stop." Delilah held out her mushroom covered hand. "No, closer."

"It's ok, Brutus, they have treated me well and are medicating my sickness," Claire said.

"So you left willingly?"

"No, not exactly. You know how ill I've been, they helped me."

"They took our food and our guns."

"Guns, not yours," said Saxon. "Food, will return, if, co-operate."

Brutus glared at Saxon and stomped closer. "You're not the brains of the operation. I think you'd best lead me to the person who is."

Adder was forced to discontinue her work again. The mess hall was filled with the Brutes and enough Mushroommen to stop them trying their luck.

"I see you have located us before we could locate you. We have much to discuss," Adder stated.

"No we don't. You give us our stuff, let Claire go, and pray that we don't hold a grudge," said Brutus.

"It is not that simple," said Adder. "Claire needs medication, which we will provide. In return I need you to help me capture live mutants for study."

"Why do you need us? You have mushroom freaks for that."

"They were once Authority soldiers, highly trained, highly capable. Do you know what they are now, Michael?"

"How did you—"

Adder flashed him a warrant card. "Now they are drones. With their current level of programming, they are inept at adapting to situations that deviate from their instructions.

Their success rate outside of protecting this building has been poor."

"The dead mushroom freak at the Spokes?"

"Yes, Sage Garven, and three more when we tried to rescue the inhabitants of Sycamore Close and quell the horde you built."

"You rescued them?"

"No, it would seem they were quite capable of doing that themselves, Michael."

"Brutus, I don't go by Michael anymore."

"Do you see the arrangement we can forge between us?"

Brutus frowned. "Claire gets meds, we get food, and you get test subjects." The Brutes huddled together and discussed the arrangement. "Claire comes with us though, we'll work for her meds, but she stays with us."

"She can go with you, so long as she returns weekly for her meds and allows me to take bloods and vitals." Adder held out her hand and Brutus shook on it. "Jenna will give you all a shot before you leave."

"You best mean booze, 'cause none of our lot is being a pin cushion for you."

"The shot, Mr Brutus, is a booster to keep you human. I assume this is something that you want?"

Jenna stepped in. "No decisions have to be made just yet, and it's not compulsory. The inoculation you already had will wear off, but it's still your call. Stay, eat, ask questions, and leave on your own terms with all the facts in hand."

Brutus sat down next to the tray of needles and pulled his sleeve up. Jenna smiled, she levelled her low cut top with his eyes, swabbed his arm, and jabbed the needle in. The rest of the Brutes fell in line to follow his example.

"Damn, is it supposed to feel like ice?" Leighton rubbed his arm.

"The first jab we got was cold too," Joel reassured him.

"Yeah, but I don't remember it being this bad."

Jenna hugged Claire before leaving them alone with the Mushroom-men. "Take care, I'll see you soon."

Saxon dumped two packs of food at Brutus's feet and handed him a clear bottle labelled *Claire Ivanthor's pills*.

"What the fuck is this?"

"Food, pills," said Saxon.

"Where's the rest of it?" The Brutes surrounded the simple giant.

He handed Brutus a handwritten address. "Earn, rest."

"What about instructions for the meds?" asked Joel.

"No, instructions, just pills."

"I have to take them three times a day, before food," said Claire.

Joel jabbed her with his elbow. "If we know what they're called, we can get our own," he hissed.

"Forget it," said Brutus snatching the paper out of Saxon's hand. "We'll earn it, for now."

Chapter 9: Chris

Chris left the stall and pressed his ear to the bathroom door. There was shuffling. The roar of engines had petered out some time ago. *'Why are they still here?'* He had been banking on the Wailers following the cars away from the diner.

On the other side of the door the Wailer's paced, in their frenzied state their senses heightened, the lingering smell of human presence caused them to pull through the cupboards, and slither under tables. The sewage cologne that Chris had doused himself in, was the only reason they hadn't found him.

There were no windows in the bathroom. The door was his only way out. *'Maybe they'll come back for me.'* It was a weak thought. Chris was alone. Well almost, eleven surviving Wailers shuffled and squawked in the next room.

***

A white-eyed male with freckle clusters sniffed along the edge of the kitchen counter. Minute particles of dried food lingered in the drawer beneath his nose. Freckles opened it up and rummaged inside. He sped back to the central table with a rusted tin opener and slammed it down. A Wailer child picked it up and attached it to a tin, he mimed the way the hand would need to twist to operate it. Freckles took the tin from him and twisted the opener, slowly slicing through.

A scraggly haired girl dragged more tins out of Chris's discarded rucksack and towered them. Human flesh was not their only food source, their living bodies needed sustenance.

She pulled out a bottle of water and swirled the dregs that remained. She rushed it to the kitchen taps and slammed them round, grunting at their refusal to flow. There were many things that Scraggly could no longer read or recognise, but the universal picture for a bathroom was something she understood.

***

Something tried the handle, wrenching it up and down. It sounded like just one for now, but if it became agitated, they might all bang down the door. Chris slid the bolt across silently and braced himself against the wall. The door flung into him and the scraggly Wailer woman walked in. She tried all three basins, none of them had water.

Chris sipped only little breaths of air, desperate not to push the door with his rising chest. Pinned between the wall and door, he watched Scraggly pick up the bottle he had emptied earlier. She pressed the rim of the upside-down bottle to her nose and snorted as a drop of water followed the scent into her nostril. She kept hold of it and checked the stalls.

Chris stopped breathing altogether as she walked past the door and exited the bathroom. He peered through the slit that ran between the hinges. The Wailers were all interested in the tins on the table. Scraggly joined them.

This looked like his chance. If he stayed low, he might make it to the door while the food distracted them. He edged out listening to the clattering of cans and the slapping of lips. He made it to the second table and peeked up over it.

That's when he saw her. Their eyes met across the crowded room, her mouth stained red with her last meal, his trousers stained brown by his. He could not take his tired eyes off of Lara's large oval ones. He backed into the bathroom and she followed him, staring at her prize with venomous intent.

She lunged through the door at him. Her throat rumbled with a wail. Chris flipped her onto her back and smothered her mouth, stifling the cry. She thrashed and hit against him. He pinched her nose closed with her mouth still smothered. He didn't remember his petite girlfriend ever having this much strength. Her body went slack underneath him as she lost consciousness. She was breathing steadily. Her eyes closed. Without that milky hue on show, she looked just like the Lara he knew. Her skin was hot to touch, like she was still running a fever.

Chris checked on the other Wailers. They were still engrossed in their tinned meal. He softly closed the door, took off his belt and used it to bind Lara's hands behind her back. There wasn't a great deal to improvise with in the bathroom. There was an unopened pack of toilet rolls, and it turned out that's all he needed. He ripped a strip off of the plastic wrapper and placed that over her eyes, then he wound toilet paper around her head to bind it in place. He balled more of the toilet roll and twisted it inside of small squares of wrapper and popped one in each of Lara's nostrils.

After an hour, the Wailer group left. A passing doe and her fawn drew them out of the diner and they chased the pair into the Eaves. Another hour passed and Lara regained consciousness.

Chris touched her cheek. She nuzzled against him. "Lara, honey, it's me, Chris." She launched at him, snapping her teeth and wailing. *'Touch fine, speech bad,'* Chris thought. He had spent hours listening to the grunts and moans of the contented Wailers in the diner. He tried to copy them now.

Lara calmed, she allowed Chris to take her elbow and help her to her feet. He linked his arm through hers and led her out into the gravel car park. *'I was right,'* he thought. *'I couldn't help you back at the flat, but I can help you now. We're going back to Soarken, to Dr Adder. I will save you.'*

Chapter 10: Prospect Heath

Bright light dug into James's eyes as he opened them. He was not alone. Graham was by his side and yammered away the second James woke up.

"They're up to something, meeting together thick as thieves. They won't even let me visit the girl we rescued at the school. Jenna idolises Adder, she doesn't want to see it, but I see it. Adder is up to something. She blanked me when I mentioned your findings on the woman's hair. The ones you pulled off Luke. There is potential for a cure in that woman's DNA, she must see it. She's not done anything to work on the cure, she's just obsessed with the mutations. The guy who killed you got away, well not killed you, but you know what I mean."

"Luke, Luke killed me." James shielded his eyes but the light still burrowed into his head. "Look, Graham, I just woke up—"

"I know, Luke broke your neck, but you're healed now, it's all good."

"No, I mean it's a lot to process. My head is banging and your words are painful. Thank you for coming to me with this, but can I wake up first?"

Graham sank. "I... I just need a friend."

"I am your friend, Graham, but I need a little time. Come back in an hour, and we'll talk as much as you like."

Graham hesitated in the doorway. He spoke in his smallest voice, partly not to further James's headache, but mostly because the words frightened him. "Are we still the good guys?"

"Me and you? Yes, we are."

Graham mumbled to his feet as he walked down the walkway, before he crashed into Jenna.

"Easy there, friendly," she laughed and steadied him. "Are you ok?"

His heart raced from her lingering touch. "He's got a headache, but he'll be fine."

"You went to visit James? I'm glad he's recovering, but I was asking about you. You look washed out."

"It's just..." Graham sighed and retreated from any further explanation.

"How about you come over to my place and chill?" Her broad smile drew him out of deep thought and into shallow desires. "I have a coffee machine in my room."

"How did you get a coffee machine? My room is beyond basic." He looped his arm through hers and allowed her to drag him away.

"Perks of being an assistant. I sent out the final inventory request and snuck a few luxuries on for myself."

Her apartment reeked of personality. It was fully decorated, although the furnishings were the standard plain ones. "A few luxuries?"

Jenna shrugged. "We had a suitcase allowance. I used one of my bags for wallpaper rolls and paint." She collected up some discarded clothes and paperwork to make a space for Graham on the sofa. The papers caught his attention, at a glance he made out some difficult formulas, and a few noteworthy SIA (Scientific Initiative Alliance) names in the crediting title.

"Are these from the lab?"

"No." Jenna hid them under a cushion. This made him glare at her more. "It's kind of embarrassing," she said. "I was doing distance learning before we set up here, and I've been continuing with the coursework in my down time. I know I won't get my Masters with everything that's going on." She flicked on the coffee machine, which took pride of place on her coffee table, and prepared the grounds. "It gives me something to do. And who knows, maybe I'll be able to contribute something to Adder's work. The way you do."

Graham often teased her about being of a lesser intellect, he didn't mean it maliciously, but now he felt guilty. "I think it's great, and I'm always available if you need some tutoring."

"I will definitely take you up on that at some point. Not right away though, I want to get through as much of the material as I can on my own."

Even though Graham was seated and now smiling, he was still fidgety and agitated.

"Latte for me, and for you, my high strung friend, hot chocolate." She served it beaten not stirred, to maximise powder absorption, and topped it with whipped milk.

"Is Adder still even working towards the cure?" Graham blurted.

"No doubt, top priority."

"It's just, James found that hair, recovered from Luke's clothing. Adder won't talk about it. That girl, Claire? I haven't seen her since we rescued her. And Adder is so obsessed with the mutants. Nothing else seems to matter."

"All genuine reasons to be concerned. I'll start with Claire. She's pregnant, a delicate situation, one which I advised Dr Adder, would be easier to handle with a female only presence. You can blame me for that. Claire is a Wailer in waiting. Her pregnancy has stopped the progression of symptoms though, and Adder thinks it may give a clue to a cure."

"Are we keeping her prisoner? Experimenting on her?"

"No, Adder released her back to her group today. She will come back every week for sickness meds and allow us to take bloods and vitals, but that's it, all on her terms."

Graham relaxed back into the sofa. "And the hair."

"Reese traced all bills and tenancies in the block. Luke was living at number nine, with a woman named Sadie Ratcher, aka Scratcher, the graphic novel artist? No? That's ok, you don't have to know her, her work is obscure. Anyway, Sadie's record photos show she has long mahogany hair, consistent with the ones James found. Reese is going through her logged text messages on the system and Luke's too. We know they planned a boat ride with two men, Kronic and Tyde, but both those names are pseudonyms, and they wrote in code. They were to rendezvous at the diner, go on to the village, and then to Tyde's boat. Thing is, there are a lot of diners and villages scattered about. So, nothing to go on yet, but Reese is still working on it. Dr Adder concurs with James that this could be a lead on the cure.

"Finally, her obsession with the mutations is down to the last paper James wrote back when he was known as Tobias

Davidson. He said that the mutations themselves hold the cure. That one or more of the mutant variants could produce some kind of secretion or chemical that would reverse engineer the Wailerism."

"Dr Adder let *you* read this paper?"

"She left it out on her desk. To be honest, I didn't understand most of it. It was..." She waggled her fingertips in front of her, like she was about to perform a magic trick. "A bit too wordy for me to get a proper grasp. I made a copy, you can have it."

"So, Claire, the mutations, the hair, they're all leads for the cure and Adder is chasing them down?"

"Mm-hm."

"What about the Mushroom-men? I've never been happy with using them as an experiment."

"It's reversible, Adder said so. She only did it because Minister Farr was trying to shut us down. Without the lab and us there's no cure, so Adder improvised."

"Four of them have died, Jenna, that's not reversible."

"No, but we won't be using them like that again. Adder is getting Claire's group to help with survivor rescue and Wailer capture."

"Not a bunch I'd trust, I doubt that will play out as planned." Graham downed the last of his hot chocolate. "I suppose we had best go back to the lab."

Chapter 11: Mallard Hill

A large section of the tree-like wall in front of them swung inwards, allowing the returning cars access. Once closed, it flushed against the rest of the wall giving no visual clues to the gate's existence.

The vehicles parked up in a lay-by close to the entrance. The Odd Blockers filed out. A woman with a wheelchair raced towards them. Her already pale Marazsian face, drained white at the sight of the new arrivals.

"Can I help you, Lashale?"

"Paul," she said, stringing relevant words into a nonsense sentence. "They said, Paul, injured man. Collect Paul for treatment. I'm here." She made no effort to hide her stares. "What are they?"

"Paul is in here. He's not like them." Mal guided Lashale away from the Odd Blockers. They stood and listened to Paul making a grand first impression.

"Help me, young lady," he squealed. "My leg has fallen off and it won't stick back on."

Lashale ran screaming from the patrol car.

"I'll take him," said Mal. He lifted Paul into the wheelchair and placed his unclipped false leg across his knees.

"Excuse me, good sir," Paul said to a random passerby. "Would you hold on to this for me?" He thrust his leg into the man's hand before he knew what was happening. "Mind you don't let it hop away."

"Doc's gonna have his hands full with that one," Digger said shaking his head. "Right, I'll take you to Kronic and Tyde. Stay together, no wandering off." Digger took point and Elaine and Tori stood further back ensuring they had a good view of everyone.

The roads in Soarken were straight and flat. They conformed to a grid-like pattern. The Roads in Mallard Hill curved, rising and falling with the contours of the land.

The Odd Blockers walked down what they assumed was the village's main artery.

"Hey, Anglo," a man shouted over his neighbours fence. "Your long johns are getting frosty."

"Just the way I like them," Anglo called back. Anglo had an array of washing hung in his front garden. All of it had frozen solid.

The garden a few doors down had hundreds of brightly coloured mushroom statues, little and large, covering every inch of the patio. Sadie was sure this was a symptom of mental illness.

A large cat crossed the road. She had wrestled a bright orange fish out of a garden pond. It was easily half the size of the wet feline and she carried it proudly in her mouth. She stopped in her tracks to glare at the newcomers, before disappearing under a hedge with her wriggling prize.

"Welcome to the village of the mad," Sadie said aloud. Elaine jabbed her in the ribs with the butt of her gun. "What, so I can't talk?" Elaine jabbed her again. "Use your big girl words, so I can understand you," *The Bitch* said through Sadie, in her most condescending voice. The third jab was forceful enough to shut Sadie up.

They stopped outside of the most modern looking building in the village. Mallard Hill's Authority Station. There were usually separate stations for policing and military units, but Mallard Hill was so small, all divisions made use of the one building. Spear, Tyde, Kronic, and Cleaver waited inside of the gym like training room.

"So, hose-hands, you can vouch for every one of them?" Spear glared at Tyde.

"Yes," said Tyde hesitantly. He looked from stranger to stranger. He had not met a single one of them before.

"Are you sure about that?" Spear glared at him.

Tyde looked to the only face he needed to see. He trusted Kronic. "Yes," he said with more assertion. "I will vouch for them."

Spear took out a warrant card. Walking down the line, he scanned each of the Odd Blockers' faces and locked their details into his save folder. None of them had flashed up with anything serious; even so, their files would make for a long night of study. "Tori, you're dismissed," said Spear. "Elaine." She smiled and stood to attention at her name. "Cleaver left a mess in my office, go clean it up." The woman's face dropped, and she skulked away.

"As for the rest of you, you will get three houses on the outskirts to live in until the thaw. You will contribute to the survival of this village and the well being of its inhabitants. If you cause any problems, I don't care if it's by accident, I will evict you all. Understood?" They all agreed to the terms.

"Digger will show you to your new homes. You will report to me here in the morning for assignments."

Digger walked them to the edge of the hill and showed them the three house cul-de-sac. He gave out three boxes of rations, one for each home, and warned them that they would turn all gas and electricity off at dusk.

"Fliss," said Kronic. "You can come out now."

"She's not here, mate," said Luke.

"What do you mean she's not here?"

"She went back to Soarken, something about unfinished business on an old case. She said she'd come back before we leave for the island."

"You let her leave?"

"Like I could have stopped her, she's as stubborn as you."

Kronic glared at his friend. He grabbed his box and stormed inside the house furthest away. Tyde and Cleaver followed him.

"Shall we share this middle house?" Serenity broke the silence.

Rapz took a moment to realise that her proposal was aimed at him. "Sure, you and the kid can take the bigger room. I don't need much space."

Sadie, Luke, and the kids were left with a house to themselves.

"They didn't leave keys." Sadie looked in the door and on the key hooks hung on the wall behind it. No keys.

"I guess we're not supposed to lock up," said Luke. He took their supplies through to the kitchen.

Sadie walked through the house with a growing unease. This was someone else's home. Framed and mounted photographs hung on the wall. Sadie stroked her fingers over the ornaments above the mantel. A little dust had settled, but not much. Every draw and cupboard was stocked with utensils, clothes, stationary, toys.

"Did they die?" Kyan asked.

"Did who die?" Sadie said.

"The people whose house this was. All their stuff is still here. It's kind of creepy."

"Well—"

"Kywam no have a bed," Madam sang as she crawled down the wall from upstairs.

Sadie held out her arms and Madam fell into them. "Shall we figure out sleeping arrangements?"

"Madmam have a bed, Kywam sleep on floor."

Kyan glared at his rosy cheeked sibling.

"Kywam no have a b-ed, Kywam no have a b-ed," Madam sang as Sadie carried her up the stairs.

Sadie pushed open the door to the smaller room. Inside, squished between the walls was a metal framed high bed. Underneath sat a set of drawers, a small bookcase, and plastic boxes containing toys. To the side, squished between the edge of the bed and the wall, was a small desk, with a light box and a cup full of coloured pencils.

"See, Madmam has a bed. Madmam gets to sleep up high."

Sadie ignored her comment. The high bed would be Kyan's. She spotted unopened model kits under the desk. The space felt like it had been waiting for him.

There was a cramped master bedroom next door with a double bed. Too much personality drenched this room, and it felt lived in. Sadie walked out and opened a small airing cupboard, filled with sheets and towels. She mentally changed the beds and reached for the bedding in preparation.

"Not the satin stuff," said Luke as he came up the stairs. "I'll slide straight off."

Luke examined the padlock on the back bedroom. "Perfect opportunity to try out my lock picking skills." He fished the lock picks that Paul had given him out of his pack and practised what Paul had taught him back at the flats. His elongated mutant fingers struggled to even hold the picks let alone angle them. He dropped them again. Having an audience wasn't helping.

"Come on, you two. Let's go see what we can make for dinner." Sadie ushered the children down the stairs.

Luke dropped and fiddled and swore, but after an hour his persistence paid off. "I got it open," he yelled over the banister.

Sadie came up the stairs and picked up the plate of pasta she had left on the top step. "You didn't touch your food," Sadie said.

"You made me food?"

"Yes, I left it on the landing. I told you it was there."

"I'm sorry I don't remember you coming up. It'll still be good cold though. Are the kids ok?"

"Yeah, they're crashed out in front of a film."

Luke opened the door. Thick musty air escaped. Someone had painted the room in a deep pink. The wall tucked behind the door had photographs of a young girl pinned all over it. The girl had black hair and eyes, and a cheeky smile. The oldest she looked in any picture was six. These dominated the wall, although there were some younger pictures, even the odd baby one.

Boxes stacked against the wall opposite the door were labelled, clothes, toys, drawings, books. The wall facing the photographs had a window. Underneath it, sat a sofa that had turned grey with ash. A huge glass ashtray overflowed onto the seat. There was another photograph, facedown under the ashtray.

"I can't imagine losing a child." Sadie wrapped her arms around herself as she entered the room.

"What makes you think they lost a child?"

Sadie lifted the ashtray, dusted off the picture and turned it over. The same six-year-old stared back at her. Her eyes were lighter, not quite white, more like the palest of greys. She had a blank expression. Clasped around her neck was a collar. The green light showed it to be in good working order. Sadie recognised the shape in her peripheral and turned towards it. On top of a box lay an unhinged collar. Its lights were out.

Luke took the photo from Sadie and held it up at the pictures on the wall. It was the same little girl, but at the same time, it wasn't. All the joy and cheek and life were missing from the ash covered photo.

"I don't want Verity-Elise sleeping in here."

"It's just a room, Sade. All houses have some history, maybe just a little less obvious than this. We'll clear it out, clean it up, and make a nice big hammock to hang across these two walls."

As Luke described it, she could see the room being transformed and the negative energy it held fading into something else.

"She sleeps in with us tonight though."

Chapter 12: The Brutes

"I'm not going back to the school. By all means, we'll keep our deal until we can get our hands on meds for Claire, but I don't want to sleep where they can find us." The others felt the same as Leighton. "We need a new supply stash too. I'm not relying on them for food."

He talked with Brutus, Joel, and Caleb as they neared the van.

"I know a place," said Claire. "A bunker in the grounds of a mansion, filled with supplies."

Brutus laughed. "You must be delusional from the meds. You'd have told me if a place like that existed."

"I didn't tell you because people I knew died there. I didn't want to go back."

"But you do now?"

"Not really."

Claire sat shotgun and gave Brutus directions to the Ivanthor Estate.

"Damn it, Caleb, get your boney 'bows out of my ribs."

"Did you say the second or third right?"

"Yeah, Caleb, and get off my foot!"

"Knock it off. I can't hear Claire's instructions."

"Sorry, Brutus, but it's cramped back here."

"We're here," said Claire. "I'll just put the code in the gate."

Claire got out and punched in the code. The gates swung open. She jumped back in and Brutus carried on up the drive.

Ethan, George, Joel, Leighton, and Caleb all strained to see the mansion which was still some distance away.

"The Ivanthor Estate has always prided itself on its independence." Claire pointed to the wind turbines in the distance and the solar panels on the roof. "We'll have plenty of electricity."

"For how long?" said George. "These things need maintaining. You can't just lay some solar panels and wind turbines and expect them to work forever."

"Well, the power is working now otherwise the gate wouldn't have opened."

The Brutes parked up the van and stepped out. The grounds were so substantial it was hard to make out the city from here. Brutus pushed the doors that towered over him open.

Claire hung back. "I don't want to go in."

"How many?"

"Just two, but, Brutus..." She grabbed his arm. "I knew them, I know that they're dead, but please treat them well."

***

The bunker had been home to the man for seven weeks. With its extensive supplies, he could survive down here for decades. These last few weeks he'd wondered why he would want to. It was isolating underground.

The first few days after the Great Wailer Regression, he had driven around Soarken. At first he hunted for friends, family, acquaintances, soon after he would have taken anyone at all, just for the company.

The last time he went out, he found an un-regressed Collar clearing bodies at the side of the road. For a moment he thought the Collar had a golf club. It turned out to be a litter picking arm, but after that first glance the man named the Collar, Golfer. He ordered Golfer into the car. On the way home he grabbed some serum and collar maintenance packs. In hindsight, he should have rescued a dog.

The white-eyed Wailer stayed submissive at first. Golfer sat patiently in the bunker, listened to the man speak, he ate his food supplements when ordered to, and was generally a delight to be around.

When the headaches came, the man was sure he was becoming a Wailer himself. He felt as though he was leaving his body for short bursts, or rather, another body was visiting him in spirit form.

He concentrated hard. The visiting spirit was dark for a long time. When the light switched on, the image was of a bird fluttering by the window. He was both hungered and excited by the bird. His hands, no hers, he could see a delicate ring on the rotted lumps of hand pounding on the window in response to the bird. He recognised the garden that the window overlooked and he ran from the bunker. Sure enough, when he rounded the corner he saw a female zombie banging her rotten hands on the window. He closed his eyes and concentrated. Again he saw the world through the zombie's eyes. He saw his confused face staring through the window. A second presence, a male this time, roused by the female's noise, joined her in the kitchen. The man was now seeing himself simultaneously through both the dead things' blurred vision.

The resulting headache was catastrophic, he tried to pull himself away from their minds but he struggled. Their pull was too strong.

He needed somewhere quiet, and this was the moment where Golfer turned out to be an asset. The snarls and murderous intent of the beasts dropped away, as he concentrated on Golfer. He could see shelves stacked with tins. Golfer's vision remained fixed, and his mind was empty. It was numbing. The more the man concentrated on Golfer, and only him, the more his mind slipped back into his own body. When he fully inhabited it, he found blood pooling under his nose and on his earlobes. It had been one bitch of a headache, but it was gone now. He Left the zombies, who had once been Sophie Whittle and Gerald Mace, to bang on the window, and retreated to the bunker.

He tried many times after that to touch the minds of the dead butler and cook from the safety of the bunker. More often than not, their minds were a void. They only flicked on if something caught their attention. Sophie stayed put in the kitchen, stationary in front of the window. Gerald was a shuffler. A few times when boredom set in, the man took a very slow tour of the Ivanthor manor through Gerald's eyes.

Something new woke him one night. It was ravenous, high on anticipation of death and gluttony. He sensed the veracity of Golfer's intent. The man was the meal, and as soon as he spied himself through the Wailer's eyes, he knew it was too late to run. Golfer ripped into him, and although he had loosened the mental tether, the man still felt both his pain and Golfer's delight. This frenzy state for Golfer was so all consuming he was prepared to die in it. The man had little to hand. He took the largest can he could keep grasped and plunged it against the side of Golfer's head.

Golfer's death brought the strangest relief, he was no longer keenly aware of how delicious his own flesh tasted. Blood poured from the man's wounds. He pulled himself between the shelves and grabbed at the first aid kit.

The loneliness resumed. Recovery from his injuries was the first priority, when he was well enough he would search for company beyond his bunker. For weeks though, the only contact he had was with Sophie and Gerald, his mind touching theirs briefly like he was scanning through radio waves, but he didn't tune in, he didn't have Golfer's quiet mind to fall back on.

***

Brutus walked through the Ivanthor Estate in awe. Painted portraits that stood taller than him, lined the entrance hall, portraits of Claire and Terry and of their stern looking parents. The siblings looked separate from their parents. They had posed in pairs, and although the artist tried to merge the image, Mr and Mrs Ivanthor had been painted abroad in their second home, where the light quality was very different. Harder light and shadow defined them, while Terry and Claire seemed to fade in the softer Soarken light.

"Clear," George shouted from the landing.

"All clear," Joel shouted from another corner of the house.

"I gots nuffin. I fort there was bloods in 'ere?" Caleb called from the kitchen.

"It's all good," Brutus said, pulling Claire into the house. "It's safe."

"Where are they then? There should at least be bodies."

"Authority must have cleaned it up, before the Wailer Regression."

"I doubt it. They died mere days before the Regression."

"What do you want me to say, Claire? There are no monstrous maids. Let's just go find the bunker, shall we?"

"Ok, go straight through and across the grounds, it's quicker than walking all the way around the mansion."

"You're coming too, Claire."

This was her home, a large and unfeeling place, but it was still her home. This had been Terry's home too. What little personality this labyrinth of rooms had, belonged to Claire and her brother.

"Through there." Claire pointed at the door she had run through when trying to escape from Gerald. "I locked it though, so the key is still on the outside. You'll have to break the glass."

Brutus pulled the handle and opened the door. "It's not locked."

"But..." Claire was confused. She was sure she had locked it. There was something else wrong with this picture. Something had changed in the landscape. Claire ran out of the door.

Someone had hacked a bench to pieces. An axe stuck out of the remaining strut. The re-appropriated wood made four crosses. They were named, and each had flowers placed at its base. Sophie Whittle, Gerald Mace, Golfer and... Claire broke down and hugged the dirt beneath the fourth cross titled Terry Emanuel Ivanthor.

"He's not under there." Brutus tried to lift Claire from the ground. "Claire, he's not—"

"He is." The bunker man strolled up to them with confidence, his immense reservations buried deep. "When you didn't come through the back gate, I drove around through the chaos looking for you. For days I looked. After I found Terry's body, I brought him home, and buried him first."

Claire raised her dirt tinged face from Terry's grave. "Brett? You're alive?" She curled her fingers around the flower heads, stroking the midnight blue petals. "Terry loved this colour."

"Who's this prick?" Caleb, as usual, was eager to escalate things.

Brutus glared. "This, if I remember correctly, is one of Claire's butlers."

"Technically an employee of the Estate," said Brett. "But are any of us defined by our jobs or social classes anymore?"

"Is there anyone else here?" Brutus gripped the hammer suspended in his belt loop.

This gesture alarmed Brett. He searched for Brutus's intention in his facial expression and found himself being drawn into a corner of Brutus's mind.

It was a memory. *Brutus had a box tucked under one arm, the Soarken Authority station was at his back, and a female officer stood before him. She had no love for him, Brutus sensed that. Brett felt something in that memory, something about the woman's hatred. Brutus had done something she found horrif-*

ic. Her dislike pleased him. The conversation happened as it always had and Brett experienced it through Brutus's eyes.

"Where'd you get that scar, Michael?" Brett spit the words aloud without meaning to. His tone and pitch matched the female officer's words as they existed in Brutus's memory.

"What the fuck did you say to me?" Brutus screeched.

Brett snapped out of the memory and back into his own body.

"Leave him alone, he just asked a question." Claire stood between the two men. Brett saw that Brutus had his hammer raised above his head. From what little he gleamed from that memory, he knew Brutus would use it without hesitation.

"He knows my name, but I've never met him."

"The pane on the front door is one giant warrant card," said Claire. "There's a receiver panel in the food store. He knows all of your names. Is that a reason to kill him?"

Brutus stood down.

"I'm sorry," Brett said. "It's been a long time since I had contact with anyone. I should have let you introduce yourselves. That scar looks like it has a story, perhaps you'll tell me about it one day."

"Sure," said Brutus, narrowing his eyes. "Maybe I will."

***

They ate a feast that night. It turned out, that as well as being a scrawny psychopath, Caleb was a pretty decent cook.

"This is amazing," said Leighton gorging on his third helping. "How can a guy like you cook like this?"

"Jus good a mixin shit up, I guess."

"Used to be a different sort of cook, didn't you?" Joel said.

"More cash for drug cooks, ain't it?" Despite cooking copious amounts of food, Caleb only picked at his.

Brett ate in silence. If he engaged with them, he may end up being pulled into someone else's brain. Wailer and zombie minds were easier to navigate. He found being forced into random memories terrifying.

Claire had taken her last anti-sickness dose of the day and eaten as much as her appetite would allow. She was absent from the group now. Brutus found her in Terry's room. He sat beside her on the bed and cradled her against him.

"Things have been worse than shit, babe, but they will get better. We can stay here if you like. The P Heath guys can't find us here, or if all these reminders are too hard, we can pack up and move anywhere you like." He took the bottle of pills out of Claire's hand, and tipped one into his palm. "We'll raid the pharmacies tomorrow, rip open every blister pack and pour out every bottle till we find out what these are."

"They called me a Wailer in waiting," Claire sobbed. "I have to go back to Prospect Heath. Dr Adder is mental, but Jenna, the one with the piercings, she's nice and she wants to help me."

"You really think you're going to turn? If you do, what help can that mad scientist be?"

"I'm pregnant. The baby has stopped my transformation for now, but they don't know why. If they do, they can synthesise a cure. I believe it. I have too. What if our child gets my genes? What if it's destined to be a Wailer? If I can help to make a cure for our child, then that is what I have to do."

Brutus let her finish but from those first two words he was overcome with emotion. "A baby," he said with tears flowing down his cheeks. "We're going to have a baby?"

Claire nodded. "It's early, but Jenna says everything is on track."

"This is amazing, just amazing, come here." He kissed every inch of her face. When he reached her lips, he pushed a lasting kiss on them. "I have never been happier."

"I want to name it Terry, after my brother, Terri with an 'I' if it's a girl." She snuggled into him and let his scent fill her up.

"It's perfect," he said. "You're right about needing the cure just in case, but for the safety of our child, we need to bend the agreement a little. Take away their leverage." He held the pill out. "Then there will be more room for negotiation."

Chapter 13: Felicity

I can see the smug bastard breathing in his freedom. Slamming the patrol car into the nearest spot, I step out to greet him.

"Officer Grange, how nice of you to come see me off."

I want to hit him. I want to ram that box down his throat. What I want and what I can do, while still keeping my job, are two different things.

"I work here, Michael, although I must admit it pains me to watch you go."

"I'm sure we will see each other around."

"Oh, count on it." See him around? He isn't getting off my radar, not for one minute. "Hey, Michael." I call after him. He keeps walking. "Michael?" I call even louder. "Hey. Where'd you get that scar, Michael?" He wears it like a badge of honour, but we both know where it came from. That gets his attention. He turns to face me, but keeps backing up.

"I told you it was a shark attack. The toothy bastard was this big. I fought him off with a toothpick and a power ballad." He starts to sing, his outstretched arm mimes his imaginary shark.

"Careful," I yell with a grin. "Carry a tune that badly and you'll be mistaken for a Wailer."

I hope he is. He went down for assault before the Calamity. He's never even seen a Wailer or a zombie. I'm hoping his inexperience will be his downfall. I don't bank on it though. His downfall is my responsibility.

He's long gone from my sight before I walk on in to headquarters. I sign in and head straight to my desk. Her pictures are still in the top drawer. Two of them, one of the smiling petite blonde in life, the other is of her corpse. The former couldn't be used to identify the latter. Nicole was beaten to the brink of death. Thirteen fractures, bruising to most of her skin, and her organs had been viciously tenderised. Despite all this, her injuries hadn't killed her. Nicole's battered body had been rolled in to Soarken's river, her last breath filled her lungs with its watery sludge. I worked plenty of murder cases before the Calamity, but this one haunts me still. It's the suffering. I've never seen that level of hate inflicted on a person, before or since.

Bill, my Infection Control partner, places a cup of get-up-and-go on my left. He looks at Nicole's picture. "We'll get the bastard," he says.

"We had *the bastard. He just walked out the door." I know Bill doesn't want to hear it. He's heard it a hundred times before.*

"Felicity, you have to get past this. Michael Brutus is not Nicole's killer. He has an air-tight alibi."

"It's not air-tight." I'm sick of this argument, we've had it too many times before, and it drains me.

"Thing is, Lissy." He softens his voice and covers the crime scene photo over with the perfect portrait of Nicole. "He pleaded guilty to assaulting Joe Byrne. Joe identified him as his attacker. Shawn Mayer says Michael showed up drunk and bloody at his, and confessed to the attack. That puts him on the other side of Soarken when Nicole gets attacked and in Shawn's house when her body's placed in the river. He can't be guilty of both crimes."

I uncover the photo of Nicole's body and point to the ring on her left hand. A diamond fitted in a star shaped setting. "She fought back, Bill, she hit him."

"Yeah, Lissy, she hit him. That's why he walked out, got drunk, and brawled with Joe."

"I don't buy it." I never have. "He's our man, I can feel it."

***

'He's her killer, I still feel it,' Felicity thought. She hadn't seen Michael Brutus since that day at the station. He'd walked out of her life in his parole suit. She hoped whoever crossed his path recognised him for what he was. After the Great Wailer Regression, she looked for him. There was no sign of him at his old flat. She hoped he had been back and found all of his mementos of Nicole torched. The memory of the flames licking away his time with Nicole brought a smile to her lips.

The room she spent last night in was bare. Felicity had been part of the unit that decontaminated it months ago. It had taken her two days of cautious travel by foot and pushbike, to reach the outskirts of Soarken. After her long trek from the forest diner, she needed to rest and get back to full strength.

Kronic had described the group at the school to her a few times, a group of four men, two teenage boys, and a petite blonde. The leader was big, but when she made him go over his story again, a new detail arose. The big guy, the blonde's boyfriend, he had a scar like a shooting star under his eye. Michael Brutus was alive, and he had a new girl in his clutches.

After food and a two hour snooze Felicity was ready to move. She avoided using her camouflage and relied on her Authority stealth training to get her close to the school. She watched from a distance until she felt confident enough to walk in.

Kronic had told her about the school, the rooms he had seen, and their layout. Stacked chairs and tables had lined the corridors, acting as pull down barricades. This was what Kronic described to her, but it wasn't what she found. The tables and chairs lay haphazardly across the floor, making progress tricky. In the first room Felicity saw obliterated tech, she only discerned it was a gaming console by the half a controller, nestled amongst the plastic fragments and wires.

She raised her leg to hip height and arched it over the next table. Her back foot jerked against a chair leg. The chair squeaked and scraped against the floor. A clatter rang out from one of the far rooms. *'Damn it.'* Felicity shimmered out of view and found more stable footing.

A man stumbled out of a side door. Thick foam filled his mouth, which was more dust than saliva. He was one of the dead ones. A phantom taste of iron swilled in his mouth, he craved the taste and texture of blood more than anything he'd desired in life. Incapable of processing pain, his flesh withered and rotted, without acknowledgement or consequence.

Sla-ck. A lump of the dead man's flesh slid from him and slapped the floor. He was blackened and putrefying, close to completing his undead lifecycle. His senses were mush. Felicity was surprised that her chair scrape alerted him — or perhaps it hadn't. A second creature entered the hall. Her sleek black fur had no way of camouflaging in these whitewashed halls. Shadow, Ethan's cat, strolled out catching the attention of the zombie's failing vision. It leaped at her. More flesh slipped from its bones.

The raven cat danced around the zombie. It lurched and flailed trying to catch her. The more the zombie moved, the more it fell apart. Within minutes it was immobilised. Shadow looked very pleased with herself. She strutted with the end of her up-stretched tail flicking from side to side. Then she stopped and stared in Felicity's direction.

'Can the cat see me?' Felicity was grateful not to have said that out loud. From behind her came gentle scrapes, scuffs, and the miniscule sound of fabrics gliding. Something was navigating the barricade more swiftly than she had. It would not be easy to slip out through the jumble. Three tables and seven chairs, was the least cluttered route.

'I can make it, if I'm quiet, slow, and considerate, I can make it.' She planned how to mount each obstacle for speed and silence.

The warmth of a breath left her frozen to the spot. Felicity held hers and listened to the rhythmic breathing of the Wailer that passed her. He was agile. His socked feet gently nudged each obstacle before he put weight on it. He clambered at pace. Some of his followers were not so light-footed and manoeuvrable. The soft scrapes and scuffs edged closer. It sounded as though they were taking the same line through the debris that their leader did.

Felicity dared to swivel her head, really slowly. Kronic had said he could see through her camouflage when she went too fast. *'I wish he was here with me now. There's no need for quiet with Kronic around. One, two, three — Shit.'* A Wailer woman crawled inches away from her face. It took all her will not to jump and give away her position. The Wailer's white eyes darted through her, and she sniffed and bit at the air around Felicity, then she let out a noise, in the same vocal range as a wail but it was quiet and gargled in the throat. The rest heard and favoured haste over discretion. Each time a Wailer passed Felicity, it spent a little time snorting in her scent.

Shadow hissed, her hunches were up, but the Wailers seemed uninterested in her presence. Felicity seized this opportunity and started to mount the barricade.

One member of the Wailer group was still making her way. Her little fingers curled over the edge of a table top and after a few attempts, she hauled herself onto it. Her pale inhuman eyes hid underneath a mat of hair. Felicity knew to be cautious around Wailer children. They adapted quicker, held more memories from their previous lives, and were much more intelligent than their adult counterparts. Although Felicity had to admit, these adults were acting differently than the ones she was used to. Their movements were strategic and careful, even after they got her scent they restrained themselves. Then there was the cat, none of them chased it.

'Follow the cat, follow the damn cat.' Two tables stood on their legs. Felicity slithered over the tops to the other side of the corridor. This put her on a different path to the child.

At the foot of the tables were chairs, tilted and precariously balanced on each other. Felicity placed her bare foot on a chair. It was solid so she stretched out her leg and tested the next one. It seemed sturdy, until she put her weight on it. Felicity hurtled forward, knocking over a chair tower. Her camouflage struggled to keep up as she fell. All heads turned to the cascading chairs which pushed open a door and poured through its opening. Felicity's blurry body had been spotted. Darting through the open door, she didn't give her camouflage a chance to catch up. The Wailers raced to catch her.

Felicity retched. It was involuntary. The smell in here was overwhelming. Claire's sick bucket was full to the brim. Vomit and tiny dog faeces lay on the floor too. All left to stew in the unventilated room.

Felicity threw the nearest chair and stood still. The chair cracked the window and rebounded off it. *'Oh, come on!'* She pressed herself against the wall and blended into it and was invisible again by the time the first Wailer crashed through the door. The adults spread through the room. They couldn't pick her scent out of the sickly aroma. The child strolled in. She cradled Shadow in her arms and stroked her then placed her on the ground. Shadow rubbed herself against the girl's legs. The little Wailer dug a handful of fish shaped biscuits from her pocket and placed them on the floor.

Felicity watched with interest. *'Are they going to kill the cat? Do they think I will try to save it?'*

Shadow crunched her biscuits while the Wailers watched. When she'd had her fill, Shadow strolled over to Felicity, and sat at her feet. She stared up and purred. All white eyes moved to the bit of wall that the cat sat at.

'Screw it.' Felicity picked up Shadow and dropped her on the girl's head. The distraction was fleeting, but she had no option now. She ran through the door and waded through the

tumbled chairs. Giving up on the camouflage, she put all her energy into speed.

Screeches raged just behind her. A hand grasped at her scaly thigh. She shoulder barged a table stood on its end and twisted it behind her. The table slowed her would-be attacker, but not by much.

Once outside, Felicity ran full pelt. She tripped in a trench that had been dug in the verge outside the gate and glanced at it before picking her pace back up. Large wheels had made the trench. The distinctive tread was frozen and pristine. *'Authority patrol car, made within the last few days. Can't be older than the last storm.'* Felicity only knew about one active Authority unit in Soarken. *'Anyone could have stolen a patrol car,'* she thought, trying to argue every angle, but Prospect Heath had motive to be at the school. They wanted the Odd Blockers for their experiments, and Brutus's actions had thwarted that plan. It was a lead.

Prospect Heath was her new destination. She zigzagged through the streets, trying to lose her growing entourage.

Chapter 14: Chris

The forest was reclaiming the land of this long-abandoned farmhouse. Knotted roots and brambles dominated the wilderness, and strangled the once neat wheat fields. The house itself was crumbling. Chinks in the wall and the holes in the roof's thatch revealed the glittering night.

Chris clutched Lara to his chest. Her warm body rose and fell against him. Many empty burlap grain sacks weighted her to him, and shielded them against the chilly wind. Fate had gifted him this second chance to save her. With her held tightly in his arms, he fell asleep.

He awoke to unfamiliar bird song. Soarken had birds, but nothing to match this chorus. He unwound his arms from Lara and kissed her head. *'Soarken is eighteen miles away, I'll need a vehicle.'* He made Lara a new, more durable blindfold from the burlap, drew her up to her feet, and led her by her hand.

The stairs were a challenge for her. Chris crawled down backwards. Facing Lara, he grasped her ankles and guided her feet down the steps. He had piggy-backed her across the overgrowth in the dark last night. In the light he looked for a flattened route but couldn't find one. He wore his backpack on his front. It was empty all bar a roll of toilet paper, aka Lara's fresh nose plugs.

He pulled Lara's arms over his shoulders. As he tilted forward, she instinctively rounded his hips with her legs and gripped. He trudged through the field, being pricked and stung. Chris pushed through the boundary hedges and stood on the country lane. As he straightened, Lara plopped onto her feet. He held Lara's hand and guided her. Abandoned farmland surrounded this stretch of road on one side, and forest dominated the other. They would have to walk hand in hand for some time before finding a ride.

The sign pointing down a single lane track read *Cattle's Gate ½ mile*. *'Another forest village?'* Chris thought. It sounded like the type of name the foresters gave their villages. *'Someone there has to own a car. You can't live this far out and not own a car.'* The track was winding and the dense trees lined either side of it. If there was a village around the corner, arriving at it and seeing it would be the same thing. Tyres had worn the dirt. That was all the encouragement Chris needed to lead Lara down the track.

Even this close to the road, the forest's eaves were thick and twisted. The trees offered them cover, but they walked in the middle of the lane. *'Because Lara would trip in the forest, it would be harder to navigate,'* Chris told himself. The forest was foreboding and had the darkness of dusk even at midday. Rustles and flickers reminded him that the forest was alive.

A wail called out in the distance. Lara stopped and tilted her head to one side. Chris dragged her into a jog. The track rounded right and then turned left. The dirt dropped away into a large ditch. There were bars across the pit spaced out with ample gaps between them. *'A cattle grid? Is this it?'*

A wail rolled out on the wind, and this time Lara responded in kind. Chris wrenched Lara's arms over his shoulders and tilted forward. Once again she mounted his back, and he precariously crossed on the cattle grid's bars. Each foot-plant had to be solid. He wobbled on the second from last bar as Lara twisted and wailed into the wind once more. He stretched his leg over the final gap and planted onto the solid earth.

Lara reached her head round to catch the growing sounds behind them. Chris darted up the road, and to his relief, behind the next corner was the village. The Wailers would search the houses. He could run on through and hide in the woods, but Lara's squealing, pinpointed their location. A Granny-house stood at the top of a steeply sloped garden, set back into the woods. Chris kicked the little gate open and ran past the house. The length of the steep garden seemed endless, but he made it. He opened the door and dropped Lara inside, smothering her wails with his hand.

The Granny-house was not what he had expected it to be. Too small to be a cabin or bungalow for the elderly (as first perceived), it was more like a long shed with a single window and a glass-paned door. The main feature of this room was a desk. Upon it, sat an ornate ceramic sewing machine with a hand-crank. A padded rocker stood behind them. Next to it was embroidered fabric and a sewing box. The contents orbited the box, which sat empty.

The Wailers had reached the village and tore into the house at the foot of the garden. "Shit." It was a word, a single human word, but enough for Lara to drench his hand with wails and cause her to fight against him. She thrashed her head beneath his grip and tried to bite his palm. They wrestled and rolled. Chris grabbed the back of her head with his free hand and pushed her face into a pillow. He pinned her arms under his knees and sat on her back, weighting her to the floor.

The Wailers were so close. If she wailed now they'd hear her, and he'd be forced to abandon her and run. The contents of the table rolled around on the floor from where their scuffle had disturbed them. *'They said on the news, that Wailers don't feel pain, not the way we do.'* He grunted, making the same sounds that the Wailers did to calm Lara back down. The Wailers outside ransacked the houses. *'If they stay quiet so should she.'*

Minutes slipped by. The Wailer group carried on down to the other end of this single road village. They overlooked their hiding place. Lara had calmed. Chris took his hand away from her mouth. He found a bag of cookies and fed them to her. A camping stove under the desk had an old fashioned kettle. It was full of un-brewed water that smelt ok. Chris dipped his finger in, it tasted fine and he gave all of it to Lara.

Then he found the thickest needle, and wire like thread. He placed the tip of the needle under her bottom lip and pushed it through. Lara didn't complain as he sewed her mouth shut, he couldn't hurt her, not with her condition. The wounds bled though. Chris kept pausing to mop up the blood with scrap fabrics. He needed to remove her nose plugs so she could breathe. He would have to mask his scent.

'It's just until we get to Soarken,' he told himself as he slipped the needle once more through her beautiful lips. *'Just until we get to Prospect Heath.'*

Chapter 15: Mallard Hill

'We need to make the best out of this.'

'Bullshit,' said the Bitch. 'Tyde said we could go. This treacherous winter water thing is utter crap.'

'So you think he's lying? That there is some big conspiracy to keep us here?' The Brain was fighting a losing battle.

'Yes! Never trust the Authority. They're not rebels, they're just trying to keep us here. I bet they're in league with Adder. One night they'll feed us sedatives, the next thing you know our brain is being delivered to P Heath in slides.'

'And Tyde has orchestrated it all?'

'Not exactly. He strikes me as a weak man. Spear tells him to stay here for the winter, and he does.'

'You can't call a stranger weak. What are you even basing that on?'

'He has weak eyebrows. They're going silver and his hair is having trouble holding on to pigment too.'

'He's an older gentleman with a high-stress manual job, silver is to be expected.'

'Gentleman? And what are you basing that assessment on?'

'You are impossible, I can't reason with you when you're like this. Go take a nap with the Child and let me take the wheel for a while.'

'Not a chance.' The Bitch smiled. 'I'm the best at making first impressions. Wouldn't want these people thinking we're a push over, would we?'

"You shouldn't be touching that."

"Excuse me?" Sadie turned to see a woman standing in the doorway.

"Those are Farrow and Wingan's possessions. You shouldn't be touching them."

"I'm just boxing them up, to keep them safe. If someone takes up residence in my old place, I hope they'll do the same for me." Sadie continued to wrap and pack.

The woman remained. "They'll be back soon. They won't take too kindly to strangers touching their things."

"Spear put us up here for a reason. Are you sure they're coming back?"

"They left a fortnight ago. They'll be back any day now."

"Ok. In the meantime, I have two children, and would feel more comfortable packing this stuff away, where it won't get broken."

The woman stared at her as she packed the box. Sadie taped it, doing her best not to engage with the intruder, then she opened another box and placed a large photo inside.

"You shouldn't be touching that," the woman said.

Sadie was still more *Bitch* than *Brain*. "Uuugh. Is there somewhere you should be right now, like, I don't know, some sort of facility? Is there a regiment of drugs you have neglected today, or a full-time aid you slipped away from?"

"Are you implying that I am mentally impaired?"

"With all the subtlety of a sledgehammer. Now if you don't mind, or even if you do, could you be a dear and get lost? Magic, thank you."

"You're not very nice."

"And you're not very bright. Got anymore statements of obvious?"

"We don't like you, and we don't want you here." The odd woman stormed out.

"Shocker," Sadie hissed, "and what's with the 'we' crap? Does crazy multiply if you get it angry?" She continued to pack up anything that looked sentimental.

"Talking to yourself again, sexy?" Luke closed the front door. "Did you know this was open?"

"Yeah, apparently the locals don't knock. Was the water hot?"

Luke rubbed his hair and then draped the towel over his bare shoulders. "It was. Did you play nice?"

"For as long as humanly possible."

"I noticed you've been a little moody lately. You can always be yourself around me, but we have to pedal sweetness with these guys for now."

"I'll try."

"Thank you." He wrapped his wings around her. His hugs were so different now, Sadie was glad his kisses remained the same.

The door swung open once more. Sadie rolled her eyes. "It's time," said Tori, "I'm to escort you to Spear for assignment."

As they stepped out, they saw Elaine collecting Serenity and Rapz. Mal was frantically knocking on the end door. It seemed Kronic had come up with a way to lock it.

"Open up."

There was a loud crash as something heavy was moved behind the door. Kronic stomped out. Sleep had done nothing to lighten his mood.

"Cleaver stays behind. Spear's orders."

"Spear can lick my left nut, where I go, Cleaver goes."

"I will drop the children off to the village nursery and school on the way," Tori said to Sadie. "All parents have a job to do and Spear feels it's safer to keep the children all in one location."

"What about their…" Sadie paused unable to word it right in front of Kyan and Madam. "What about their abilities?"

"Their files have been passed on to the teaching staff." Tori turned and addressed Kyan and Madam. "Ultimately though, you need to keep those sparks under control. If you need to vent it, there's a designated spot for you. Your teacher will show you when we get there. And you, little miss, need to keep two feet on the floor."

Kyan smiled and nodded, and Madam giggled.

Sadie wanted to go in to the school, to talk to the teachers, and understand their curriculum. Tori insisted that there was no time for that. Sadie said goodbye at the gate as a stranger took hold of Innocence and led Kyan and Madam through the door.

"Even the babies?" Sadie gasped.

"It is safer for all. Who knows, your job may be within the school. We'll find out when Spear hands out your assignments."

This was of little consolation. All Sadie could do to stave off the tears, as they headed to the Station, was to assure herself that this place, and these requirements, were temporary. The thaw of spring would be upon them soon.

They filed into the training room and lined up where they had the previous night.

"Serenity," Spear called. Serenity stepped forward. "Your file says you spent four years in Conclee on a humanitarian visa, in one of their most impoverished areas."

"I did. I was helping with the schooling of the children and the betterment of their town."

"Indeed," said Spear. "It says you helped with irrigation, well building and the erection of shelters. When you returned, you ran a Lord's prayer group in a Soarken church. Of your many skills, you would best serve us by working in the school. Although we may call on you to get your hands dirty, if you're needed elsewhere."

"I will help where I can."

"Laurence Tanshaw, aka Rapz. You were under investigation for inciting hate against the Authority through lyrics.

You were also associated with several activist groups, making your loyalties clear. You will be my personal assistant. I'd like to keep you close."

Rapz looked blankly at him.

"You're welcome." Spear continued down the line. "Tyde we've discussed your roll at length in the past, you have knowledge in many areas, so you will join the village maintenance team and help where they need you."

"Thank you."

"Sadie Ratcher, artist, hmm, we'll circle back to you. Kronic, we want you on the frontline on forest clearing duty. The dead and Wailers can become herds if we don't keep clearing them out. Luke, if your wings won't get in the way, you'll join him. You're previous martial arts training, and the fact you were a successful vigilante known as the Silver Dragon, mean you're capable of such duties." Luke opened his mouth to protest his role as a wanted criminal, but Spear shut him down. "Don't try to refute it, my research is solid. So, Serenity follow Tori, Kronic and Luke, you're with Mal, and Elaine will take Tyde to maintenance."

The room cleared. Only Rapz and Sadie remained. "So, artist, do you have any useful skills?"

"My last job was in a Collar care home."

"Yes, I saw that. Sacked for punching your boss in the face, broke his nose in fact. I don't trust you in a caring position."

"Besides that, I've only worked retail, I cook and clean at home and—"

Spear closed his fingers onto his thumb. "Zip it. As you have no useful skills, you will be confined to your house without a job, lucky you." He smirked. "I'm sure you can find the way back on your own."

"Is this because I lost my patience with that crazy woman?"

"You're dismissed."

Sadie saw how pointless it would be to argue. Though she wanted to, she wanted to verbally assault Spear until that smug smile was torn clean off.

"I said dismissed, that means you leave."

Sadie glowered and walked out.

"As for you, Mr Tanshaw, I think we should grab a coffee and have a nice long chat in my office."

***

It took Sadie an hour of walking through Mallard Hill's windy streets to find her cul-de-sac. She had passed many of the villagers on the way. None of them were friendly enough to ask directions.

Eventually she stumbled across her designated home. She walked in, fingers still frozen from her hour-long walk in the cold. Grabbing an empty box, she stormed up to the pink room. She took pictures down, pulling the tacks out and collecting them into a pile. One by one she piled the little girl's pictures up in the box.

The stairs creaked as someone approached. Sadie grabbed the glass ashtray, spilling butts and ash all over the floor. It was the only thing in sight with enough weight to cause damage. The footsteps continued. Sadie tucked herself behind the door and the intruder strolled in.

"You shouldn't be in here, and you shouldn't be touching those pictures."

"You again," Sadie growled at the odd woman. "Haven't you got a job? You know, like everyone else."

"My current job is to keep an eye on you."

"Oh goody." Sadie sighed and lobbed the ashtray back on the sofa. "Do you have a name?"

"Cynlear, Cynlear Spear."

"You're lieutenant Spear's wife?"

"No, his sister."

"Should've guessed, you're equally likeable." Sadie pulled another picture off the wall. The little girl was posing in it, she had on oversized sunglasses, pursed her lips in a kiss, and fisted her hair up in two uneven bunches. "Did you know the family well?"

"Farrow and Wingan took their daughter Shale to doctors in another town to get her and her brother vaccinated. They had found out that our Doc was issuing placebos. He wouldn't give them Adder's poison."

Sadie remembered what Luke had said about Adder's serum being a slow burner cause of Wailerism, but feigned ignorance. "You think Adder's inoculations made the girl, Shale, into a Wailer?"

"I'm certain. My brother has tapped every Authority line. Adder's inoculations make you Wailer or mutant, there is no in-between."

"Did you know this before the regression? Before the world went to shit?"

"No, transmissions confirmed our fears last week, but our suspicions were strong enough to forbid inoculation."

"Were they exiled?"

"The family was housebound, but they didn't follow the rules. They had the girl at the dinner table, and they would cosy up in front of films. She was supposed to be locked in this room."

"You watched them?"

"I was assigned to keep them under observation, before they assigned me to you."

"Of course, Mallard Hill's resident stalker."

"I liked watching them better." Cynlear picked up the Wailer photo. "Her collar failed. Shale escaped into the forest. Our cleanup crew caught her and disposed of her in the normal way." Cynlear saw the look of disgust on Sadie's face. "She wasn't a child, she was a threat. The younglings are always more resourceful and she had inside knowledge of our village and our wall. She already had six followers when we put her down. Cobalt, the son, he started getting headaches a few weeks after Shale died, an early Wailer symptom, we intended to imprison him for our safety, but the family fled. They never should have trusted Adder's formula, we told them that. No doubt when the boy turns they will come home."

"In their time of grief, you tried to rip another child from these parents and offered them an, *I told you so*, as a condolence?"

"We did tell them so. Their actions put us all in danger and their son's transformation would endanger us further."

Sadie sighed and rubbed her temples. "Could you watch me from over there, and in silence? Every time you speak I have to swallow my throw-up. It's starting to burn."

Chapter 16: The Brutes

"Come on, babe, you need your rest." Brutus scooped Claire up and lifted her off Terry's bed.

"I want to sleep here," Claire protested.

"It's not healthy, for you or the baby." He carried her out of Terry's room. "Now which of these rooms is yours?"

Claire pointed listlessly towards a door at the far end of the hall. Her room was easily the same square footage of his old flat. He crossed the threshold and placed her on the bed. She wriggled, carving out a Claire sized hole in the herd of scatter cushions. Brutus tilted her chin. "Night, beautiful." He pushed his lips against hers. Claire returned his kiss, daring to slip her tongue past his lips. It had been days since she could stomach saliva exchange. Brutus pushed away. He smiled at her and stroked the length of her cheek.

"Are you not coming to bed with me?"

"Not tonight, I'm going to stay down with the guys. That way I can let you sleep and help them settle in."

"You want to keep an eye on Brett, don't you?"

"You asked me to trust him, and I will, but do you really think I should leave him alone with Caleb?"

"Hmm, ok. Enjoy yourselves."

***

That first night in the Ivanthor manor was a riot. While Brutus tucked Claire in, the others had pulled antique loungers from the lobby, and ornate settees and chairs from the guest rooms. Bottles and beer cans lined the tables and the floor space around the seats, waiting to be consumed. They could have separated, had their pick of the rooms, but the lads had become accustomed to communal sleeping.

Brett perched on the window box looking out onto the darkened lawn. He set himself apart from the others. Their thoughts were frenzied. As much as he tried to keep out of their heads he was owned by their thoughts. He waited for the right moment to slip out unnoticed. *'A few more drinks should do it.'*

His mind focused on Brett before he even stepped through the archway. Brett saw the room being scoured through Brutus's eyes. When they fell on him, they stopped hunting.

"Brett, come join us." It required no mind reading, this was not a request. Brett walked over and sat opposite Brutus. Caleb jumped into the spot next to Brett and sat uncomfortably close. "Caleb, shift over," ordered Brutus. Caleb gave Brett a little space. "Brett, Claire tells me you worked here on the Estate. What were your duties?"

"It varied, depending on the needs of the Ivanthors and the manor itself. I worked on maintaining the grounds, I did odd jobs around the house, and also coached Terry in tennis."

"They paid you to play tennis?" Brutus uncapped a bottle with his teeth.

"My official job title was groundskeeper, but I did a variety of jobs." Brett shuffled in the seat. He fought hard to stay out of Caleb's head. There was a mist in Caleb's mind, what it concealed was unclear, and Brett fought hard to keep it unclear. It felt like violence, drooling with maniacal joy.

"Groundskeeper. So the skills you bring to this group are what, mowing and topiary?"

"I bring adaptability. My skills are in basic plumbing and electrical maintenance, including the renewable power systems. I can repair and sustain the wind turbines and the solar panels."

'This isn't a job interview,' Brutus thought.

"I might not be what you'd want, so far as group members go, but I don't want to be forced out. There's plenty of food and power, which I can help to keep going." Brett looked down and peeked in Brutus's thoughts. He didn't get words, just a sense of his feelings. "Please let me stay here. I can follow your lead."

Brutus enjoyed being placated, it spoke volumes to his ego.

"Perhaps there's room for you, if you — Ah, holy fuck!" Brutus gripped his head.

Brett stood and backed away. All around the Brutes curled up in the foetal position and squealed with pain. Their pain slowed his steps as it filtered into his unprotected mind.

"You..." Caleb stumbled forward, hands reaching for Brett. "You done this."

"He poisoned our booze," George agreed. "The only, ahh, thing that makes sense."

They slipped to the floor, the pain brought on spasms. Their anguished screams boomed and echoed.

Brett was force fed their thoughts and pain, despite his will to resist. Something started to filter through as he reached the staircase. Grogginess and concern.

"Brett, are you ok? What's going on?" Claire hurried to his side. "Why is everyone screaming?"

"It hurts, it hurts." Brett fell to his knees. Claire bent down and placed a sympathetic hand on him. "No, not me, them, it's unbearable. They hurt." Brett fought the multiple surges assaulting at his mind. "Claire, we need to move, now."

Claire looked at the Brutes. They were floor-bound, squirming and writhing. "What are you talking about? They're my friends, I'm not leaving them."

"One of them isn't himself anymore. We have to move!"

Claire weighted her stance and countered his pull. "No."

"I don't have time to argue with you. One of them is Wailer. He has woken ravenous, a hunger that hurts, and of the bunch of us, you smell the most delicious to him. Or rather your child does."

"How did you..." Claire grasped at her still flat stomach. The Brutes started to rise

"I know because *he* does. I can smell you, sense you through him. Oh Lord, I can see you, Claire, he sees you. Move!"

"Kwrraah." The newly minted Wailer bounded forward.

"Are you tweaked? What do you mean, you can see me? I'm stood right here."

Brett said nothing. He grabbed Claire's hand and her feet slid across the marble entrance hall and through the heavy front door. They both jumped as something collided with the closed door. The night was cool and refreshing. Brett's tie to the minds left behind loosened.

"What is going on?"

"They're transforming."

"You mean they're all Wailer?"

"No, only one, the others are turning into something else." Brett took off his jacket and draped it over Claire's quivering shoulders. "Let's get into the food store where it's safe. We can watch the others on the security screens down there."

***

Brutus started his change first. The bones in his arms splintered and slid into his lengthening arm cavity. Strong muscle fibres extended down his reforming humerus, radius and ulna. He propped up on his lengthened, muscular arms. All around him were screams. Brutus spat out blood and teeth. His jaw dislocated, the socket grew, as did his distended jaw. More teeth spilled out onto the floor allowing his jaw to slot into its new fitting. Muscles all over his body swelled and densified, ebony hair thickened and spread over his skin, new teeth pushed through his gums, and huge overlapping canines completed his new overbite.

Birth wasn't designed to be painless. Gnarled, breaking, twisting, transforming, the Brutes' screams beat against the walls, and echoed through the Ivanthors' lavish home. The first to emerge from the mass rebirth was the Wailer. His debilitating headache had subsided and his milky eyes focussed on Claire. She stood at the foot of the stairs in satin pyjamas and thick slipper socks. There were closer victims, sprawled out around him, but they smelled broken, wounded.

Claire smelled irresistible. He skulked over the squirming bodies, when he saw Claire being dragged away, he picked up speed. He skidded across the marble floor and slammed into the door as it closed. His full frontal plant should have smarted, but Wailer nervous systems are rewired to bypass pain. The Wailer reassessed his options. As Claire's scent in the air diluted, the Brutes became much more inviting.

Ethan tried to stand. Like Brutus, his arms had lengthened and his body was more muscular but still lean. A brown fur covered most of his body. The muscles in his legs burned, he stopped trying to put weight on them and sat cross-legged. "Ow!" Ethan reached down and ran his hands over his tight trainers. The laces were tricky, his hands were larger, and it felt like they were on stilts. When he freed his feet from the shoes, he found them transformed into a second pair of hands. "Brutus," he called. "George, Joel." The words were hard to form and he sounded like his mouth was numb from dental work. He stroked his muzzle, running his hands over his whole face. His tongue probed at his new teeth. They were huge.

The Wailer sank his teeth into Ethan's neck. The blood that spurted out tasted more animal than human. An alien noise escaped Ethan, he was screeching a call, like that of a chimpanzee, and his troop responded. Brutus came running on his knuckles and feet. Larger than his subordinates, Brutus picked the Wailer up and tossed him across the room. He bounded over and stood on the Wailer's legs. Brutus pulled both his arms out of their sockets and then dislocated his legs.

Sophie and Gerald's eyes. I thought I was hallucinating at first, but then I realised I hadn't imagined it."

"What are you saying, Brett?"

"I can experience thoughts, see, hear and smell through other people. I slip into minds and it's not always voluntary, I'm learning to control it."

Claire looked back at the screen. "Will they try to hurt us?"

"I don't know."

Claire scowled at him. "Then why don't you look in their heads and find out."

Brett was nervous. Brutus's mind was the only one he had slipped into fully so far, and it felt dark. He focussed on the boy, on Ethan, he seemed the safest option. *'I'm hurt, my neck is bleeding. My arms feel long and weird. George is dead. I liked George. Brutus hates mutants. He killed two, the little boy who spit acid and his mum when she shot thorns from her fingers at him.'*

"Brutus killed two mutants."

"He killed them defending himself."

"Then why am I, I mean he, why is Ethan so scared?" Brett slipped back into Ethan's thoughts. *'I have seen other mutants, too.'* This brought a smile to Brett's face. He was not alone. *'I've seen a huge, strong man who could break through walls, and a lizard lady. Brutus is a mutant now, the same kind as me. I'm not scared for me. I worry about Claire.'* Brett opened his eyes. He pointed to George's corpse on the screen. "Ethan's scared they will do that to you when you turn Wailer, because you will turn. Somehow he knows this."

"It was like, I don't know a negative energy or something, coming off of you guys."

Brett lied so effortlessly. Claire wondered if she really knew this man at all. What else could he be lying about? Brett glanced at her pleadingly. Brutus also looked to her for input.

"I felt something. Maybe it was stronger for Brett, he was closer to you." She wasn't comfortable lying for him. Brutus held her gaze a moment longer and then backed off.

"Brett, you know this storeroom, get medical supplies, Ethan's hurt." He draped his long heavy arm over Claire. "We lost George."

He said it so matter of fact, as though he hadn't been the one to snap his spinal column. Claire felt sorry for him. *'It had been to save Ethan,'* she rationalised. *'He needs to distance himself from the act. I can understand that.'* Claire snuggled his arm and placed a kiss on the fur that covered it. "Will Ethan be ok?"

"Yeah, I think so."

***

Ethan lay shivering. Joel had given him a lace doily and told him to hold it on his neck. The flow had stopped. Despite the lack of need, Ethan held the sodden rag against his wound. The ceiling was so tall, the floor was hard beneath him, the room had its own little hum he hadn't noticed before, and it smelt strongly of spilt beer. Ethan focused on all these little things. His injury, George's corpse, his alien and ungainly body, these were things he shied away from.

The large door slammed open. A cold breeze rushed into the room and Ethan's fur stood on end. Joel galloped on his knuckles, wearing the strap of the first aid bag like a bulky necklace.

"You ok, little bud?" Joel placed the bag next to him. Ethan nodded. The skin on his face was drained and pale under his fur. "Let me see what we've got here." Joel spilled the contents out of the bag for easy access and pulled off the doily bandage. It was sopping, but the wound seemed to have stopped bleeding. Joel uncapped some antiseptic fluid and tipped it onto a large cotton ball. Ethan winced. "The stinging is good, means it's doing something right." Ethan recalled his mother saying something to that effect, when she had tended to his grazed knees. "There you are, good as new." Ethan returned Joel's bright smile and allowed him to sit him up.

His view of the ceiling turned to wall and then to George's sprawled corpse. Behind it, stood the rest of the troop, Brutus, Leighton, and Caleb. Claire and Brett were there too, but he focused on his fellow Brutes. Ethan saw his new form reflected in theirs. He was no longer human.

Chapter 17: Prospect Heath

"Someone, out front, wants, to come, in." Saxon's slow voice boomed through the intercom.

Jenna pushed the speak button. "Graham and I will attend."

"Will we now?"

"Oh, don't look so sour, it could be someone fun." She pulled Graham's coat off of its hook and threw it at him.

"What like Moira? She's a barrel of laughs. Do you know they put her food in the entrance and leave? She bites anyone who comes through the door."

Jenna looped her arm through his and skipped him down the passageway. "Afraid it will be someone more exciting than you? A dark and handsome stranger, perhaps?"

Felicity followed them out of the lab. She was grateful for the change of pace. Maintaining her invisibility and watching the tedious lab work had made her sleepy. She shadowed the pair down the stairs.

A tall Mushroom-man with platinum-blond hair stood arms crossed next to two figures. One of them Felicity recognised. She had to admit it surprised her that Chris had made it. Though thinking harder she shouldn't have been. He seemed to be good at running away. The figure next to him was a mystery. Brightly coloured embroidered bandages covered her eyes. The same fabric bound her hands, Chris held onto the excess like a lead. There was blood around the woman's mouth. When she turned, a ray of light fell onto her lips. They were sewn shut. The prisoner jostled and lunged on her leash at the sound of human voices.

"I'm Chris and this is my girlfriend," Chris explained to Jenna who inspected the woman. "Her name is Lara, she is a Wailer. I brought her here because I thought you could help her."

"We will offer sanctuary to you both," said Jenna. "We have a dedicated floor for Wailer refugees."

Graham raised an eyebrow, refugees was a stretch, more like caged test subjects.

Chris folded his arms and glared. "I won't part from her."

"The thing is." Jenna put a hand on his shoulder and smirked at him like he was a little on the slow side. "She needs to eat. We can't keep her like this."

"The stitches need to be unpicked, that's fine. We slept in the same room without the stitches, it's just, we ran into a Wailer group, they yelled, she yelled back. I did it to stop her from calling, but she can yell in here, right?"

"Ok, we'll get you a room together."

Graham stepped in. "Don't make promises, Jenna. Look, Chris, we're what you would call middle-management, we need to check with the boss lady before confirming living arrangements."

Felicity backed up the stairs and ducked into an alcove. She waited for the group to pass and then followed them to a furnished apartment. The rooms were small and crowded. Felicity could get trapped in there, so she hung back and watched through the kitchen window.

"I'll bring up scissors and a first aid kit," said Graham. "The unpicking won't hurt her but she may still be susceptible to infections, so you need to keep the wounds clean."

"If there's anything else you need, just push this button and ask." Jenna pointed to the intercom on the wall. "We'll lock the door for the safety of others, because of Lara's condition."

"I understand."

The two locked up Chris's flat and walked away. "We should inform Dr Adder."

"She was visiting with James, we'll try there first."

Felicity followed close behind. If anyone knew the whereabouts of Brutus, it would be Dr Adder. Felicity would follow her. Hopefully Adder would discuss this information with a colleague. If she didn't, Felicity would force the Intel from her.

***

He had been offered help, but Chris had wanted to do it himself. The scissor arm slid through and popped the stitches one by one. The first stitch being whipped out caused Lara to jerk away. Painless, but the foreign touch spurned her instincts. She snarled and wriggled against her tied hands. Chris stroked her face, calming her, and then pulled the rest of the stitches out, taking greater care.

He winced as he cleaned her wounds. Her lips were weeping and red. Chris could not tell her he was sorry with words. He undid her restraints and held her, soothing her with grunts, they fell asleep in one another's arms.

***

"So you're telling me that there is no correlation between your inoculations and the mass affliction?"

"No, James, my inoculations are responsible, however, I did not design them to be that way. Someone has corrupted the stock during production."

"Bullshit! I read *your* notes, and have deconstructed *your* formula. *You* created the slow burn formula, you engineered it to cause eventual Wailerism, and then you distributed it to the world as a cure. Do you have a soul? What was the point? Was it an enslavement technique, population control, financially lucrative? Explain to me how creating a zombified populace could be deemed useful?"

"That seems a little judgemental. An Authority Minister paid you and your team to engineer an army of dead. Their purpose was to exterminate a rebellion, made up of oppressed and persecuted people. How did you justify that as useful?" Even now confronted by her father, Loralias Adder's voice was even and unfeeling.

"I've had thirty years to repent for that, Loralias. I lost the chance to be with you and your mother. Maybe you wouldn't have turned out so cold and emotionless if I had been there to help raise you."

"You and your team created this formula. I altered it and utilised it."

"A cure was written into the original mutation sequence. When you create something deadly, you always make a way to undo it. You tweaked the formula, made it slow burning, you screwed us out of our cure."

"We can undo it. We just need time to resolve the aberrant variables."

"You don't have a cure. You made this with no way to unmake it."

"I am perfectly capable of finalising a cure. If you are feeling rested, you may return to the lab and assist me."

James lunged past her. "I'll find my own cure. I will not work with you anymore, the Authority was right to try to shut you down."

Adder let him pass. Her mushroom bodyguard stood without opinion in the shadows waiting for instructions.

***

"I've had thirty years to repent for that, Loralias. I lost..."

"They're arguing again," said Jenna, with her ear flush against the door to James's room.

"Again? Go to the Lab?"

"Go to the Lab," Jenna agreed.

Felicity stayed behind as her unwitting tour guides disappeared down the stairwell. She was exactly where she needed to be.

"... You tweaked the formula, made it slow burning, you screwed us out of our cure."

"We can undo it. We just need time to resolve the aberrant variables."

"You don't have a cure. You made this with no way to unmake it."

Felicity gasped as she realised what she heard. The mastermind behind this hell was behind this door. *'Are they searching for a cure for Wailerism or mutations, like mine? Could I be remade?'* It shocked her at how much she disliked the thought of reverting to human. She missed her smooth skin and her hair, but the idea of being human and vulnerable in this world terrified her. Her invisibility had saved her life and her scales kept her warm and provided a layer of armour. She felt more than safe in her new skin, she felt superior.

The door was thrust open and Felicity flung herself back. The speed of her movement had made her visible, but James huffed off in the other direction and saw nothing.

Dr Adder stood in the doorway. Mervin Hatter, her escort, still wore his Authority Khakis with Minister Farr's Red logo on the shoulder patch. Bright orange mushrooms grew all over his skin. "Follow James, enlist help. Return him to his room and confine him there." Her instructions were clear. Hatter marched down the hall.

Adder went back into James's room. Drawers were turned out, his mattress was flipped and his bedding stripped. The key slipped out of the pillowcase and clinked on the floor. Adder picked up the key and put it in her pocket. James's freedom had been revoked.

Felicity followed Adder as she left the top floor. Her footfalls were gentle thuds that became lost in the rhythm of Adder's. Hatter and Field, two Mushroom-men, strong armed James up the stairs.

"You can't do this, let me go."

Felicity flushed herself against the rail knowing that their pass was imminent. A Felicity shaped distortion of the stairwell became visible in her haste.

"There," yelled James. "There is something there, some kind of mutant."

Adder turned and inspected the empty stairwell. "Hatter, did you strike him in the head?"

"Possible, he did, resist."

"I'm telling you there is a person, an apparition, a camouflage, something. It was right there."

"You are stalling, James. I have no interest in your concussion induced delusions. Take him to his room and lock him in. Stand guard, no visitors are permitted without prior authorisation."

"But…" James extended his arm as he walked past the spot he had seen shimmer. It slipped through the empty air.

***

"Good afternoon, Chris is it?" Adder took a syringe out of her supply box and filled it with a solution. She pushed on the plunger until no air bubbles remained. "I have been informed that you wish to share your provided accommodation with a Wailer."

"Yes, my girlfriend." Lara was tied to the bed. The sound of human words turned her to a frenzied beast. "She stays calm if no one talks."

"I understand, however I need to be sure you understand the inherent danger that her proximity puts you in. Arm please."

"I do, I — wait, what's the shot for?"

"The immunisation for Wailerism that you had will wear off. If you are to stay here, you will need a booster."

Chris pulled up his sleeve and produced his arm.

"Where did you live prior to the mass regression?"

"In some flats a few blocks from here."

Adder already knew his address. Chris was a registered citizen so all of his information was readable through a warrant card.

"The same apartment block that was attacked the other night? We had plans to rescue you all the following morning." Adder plumped a vein by flicking it and plunged her serum into him.

The injection felt like ice. Chris winced. "That's why I came here."

"Were there other survivors? Will they be joining you here?"

"No." Chris shook his head. "They've found sanctuary in a village, in the Forest of Eaves, they won't be coming here."

Adder capped the empty needle and removed her gloves. "There is a woman, with long mahogany hair in that group. We believe her DNA holds a link to the cure. I need the exact location of that village."

Felicity materialised behind Adder. It was a huge risk. Her camouflage would take seconds to kick back in. She mimed for Chris to keep quiet and enforced it with a glare.

"They, they." He looked at the floor. "They never told me the name of the village. We weren't exactly friends. They ditched me before we got there and I found Lara like this. She is all I care about."

"Sadie is alive?"

"When I left them she was."

"They are in a forest village close to the river."

Felicity glared at him again. "They never mentioned the river to me," he said.

"It would need to be close, because of the boat."

Chris stayed quiet. Adder stood up and Felicity shimmered out of view and prepared to follow her. "I need to find Sadie, if I am to cure your Wailer."

"I've told you all I know."

"How many mutants are in their group?"

"Six. One super strong, Luke you know, he has wings, and a woman who repels the Wailers. The other three are children. One can climb walls and hang from the ceiling, a boy that shoots electricity from his hands, and a baby that glows. Plus three regular humans, one of them being Sadie."

"No other mutants?"

"Those are the only ones in the group right now." He hadn't mentioned Felicity and thought this would placate her, if he could have seen her, he would know how displeased she was. He had handed over the Odd Block and secured his place at Prospect Heath.

"Thank you, Chris, please, rest for now. My colleague, Jenna, will come and talk to you in a while."

***

James had returned his room to its original order. He was not surprised to find his key missing. *'What did I expect? I outed my daughter as a traitor to her own species.'* He sat with his head in his hands for a long while, contemplating Adder's next move. *'She will calm down eventually, she needs me,'* he reasoned.

His cell inside of the Authority institute had been larger. It had been furnished with more mod-cons, puzzles, and games to keep his mind fresh. While there had been no access to live streaming or the internet, they had provided him with a great deal of pre-approved reading and watching material. There was nothing to do in this room. Every other room on this level had Wailers in, screeching to one another incessantly.

James began to hear pain, longing, connections in their calls. Unable to drown out the noise, he focused on it, trying to decipher the meaning of each tone, to find the language in the noise. It was repetitive, yet pattern-less. Droning on through the night, James found himself rocking back and forth to the nightmarish lullaby, until he fell asleep in his chair.

He awoke in a daze. His head felt strange, like he had been drugged. He opened his heavy lids. Someone sat at his feet with their hands held in front of his face. There were open slits in their fingertips, which followed the curves of their fingerprints, and bright orange spores poured out of these slits. The more he ingested, the less he wanted to fight. His pores widened as mushrooms shot out and grew upon his skin.

James the scientist, the absent father, the genius was gone, in his place stood James the Mushroom-man, complacent and ready for his handler's instructions.

Chapter 18: Mallard Hill

The odd bird, hardy enough to winter at home, called through the trees. Luke was out with the forest clearing crew. He saw this as training, a way to regain some of his lost skills and familiarise himself with the abilities and limitations of his new body.

Kronic led the group. He was an outsider, but he was Marazsian like them. Besides, you only needed to see him punch a rooted tree into the air once, to know whose side you wanted him on.

As they entered a clearing, Digger put his fist up, signalling for them to stop. "We'll have lunch here, usual formation."

The ten men sat in a circle facing outwards. Luke took out his rations. He ripped into the packets with his teeth. There was no way he was using his hands. His wings didn't fit into normal clothing, so he wore tank tops under body-warmers, the long fingered gloves he had fashioned gave him a little extra warmth and he wanted to keep them on.

Digger sat next to Luke. "How long have you had that body?"

"Four days."

"Huh." Digger stared out into the trees. "Can you fly with those things?"

Luke shrugged and finished his mouthful. "I can glide."

"Show me."

"What, right now?"

"No one will steal your lunch. I need to know my men's manoeuvrability, so I can direct you in the field."

Luke squinted at the man. *'Manoeuvrability or curiosity?'* It didn't matter. He was under this man's command. Luke started to climb a tree.

"Do you have to be up high?" Digger asked.

"I'm not sure. I've only ever done it from rooftops."

"Continue."

Luke climbed up the tree. Height was never an issue for him, but falling made him nauseated. "I'll jump from here, my wings will get tangled in the higher branches."

"As you wish."

Luke leapt from the branch and glided to the ground.

"Ok," said Digger, he moistened his finger and placed it in the air. "I need you to run, wings outstretched, across the clearing to that stump over there." Luke looked at him blankly. "Fast as you can."

Luke couldn't help feeling like he was the butt of a joke, but he did as Digger asked. Running as fast as he could, he kept his eyes on the tree stump that Digger had pointed out. The wind picked him up, and he glided in the air. The shock was followed by something else. This wasn't falling, gliding over the ground like this, it felt right. Luke had no fear. He turned before he crashed into the tree line. When he started back for the patrol, the wind crashed against him. His wings bellowed out and the air current dragged him back.

"Flap your goddamn arms," Digger yelled through cupped hands.

It was hard, but Luke started to find the wing shape and the movement that could cut through the wind, and propel him forward. He dipped them as he got closer to the group and landed on the ground.

Luke sat down and started back on his rations.

"What about fighting, are those wing bones hollow, fragile? Throw me some shapes, show me how you spar."

Luke glared at him and exaggerated his chews.

"Doesn't bother me if you speak with your mouthful."

Luke swallowed hard. "Can I eat? I appreciate the interest you're taking, and I want to improve my fighting skills, but you called a lunch break, and I'm hungry."

"Ok, ok, you've got ten minutes then I'll train you hard. You'll be my project and I won't stop until you're exceptional."

"Wailers, in the trees, two o'clock."

"I got it," Kronic said, as he hoisted himself off the ground.

"There's at least six—"

"I said I got it. Go finish your muffin."

The frustrated recruit got out of Kronic's way. The heavy man thundered over the frozen ground. From their luncheon spot, the men watched trees rattle, as Kronic destroyed the group.

"That man," sighed Digger, "is going to put us out of a job."

"We leave in the spring," said Luke, "your job is safe."

***

"My leg hurts, Doc." Paul was a known practical joker. Though his pain looked real, Dr Hern suspected it was the set up for another punchline.

"Many amputees complain of phantom pains." Hern looked at the notes that his acting nurse, Lashale, had added to his. "You are due some painkillers. I can get those for you now."

He hung the clipboard on the end of Paul's bed and unlocked the drug cabinet.

"Seriously, Doc, please take a look. I don't know what's happening, but this leg is freakin' killing me."

Hern shook his head and pulled back the covers. "Is this a joke?"

"What is it, what do you see?"

"This isn't funny, Paul. I put you on bed rest for a reason. Where did you even get the materials to make something like this?"

"What is it?"

"Like you don't know." Hern sighed and pulled at the fleshy toes and poked the ball of the foot that had sprouted from Pauls stump.

"Don't, don't. You're tickling me."

The toes wiggled. Hern shot back so quickly that he fell over a stool and became tangled in its legs. "How in the world?"

"Is everything ok, Uncle?" Lashale walked in, looked at the odd appendage, screamed, and fainted.

"Will someone tell me what the hell is going on down there? Uh, fine." Paul rocked himself into a seated position.

He stared at the half a foot sticking out of his stump. "Would you look at that?" He wiggled his toes and grinned.

***

The preschool room was neat. Box shelves lined the wall, and they had order. The toys were arranged by purpose. Cars stood in neat lines in descending size order. Paint brushes cleaned and conditioned were rowed in pots, again, in descending size order.

Sadie looked around the room and shuffled in her child-sized chair.

Mrs Best frowned down on her from behind her desk. "My concern, Miss Ratcher, is well founded. I observed her today. Verity not only refers to herself in the third person, she refuses to use her given name. She calls herself Madmam."

"Her previous nursery setting had no issues with the third person stuff, they said it's normal for a child her age. And it's not Madmam, we call her Madam."

"But you don't correct her when she calls herself Madmam. Is she mad? Do you want her to believe she is stricken with madness?"

"No of course not, we just thought the way she said it was cute."

Mrs Best sneered at her. "She is closer to her third birthday than her second. All the Marazsian children in my charge have no issues using *I* and *me,* none of them lack the verbal skills that Verity does."

"There were some children back home, Verity-Elise's age, who barely spoke at all. They were referred to speech therapy, my daughter wasn't. The staff and health visitor said she expresses herself well enough. I think she's doing fine, maybe it's your children who are too advanced."

"Let's not make this a race issue, Miss Ratcher. Marazsian children develop no differently than those native to Tave."

"I wasn't—"

Mrs Best gave Sadie no chance to continue. "I can only do so much. Here is what I need from you. No more 'Mummy will be back soon' or ' Mummy loves you'. Use the correct pronoun. 'I will be back soon', 'I love you.' You need to accept that your daughter has a problem, accept that you cause that problem, and adjust your behaviour accordingly. No more nicknames and correct your daughter. Mistakes are not *cute*."

"I am trying my best, do you have any idea what it's like trying to keep her off the ceiling? To keep her safe?"

"We have no issues like that here. She plays on ground level with the other children."

Sadie's lip quivered and her voice cracked. "So my daughter is broken, and it's all my fault?"

"Acceptance is only the first step in this process." Mrs Best circled her hand in the door's direction. "Good day, Miss Ratcher."

Sadie sobbed all the way home, cloaking her face in hood and sleeve. The *Bitch* and *Broken Child* argued in her mind. Sadie choked out both rage and sorrow filled tears. This felt like the old days, the days before the *Brain* restored order. Sadie was slipping into a darkened place where she would enjoy less and less control.

She closed the front door behind her. Giggles and cheerful voices filtered down from upstairs. Sadie walked through the living room, dodging scattered crayons and paper. She glanced at Madam and Kyan's masterpieces and stepped over them. Tears still streamed down her face.

Pots and pans cluttered the kitchen. Sadie ran the hot tap and put a generous squirt of liquid in the washing-up bowl. She piled in bowls, spoons, and cups, and spritzed all the surfaces with an antibacterial spray. After pulling open the under-sink cupboard she paused and sat back. *'What was I looking for?'* The washing machine was idling next to her. It started up again and Sadie was mesmerised. The clothes tumbled and turned lulling her into a trance like state.

"Sadie."

The washing machine whirred, matching the pulse in her head.

"Baby, talk to me, look at me."

Luke put his hands on Sadie's shoulders. She looked right through him.

"Damn it." He jumped up and twisted the tap, as water flowed over the bowl. Sadie stiffened and frowned as Luke sat down and wrapped his wing round her. "Sadie, you worry me when you just sit here like this, it's not normal."

"I'm fine."

"No, you're not. I've seen this cycle before. You get snappy and confrontational, and then you just sink into depression. You took ages to pull yourself out of it last time."

"Don't you think I have reason to be angry? Everyone here hates me. Within an hour of getting here, Elaine struck me, three times, Spear was a dick to me, his psycho sister is stalking me, and Madam's teacher just told me I'm a bad parent."

Luke stroked sodden loose strands away from her face. "You see hate everywhere because that's what you expect, then you go on the defensive and rub people up the wrong way."

"You have no idea what it is like inside of my head. My anger and misery are so big, that they take on personalities of their own. I mean they are me, they're a part of me, but they're not all at the same time."

"Anger and misery are not personas they're feelings. They are your feelings, Sadie, you control them."

"It doesn't feel like I'm in control. It feels like I've split into three, but the pieces changed shape and they won't fit back together anymore."

Luke tried to approach imagery with imagery. Sadie was an artist, sometimes she heard him more clearly when he spoke in pictures. "Just imagine the pieces are squishy, they don't have to be the right shape, just smoosh them together."

He hadn't heard her, or perhaps she hadn't explained it right. You couldn't just smoosh the *Bitch, Brain* and *Broken Child* together. They resulted from a personality fracture that had been there since childhood. They had evolved to protect her.

A breeze swirled into the house. The front door shut and Cynlear strolled into the living room.

"Is she changing?" she called through to Luke.

"No, just having a good old cry, you heartless bitch," Sadie snapped.

"I will return to check on you again shortly." Cynlear walked back out of the house.

"That woman is crazy, and do you know the worst part? Her whole job is to watch us. Who gives out these assignments? The God of anarchy and turmoil?"

"Not us," said Luke, "You."

"What?"

"You were inoculated. They say it could go either way, Wailer or mutant, there's no way to tell. I mean, it's not *just* you. They're watching Rapz too."

"What about Paul?"

"Oh yeah, I can't believe I forgot. The old coot grew himself a new foot today. They're not watching him anymore."

Sadie studied Luke's profile, his eyes shifted. "What aren't you telling me?"

'Oh, I don't know, that you may not change at all. You and these Marazsians may be the last of humanity, that scientists at Prospect Heath believe that you're the cure, and they'll dice you up if they get their hands on you.' He thought it, but he couldn't say it. Stable Sadie could handle it, but when she was already on the edge, it was too dangerous.

"Luke, please, we don't keep secrets from one another."

"I'm just worried because it hurt for me, the change, because it was so quick. I worry about you going through it, but I don't want my worries to be your worries."

Sadie smiled and twisted onto him wrapping her arms and legs around him. "You'll love me even if I become a swamp monster?"

"I'll flood the garden and we can wallow together." She hugged him tighter. His wings enveloped her like a silvery blanket. "I need you to try harder to get along with Cynlear, though."

"Bring her to the wallow. She'll make a great swamp monster snack."

"I mean it, Sade. The woman is highly trained Authority special ops, stop pissing her off."

"Awesome," groaned Sadie. "Just what crazy needs, a dash of deadly."

Chapter 19: The Brutes

Caleb's morning breath was stale and rancid. Brett didn't feel its warmth, but Caleb was still much closer than he'd have liked. Brett rubbed his eyes and stretched. Heating ran under the hard floor he had slept on and beckoned him back to slumber. The food store was a repurposed bunker, its sleeping quarters furnished for comfort. They all stayed the night. No one wanted to return to the room where George died.

Brett stretched again and yawned. *'Ew, I could benefit from a toothbrush myself.'* Brutus and Caleb stood over him, staring. "Good morning, Brutus, and Brutus's guard dog."

"Caleb, go make us some coffee," said Brutus. Brett couldn't make out Caleb's expression from his chimp-like muzzle, but his human eyes had a touch of manic glee.

"I need to know what you are, Brett."

Brett squinted at Brutus. "What do you mean?"

"When I look at you, if I really try to sense you, all my fur stands on end. You're not human. You look it, but you're not. What, are, you?"

Claire peeked round from behind a bunk, she looked pale today and drained. Brett watched her mime the words, "Just tell him," and got a horrible feeling that she already had.

Brett rubbed some sleep from his eyes. "I see things. I thought I was hallucinating at first, but I seem to be able to see thoughts, memories. Just snippets, sometimes I glimpse an image, then it's gone."

Brutus lowered his voice and puffed out his fur. "When we first met, you asked about my scar. What did you see?"

"You talked with an Authority officer, she asked you about the scar under your eye and you gave her some bullshit answer about a shark attack."

"That's it?"

"That's all I saw, but I sensed you knew she hated you, and I sensed it was for a good reason."

Caleb appeared with two steaming cups.

"Leave the coffee, Caleb, take Claire and get some breakfast." Caleb looked hurt but did as Brutus asked. Their steps echoed up the metal stairs, and the hatch opened and banged shut. Brutus leaned in closer. "What I'm about to tell you, stays between us."

Brett stayed quiet, he had no desire to hear the deep dark secret, a glimpse of it had chilled him.

"Four years ago I lost my love, Nicole. She was beautiful, funny, and came from a good Authority family, so you can imagine how surprised I was when she chose a Moorland grunt like me. It was perfect, for the first six months. Then her mental health issues started to rear up. She would fly into fits of rage for no reason, beat me, scream, shout, smash up our flat." Brutus felt a lump form in his throat. "Anyway, the day I got this." He traced the star's tail with his finger. "She punched me in the face. Caught me with her ring, blood pissed out everywhere. I was furious, and it took all my strength to walk away. I slammed the door as I walked out. She screamed something after me, but I didn't hear what she yelled. Her last words to me are lost forever. After I left, she must have taken that rage out on someone else, and it got her killed. Someone beat her to death and drowned her in Soarken River."

"So your guilt is from walking out?"

"I did time, that memory you glimpsed was the day I got out. My crime was assault, just not on Nicole. I got drunk and beat a man to the brink of death." He let out a laugh. "Do you know the best part of it? I can't even remember what this guy did to deserve a beating."

His face sobered again. "While I was punching this nobody, on the other side of Soarken, my Nicole died. I spent four years in Soarken prison for the assault. Felicity Grange, the officer you saw, came down to the lower levels to harass me every day. She didn't even work in corrections. I told Claire I was ex-Authority. There's some truth in it, I did the training and spent two years in the reserves. That's why I need you to keep it between us, she deserves to know the man I am, not the man I was."

"You were brutal. Claire turned away, but I watched what you did to George. Wailer, zombie, human, does it even matter to you?"

The growl Brutus let out made Brett regret his words. "This is the way we survive and I get that I'm forward thinking. You still dream of reprieve, of an understanding, a cooperative. That's not happening, Brett, we have to fight, to bludgeon. You hear the thoughts of others do you really think there is any other way?"

He heard Brutus's thoughts clear enough. There was only one answer he could give. "It's a brutal world, we have to be brutal."

"Exactly."

Brett picked up his coffee and sipped it.

"I need a promise from you, one your life depends on. You will never go in my head again. My thoughts, my memories, are out of bounds."

'If I could control it, I would never venture into such a horrible place.' Brett reached for Brutus's outstretched hand and shook on a deal he had no way of keeping. "I promise."

***

The walls had never seemed so far spaced, the ceilings never looked that high, her footsteps rebounded and echoed. *'What a large and foreboding place my home is.'* Claire stepped past a massive archway and looked into the room, the one that had been the stage for last night's nightmares. Joel pushed a bloodstained mop around the space where George's body had been. The soapy water soaked into the more stubborn blood stains that had dried on the heated floor overnight.

"I want to help," murmured Leighton. He stared at the floor.

"You wrapped the body, leave this to me," Joel said.

"But I want to help." His murmur was quieter this time. He looked at the blood on his hands and willed himself to move, to clean himself up, but a small part of George lingered on that floor and he was mesmerised by the mop that cleared him away.

Claire continued her pace. She went into the kitchen and stopped. Kneeling down, she ran her hands over the tiles, tilting her head to see the floor from different angles and in different shades of light.

"Brutus said you gots ta eat," said Caleb.

Claire ignored him. "He did a good job," she said to herself.

"What you chattin' on?" sighed Caleb.

"Brett, he did a good job. There's no evidence, no blood stains. It's almost as though no one ever died in here."

She got up, grabbed a glass, filled it with water, and gulped down her anti-sickness pill.

"Hey, what about munch?"

"I can't eat yet, Caleb, my medication needs time to work."

Caleb shrugged and started to fix his breakfast.

Claire left the kitchen and found the room where Gerald had turned. Her picnic was gone but her book remained. *'Gerald called me Miss Ivanthor, he was doing a job, trying to get me to eat, and I was rude to him. Those were his last moments.'* She started back down the hallway, and weaved in and out of the side rooms, walking the haphazard route she had raced through, to evade Gerald the Wailer. When she came to the back door she had escaped through, she walked out.

This felt like a trance. She headed toward the tennis courts. *'It was here,'* she thought. *'This is where I stood when Sophie screamed. This is where I was when she died.'*

Scrape, thunk, scrape, thunk, scrape, thunk. The rhythmic noise was close. Claire walked towards it. As she got closer, she heard sobbing. Ethan dug the spade into the ground. It made a scraping sound. He tossed the dirt in clumps onto a pile. Thunk.

Claire ran her eyes down the line that Ethan was adding to. Terry Ivanthor, Sophie Whittle, Gerald Mace, and Golfer. George lay wrapped in blue tarpaulin next to the widening hole. Claire's sense of smell was acute. Pregnancy made sure of that. She could smell George, his faint unique pheromones, his lingering cologne... and his blood.

There was a trowel propped against Golfer's grave marker. Claire picked it up, got on her hands and knees, and started digging.

Scrape, thunk, scrape, thunk. Claire watched the trowel dig its tiny holes in the ground. She had never dug in soil before. It reminded her of the buckets and spades she and Terry had used to make castles on the beach when they were young. The grass under her knees was cold and moist, not at all like the warm sands of her childhood.

She glanced at Terry's grave. Brett had made an offering on it. Terry's tennis racket, some laminated photographs, a can of his favourite soda, and some trinkets from his room. Terry was so close.

"Claire? What are you doing?"

Brutus stood at the foot of George's partially dug grave.

"I'm helping," she said and held up the trowel.

"You're sat on the cold ground, and you're not wearing a coat. You will make yourself ill."

"It's George, I wanted to help."

"We've got this, you need to get inside and keep you and that baby warm. No more fucking about, you've got responsibilities now."

Claire got up. Ethan kept shovelling and didn't make eye contact with either of them.

"I'm sorry, Brute, I didn't think."

"It's ok, babe. Just go inside, get warm, and eat some breakfast."

Chapter 20: Prospect Heath

"Keep, reports, in better, order." Hatter delivered Adder's message and marched off, he was not instructed to take a response.

"Gah, really?" Graham watched the Mushroom-man walk away. "Can we not train them to talk a little faster, to talk good?"

"You want them to talk good?" Jenna giggled. "Or maybe gooder? Who taught you how to speak, Graham?"

"You know what I mean. It takes ages to get a single sentence out. If they've been programmed, then they need an upgrade."

"Firstly, your reports are shocking, get into the habit of typing because your penmanship sucks. Secondly, do you know what would go into programming a Mushroom-man so he was better spoken?"

"No, I have no idea, do you?"

"To rewire the brain to complete compliance and self-awareness would take years. The spores carry data packets that are broad enough to make basic Mushroom-men. You would need to insert spores directly into the brain stem and instruct them to rewrite personality, and habitual responses, basic instinct even would need to be bypassed.

"There would need to be frequent updates with spores to keep the subject complicit. Then, there would be the trial and error of writing programs to replace the lost pathways. All of those pathways would need a rewrite for a Mushroom-man to walk among us unnoticed. He would need to keep knowledge and memories, his entire vocabulary, and use these tools to interact, and form conversations, whilst still acting out the will of his handler, keeping their agendas at his core.

"It would take years to undo a person with that precision. It is far simpler to shut down most of the brain and impose simple programs onto it. We must keep the stumbling buffoons and hope they strike more hits than misses in their tasks."

Graham's jaw dropped. "How do you know all that?"

Jenna laughed. "Your face is priceless. I'm almost tempted to tell you I'm a secret genius."

Graham's eyes rolled. "I get it, you asked Dr Adder the same question and you've regurgitated her answer."

"Not word for word, but yeah, that's what she said."

Graham caught her eye again. "Secret genius," he scoffed and started laughing.

"Hey, it's not that funny," she said pushing him.

"I trust you are finding time to complete your tasks, while socialising with one another?" Adder stood in the doorway.

"Dr Adder, yes, sorry, I didn't realise, I mean, yes we are."

"Very well, I expect an update on your progress in an hour."

Adder left the lab with the same swiftness as her arrival.

"Did it get colder while she was in here? I swear it got colder." Graham jumped as someone walked past him. "James, you scared the life out of me. She let you out then. What did you do to piss her off this time?" James slowly turned. "James?" Graham gawked in abject horror at James.

His expression was bare, and bright orange mushrooms grew from his neck. "No," Graham gasped. "No, she can't."

Jenna placed her hand on his shoulder and squeezed it. "Graham," she whispered.

"No, don't tell me this is ok, nothing about this is ok." He threw his shoulder back dislodging her hand. "We're next, you get that right? One false move, one cock-up, and we join the mushroom ranks. I can't stay here, I can't do this anymore."

"Take a breath, Graham, please." Jenna threw her arms around his neck, he struggled to break the hug, but sweet little Jenna was stronger than she looked.

"Let go, let me go." Graham's head flopped and Jenna pulled it down to her shoulder. "He was my friend."

"I know he was, shh, quiet now."

Graham straightened out of the stoop.

"Socialising again? It is a wonder you two accomplish anything," said Adder. She hurried over to James and placed a set of slides in front of his microscope. "Analyse, catalogue, then complete this list of additional tests." Adder handed him a piece of paper.

"As, you, wish." James inserted the first slide and looked through the eyepiece.

Jenna walked over to Adder and confronted her with the questions that Graham was afraid to ask. "Will you do that to us?"

Adder stayed calm, not reacting to the fierceness in Jenna's voice. "To Graham I cannot. His latest screening has shown he is in the early stages of mutation."

"James is a mutant, that hasn't stopped you doing it to him."

"This mushroom species destroys all plant life in favour of its own. Graham has developed plant cells, his final form is still unclear, but I cannot infect him. The mushrooms would eradicate his mutated cells and probably kill him."

"And what about me?"

"You have done nothing to warrant such an action."

"What if I do? What if I step out of line?"

"Continue with your work, Jenna, you too, Graham." She walked past Jenna, her face still cold and unfeeling. "I shall conclude my autopsies on Hemella and Jayron."

Graham listened to the clips of Adder's sensible work shoes, grow distant.

"She's a psychopath," said Graham.

"No, she just struggles with social interactions. I'll talk to her again on her own, I've known her most of my life, she should listen to me."

"She just threatened you, and you think you can talk this out with her?"

"She didn't threaten me—"

"You asked if she would do the same to you, and she said to get on with your work, how is that not a threat?"

"She's cold, not dangerous. We are here to make a cure, and the way I see things, we have a duty to put up with her. She is humanity's last hope."

"No, she's gone too far. The Wailers I got. Controlling them is a useful stop gap until we can cure them, and as for the military, Garven and the rest? They threatened our work, our progress. But James? James was hungry for the cure, he was working hard for it, harder than Adder even. This makes no sense."

"We don't know why she did it. He might be your friend, but he's still a war criminal, he's still dangerous. This makes sense to me. If he's locked away he's useless, at least in this condition, we still get his knowledge, still get that hard work out of him."

"You are unbelievable."

"Graham," Jenna reached for him, but he evaded her touch.

"No, you're as bad as her, leave me alone."

"Graham," she tried again.

"Go to the storeroom, Jenna, we need more gloves and sterilising spray. Take your time. Get a manicure on the way back if you like."

Jenna opened her mouth to defend herself, but decided to give Graham some time. He liked her, but without being able to dump his frustration on Adder, she was his substitute target.

Graham refused to acknowledge Jenna when she returned. He stomped about the lab all afternoon, completing his work in huffs and groans. When he finished, he placed a typed report of his day's progress on Adder's desk, and scurried away to his apartment.

He scavenged a meal, of sorts, from dried and sustainable goods. Slamming the kitchen cupboards, he thought of the meal that was being served in the mess hall. It would be edible, delicious even, some days, but there would be rows of blank Mushroom-men eating efficiently. Behind the counter, mushroom riddled automatons would cook the food and serve it. He was happy to eat his biscuits, crisps, and canned pasta alone.

Picking a film required more thought than he cared to give, so he just played the first thing that popped up. It was a period drama, in which the Authority, in its infancy, educated and guided the savage locals. Graham wasn't watching it, just allowing it to stream in the background. *'What the hell am I going to do? I don't have the skills to survive out there. I don't have the stomach to survive in here.'* He hashed out the same arguments in his head. He made plans, then found flaws, and abandoned them. The room had darkened around him. One film finished, and the next in the queue played. The security lights outside glowed.

Graham closed his eyes and sunk a little deeper into his crumb covered bed. It was quiet. Graham sat up and listened hard. There was a faint hum of electric and if he strained hard, he was sure he could hear one of the mushroom security guards pacing the perimeter. What he couldn't hear were the calls from the top floor. None of the Wailers sounded off. Not a single one. *'How is that possible?'* Graham leapt from his bed and pulled on a jacket. Not being light of foot, he forced the toes of his shoes into his slippers.

His front door creaked a little and the click of its close seemed to echo. Graham stood just outside of the door clinging to the handle, ready to run back inside. No one came. Out here, where their wails should have been louder, the silence was all the clearer.

Graham walked to the nearest stairwell and snuck to the top. The slippers worked great, his footsteps were almost inaudible. He ignored the first door. Adder assigned James those quarters and in his current state, they were not on the same team. The second should have had a full complement of four Wailers. Graham opened the door and stepped in. They had stripped all four rooms in this one bed flat and turned them into cells with barred doors. It was dark. *'Damn it, I should have brought a flashlight.'* Graham stepped further into the hall and closer to the bars. If they lunged their arms through they could reach him, but he needed to see.

From the bundles on the cot beds, he assumed that three of them were sleeping. In the kitchen the fourth stood upright looking right at him. Graham's presence alone should have sent this thing into a frenzy, but it just stepped closer. The dark muted the colour, but the shapes were distinctive. Mushrooms infected this Wailer. Adder had shown them the spores and demonstrated their effectiveness on two Wailers. This was not one of them.

Graham backed out and went into the next holding. Four full cells, four mushroom ridden Wailers. *'Compliance, compliance makes them quiet.'* He approached the next flat. He was unsure why he needed more confirmation; the silence should have been proof enough. He reached for the handle. A hand smothered his mouth, and a second wrenched him away from the door. Graham didn't struggle, as someone pulled him back down the walkway.

"There was a child in there," a hoarse voice whispered. "Wailer kids are of greater intellect, even the mushroom kind, one look and he would have known you didn't belong, and screamed holy hell." Graham was pushed through the door of James's flat. "The kettle's freshly boiled, help yourself to a drink."

"James? Is that you?"

"Yes. Keep it down, a guard still patrols this level once an hour. No lights, hushed voices, and we sneak you back to your room as soon as we can."

"I don't understand?"

Graham took the seat that James offered him and waited to be enlightened.

"Last night someone came into my room while I was sleeping. They infected me with mushroom spores, it worked, and it was hell for a few hours, but my regenerative ability fought the spores off."

"Did you become yourself in the lab, while I was there? You should have given me a sign or something that you were ok."

"I couldn't risk it." James watched his face sour. "I appreciate you sticking up for me, I know how much you like Jenna."

Graham smiled. "She's hot, and funny, caring, but she lacks intelligence sometimes."

"You can't tell her I'm healed. You can't tell anyone. If they figure out they can't control me, they will kill me."

"Why, what the hell did you do?"

"I decoded Loralias's research. Her inoculations were slow burning versions of the project re-gen formula. I'm not saying this is all her fault. There must be someone higher up, behind the scenes, someone hiding in a bunker."

"You must see how stupid that sounds. She made that formula, she pushed for its distribution, and branded it with her name. Adder isn't that little girl you weren't there for. She's a fully grown, unfeeling, psychotic woman."

'My daughter is not beyond hope.' James thought about Adder as the smiling child in the photos he'd been given, whilst imprisoned. "We'll agree to disagree on that one."

There was an uneasy silence. Graham was the one to break it. "What happened to the Wailers?"

"They're all Mushroom-men, I'm not sure why yet. We'd all agreed that the mushrooms could throw off the cure's results. You remember that Roger Smiles guy? Real piece of work, he's the one who ran the collar care home. He and his goons are spore ridden now, and that strange woman Moira, the one who had an unnatural obsession with tinned peaches."

"Oh yeah, she's an odd one. Is she mushroom infected too?"

James nodded. "Officially, you, Jenna and Loralias are the only ones at Prospect Heath who aren't."

Graham let that sink in for a moment. "You have a plan?"

"We need to take back control. This place has all the resources we need to make a cure, and we have the knowledge. I have to keep up the charade for now. No one must know that I'm me again."

"Where does pretending get us?"

"My mutation cures the mushroom spores, if I can synthesise something from my cells I can wake up the Mushroom-men. We'd have to do it strategically, help those who would be most useful to our cause first."

"Adrienne Reese is a computer genius and engineer. She'd be a good one to get on side."

"Yes, apart from the fact she vowed to beat me every day, and have a hand in my death. Mervin Hatter is a good first candidate. Pro cure, and Loralias keeps him close, we could get a lot of leverage through him."

"We're really going to do this?"

"It may take weeks, months, but yes. I'll need you to synthesise mushrooms for me, fresh ones to stick on every day, we must match shape and positioning."

"That will be easy enough if I get access to spores. Do you know where they're stored?"

"You shouldn't go anywhere near the spores, not if what Loralias said about your mutation is true. You could craft them out of papier mâché. Besides, the spores are not stored, they're produced. A mutant infected me with them. My assailant released them through tiny slits in its fingerprints."

"Adder, you can say it, your daughter's the mutant."

"No, I mean I'm not sure. I didn't see who it was I just saw the fingers and the spores."

"Who gave you instructions? Who was your handler?"

"Loralias, but that still proves nothing."

"Ok, believe what you want, I'm going back to my room. Enjoy your denial and selective memory."

"You'll help? You'll keep quiet?" James asked as Graham got up to leave.

"I don't have a better plan, and the cure has to come first."

Chapter 21: Mallard Hill

Serenity hummed one of the Lord's hymns as she readied the school room. She felt so contented. Soon the room would fill with eager pre-schoolers. Her views were respected, wanted, they valued her experiences. She woke up with a smile every day and maintained it with ease.

"Good morning, Serenity, bringing cheer into my classroom as usual I see," said Mrs Best.

"Good day, yes, this truly is a joyful place. Would you like me to get you your fruit tea?"

"In a minute, could you take a seat, there's something I would like to discuss with you."

"Of course." Serenity perched on one of the child-size seats with grace.

"It's about Verity, as you know I have raised some developmental concerns with her mother, but what I want to talk to you about is of a more serious nature."

"I will answer what I can."

"Have you witnessed any physical harm being inflicted on the child?"

"No, never."

"Verity has a serious blister on her arm, I have heard the family's version of events, but would value your unbiased opinion on how this happened."

"It is my understanding that Kyan grabbed her, his mutation was unknown at that point. The injury was caused accidently."

"You believe this story?"

"I do."

"But you didn't witness the injury?"

"No, it happened before I arrived. I did however, witness Sadie taking great care to keep the wound clean and wrapped in film. The family has also taken strides to help Kyan learn to control his ability."

"I see, thank you, Serenity. I will take that tea now please."

Outside, the playground supervisor waved the school bell back and forth. The chimes echoed and Serenity beamed. The children would be here soon, to receive her help and guidance.

When she returned with Mrs Best's tea, the register was almost complete. Mrs Best called out their names, and the children responded with, "Good morning, Mrs Best."

"Verity-Elise Ratcher."

Madam didn't respond. She was examining the nose nugget perched on her fingertip.

"Verity-Elise Ratcher," Mrs Best said more forcefully.

Serenity put her hand on the little girl's shoulder and pointed at the frustrated teacher. "Madam? You must answer with, good morning, when Mrs Best calls your name."

"Huh?" Madam wiped her finger on her knee. "Good mornin, Srentay."

"No," said Mrs Best. "She must answer to her proper name and also address you accordingly. In this school, Verity, you must call our teaching assistant Ms Feldon, not Serenity."

"I would prefer Mrs, if that is all right. I am widowed not divorced."

"My apologies, Mrs Feldon. Could you prepare and lead a crafting session, it would appear that I need to spend more time re-educating Verity."

Mrs Best led Madam into the small side room used for quiet reading.

"We have been learning about winter and hibernation. With these materials..." Serenity dumped a box of craft scraps onto the middle table. "I want you to make an animal that sleeps through winter. If there is time we could try to make their homes too."

Serenity busied herself helping the children cut and stick. Her eyes drifted toward the closed door when she heard Madam screaming out and arguing with Mrs Best.

"Mrs Feldon?"

"Yes, Myrel."

"Why are you so dark?"

"Hmm, in what way do you mean?"

"Your skin is really brown, I've never seen anyone like you before."

"Your eyes and hair are really black." Serenity smiled and helped to tie together some coloured straws with wool. "We both look different from the native Tave people, because our ancestors and their homelands are on the other side of the oceans. We do not look the same as one another, because our ancestors lived across different oceans, far away."

"Oh, ok." Myrel twiddled some pipe cleaners. "What's an ancestor?"

"Someone in your family, who died long ago, like a great, great, great, grandma or grandpa."

"Madmam no listen! Madmam wan Mummy, Madmam wan Cat!"

"You infernal child, get down from there!"

Mrs Best opened the door to the reading room, and Madam sprung out. She climbed over the top of the door frame and continued across the classroom ceiling. The children dropped their craft and shouted and cheered.

"She's removed her shoes. Help me find something to knock her down with."

"I will not," said Serenity. "She is a child not a rodent." Serenity walked underneath Madam and held up her arms. "Do you need a cuddle, little one?"

"Madmam no little one," she sniffled, "Madmam no Verity, not third person. Madmam wan Mummy."

"I know, but Mummy is not here, I can still give you a cuddle."

"It is forbidden to touch the children," said Mrs Best.

"She is two years old, the youngest in this class. If we cannot offer her comfort, it might be better to place her with the infants."

"She is three in a fortnight and belongs in the pre-school class. Get her down, I don't care how."

"As you wish, Mrs Best."

Serenity tried to coax Madam down. She refused to move, so Serenity decided to ignore her and allow her to come down when she was ready.

Madam watched them make crafts, she listened to a story being read, although she was too far away to see the pictures, and she watched Serenity wheel in a tray of lunchboxes. The children tidied away their things, went in twos to the sink to wash their hands, and then ate their lunch.

Madam's lunch was on the table waiting for her.

"Would you like to come down to eat?"

Madam didn't respond, her eyelids were at half-mast and her suckers were slipping. Serenity caught her as she fell from the ceiling. She let her nap in her arms until Mrs Best suggested that she go into the sleeping area in the infant room.

Serenity carried the sleeping babe and placed her on some cushions. She covered her over with a blanket and brushed the curls out of her eyes. "Defiant," she whispered with a smile, "and stubborn. Just like your mother."

***

"We are unable to contact anyone at Prospect Heath. Underground facility five has had great success in counteracting the formula, if administered before any change occurs, but once the mutation has begun, it is useless. If we can reach the doctors at Prospect Heath and pool our intelligence, we may be mere weeks away from a cure."

"Prospect Heath is lost, forget it, and continue to pool the resources we still have."

"But the satellite footage, sir, it shows life in Prospect Heath, power still exists in that area. We have every reason to believe that this is just a communications error."

"No. If a single one of my men survived there, they would have made contact by now. The Moorland estate was overrun. I don't know who is surviving in that building now, but I can say for damn sure it's not our men."

"But Dr Adder—"

"If I believed for one second that Dr doomed-us-all-to-hell Adder, was still alive and in Prospect Heath I would have trained missiles on it by now."

"How are you getting on?" asked Spear.

"Great." Rapz took off his headphones and put his pen down. "There has been non-stop Authority chatter today. I've transcribed so much my wrist hurts."

"Good man. I knew this would be a good fit for you. I followed your career and I've got to say your anti-Authority lyrics hit home with people round here. You've been singing our cause."

"It still seems so hard to believe, a resistance of your size, hiding in the shadows, infiltrating the military, waiting to pounce. It's the stuff of legends."

"Speaking of legends, we have a winter fair coming up. Some of the local talent will show off their skills, and I hoped that you would join them."

"Ha ha, yeah for sure, let me see your decks, before I fully commit."

Spear patted him on the shoulder and walked out of the communications room.

Digger caught up to him in the hallway. "How is our new listener settling in?"

"Perfect, just as predicted. He has been instigating Authority dissidence through his music for years. Growing hate is easy, creating comradery and purpose through that hate? That takes skill."

"The others may not accept him so readily, he's not Marazsian."

"Most of the resistance were from Tave and Conclee. Marazsha was just a base. If any of our people want to make this a race issue, they should bring it up with me directly. As far as I'm concerned, there is Authority and there is us. They are underground, but they're not gone, this is the best chance we've ever had to wipe them out."

"I'm with you one hundred percent, sir. I just thought you should know that there is unease in the village, and it's growing."

***

They had taken the fences down, turning the three gardens behind the Odd Blockers' houses into one giant garden. Luke was sparring with Kyan. The space was great for Luke to engage with his wings and practice gliding. Kyan was enjoying the session, he could sense if his electrical charge was building, and discharge it safely, without risk to Luke.

"He is getting the hang of his new body," Serenity observed, joining Sadie at the window.

"Hmm, oh yes, he is starting to get the hang of those wings. He still struggles with positioning the tail for balance, but he's getting there."

"How about you? Are you accustomed to his new appearance?"

"I fell in love with *him*, not his biceps. Though, I have to admit the tail is annoying, I used to enjoy staring at his arse, now it's hidden."

Serenity blushed. "I cannot say I had noticed his backside."

"His hugs still feel weird." Sadie stared out of the window, never engaging Serenity in eye contact.

Serenity studied Sadie's face. Her weak smile was hiding a deep sadness, and her blue eyes with a yellow circle around the pupil, a trait that her children had both inherited, were glassy now and covered in a watery film.

"You are not happy here?"

"They're telling me I'm raising my kids wrong, that I'm living my life wrong. Cynlear follows me everywhere. She thinks I'm a threat." Sadie flopped her head against the window. "No, I'm not happy here, everyone else is, but I'm not."

"It is just for the winter, and then you shall move on."

"You're staying?"

"Innocence and I are thriving here. Meeting you was the Lord's will, and you have led us to the place we are meant to stay."

Sadie took it as another blow. Her friend was choosing this horrible village over her. She felt even more alone. "I should check on Madam."

"Mrs Best has requested that you use her given name."

"Mrs Best doesn't dictate what goes on in my home."

"Sadie," Serenity called, but Sadie didn't slow. Serenity turned back to the garden and watched Luke offer Kyan in elongated hand and help him back up to his feet.

Chapter 22: The Brutes

The Brutes spent a week, mourning and drinking. Claire walked around the carcass of her home. There was nothing stately or refined about it anymore. They smashed furniture, scuffed and stained the floors and destroyed artwork. Claire felt weak and emotional. She could see the lawn from the massive landing window. The Ivanthor grounds stretched on for acres, but the five graves were all Claire could focus on.

"Claire, they're preparing to leave." Claire continued to look out of the window that towered over her. "Claire," Brett repeated, "they're leaving."

"The lawn looks appalling. When's the last time you mowed it?"

"You're deflecting."

"And you're a terrible groundsman."

"They are going to Prospect Heath. They will kill people. Talk to Brutus, he'll listen to you."

"He doesn't listen to me though, does he? He tells me what to do, how to stay safe, how to keep our baby safe." Claire scowled. "He listens to Joel sometimes, if you want to gain Michael's ear, bend Joel's first." Brett started back down the curved staircase. "And mow the lawn, it looks atrocious."

Brett hadn't spoken to Joel much, but he struck Brett as one of the most reasonable of the group. "Joel?"

Leighton looked up at Brett. "He's over there."

"Right, thanks." The brothers had a resemblance, it hadn't been that strong before, but now they'd mutated, Brett found it hard to tell them apart.

"Joel?"

"What can I do for you, mind reader?" Joel said, hauling a bag of knives and blunt weapons into the van.

"I hoped you would talk to Brutus."

"About what?"

"About this trip, about planning murders. Aren't you involved in some kind of deal with these people? Doesn't Claire's continued health rely on their medication?"

"You spoke to Brutus about any of this?"

"Do you think I would still be breathing if I had?"

Joel raised an eyebrow and smiled. Their illustrious leader was an open book. "They gave us injections and forced us to mutate. I for one don't mind this body, I'm stronger, faster, and I can climb shit with ease. But George died. I get you didn't know him that well, but that boy had brains. Every time there was a hole in our plans he had an idea to plug it up. He was smart and brave. I can't forgive his death."

"Brutus killed him."

Joel thrust out his arm and pinned Brett against the side of the van. "Brutus killed a Wailer, our friend was already dead. Adder did that, not Brutus."

"Sorry, I just, I mean Adder sped the process up, but it's a genetic lottery, right? George probably would have turned at some point."

Joel put his hairy muscular arm down. Brett steadied himself against the van. "We could've had days left with him, weeks, months even. He had no symptoms. Those so-called scientists should have let it take its course. They didn't test us, they jabbed us all under a pretext. We might all have been Wailers. They are playing god, and I for one, am all for some payback."

"But Claire, the meds, the arrangement."

"You want someone to argue those points? Do it yourself. Brutus wants you with us, so you can use your mind mojo, and give us an advantage. Speaking of advantages, I hear that Claire's dad was big on guns, but we haven't found a single firearm in the house. You wouldn't know anything about that would you?"

"Mrs Ivanthor wouldn't allow them in the manor, so he kept a lockbox down at the shooting range."

"Of course he did," Joel sniggered. "I think guns would hinder us, so I won't press further, but you don't have to be a mind reader to see through that bullshit. I'd work on your technique before Brutus asks you the same question."

The Brutes filed out of the manor and crammed into the van, Claire included. The last time he left Claire alone she was kidnapped, Brutus would take her with him everywhere now.

"Start her up, Joel, you're driving."

Brutus sat shotgun. He stuck Brett in the back, squeezed between Leighton and Caleb. They sat closer to him than they needed to, pinning him between their shoulders. They smelled awful. Not of sweat or lingering beer. It was an animalistic smell, the kind of thing you notice when a dog or a cat was near. *'The oil in their fur, maybe?'* He looked at Claire and Ethan. They huddled, but not together, they sat hugging themselves, and staring at the floor.

"I'll park a few blocks away."

"Good idea," said Brutus. "Brett, you're going in first."

"What?"

"They don't know you. You can go in, read their thoughts, get the low down on numbers and positions within the building. You'll be the most successful at reconnaissance."

"And if they capture me? Kill me?"

"It won't be the greatest loss."

"Michael," snapped Claire.

"He knows I'm joking."

One glance at that scarred monkey face told Brett he was deadly serious.

"We're close enough. Brett, if you take this road up to the bookies and hang a right—"

"I lived three blocks from here. I know how to get to P Heath."

The back doors to the van opened, and they shoved Brett out. "Good luck."

It was quiet. Much quieter than when Brett had come here looking for Claire and Terry all those weeks ago. There were no walking corpses, plenty had frozen to the pavement, but none of them walked.

Brett stopped in his tracks, his heart beat faster and he panted, gasping for air. He could see himself, through so many eyes. They surrounded him, watching him. Brett pushed all of those hungry Wailer eyes from his mind and he ran. By the time he reached the fences that surrounded

Prospect Heath, scores of Wailers had filed out of houses, flats, and shops to chase him down.

Brett scaled the fence, but so did the Wailers. Once he tumbled onto the grass below, someone turned the fence on. Many volts ran through that metal fence. Anything unfortunate enough to be touching it died instantly.

A few of the Wailers made it over when Brett did. They regained their footing and prepared to pounce. Two men came out of nowhere. Neither one was short but the one on the left was monstrously tall. The men ran at the Wailers and threw one at the fence. The remaining two assumed a submissive position. Hatter cable tied the Wailers' hands and led them inside.

"My, name Saxon, who you?" The tall man with white-blond hair held his hand out to Brett.

"Brett, my name's Brett." There was an alien sensation when he looked into Saxon's eyes. The man seemed to have no thoughts. *'A simpleton perhaps?'* Brett let go of his hand and stepped back. "Are those contagious?" he said, pointing at the orange mushrooms growing in patches over his flesh.

"Have, to ask, Adder, I not sure."

Brett followed him into the complex. He had been in Prospect Heath back when it was flats. As a teenager he had come in here to buy cheap booze and cigarettes, from a man who never asked for proof of age. It smelt different, like disinfectant, rather than urine. The stairwells and walkways seemed the same, but he glimpsed pictures of rooms from people who were in them. A lot of these glimpses came from brains with as little activity as Saxon's. *'A community of simpletons?'* It seemed unlikely. Something else was going on here.

His hairs stood on end and tingled. He touched a presence, a person so remorseless they would watch the world burn and die, with no regret. Brett pulled away from this mind. There was another that stood out from the crowd of blank minds, a person he had seen through Brutus's eyes. Officer Felicity Grange hid somewhere in the building. She was alone, skulking in the shadows.

Brett dabbed the blood trickling from his nose. He had overreached and been so absorbed, that he hadn't paid attention to where he was in the building. How many flights of stairs had he marched up? He wasn't sure. Saxon ushered him into a room.

Her posture was perfect, her hair tied neatly for practicality. Dr Adder produced a facial expression that imitated a smile. Brett didn't buy it, but he tried to sell his own smile as genuine.

"Are you here seeking sanctuary?" asked Adder.

"Erm no, I guess I'm here to discuss the terms of your surrender." Brett shuffled his feet. No one reacted to the comment. "Although some context may help this conversation run smoother."

Loralias Adder addressed the large man. "You may leave us to talk alone." The mushroom escort filed back out of the room.

There was a living corpse strapped to a chair. The zombie woman had one hand attached, the other was on a metal tray next to her. Her fingernails were peculiar, dark, hard, and pointed like thorns. The zombie stared at Brett with a hunger in her gaze. Brett stared back at her. He entered her mind and dived past the hunger to a memory that remained intact. The zombie brain bypassed it, the content had no relevance to its existence, but Brett could see it. He replayed Hemella's last moments as seen through her eyes.

Brutus was there, he was killing her son. Brett watched the young boy being pummelled with a hammer until little remained of his head. Brett was beyond grief stricken. In that moment, the mother's loss was his own. Ethan stepped forward and tried to hold the mother back. He was trying to save her. She knew and appreciated the kindness off his efforts, but she had to fight, she had to avenge her baby. Her fingernails shot into Brutus's face. A barrage of scratches, nothing more. Brutus pulled out a knife and put it to the woman's throat. Hemella welcomed the blade.

"Michael Brutus killed them," Brett whispered, almost forgetting where he was.

"You were with him when he did this?" said Adder.

"No, we met more recently, but events have been described to me." He glanced from the zombie to her severed hand. It felt strangely wrong for Hemella and her hand to be rotting at the same pace. Her movements gave the illusion of life, her hand, in its stillness, pretended to be nothing other than dead.

"You said you would contextualise your absurd demands." Adder draped a sheet over Hemella.

"Right, yes. Brutus sent me. He and his friends mutated into monkey hybrids after your injection. Thanks for that, what these guys needed was extra strength and manoeuvrability. They didn't all mutate, George became Wailer and died. Brutus holds you responsible for that. We want Claire's pills, that's the one thing I will fight for off my own back, and they also want blood, yours preferably, spilled everywhere."

"Are you saying they all mutated into the same subspecies?"

"More or less, some colour and size variants, and obviously not George, but yes. You're missing the point though."

"I hypothesised that coordinated mutations could occur. The circumstances would have to be just right. The group would need to be close, in proximity and social bonding, and they would also need to mutate at almost the exact same time." Adder scribbled some notes down on a pad. "How much time passed between the first mutation and the last?"

"The mutation itself took some time, but they all started to change within minutes of each other."

"The dominant male, Michael Brutus, did he start the transformation first?"

"Yes." A slight crackle came from the intercom on the far wall. "Is someone listening to us?"

"More than likely it is Jenna. She is a little too curious for her own good." Adder's eyes darted from Brett to the intercom. "Jenna?"

"Yes, Dr Adder?"

"Would you join me?"

"Yes, Dr Adder."

The voice on the end of the intercom sounded nervous. This didn't surprise Brett. Adder was cold, unfeeling. Even when she talked about the group mutation, a subject that clearly interested her, she had no joy to draw from. Her face remained wooden.

"I have work to be getting on with, explain your demands to Jenna. I'm sure she has the time to tell you why they are ridiculous."

Brett dared a quick glance inside of Adder's mind, and retreated immediately.

Chapter 23: The Brutes

Jenna walked in with a smile. "Hi, I'm Jenna." Brett shook her hand. The colour drained from his face.

"Jenna, I have work to do. Please take Mr..." Adder realised that she had not gotten the man's name. "Take him away and speak with him. He represents Michael Brutus."

"Okie doke, this way," Jenna said. Brett stumbled through the door in his eagerness to get out. "Do you like tea? I have coffee but you seem strung out."

"Oh Lord, oh Lord, I have to get out of here, Brutus was right, that thing needs to die."

"Hemella? She is starting to smell a little. I told Dr Adder we've learnt all we can, but she insists—"

"No, not Hemella, Dr Adder, she's not human. Do you know? How can you not know, you work with her?"

"Whoa, slow down, breathe deep, what's wrong with Dr Adder?"

"She's not right, there is something so off about her, and those mushroom people too. You don't sense it? I can, I can sense it. My senses are strong."

He wished he could say more. *'Don't trust Adder. I can hear cogs, and information being processed, but I can't hear her thoughts. It's like she's a void, soulless and emotionless. I imagine this is what a sociopath's mind would sound like. The thoughts, or lack of, are similar to the mushroom people. She is modelling them on herself, recreating her way of thinking within them.'* He thought it, but he couldn't tell Jenna that, he needed to hide the full extent of his ability.

"Is it like a mutation, can you hear, see, smell better?"

"No, it's more like a sixth sense, like a feeling I get, and around her that feeling is bad."

"Ok, I believe you, but you need to tone the volume down. All those Mushroom-men are under Adder's command. They'll report anything you say to her, albeit slowly and in stutters, still they'll tell her, and then we'll both be screwed." Jenna pulled out a key and unlocked the door. "This is me, so come in, excuse the mess." Brett stood uncomfortably in the entrance. "Take a seat." Jenna gestured to the one cushion on the sofa that didn't have papers stacked on it. "Please."

Brett moved to the seat. He was too shaken to read Jenna's mind, he was too shaken to read Felicity Grange, who had followed them down into Jenna's apartment, and found a corner to squat in.

"Do you take sugar?"

"No thanks," Brett said.

"Here you go, that should settle your nerves." She gave him the cup handle first and cleared a space to sit in. "Now, Adder said you were representing Michael Brutus, why don't we start there before we get into the politics of this place?"

'Yes.' Felicity grinned. *'Let's start with Brutus.'*

"He wants Adder dead, he's mutated, they all mutated, one turned Wailer—"

"Is your Wailer with you? We can offer him sanctuary, and he will be one of the first to get the cure."

"No, Brutus killed him."

"Oh." Jenna looked sorry for his loss, although she didn't patronise him by saying so.

"So the demands are: Adder dead, potentially you scientists too, depending on how much blood lust he has in him today, a lifetime supply of pills for Claire, and then if any of you survive, leave us in peace."

"Here's the problem with that, we made a deal with Brutus to bring us more Wailers, to advance the cure, and to bring more mutants too. Dr Adder believes that the cure already exists in the form of a mutation. We need him."

"You tricked him."

"Not my call." Jenna held up her hands defensively. "Adder is being, well, difficult of late. She's been creating more Mushroom-men, I fear out of boredom. She's hit a snag in her research, and has lost the plot a little."

"How is that my problem?"

"It's your problem if we don't find the cure. Life expectancy in Wailer territory for mutants, with useful mutations and survival skills, is two years, for humans its two days. She can figure this out, but she needs things and Brutus can get those things. That's why we made the deal."

"Pretty sure you burned that bridge when you turned them all into monkeys."

Jenna sat with a pensive look on her face. She used her feet to guide scattered papers into a pile. Brett sat quietly while she did this. "Take me to them," Jenna said finally. "Take me to Claire. I will give you more than enough medicine for her, if they will hear me out on a new deal."

"He'll still want Adder."

"We need her for the cure."

"You're smart," said Brett pointing to the books and papers. "You can do it without her."

"I'm bettering myself, like a student. I wouldn't have the slightest chance of curing this thing without her."

"Ok, you tell Brutus that, see what he says."

Jenna led Brett down to the supply room. They filled a bag with prenatal vitamins and anti-sickness meds, and then they went out through the back. Hatter was on guard at the gate.

Jenna commandeered a vehicle and approached him. "Hatter, let me out. I have business in the Moorland estate." Hatter didn't question the orders. He pulled the gate open and let them pass. Brett got the sense that there was someone being left behind, someone who very much wanted to meet with Brutus.

"Felicity Grange," Brett said under his breath.

"Hmm, what was that?"

"Oh, nothing." Brett locked on to Felicity's mind. She was racing behind them on foot, moving so fast that Brett could see her in the passenger wing mirror. Her form was shimmering in and out of view.

They lost her as they turned the corner, but Brett could sense her lack of concern. They were in the only vehicle on the road. She would follow the sound of the engine.

"Pull up over here."

"How deep in are they?"

Brett's mind darted through the writhing mass of Wailers and dead and built up a picture of their surroundings. "They are parked about fifty meters away."

"Can they survive this?"

Brett touched the minds of the Brutes. They were fighting hard. Claire was scared, but safe inside of the van. The surge of testosterone in the others was inhuman, so was the pack mentality that guided them. Heeding Brutus's words, Brett avoided him, and took a peek through Caleb's eyes. He and the others were bouncing around, hooting to one another, and ripping their prey limb from limb. "They're doing fine," said Brett. A severed zombie arm bounced off of their windscreen. "It looks like the mob is pulling back. It's us I'm worried about."

"So this sixth sense of yours? It's that strong?"

"I can feel they are all well and fired up."

"And our predicament?"

"I don't know about you, but I've never *sensed* my way out of a fight. Wait, don't retreat," Brett said sharply, grabbing her hand.

"Can you see my thoughts," asked Jenna, alarmed.

"No, you were shifting the gear stick into reverse. They are running away from the Brutes, if we edge in closer, they should back away from us too, you know, because of proximity."

"Sure, makes sense." Jenna edged the patrol car into the crowd. The Wailers were now retreating en masse. The dead had no such self preservation, but there were fewer of them, and the Brutes and their van, were now visible.

"They're incredible," said Jenna. She watched the troop, jump, and tear, and stomp. Their agility and strength was exceptional. Leighton and Joel worked together, linking arms to swing the other into the mob. Brutus and Caleb worked alone, they both stood as forces to be reckoned with.

While Caleb was wiry, slender, and tan coloured, Brutus was huge both in bulk, and height. His black fur was thick with a satin sheen. Under his eye was that shooting star, branding his face in purple and white scar tissue.

Brett ignored the warriors. At the back, fighting only in defence, was Ethan, his cheeks were wet with tears. *'Hide them,'* Brett thought. *'Wipe them away before he sees.'* As though sensing Brett's thoughts, Ethan wiped his face and launched himself at a zombie. Brutus saw this proactive attack and smiled.

"A clear leader and subordinate hierarchy, just like in the animal kingdom, how fascinating."

"Avoid words like animals and fascinating when you speak with Brutus. He already thinks you see him as an experiment."

"Oh, right, I didn't mean—"

"Of course you didn't. Just remember that Brutus is ruthless and he will happily do to you, what he just did to that zombie."

Jenna gasped. Brutus grinned at the zombie head he held in his hand. Its torn, ragged flesh had been ripped, not cut. "I'll be more careful with my words."

"Come on, let's go."

Jenna stepped out and started to hop over the body parts. Brutus raced over, running on his knuckles. "You!" he yelled.

"Wait," Brett stepped between them. "Please, just listen to what she has to say."

Jenna started off by handing the bag to Brutus. "Meds and vitamins, enough for the duration of Claire's pregnancy."

Brutus glared. She was the one that stuck him with the needle, the same smiley, pierced, make-up wearing snake. "You just handed over your only bargaining chip."

"The meds are my way of apologising. Dr Adder told me you all had tested negative for the Wailer gene. I would never have injected him if I'd known."

"But you still would have injected the rest of us," Brutus growled.

"Well yes, I follow orders and agree with Dr Adder, to some extent, that mutants have a greater chance of survival. Although asking first would be my policy, if I were in charge."

"You took away our right to be human."

"No, I didn't, you would all have changed eventually. Mutating quicker gave you a fighting chance."

Brutus dragged his monkey knuckles down the curve of Jenna's jaw and shoved her chin. "Did we look like the kind of men that needed a fighting chance?"

"No, but this new form seems to suit you. Your fighting skills were remarkable, I watched in complete awe of your magnificence." Jenna worried she had crossed the line from complementary to condescending. The flattery seemed to have stuck, so she continued. "I need your help and I will pay dearly for it."

"I doubt you have anything to offer."

"Passage," said Jenna, "on a cruise ship. It leaves in a few months, after the thaw. I can get your names on the manifesto."

"What makes you think we want to go on your mystical boat ride?"

"The trip ends on an uninhabited island, completely isolated, surrounded by sea mines. Very few people can navigate to its location. There will be no Wailers, no zombies, just humans and mutants. I know you like the fight and struggle, you thrive in it, but will your child?" Brutus wrapped his hand around Jenna's throat and squeezed. "Your baby..." Jenna gasped. "You'll need... somewhere safe... to birth... safe..." her voice became more strained as his grip tightened more. "Ugh, to raise, him." Brutus released her. She flailed and gasped on the ground.

"Brutus," Claire said as she jumped out of the van. Reaching Jenna's side, she cradled her. "This woman is my friend."

"This woman made us what we are."

"Stronger, fitter, more arrogant, I should think you'd shake her hand, not squeeze the life from her."

"What's the price?" asked Joel. "For getting on that ship?"

"The deal is the same as you made with Adder. I need Wailers and mutants delivered alive. Pretend as though you are doing it for her. She never needs to know about this meeting."

"What do you need them for?" Joel glared at her with arms folded.

"The Mushroom-men, you've seen how effective they are, when the time comes I will need a group for protection, a bodyguard detail."

"We can escort you to the boat when it's time," said Brutus. "There's no need to build bodyguards."

Jenna shook her head. "That won't work. I have a task that will require me to go on an excursion before the ship launches. The boat will be the easiest way to transport Wailer samples and a variety of mutants, but I need to complete my task first."

"Two questions," said Joel, "what is the task? And why do you need Wailer samples?"

"There is an underground facility on the island, it's disused, but will have the space and equipment we need. I am to join other scientists there, and bring all of Dr Adder's work with me. I will work underground. You and the other survivors would have free reign on the surface."

"And the task?" Joel pressed.

"There is a woman, she has both Wailer and mutant genes, a rare combination, but neither one is finding dominance. There is talk among the academics, she could be the cure. That is the reason for all of this. My loyalty is to the cure."

Brutus sneered. "I thought you were loyal to Adder."

"I care for Dr Adder as though she was my own highly demented sister, but the cure has to take precedence. It's clear she has lost her way. I hope she will regain her path, and in the meantime I need all the work she has, and will have over the next few months, copied and ready for transport. I have to stay close to her for that."

Brett tried to glimpse inside Jenna's head, to gauge her honesty, but he hit a wall. Then he found himself in someone else's head. Felicity had caught them up.

'I can't take them. How would I even get close to Michael? That scar dominates his face, owns it, as it bloody well should, scummy, murdering, bastard! Damn it, what do I do now?

'I'll wait for my chance, if they broker a deal, he'll return to Prospect Heath, maybe on his own next time. My Authority codes should still work on their guns. I need to follow this Jenna too. She will try to get Sadie's location again from Chris. I need to ensure the Odd Blockers stay safe.'

Brutus frowned. "We agree to your terms and will bring you the first lot in a fortnight."

"Thank you." Jenna jolted, it sounded like the patrol car door had clicked open.

"I'll check it out," said Brett. He walked over to the patrol car and opened the door. He could sense Felicity lying on the backseat. Her camouflage was seamless though, she was invisible to him. "We should talk sometime," Brett whispered, "our interests may coincide. I'll return to P Heath in a fortnight, with that monster Brutus. If you're still there, find me." Felicity stayed still, wondering what kind of trick this was. "See you around, Officer Grange."

Brett closed the door and yelled out, "All clear." He returned to the van and Jenna got back in her car, oblivious to her stowaway, and drove back to Prospect Heath.

Chapter 24: Prospect Heath

Chris knocked on the door excitedly. "Get Dr Adder, quick, something amazing has happened."

"Okay," the slow-witted guard responded.

Chris listened to him shuffle off to get his master. "It's amazing," he said to himself, "just incredible."

A short time passed before Dr Adder walked in. "You made a request for my presence."

"Yes, please come see, it's amazing, she's cured."

"So long as infection did not intervene, I expected her mouth to heal quickly."

"No, not that, I mean she is cured. Come see, she's right through—"

Lara lunged at Adder, screeching.

"No," said Chris stepping between them. Lara calmed at his presence. "Come sit down." He led Lara over to a cushion pile and stroked her hands. "She's much calmer and doesn't become aggressive at the sound of my voice or the sight of me. She's becoming herself."

"I am afraid you misinterpret." Lara snarled at the sound of Adder's voice and tried to make a move, but Chris shushed her and soothed her. "She has not changed. She is still Wailer and she will still slaughter humans if the chance should arise. It would appear that you have mutated into something non threatening to Wailers."

"Mutated? But I feel fine."

"The day you arrived, you received an injection described to you as a booster. This injection speeds up the mutation process. Your greatest desire was to be around Lara without her killing you. Your mutation could not change her nature, so it has changed yours. I shall mark you down as a defensive mutant as opposed to an offensive one."

"But," Chris whimpered. Adder walked out of his apartment and had the Mushroom-man lock it behind her.

Lara snuggled into him, to her they were alike. Chris was part of her Wailer pack.

***

"Jenna," Adder said as she walked into the lab. "I would like an update on the man who came here yesterday."

"Yes, Brett, he helped me smooth things over with Brutus. He has promised to deliver us Wailers and mutants in thirteen days."

"The deal remains the same?"

"No, I gave them all the medicine, as a show of trust."

"Then what assurances do you have they will stick to their word?"

"They would like help and protection when it is time for Claire to have the baby."

"That seems reasonable. There are notes on my desk which need typing up. I finished my experiments with Jayron and Hemella, have their corpses burnt off site."

"Of course, Dr Adder, I'll see that it gets done."

Adder turned to Graham. "Chris has mutated as expected. He has become nonthreatening, accepted even, by the

Wailer he shares his home with. I doubt that this is the mutation we are looking for, but I would like samples catalogued and collected."

"I thought you had infected all the civilians with mushrooms?"

"Not Chris, he had yet to mutate, although now he has, I may well find him more amenable in orange. Take James with you, even in his mushroom state, he should heal if the Wailer woman bites him."

James turned around at the sound of his name. A well rehearsed blank stare stained his face.

"James, you're with me," said Graham. He scratched his arm. Not all, but some of his arm hair had thickened and turned green.

"I can give you an injection and force the mutation," Adder said. "I can spare you for a few days while you recover."

"No thanks," said Graham. "If it's all the same to you, I would rather mutate slowly."

"It is indeed all the same to me." She flipped through James's notebook and left with it.

"Come on, James, bring that bag, we'll need it to take the samples."

"Bringing, bag," said James slowly for Jenna's benefit.

Graham suppressed a knowing smile. The two of them made their way down to Chris's flat and Graham knocked on the door.

"Go away," Chris called.

"We need to take some samples from you."

"No, just let us go. The Wailers won't hurt me now. Lara and me, we can live our lives, and be free together."

"We know one Wailer in particular won't hurt you, I can't vouch for the others, and as for the dead? Pretty sure you're still on their menu."

"There can't be that many dead left."

"You'd be surprised, the cold slows the rot." Graham paused. Perhaps fear was not the way to go. "Look, Chris, you came here to save Lara and we are still your best bet for that. Just because she isn't eating you, doesn't mean she's human." Graham waited for a response, when he didn't get one he continued. "This mutation of yours may come in handy. When we have the cure, you could walk among the Wailers administering it. You can bring us back from the brink. Think about it, Chris, you have the potential to be humanity's hero."

Chris had always known he was meant to be a hero, but hearing it from someone else was humbling. "You know I don't have the key."

"I was looking for permission not accessibility."

"Well thanks, everyone else just walks on in. You have my permission."

"Great, also as I'm still on the Wailer menu, could you shut Lara in the bedroom please? Just while I take some bloods."

Chris took Lara's hand and led her into the bedroom. He closed the door and slid a bolt across. "It's safe," he called.

Graham walked in. "Thank you, Chris, do you mind if my bag carrier comes in? It's fine to say no."

"I don't mind."

James followed Graham in. He was impressed with how he had handled the situation. Chris got comfortable and Graham drew his blood. "Sharp scratch, perfect. You have good veins, makes this thing a lot easier." Graham filled four vials and labelled them. He passed Chris a carton of fruit juice and some sweet biscuits. "Take these for your blood sugar, and try not to get up too fast."

"So when do you think you'll need my help, distributing the cure?"

"We're a little way off that yet, but I've been thinking about sending some Mushroom-men out to study the Wailers. Their behaviour is changing and that could provide useful data for making the cure."

"How does that involve me?"

"The Mushroom-men are morons. You would do a much better job of fact finding, and just use the Mushroom-men as backup. They'll kill all the dead things."

Chris smiled. "Watch and take notes in hostile territory? That sounds like something I can do."

"Let me run it past Adder, I'll get back to you with an answer soon. Remember, get up slowly."

"I will, thanks." Chris sank deeper into the chair with a wide grin. A hero, the saviour of all humanity, somehow he'd always known this was his destiny.

***

Jenna typed up Adder's notes, when she finished, she took a stick drive from her pocket and saved a copy for herself.

"The double agent," whispered a voice.

Jenna's eyes darted around the room, she couldn't see anyone. "Who are you? What do you want?"

"Two things," said the voice. "Michael Brutus's completely warranted demise, and for you to lose interest in the Odd Blockers."

"Odd Blockers, Odd Blockers..." Jenna rolled the words around on her tongue until she placed them. "The odd numbered block of flats on Sycamore Close, the block that was overrun."

"That's the one. I won't let you hunt them down. They are happy and safe. Leave them alone."

"I just want Sadie, she might be the cure."

"Because she is neither Wailer nor mutant but has the potential for both? I've listened to more than one person make that case since entering this building."

"Yes, when the mutation wins out, it will have overridden the Wailer gene, that's what my colleagues think, anyway. The resulting mutation should be a self-replicating cure. At least that's how it was explained to me."

"She is a mother, a girlfriend, a friend, I'm not her greatest fan, but I wouldn't see her in pieces on a metal table."

Jenna slid her fingers under the desk and fumbled with the sensor embedded in the wood. "How long have you been here?" She moved around the desk and scanned the room to locate the voice's owner.

"I arrived a little over a week ago."

"Did you get here before or after Chris? It seems strange that you'd both arrive around the same time." Jenna had narrowed down the part of the room her intruder was occupying.

"He listed all the, what did you call them, Odd Blockers? You were not in his list."

Felicity looked beyond her words, Jenna was stalling, and help was on its way. Felicity rushed to the door, but it was too late. Mervin Hatter and Roger Smiles entered, their stares were blank, under the mind control mushrooms. Hatter was still a man, he wore his Authority uniform, but despite having Minister Farr's logo stitched on him, he was a dog of Prospect Heath, not the military. Roger Smiles was something else. Both of his legs were long, thick articulated muscle. He slithered on them. They held his weight and propelled him forward, whipping back, forth, and round. He looked like a torso, sat upon two massive snake bodies.

Felicity's haste had revealed her location. She tried to barge past the two slow witted Mushroom-men, but Saxon's massive form filled the doorframe. Hatter caught her by the arms and twisted her around to face Roger. She stared into his face. His pupils were elongated slits. Inside his mouth, his teeth were all flat and short, barely protruding from his gums.

Roger looked to Jenna for confirmation. Jenna covered her mouth and nodded. "Do it," she whispered and turned away. Thin needle like fangs shot out from Rogers gums. He bit into Felicity's palm, one of the few areas of flesh that had finer scales. Felicity felt intoxicated, the room swam and blurred and her whole body tingled and went numb. "You'll wake up, I promise," Jenna said. "We have the antidote. You will be fine." Felicity didn't hear her, she was already unconscious.

Chapter 25: Mallard Hill

It was fate, Luke had always believed that. What other force could have caused her to open the door in that state?

Sadie stands in the open doorway with a faded black eye, a positive pregnancy test dangling towards her toes, and a red puffy face drenched in tears. I smile at her and hold out the hand that would pair with her empty one. "Good morning, beautiful, and how are you, on what is clearly a shit-storm of a day?"

Sadie takes my hand and shakes it. "I'm fine, I guess," she sniffles.

"May I come in and talk to you about the mighty fine fight school I'm affiliated with?" Sadie stands numb and hollow, she steps aside to let me pass. All reasoning power has gone from this woman. "This is me." I show her the lanyard which has my photo and information on. "I'd be happy to show you a few defence techniques, free of charge, to help you floor the bastard that blackened your eye."

Sadie shows me into the living room, I'm beginning to feel like I'm being led around by a ghost. She waits for me to sit and then takes the seat that is furthest away from me. I look around for my angle. There are boxes stacked to one side of the room. "Just moving in?" I ask. Sadie nods. The room is almost empty but there are photos around, every one of them is of a young boy. He has dark hair, and striking eyes like his mother, dark blue with a yellow ring circling the pupil. I look over at the empty woman. "That your son?"

"Yes," she says. "His name is Kyan."

"Awesome, how old is he?"

"Five, nearly six."

"That's the perfect age to start a martial art, and if you're new to the area, it would be a great place for him to make friends."

"What makes you think we're new to the area, we could have moved across town?"

"This is the Moorland estate, and you let me in after a few sentences. No local would be that trusting."

"This was our fresh start. I had Kyan young. I've been more off than on with his dad. We moved here to make a go of things." I let her talk. She stares through the carpet. *"It didn't end well, he'd never hit me before, and he never will again, he doesn't get another chance."* She looks down at the test, the bottom half of it glows green. *"This complicates things."* Sadie looks at me for the first time. *"I'm sorry,"* she says, *"I shouldn't be unloading this on you."*

"If I wasn't prepared to listen, I never would have come in. Pour your heart out, I don't mind." Sadie smiles weakly, I can tell that when that smile is strong, it will brighten her whole face. *"Are you going to tell him?"*

"I tried before you knocked, he blocked my number. I rang his mum, she told me to forget about him, that he's back with his other baby mamma, and they renounced Kyan. I told them about the baby, they disowned that too."

"What kind of twat disowns a baby before it's even born?"

She fidgets in the chair and looks back to the floor.

"Fuck him," I say. *"Well, not in the way that got you pregnant, just fuck him, I guarantee it won't be a great loss."*

"I don't know anyone here," she whispers.

"You know me, but in case you didn't memorise my ID card, my name is Luke. I'm a martial arts instructor in training and sales man, and proud to be your first friend in Soarken." I dig around in my satchel and pull out the fight club leaflet, with the address and class schedule. "What's Kyan's last name?"

"Ratcher, but I don't think I can afford—"

"Here's a voucher for five free lessons, no obligation after that." I scribble Kyan's name on the voucher. I'll pay for it out of my own pocket, but I don't tell Sadie that. She is becoming uncomfortable, so I tell her, "I look forward to seeing you," and take my leave. She warns me not to knock on opposite, the guy who lives there has a vicious rescue dog. So I head down from the top floor and out of the block.

Kyan takes up a weekly class, he's a good kid, and I enjoy sparring with him. I see Sadie with an orange and cucumber smoothie, gross, but it becomes a craving. I show up with a weird smoothie combo every lesson for her to try. Three months later, my hard work pays off and Sadie falls for me. I couldn't imagine my life without her.

Sadie reached a mega low when the Calamity hit, but the lowest Luke had ever seen her, when she was completely hollow, was the day they met. She was hollow now. She lay on the sofa in their Mallard Hill house, pushing herself against the back cushions, hoping that they would swallow her. Luke curled her hand around a cup. She gave no resistance, allowing him to manipulate her fingers. "Drink up."

"What is it?" Sadie's mumble was muffled.

"It's a pineapple and aubergine smoothie."

"Ugh, I'm not pregnant."

"Pregnant, sad, I sometimes get those two mixed up."

Sadie twisted her head round and looked at the curdled mixture in the cup. "That's a waste of food." Her voice was monotone. Those beautiful eyes were hazed and unfocused. Luke hoped that James had been right, that Sadie wouldn't change. He feared that if she gained the power of invisibility, they would never see her again.

He tried to reach her with their language for two "Arg huhhmoopleh fi, awplehoikeh."

"I don't feel very awplehoikeh right now," she grumbled.

"We're going out."

"I don't think—"

"You don't have to think, just chuck on a coat. Kronic is babysitting."

"Awesome," said Sadie with no enthusiasm in her voice. "Grab the car, we can have a sly fuck in a lay-by."

"Oh, baby, you spoil me." He grabbed her arm and pulled her dead weight up off the sofa. "But I have something else in mind." Sadie flopped onto the floor and buried her face in the carpet. "Sadie, come on, I'm not taking no for an answer."

Sadie found some warm clothes and pulled them on. She dug out the small bag of makeup she had found in the house and dabbed some concealer on her puffy eyes.

Kronic called both children down when he walked in. "Listen up mini twat-bags, if you muck me about while I'm babysitting, I will sit on you and it will fucking hurt."

Kyan tried to keep a straight face as Madam started to mount Kronic (aka her own personal climbing frame).

"When I say bed, I mean bed. I don't do poo or wee, so if you shit yourself you're on your own."

Madam grappled one of his eye sockets as she climbed onto his head. She then sat there cross-legged.

"No electrocuting one another, no climbing on the ceiling — Madam, what are you doing?"

"Madmam being your hat."

"I meant, what are you doing to my hair?"

Kyan had collapsed by this point. His mouth was wide with silent laughter and tears streamed down his face.

"I just makin' it pretty." She gobbed more spit into her hand and ran it through Kronic's hair. She kneaded it into his scalp and spiked up random strands of black hair.

"Well could you not, I'm beautiful enough as it is."

"Madam, no, that's naughty." Sadie lifted the toddler off by her hips and set her down. "Sorry, Kronic, are you sure you want to babysit?"

"It'll be fine, just go, and don't do anything I wouldn't do."

Luke grinned. "That doesn't narrow it down."

"Who wants to watch a bloody horror movie and eat a tonne of sweets before bed?" Kronic said, as they closed the front door. Luke knew he had said it for his and Sadie's benefit. Sadie rolled her eyes as the chorus of, "Me! Me! Me!" started.

"Scratch that, who wants half a chocolate bar and a cartoon about talking fish?" The children answered just as enthusiastically, and Sadie sighed with relief.

Luke interlocked his fingers with Sadie's. The shape of his fingers were different, but the connection was still the same. "We haven't done this since the fair."

"Yeah, that's right, Infernos. Not the best date we've ever had, what with the killer clowns and all."

"Oh, I don't know, you skipped there, we went on all the rides, and had some intimate time under a willow tree."

"Intimate time cut short by those rich kids." Sadie paused. "Do you think they made it?"

"Who?"

"That girl and her brother, the ones you saved from the clown. We walked them to the taxi rank, remember?"

"There are members of my family who could be dead or alive. I can't say I've put much thought into a pair of strangers."

Sadie withdrew. She'd done it again. *'Why do I have to turn everything into a downer?'*

"Hey, look at me. It's ok, we're ok, we're alive. The odds are that everyone we think is dead, is, but we are still here. Keep fighting with me, baby, you're so much stronger than I am. I need you to appreciate the life you have, the life we share."

"I do appreciate it." Sadie left it there. Their swinging hands pushed silence back and forth.

> *'He doesn't get it, he doesn't get us.' The Broken Child swamped Sadie's body with heaviness.*

'No, he's right, we have each other. The kids are well and happy. This should be enough,' the Bitch said in a quiet voice. In Sadie's mind's eye she lay listlessly.

'Shush.' The Child bent down to the Bitch's level and pushed a finger to her lips. 'The world is decaying around us. We're not smart or strong, eventually death will claim us, and rightly so. I still vote for a clean suicide, away from the village. The sooner we remove the weak link, the sooner the others can move on and thrive without us.'

The Child pressed the sole of her foot on the Bitch's cheek. She mumbled again. The Child had drained all of her energy. All of her spirit had been malformed and twisted into depression. 'Shush.'

'We've been quiet for too long,' said the Brain. The Broken Child was in charge, but unlike the Bitch, the Brain still got a say. 'He needs to think you are open to healing. If he figures out you're planning suicide, he will stop you. You preach about culling the weak, i.e. us, to help the strong. You can't accomplish that if you drag the strong down with us.'

"The moon is bright," Sadie said.
"It is. That's partly why I chose tonight to take you."
"Take me where?"

"Up there." A sheer hill rather than the tree imitating wall protected this side of the village. "I promise the climb will be worth it."

Luke ushered Sadie up first. The grassy hill was so steep they had to crawl up it. Luke helped Sadie. She made no objections when he cupped her butt and pushed her a little further up, so he gave it a cheeky squeeze once she was steady. She snorted out a single breath of laughter. It was a start.

Sadie fumbled on the ground for thick weeds that were strongly rooted, and used them to pull further up. When they reached the summit, both of them were covered with dirt. The view was something else. The Forest of Eaves surrounded them in all directions. Tree branches intertwined like a crowd of wizened hands. Moonlight danced on the Eaves as the wind blew through it. There was no shelter from the wind atop Mallard Hill. The concave centre on top was filled with water forming Mallard Hill's lake.

In the warmer months an array of ducks would fill the lake. Small, large, plain, colourful, but that night in the cold, only the hardiest species remained, the rest had migrated. The large grey birds kept their distance from Sadie and Luke. Luke stood behind her and Sadie pulled his arms around her. "It is beautiful up here," she said.

"It's beautiful down there too," said Luke. He nudged her scarf down with his chin and snuggled her neck.

Sadie took a second to figure out what he meant by *down there*. The surface of the lake reflected a large yellow tinged moon, rippling with the breeze. Under the surface drawn up to the light were luminescent fish. The winter had wrung so much colour out of the landscape. Orange, green, and yellow flecks of luminescence darted through the water.

"I wanted to show my colour loving artist, that colour can prevail in the grey. Winter is temporary, after the thaw, this will be one of the most colourful and beautiful places in Tave."

Sadie looked at the scene with fresh eyes. She placed an overlay from her imagination and made the bare Eaves flush with green leaves and blossoms. The lake was given a boost in wildlife. She could smell the flowers, and hear the calls of the ducks and amphibians in her imagination.

> *'We are the winter,' said the Brain, 'the ingredients for success are here. We just need to think with a little more colour.'*

> *The Broken Child banished the overlay, the scents, and the sounds. She took the luminescent fish and showed them diving deep, out of sight. 'I prefer the grey, it's honest.'*

The grey remained. Sadie couldn't conjure up a spring scene again, but the tiny fish remained as well. Sadie squeezed Luke's wrapped arms tighter, his wings blanketing her with warmth. Sometimes it felt as though she just couldn't get close enough to him.

"I've spoken to Spear. Tomorrow you will start with the local paper, drawing a daily comic strip."

"There's enough news in this village for a daily paper?"

"There's a lot of gossip and minor events. The only page I read is the Authority informer column. Spear is keeping the whole village up to date with the radio chatter."

"That's a strange thing to do."

"Not really, they're a group raised as rebels, he wants to keep them angry. I mean it works, every time I hear how those bastards have stepped on us to preserve their own, and hear of failed promises of aid, I get a little angry. They're safe, well fed, unharmed, they have written us off as dead."

"We're not dead though." Sadie wanted to fight *the Broken Child's* urges, she wanted to live. Working with people and opening up to criticism through her art sounded horrifying. That is why she resolved to do it. "Are the comics genre specific, or can I carry on with my graphic novel series in bite size form?"

"I'd say do what feels right to you."

"Huh-hmm." Cynlear had huffed and puffed her way up Mallard Hill to track them down. "I'm supposed to watch her, and neither of you are allowed out after curfew."

"Well now you're here, how about a threesome?" Luke grinned as the older woman grimaced in horror.

"She looks tired. Maybe we should give her a helping push back down?" said Sadie.

Cynlear found neither of them funny. "Both of you, down now. Anymore backchat and I will dock your rations."

Chapter 26: The Brutes

Three months had passed since they made their deal with Jenna. The thaw was already starting. Frost and snow had given way to rain, shoots had started to green the earth, and migratory birds returned in dribs and drabs.

Jenna had given Brutus locations of suspected survivors in the area, and true to his word, he rounded them up for her. Prospect Heath was brimming to capacity, but Jenna had one more target for Brutus: The Moorland Church.

Brutus surveyed the Lord's church from a distance. Made from old stone, it had stood in that spot for hundreds of years. A herd of Wailers circled it.

Leighton leaned out of the bedroom window. The house they were in overlooked the church and its graveyard. "We got three zombies," said Leighton. Brutus stuck out his hand and took the binoculars from him.

"Any idea what type they are?"

"Hard to tell from here, I keep losing them in the crowd."

All the zombies risen from dead humans had withered and rotted away. Best-case scenario was that the zombies at the church were from fallen Wailers. Zombie mutants presented an unknown element to their fight.

Leighton leaned out even further and squinted until his eyes hurt. "There are a lot of different mutations out there. Going up against them clueless could be fatal."

"Brett." Brutus stood on the landing and waved him up. Brett took the stairs two at a time. "We got three unknowns down there, I need you to read their minds and give me an idea if they have any mutations."

"Unknown what?"

"Dead things."

"We've been through this, the dead don't think. I see their hunger and what they can see, but that's it."

"Then slip into the Wailers surrounding them and get a better look."

Brett took Leighton's place at the window. He honed in, skipping from mind to mind with ease. He took a glimpse through a target's eyes, and then moved on. "There's one the Wailers are giving space. He has some kind of spiky balls all over him."

"How big are the balls?"

"An inch maybe, not big, but I can see thirty, maybe forty." The Wailer he was looking through turned away so it forced him to jump into another to keep looking. "They seem to grow out of him, on thin strings of skin. Whatever he is, the Wailers don't like it. The other zombies look normal, the Wailers aren't afraid of them, but looks can be deceiving with mutations."

It had been a rough few months. Joel had been badly injured when a mutant zombie shot out the spiky quills that grew from its arms. The rules kept changing, but the Brutes adapted.

"I suggest we split into two teams," said Leighton. "One to draw the Wailers away, and one to breach the church."

"No, we need the full team to get those people out. We clear the area first." Brutus met Claire at the door. "I'll be back soon." He kissed Claire and then bent down to kiss the tiny bump which had just started to show. "Love you both."

They filed out of the house and headed to the south side of the church. With any luck, the spiky ball zombie would stay around the other side while they dealt with the crowd.

Joel's arm was strapped up and so was part of his chest, but he had no intention of sitting this one out, and no one asked him to.

The hooting troop dived into the crowd and tore at the Wailers. Brutus was happy to use his bare hands, although he sometimes brought out his hammer for nostalgia. Caleb and Leighton fought close to Joel. They teamed Ethan up with Brett. Brutus had found that tasking him with Brett's survival as well as his own, made Ethan fight harder. They reached that pivotal moment where the Wailers started to cut their losses and retreat.

Spiky stepped around the corner. His steps were slow and laboured like the rest of the dead. As he got closer, he pulled a ball from his torso and made a pitiful throw in the Brutes' direction. The ball cracked open on the floor and a green gas leaked out of its hollow innards.

"I don't like the look of this," said Ethan.

"Draw his attention, but don't get too close," said Brett, "I have an idea." Brett rounded the zombie in a large circle. It stayed focused on Ethan and plopped another poisoned ball on the ground. Brett grabbed it from behind and tied his hands.

"Mind the balls on his back," yelled Ethan, "don't put too much pressure on them."

Brett jumped, he had just glimpsed the back of his own head through something else's eyes. He spun round, pulling Spiky between him and the new threat. It was one of the other zombies. The dead woman kept Brett's reflection on her eyes and shuffled closer. She looked normal, like a dead human, well dead Wailer as the case would be now. Then she opened her mouth. Her tongue was hollow and wide like a squashed pipe. A thick, green, smoky gas was pouring out. It looked the same as what came out of the balls.

Ethan threw a metal pole past Brett. It pierced the dead mutant's liquefying flesh. Entering through her chest, it pinned her in a backwards lean. She pumped her poisonous breath up toward the sky.

"We'll need to take these with us too," said Brutus. "Jenna said Dr Adder believes that the cure will come from a secreting mutant. Gasses and poisons are included."

"We'll need a muzzle for that one," said Brett. "This one will be trickier. It didn't take much force to crack open those balls."

Brutus said, "Let me try something." Without waiting for a response, he took out his hammer and smashed it against a ball dangling from the man.

"What the hell? You could have asked me to get out of the way."

"Stop whining, nothing happened. You have to pluck the balls first, like pulling a pin out of a grenade."

"But you didn't know that," Brett yelled.

"I strongly suspected."

"But you didn't know." As his volume increased a little squeak cracked in his voice.

Brutus leashed the restrained zombies and pulled them to his van. Once he had them secured inside, he cut off several of the spiky balls and stuck them to his chest fur. He strolled back to the group, ignoring their incredulous stares. His underlings could stare all they wanted, he wouldn't explain himself to them.

"Come on, we've got to climb." Brutus gestured and Brett jumped on his back and clung on like a backpack. "An army of Wailers didn't get through that door, it must be barricaded well. We will smash through that stain glass. Joel, are you good to climb?"

Joel winced as he circled his shoulder. "I can, but I'd rather give this chance to heal. I'll keep the perimeter clear."

"Ok, keep an eye on the house too. Make sure that Claire stays safe."

The church walls were cobbled together out of different sized rocks. The Brutes had no issue climbing the tiny hand and foot holds in the worn grouting and protruding stones. When they got to the ledge under the imposing stain glass window, they stopped and hung from it.

"Brett, I want you to listen in now, and again when we break through."

Brett started to explore the minds in the church. "Twenty-nine inside, all mutated."

"No Wailers?"

"No, when one of them turned Wailer, they dragged them up to the bell tower and pushed them out."

"Smart policy. What type of mutants do we have?"

"A mix, more defensive than offensive. The leader is big, he mutated into something four-legged with a shed load of teeth. His deputy has calcified fists, they're no longer functional as hands but they can smash through pretty much anything."

"Can he even lift them?"

"Yeah, his arm muscles overdeveloped to compensate. His other deputy is an excreter, his neck is filled with balls, smaller than the ones you've got on you, minus the spikes too, but they are still projectile gas capsules. I think those three are the most dangerous."

"Where are they positioned?"

"Twelve below us in the vestibule, the rest have been locked away. Politics it seems. Emiel Torch, a messenger of the Lord, and leader of this church attempted a failed coup. He was locked away with his parishioners and anyone else who stood up against Dane."

"Dane?" The name struck Brutus with an uneasy apprehension.

"The toothy leader, he's called Dane."

"Is one of his deputies called Shawn?"

Brett paused and examined the minds of those inside once more. "Yeah, the guy with the fists. Is something wrong?"

"I knew that crew before the Calamity, they were dangerous as humans. This won't be an easy fight."

Brett glimpsed something, a meeting Brutus had long ago with Shawn. It all looked friendly, but felt sinister. Brett realised he was seeing the memory through Brutus's eyes, not Shawn's, and backed out quickly.

"You wanna leave this one?" Leighton asked.

"Nah, we got this." Brutus looked at his small group. "We go in quick, let me do the talking, no one acts until I do, got it?" They all knew that last part was aimed at Caleb. His kamikaze approach had gotten them into trouble more than once.

Brutus smashed the pane closest to him. Beautiful shards of colour exploded into the church. A huge decorative curtain hung to the side of their entrance. The Brutes shimmied down it and stood to face the awestruck church dwellers.

"Before you say anything, Dane, we're here to talk."

"Who the fuck are you?" said Dane. "How do you know my name?"

"In a different life you knew me as Michael."

Shawn stepped forward dragging his large fists. "Fuck me, I recognise that scar. Hey, Dane, you remember Michael Brutus? He did time for that snitch getting beaten up. You came with me once to visit him in Authority holding."

Shawn took another step closer. Brett tightened his grip on Brutus's fur. He quickly released it and slid from his back.

Brutus raised his hands. "I offer you all sanctuary."

"We have a sanctuary." Dane glared at the smashed section of stain glass. "It's a little breezier than it was this morning, but we'll make do."

"But you never leave here, you never fight. We know how much food the Authority dropped here." Dane bristled at the mention of his stash. "It can't last forever and as a base this place sucks. The Wailers walk right up to your doors. How will you scavenge?"

"Cut the bullshit, Brutus, what are you offering and why?"

"Beds, electricity, running water, TVs, fences, armed support. The people at Prospect Heath have room for all of you, and with your help can find the cure."

"I ain't being no lab rat."

Dane's son Clint sat beside him etching a design into the chair with a small knife. He had a dog like muzzle, and an advanced sense of smell. Child or not, he would use that knife for more than etching if he felt threatened.

Brett could read the situation and how it would go. This one would end bloody, so he intervened. "They pay our group to capture mutants and Wailers," said Brett. "They are treated well, given food and water, and entertainment, but essentially they are prisoners living their lives in between blood tests." Brutus glared at Brett as he spoke. "I suggest that we offer you freedom instead."

Dane relaxed his stance. "Go on."

"Our reward for gathering survivors for Prospect Heath is a boat trip to a Wailer free island." Dane would have laughed, but this was the moment that Brutus grabbed Brett by his scruff and whispered threats into his ear. Brett continued despite Brutus's tightening grip. "Give us everyone else here, and we will get six of you on the boat with us." Brett started to choke, Brutus released him, and spat on his hunched back as he cowered on the floor.

"You get a room with a view at P Heath," Brutus growled to Dane. "You get safety, security, and the chance at making a cure."

"I like your man's offer better, freedom. You dream about the outside when you're locked up in a place like this for months." He smiled at his son. "But some things are too precious to risk. If you have a place of safety and freedom for me and mine, I'll take it, but I need more spaces than six."

"Eight," wheezed Brett, "that's the best we can offer. We have a quota to fill."

Brutus gave Brett a swift kick to the ribs.

"Eight it is," said Dane. "We'll discuss among ourselves who goes." The group gathered and knelt at Dane's feet and their hushed voices overlapped one another.

"What the hell was that," hissed Brutus. "On whose fucking authority do you speak?"

"We only need fifteen to reach our target," said Brett. "This is our last job if we do it right."

"You offered them travel on the boat."

"If Jenna says yes, then it's all good, if she says no, we just give them the wrong departure date. They can fend for themselves. It was the only way I saw to avoid bloodshed."

"Holiest of fucks, Brett," laughed Leighton, "and I thought Caleb was the liability."

"Fuck I did," snapped Caleb, "I ain't lied 'bout no Billy-Ts."

"Hush up." Brutus mulled over what Brett was saying. "That was smart," he said. "The kind of smarts that George had." They all went quiet. Brett felt as though he was being thrust into a George shaped void, they looked at him differently, Brutus in particular. He was seeing Brett as an asset for the first time since meeting him.

"We made up our minds," called Dane.

"That was quick," said Brutus.

"Turns out some of us want freedom, and some of us want hot water and a TV."

"Good, well we need to tie the hands of your captive parishioners, with enough spare rope to lead them."

"Not a problem," said Shawn. "There's also a girl, kinda kooky. She spends most of her time in the bell tower. She's not one of our eight."

"Ethan will go get her."

"Me?" Ethan had hid in the pews hoping to remain unnoticed.

"Yes you, Ethan," sighed Brutus. "I get you're a teenager, but do you have to moan at every little task I give you?"

"No, I mean, I'll, I'm on it."

Chapter 27: The Brutes

Ethan hesitated at the foot of the bell tower stairs. They were narrow, winding, and enclosing. *'Only children are afraid of the dark,'* Ethan reminded himself before taking the first tentative step. The darkness took the curves with him. Ethan started to run up the steps. By the time he reached the sun-bleached summit, he was panting. The bell hung high above his head, two of the walls stopped at hip height, leaving square gaping holes reaching up to the bottom of the bell.

Perched in one of these openings, sat a teenage girl with a boyish figure. She had knotted brightly coloured fibres into her dirty blonde hair, from threads unpicked from the church tapestries. Her mutation wasn't visible, she looked the same to him now as she had the last time he saw her. "Riley?"

"Do I know you, monkey boy?"

"It's me, Ethan, from school."

"Huh?" Riley stood up and walked closer to Ethan. "I think I see it, maybe under all this fur, there's a resemblance at least."

"How did you end up here?"

"I followed the flock. The Great Wailer Regression was a mad rush, right? Everyone screaming and panicking, I was like, what the hell, you guys are the grownups, deal with it, but none of them did. They just ran, or died. I ran here. What about you?" She circled the bell tower back to the ledge and perched on it.

Ethan thought of the time he spent at home with his zombie mother swinging from the beams she had hung herself from. *'I should start my story somewhere else.'* "I was alone, and these guys found me. We've made safe houses, lost them, learnt how to fight, it's been, erm, interesting."

"Yeah, see, you say interesting, but your face tells me you're a prisoner too. Your cell is bigger than mine though, so kudos on that."

Ethan felt his skin flush red under his fur. "Are you a mind reader? Is that your mutation?"

"Sort of. I deal in gossip, kinda handy that I am multi-lingual now. Morsel and Entrée are my eyes and ears. They've seen your group in action. Kaboom, bam, splat. You're brutal, is that why you're known as the Brutes?"

"No, I'm not, I'm still me."

"Tell it to them." Two birds landed on Riley's outstretched arm. Morsel was a large grey sea bird, a rare scavenger to see inland as far as Soarken. Entrée was a sleek black bird of prey.

"You speak to birds?"

"I can speak to any animal, but in the church I have a choice between the birds and the mice, and the mice are just rude."

"They told me to bring you to them."

"I know, Entrée was listening to you. But you're going to tell them you never found me. You'll tell them that because you're my friend, and you're a good person."

"You'd be all alone, you won't survive."

"Maybe you can't survive on your own, but I can. Besides, I have all the animals of Soarken to help me."

"There can't be many left after the winter and months of Wailers."

"Wailers have been eating more human food, bothering less and less with the animal population." Her stare was intense. "You want to leave your group, you want to go it on your own, but you're frightened. Don't project your fear onto me."

He had considered making it on his own before, but Claire's well being wasn't his only anchor anymore. He looked like them now. Every time he told himself that he wasn't like them, he glanced at his reflection, and it told him he was one of a new species, one of five.

The stares from Riley and her birds, burrowed into him. "Good luck." Ethan turned and raced back down the twirling darkened stairs.

"Well?" Brutus demanded.

"No one's there."

"What?"

"There was a rope leading down to the roof, I looked along the roof, and the churchyard, there's no one."

"She was up there an hour ago," said Shawn.

"Brett," said Brutus, "give me a fresh count.

'Don't you dare!' Ethan thought. It was the first time anyone had directed a thought at Brett.

"Twelve here in the vestibule, sixteen in the locked room. There's no one else."

"I thought you said that there were twenty-nine?"

"I did," said Brett, "but I must have miscounted. We have them all."

"Probably was twenty-nine, makes sense the girl ran straight after we cleared the outside," Leighton said.

"What was the girl like? Did she strike you as a flight risk?" Brutus asked Dane.

"The girl never spoke, kept out of everyone's way, never a bother. Spent most of her time in that bell tower alone."

"What was her mutation?"

"I don't know. She looked normal, bit of a recluse, but normal."

"Ok, forget her, let's round up the pastor and his crew."

Dane put up a hand in warning. "We need to subdue Emiel first. His voice is his power, it's like brainwashing, he reads scripture, and they all listen. That's how he got so many people to revolt."

Dane handed out homemade earplugs. Brutus twisted a pair into his ears and peered through a crack in the old wooden door to the rectory. He could see the reverend's mouth moving. All those around him were on their knees swaying back and forth, captivated by him. Brutus took a knife from Caleb's belt, he opened the rectory door, and walked up to the reverend. His lips were moving and his eyes pleaded, but Brutus brought that knife down on him and silenced him forever. He pulled out his earplugs and glared at the congregation.

"Do you know what these are?" Brutus held up one of the spiky balls for all the frightened mutants to see.

"Megan and Dan," an old woman whispered, "they escaped to find help last week."

"They didn't get far. Do you know what these can do?" He proudly displayed his chest, which was still covered in spiky balls. The wary crowd nodded. "Good, cooperate and you'll be safe, with your own rooms, food, TVs, the lot. Piss me off, and I will start throwing balls. Got it?"

They filed out and lined up to have their hands tied.

"You didn't have to kill the Lord's messenger. He would have come peacefully and led his people under your orders," said Brett.

"I forget that ear plugs are no good for you, his voice must have been powerful."

"It wasn't his ability, he seemed like a genuine pacifist. All of his memories corroborated that."

"Even if he was a good guy, Brett, his voice was a powerful weapon, at no point would I hand that over to P Heath."

Brett didn't argue the issue further. He was ashamed to admit that Brutus had a point. He wondered about the impact of his own ability. Would Brutus kill him, rather than see his mind reading skills fall into the hands of someone else?

"Dane and his men are off limits." Brett straightened at Brutus's words. "You stay out of their heads, the same way you stay out of mine. No sightseeing down memory lane."

"Understood."

"Go ahead with Joel, I want the two of you to pick up Claire and drop off the dead at P Heath, warn them we are bringing a large group on foot through the Moorland. They need to prepare."

Brett looked up at the smashed pane, and the damaged tapestry that hung next to it. "You want me to climb?"

"Shawn," Brutus called, "would you do the honours?" Shawn limped his heavy hands to the heavily barricaded doors. He swung his fists back and forth, smashing through debris piles, pews and nailed boards. Dust and splinters filled the air, until there was a gaping hole where two large doors once stood. Brutus smirked at Brett. "You could always just walk through the door."

Joel was still protecting the perimeter. He'd added a couple of extra bodies to the pile, but had a relatively easy time on guard.

"I need a favour from you, or rather Ethan does," Brett said when they had walked several paces away from the church.

Joel frowned. "And what might that be?"

"I need you to say you watched a girl run across the churchyard, that you didn't notice her till she was in the distance, and you decided not to give chase."

"I didn't see a girl. You're asking me to lie to who exactly?"

"To Brutus," said Brett. Joel threw his good hand up in the air and shook his head. "He keeps plenty from you, and this will be one white lie that has no bearing on our business."

"Who is the girl and why should I care? Why do you care?"

"Her name is Riley, she's fifteen, she went to Ethan's school, and they're friends. I got the impression that Ethan has a crush on her. She talks to animals, she's not dangerous, she just wants the chance to make it on her own."

Trying to glimpse Riley's thoughts, had given Brett a massive headache. Her mind held hundreds of languages, but she understood them as one. He'd seen the conversation through Ethan's mind though, and trusted his judgement.

"When you say she talks to animals, do you mean in a certifiable kinda way?"

"No it's her mutation. She can understand them and they understand her."

"I get why Ethan would want me to lie, but why do you?"

"I already backed him up. Brutus will kill us both for the hell of it if he found out." Joel didn't look convinced. "You don't have to lie, just back us up if he asks, don't bring it up if he doesn't."

"He'll ask. Brutus won't drop it if he thinks a story is far-fetched." Joel and Brett walked side by side, looking at one another. Brett's face pleaded, Joel's glared. "Stop looking like such a martyr, I'll do it for Ethan. Next time don't tell a lie if it has to involve me."

Chapter 28: Riley

Riley watched from the bell tower as the entire church community was led away. Dane and his people walked beside the train of tied up weary souls. Four of the mutant monkeys, known as Brutes, were also helping to keep the train in check. Tucked at the back, was her friend. When he was sure no one was looking, Ethan stared up at the bell tower, but Riley didn't let him see her.

"You're right, he looks sad," Riley said. Morsel squeaked in her ear again. "Well, I can't stop you going to him. Fine, if you must." Riley unwound some thick tapestry that was wrapped around her arms to protect them from claws. She sheared off a small piece with a knife. "Here."

Morsel took the swatch from her, and swooped down. She dropped it in front of Ethan, and then flew over to Dane and unloaded a massive splat that hit his neck and shoulder. Riley lay on the stone floor, laughing hysterically. Morsel flew back into the tower and perched beside Riley. "He picked it up? Yes, I'm glad, making him smile was kinda the point." She twirled a bright thread in between her finger and thumb. Morsel continued to screech at her. "I know, we'll leave when they're out of view. Let's go raid downstairs first. I bet they left some snacks behind."

Entrée clung to Riley's shoulder, he would follow her anywhere. The bell tower with its large wall openings, was all the inside Morsel could stomach, her massive wings were made for wide spaces. She flew outside and kept watch from the church roof. Riley sped down the stairs. Her feet bounced off the corners of each step, she never planted them fully.

"The mice say it's all clear," Riley whispered. Entrée squawked in her ear. "Yes, yes, I hear you, all mice are lying gits." Riley rolled her eyes. "Sure, feel free to eat one, if you can catch it." Entrée left Riley's shoulder and circled the vestibule. Riley hunched down and scurried between the pews.

In the corner to the left, was the meeting room where all the food was stored. The door on the other wall led to Reverend Emiel Torch's living quarters. His still warm body lay in a pool of blood inside. Riley pulled the door shut, grimacing as it pulled through the blood. A squeak behind her made her jump.

Entrée fluttered up and perched on the back of a bench. A small brown mouse was limp in his mouth. He grabbed it in one of his talons, tore it open with his beak, pulling out entrails, and tilting them down his throat.

"Well done, you caught one," Riley breathed the words out and pushed down on the next door handle. The door creaked open. Riley's sideways smile curled up and her eyes shone. They had left it all. Her smile flitted away, that meant that someone would be back for it.

Morsel circled the outside of the building squawking for all her might. Her intense calls trailed off and then held firm on the other side of the churchyard. Using herself as bait, she led the growing mob of dead and Wailers away from the church, buying Riley a little time.

"Bag, bag, bag, damn it. Well duh, what do you expect me to do, juggle the food? No, just help me look for a bag."

Riley backed out of the food store and paused outside of Emiel's door. "I will. I'm psyching myself up first. There's a dead guy in there, you know. No, Entrée, not scraps for you, just eat your mouse." She brought the handle down until it clicked, placed her other hand on the door, and pushed it open. An obstruction was stopping it moving all the way. Riley jolted as something pushed the door from the other side. "Entrée..." Riley whispered with a squeak.

A hand shot through the gap and grabbed Riley's arm. She screamed and tried to pull herself free from the dead reverend that was dragging her into the room. The knife Brutus killed him with was still embedded in his head, it wasn't in deep enough. The reverend had gone into shock the minute he felt the blade and died of blood loss. Riley recoiled and covered her face. She'd pictured herself killing the dead on many occasions, but practice was a far stretch from theory.

Entrée flew at Emiel's face and clawed at his eyes. The zombie released Riley and swatted blindly at the bird. A backpack lay on the rectory floor; Entrée grasped it in his claws and dropped it on Riley's head. She stayed rooted to the spot with her hands covering her face. Entrée landed on her shoulder and pecked her hand so hard that it drew blood.

"Ok, yes, fine, don't call me a moron."

The Emiel zombie lurched at the sound of her voice. Riley grabbed the bag, sprinted down the middle aisle, and out of the church. She didn't slow down in the churchyard. Entrée told her not to. He told her not to look back either. Morsel was their eyes in the sky, calling down course corrections, until they found a house to hide in outside of the dead and Wailer's search zone.

"How many?" Riley gasped in disbelief. "Well I'm glad you didn't tell me that at the time, I'd have shit bricks." Riley held up the floppy bag. "All that food," she sighed. "I suppose we'll find more. Right, let's raid the kitchen. I'm sure I can let you have first dibs on any rats or mice that might be in there. If there are some, none are talking to me right now."

The cupboards proved fruitful for Riley. Not brimming, but she found enough to fill her backpack and make a meagre meal.

An hour passed.

"Oh, will you stop going on? I know, what are the odds we would pick the only vermin free house in Soarken? If you're that hungry go hunting with Morsel. Shh. Do you hear that?"

Riley crept up to the window. Something small was scraping in the bush outside. Riley went to the back door and opened it. The rustling stopped. "Hello? My name is Riley. I promise I won't hurt you."

"My bone, get your own," came a growled response.

"I don't want your bone, in fact I saw loads of dog food in the pantry. I could get you a plate." The dog stayed quiet. Riley walked inside, opened a ring pulled can and mushed the contents onto a plate. "Here." She placed it with a clink in front of the doorstep.

The little dog poked his nose out from under the leaves. "What brand is it?"

"Are you really in a position to be picky?" scoffed Riley.

The dog dropped the bone. It had tatters of meat clinging to it and looked suspiciously human. The little terrier crept forward. He was missing one of his hind legs. Riley wanted to pick him up and give him a squeeze. As if reading her mind, the little dog yapped, "Stay back." He sniffed at the plate and tested the jelly with his tongue. Mere seconds passed after that, before the dog was licking the plate clean.

"There's plenty more, if you'd like to come inside," Riley suggested.

A huge beast on four legs jumped the fence and confronted them.

"The eunuch," yelped little three legs, "he hunts me." The tiny dog ran and hid behind Riley's legs.

"It's not a monster," Riley replied to Entrée's squawk, "it's beautiful."

The huge dog did not know its own genealogy, but if Riley was to guess she would say he was Rottweiler crossed with a Great Dane. He towered above the shrubs and bushes, his head was almost as high as Riley's shoulder. Sniffing their scent, he paced closer.

"Give me that," the newcomer snapped. "I've been tracking it for weeks." The three-legged dog cowered at his words and whimpered.

"Or, hear me out," said Riley. "We raid the pantry, and dish you both up some dog food."

"You speak our words."

"Yeah, it's kinda my thing."

"You protect the mutt?"

Riley shrugged. "If he wants me to."

"I do, I do, I do," yipped the little dog.

"Then I shall call you Terror, and we shall be friends." The bigger dog glared at her. "And you Titbit are welcome to be my friend too."

"I do not find that name suitable."

"We'll call you Tib for short, it'll be great."

Terror had survived the winter months by being skittish and employing a policy of complete avoidance, but he danced around Riley's legs now, and refused to leave her side. Tib kept his distance. He had survived through brute strength, and fought for every meal.

"Well if you want to come in, just say." Riley picked up Terror and walked inside. She closed the back door. As much as she wanted Tib to join her, it would be unsafe to leave it open.

Tib sat in the garden and watched the strange girl interact with both the shouldered bird and the small dog. He caught the scent left on the plate that Terror had licked clean. His stomach rumbled. Despite his bravado, Tib hadn't eaten since yesterday morning, and even then he'd only managed to scavenge a few scraps. He sat on the doorstep and clawed his massive paw down the door panel. The scratching was universal dog speak for *let me in*.

"Don't do it," Terror whimpered. "He'll eat me, you saw the size of him, he'll eat you too."

"Uh, you're being ridiculous, stop chewing my sock." Riley kicked out her foot, but Terror kept hold of her sock and dangled when she lifted her leg. "Terror, sit," Riley said in her most stern voice. The dog sat and trembled with his ears down flat. "Tib is coming in, maybe just for lunch, maybe he'll join us, I don't know, but you have to stay calm because this is happening."

Riley prepared a full plate and placed it on the kitchen floor before letting Tib in. He went straight for the food.

"There," barked Terror, "now you don't have to eat me."

Tib looked up from his plate. "If I had known something had already started to eat you," Tib growled, looking at Terror's missing leg, "I wouldn't have bothered."

"My leg wasn't eaten," growled Terror, "the vet took it, and he didn't eat it."

"I bet he did, I bet he took it home and covered it in gravy."

"Oh yeah? Is that what the vet did to your balls?"

Tib lurched forward baring his teeth. Both dogs erupted in angry yips, barks, and growls.

"Stop it," Riley yelled. They made their growls low and Riley lowered her voice too. "If you two keep arguing at this volume, you will get us all killed. You can either make friends or go back out there, and survive this thing on your own."

Both dogs quieted and showed submission to Riley. They weren't looking for an owner, but companionship was something they could all use.

"Great, now we're all friends, who wants seconds?" Both dogs wagged their tails and sat at Riley's feet.

"I will check again, but I'm telling you, Entrée, I saw no mice in the cupboard."

Chapter 29: Prospect Heath

"James, what are you doing?" Jenna asked.

"Gene, sequencing, spores," stuttered James.

"And who told you to do that?"

"Graham, told me."

Jenna flashed rage in Graham's direction. "Graham, what the hell? You've got him messing around with the spores."

"Well, yes, do you remember when Adder first showed them to us, she said that she had spliced them with human DNA, so they would bond with the Wailers? I think the spores are Dr Adder's mutation."

"So?"

"So I had a theory, I'm testing it. I'm a scientist, that's what I do."

"Please don't, we are so close, don't jeopardise that by pissing her off."

"What do you mean close? And how am I jeopardising anything? The spores are a form of secreting mutation, Adder asked us to explore all secretions as possible cures."

"The cure is nearly there, Adder is sure. Just hang on a little longer."

"If she's so close, why hasn't she shared her data?" Graham reached out several long green vines, curled them around a distant beaker and pulled it to his hand. He smiled. The vines had developed from the green arm hairs. Over the winter they had grown long, and he had put a lot of energy into learning to control them as extremities.

Jenna's eyes watered. "Look at yourself. If she infects you with spores, you'll die." Her voice broke. "Can't you play along with her a little longer?"

"What will a little longer really buy us?"

"I don't know, Graham, how much do you value each day or week of your life? Why are you so desperate to see it cut short?" Jenna's cheeks flooded with tears and she stormed across the lab.

"Jenna," Graham called, but she responded by slamming the door.

"She's worried about you," James said.

"I worry about her too, but we can't get on top of this thing if we sit idly."

"I finished the test, if you're interested."

"No, of course I'm not interested. Only took me three damn months to get access to a spore sample, why would I want to know the results?"

James ignored Graham's sarcasm. "It's not Loralias's DNA, it's not her mutation."

"Thoughts," asked Graham, staring at the door that Jenna had slammed.

"There were numerous reports of early mutations, people who doubled up their dose or were just more sensitive to the formula than others. My guess is our spore wielder is one of those early mutants, captured by the Authority, and utilised by Loralias."

"The mutant is hiding in this building?"

"It would have to be. I saw spores exiting fingers, not jars, when she infected me."

"Living among us? Pretending to be a Mushroom-man, like you are?"

"Possible, or kept hidden. I for one have not explored every room."

"Me neither, I always send Jenna for supplies. I've never been on the ground floor, and I haven't been inside every flat."

"A lot of hiding places."

"How do we find him?"

"It's a she, and we don't. If she infects you, all of your plant DNA becomes corrupted, you die. And I need to keep up my Mushroom-man persona. I can't just go wandering around. Plus, if I find her and she figures out I'm not under the mushroom's influence, bad things would happen." James paused and pondered their dilemma. "You have a good rapport with Chris—"

"No, finding the mutant would be dangerous. We need to override the spores. You did it. I seem to remember you suggesting we take a closer look at your mutation."

James laughed. "For thirty years, people tried to harness my mutation, but I'm sorry to say I do not ooze healing and immortality potions from any part of my being."

"None of the people who tried to figure out your mutation was you, and you can work on it legitimately, while giving your best Mushroom-man performance. Adder can't deny the value your mutation has to a possible cure."

"It's a futile act, but as a mindless mushroom drone, I don't have much of a choice now, do I?"

***

Jenna slammed the door and walked away. The sound of an engine drew her attention to the car park below. The Brutes' van pulled in. She raced down the stairs and gathered all the Mushroom-men she could find along the way.

Joel was driving the van. He wasn't wearing his sling anymore, but Jenna could tell that his recent injury still vexed him.

"What do you have for me today?" Jenna grinned.

"Two dead so far, both are zombie-mutants with poison gas abilities." Joel ignored the way she lilted against the van's hood. She had spent all winter flirting with Joel and his brother, and they had both found it to be good fun, but Joel could see that Jenna had been crying, so he stuck to business. "Brutus is bringing a whole load of living mutants over now."

"How many?"

"There were nineteen, but Brutus is herding the caravan across Wailer infested streets, so best to do a recount when they get here."

"Prepare rooms for nineteen, just in case," Jenna instructed her gathered Mushroom-men. "There will need to be a great deal more sharing." Jenna sighed. "Hey, Joel, can any of these new arrivals live around Wailers without setting them off?"

"I don't know what their mutations are, but I've never heard of anyone who can do that."

"It's fine. There's this one guy, he shares with his Wailer girlfriend. There's room for four in each unit, but this guy can't share. Not without setting off his Wailer and putting other residents in danger."

Joel watched her waffle and flick her hair a few times, he was still not in the mood for flirting.

"Big group, approach, front gate," stated Saxon.

"Wow, that was quick, I suppose I best go let them in," said Jenna

"Hey, Jenna," Joel shouted after her, "about our quota?"

"Consider it filled, I'll give the when and where to Brutus," she called back.

"You not coming out?" Joel said turning to Brett.

Brett stayed huddled in the passenger seat. "No chance. I told you before, some upper level psycho lives in that place. I can keep myself closed off from its mind here."

"See," said Joel opening up the back of the van, "I think that's an excuse so you don't have to help me unload." He grasped their restraints and pulled the two zombies to their feet with his good arm. "You gonna give me a hand, Claire?"

"Do I ever?" she said.

"That just leaves you, mushroom keeper of the gate. Help me get these inside. Up to the morgue with these ones, right?"

Hatter didn't understand the question, but he followed the command, dragged one of the zombies, and followed Joel's lead.

"Later, slackers," said Joel. He flicked Claire and Brett a V as he passed the windscreen.

Chapter 30: Mallard Hill

Sometimes I feel the weight of being me
An observant eye may even see
My shoulders slump, as it crushes me

The thaw and emerging spring colours failed to lift Sadie's dark mood. She had become better at hiding her worsening mental illness, but the more airtime the *Broken Child* got, the further into a crippling depression she slipped. She had been isolated all winter. Her children, Luke, and their friends all had their place within the Mallard Hill community, while Sadie drew storyboards for the local rag from home, often cut due to content. Sadie wouldn't be censored, though it had been weeks since she produced any drawings, offensive or otherwise.

Cynlear set up an alarm system on the house so she could keep tabs on Sadie from a distance. If anyone opened a door or window, she'd appear. For now though, Sadie was alone, imprisoned, and slowly rocking in front of the spinning washing machine.

If she could find adequate words to describe her depression, she would have said that it was like drowning. There were bubbles of air all around her that she could sip to take a breath, and relieve the pain for a moment. These bubbles were comforts: drugs, alcohol, chain-smoking, physical self-harm, and Sadie's personal favourite, comfort eating to the point of feeling sick. Taking a breath from one of these bubbles would ease the sensation of drowning temporarily, but it also weighted her deeper in the water.

Sadie learnt long ago that the only way to reach the surface, and find a normal even mood, was to allow herself to drown. To let the misery fill her lungs and suffocate her, to acknowledge the itchy sensation that made her want to crawl out of her skin, and live with it. She always rose to the air filled surface eventually if she just rode it out. Sipping on bubbles would prolong her drowning.

> *'Screw rations, I want that cake, the whole thing and those jellies in the back of the cupboard, or we could sneak out and borrow a little of Kronic's tobacco.' The Bitch was not above sipping bubbles. Only one part of Sadie's personality had the vision to see beyond them.*

> *'You feel guilty the second you've finished and hate yourself a little more. I have to live here too,' snapped the Brain. 'It's bad enough that our resident Child is always casting a vote for self-harm.'*

> *'It's just food, I'm not trying to pour boiling water on us, or get better acquainted with a knife.'*

> *'Over-eating and smoking until our lungs hurt are both forms of self-harm, a gateway to what the Broken Child is angling for.'*

> *The Bitch and Brain argued in the forefront of Sadie's mind. She saw them as versions of herself. She*

pictured them in a hollow skull with pulsating brain wallpaper decorating the walls.

Behind the Bitch and Brain, taking advantage of the argument, was the Broken Child. She looked as Sadie had as a child, though her eyes were reddened and vacant. The Child was conjuring an implement for suicide. She pulled a stalactite of brain matter from the ceiling and made two sharp blades jut out from the bottom, the tips pointed horizontally to opposing walls. This was not another ploy to tempt Sadie, the Broken Child had made it for herself. Sadie was undergoing a genetic change, and the Child was the only part of her psyche willing to accept this.

While the Bitch and Brain continued to argue, the Child brought a chair into Sadie's imagined skull room. She stood on it and thrust her arms onto the blades. They dug in just above her elbows. She kicked the chair away and put her weight onto them. The blades slid the length of her forearms and stuck in her palms. She dangled there with blood gushing all over her.

The Bitch and Brain turned to see her awash with blood. 'She can't,' gasped the Brain. 'We three are part of one mind, this place is imagined. She cannot die.'

'She has though,' breathed the Bitch as she examined the fragile form. 'Don't you feel the quiet?'

Before the Brain could respond the Child twitched. The two grabbed the Child off of her method of death, and lowered her to the floor. The Broken Child opened her white eyes, and wailed at her companions. From now on she would speak only in wails. It took the strength of both the Bitch and the Brain to bind and gag the Child, and stash her in a scarcely trodden part of Sadie's mind. They couldn't keep her there forever.

The *Child's* transformation to Wailer had a profound effect on Sadie. She writhed on the floor feeling that hunger for blood. Every muscle ached.

"Sadie!" Luke rushed to her side and cradled her. "Baby, what's going on?"

"I, I think I'm turning Wailer," she wept.

"That's not possible."

"It is possible. You need to get out of here, I won't be able to control myself when I turn."

"You're not turning, you can't. The scientists tested a strand of your hair they found on me at P Heath. They said that you had both Wailer and mutant DNA, they said that neither one was dominant. They said that you are the cure."

"They're wrong." She paused, letting his words sink in, and then glared at Luke. "They gave you this information three months ago and you said nothing." Sadie stopped talking and squealed with fresh pain.

"Mummy, I made you picture." Madam had advanced in her speech and no longer referred to herself in the third person.

"Not now, sweetie, Mummy's feeling poorly," Luke said.

"The kids are here? You're all home early," Sadie wheezed.

"We're not, Sade, it's the usual time."

Sadie did the maths. Hours, four if not five, she had sat on the floor in front of the washing machine. Trembling she raised her head from Luke's shoulder. The living room was full of people staring through to the kitchen. Cynlear Spear had her gun trained on Sadie. Kronic put himself in front of the barrel.

"Get to your rooms, kids." They both listened to Kronic without question and marched up the stairs. "As for you." He stepped closer pushing against the gun. "Get out."

"I can't do that."

"She's one of ours, if it needs to be done, we'll do it. Get out."

Cynlear scowled at the huge man for a moment longer, before lowering her weapon and leaving the house.

"Can you grab the door?" Luke asked. His wing arms had a lower muscle mass than his old arms, and he was struggling to hold Sadie. He wouldn't admit defeat though, and carried her all the way to their bed. Her involuntary writhes and jerks put even greater strain on him.

"You all right, mate?" Kronic asked as Luke closed the door to his bedroom.

Luke shook out his arms. "Yeah, just need to focus strength training on my upper body."

"Is she ok?" Kronic nodded to the closed door.

"I don't know. I guess for now we have to keep an eye on her."

Sadie wound the blind up, flooding the room with light. She pulled herself across the bed and started to rummage through a drawer in the bedside table. She found a hand-held mirror and angled her face into the light. Her irises still had the same dark blue they always had, but the yellow ring that surrounded her pupil had faded to white. *'I'm still me,'* she thought, *'I'm still human.'* Two thirds of her was.

***

Paul still spent his days in the hospital like room in the Doctor's house. After two legs sprouted from his stump, an arm had developed, growing out of his ribs. He was less mobile now than he had been as a one-legged man. Rapz was visiting with him again. Their friendship had grown from pity; pity for one another, pity for themselves. Paul's mutation made him bedbound, and alienated him from the rest of the community. Rapz's mutation had proved not only dangerous for others, it surfaced every time he rapped, leaving him unable to perform his craft.

"Tinned fish," Paul groused, "again. I get they want their space back, but poisoning me with mercury is counterproductive, surely?"

Rapz pulled out a tinned pie, and some freshly dug potatoes and carrots. "They said that you can come home for dinner with me, if you're sure you can do without painkillers."

Paul licked his lips at the sight. "I'll have to go in the chair won't I?"

"Have you tried walking?"

"What, on my three different length legs?"

Rapz shrugged.

"No," Paul sighed. "And I don't plan on it either. Grab me the chair then, boy, I'm not getting any younger."

Rapz helped the older man into his coat and then manoeuvred him into the wheelchair. Paul ripped the blanket off of the bed and covered up his legs. He had called it a cosmic joke. The first leg to emerge from his stump had grown straight for a few weeks. When the second one pushed through, it set the first on an angle giving him two strangely angled legs protruding from the same knee.

"So what's the gossip?" Paul asked.

Rapz banked the wheelchair hard left, and compensated to stop him from tipping Paul out. "Sadie is going through some kind of change, so they have upgraded her house arrest to bedroom arrest. Luke is flying more. Kronic has been taking me out to practise my rapping, where I can't hurt anyone. Kyan and Verity-Elise are both doing well — oh, speaking of kids, you'll need these." Rapz took out two pairs of large rimmed sunglasses. He wore a pair, and put the other in Paul's lap. "You'll need them on, wouldn't want you to go blind."

Paul stared at the oversized glasses, and then glanced up at the overcast sky.

Serenity burst through the door just before they reached it. "Paul, it is wonderful to have you, please come in." She had on a matching pair of sunglasses.

"Are we going to split that one pie and veggies between all of us?"

"Nah," said Rapz, "the food I showed you is your rations. I picked them up after work." Rapz dug them out of his bag and handed them to Serenity. The wheel chair was too large for the doorframe, so with Rapz's help, Paul limped through to the living room. Paul listened to Serenity peel and chop. Rapz talked about his work and the Authority chatter. Paul had protested the Authority dictatorship in his youth. He was unsurprised that they were allegedly hoarding a cure and plotting their rise back into power.

"How imminent is Tyde's boat ride?"

"They'll leave it a few more weeks to be on the safe side."

"They?"

"I'm not going," said Rapz, "nor is Serenity."

"Why not?"

"I have a purpose here. The rebels will be the only ones able to mobilise against the Authority when they try to regain power. I'm in contact with other rebel groups across the country. We are the commanding unit, and they are all ready to follow Mallard Hill."

"Did they all forego Adder's serum? Are they all Marazsian?"

"No and no. Some groups are human, most are mutants, most are Tave nationals, and all are out for blood and ready to reclaim our world."

"At least I won't be alone then."

"You're staying too?"

"They are going to a safe island to live out their lives as they are." Paul pulled up his shirt, opposite the arm that stuck out from under his ribs, toes were sticking out, also a finger and thumb was emerging either side of his bellybutton. "I need to be cured, can't just keep sprouting limbs. I need the cure that only mainlander's seem to be working on."

Paul let his shirt fall, and they both sat in silence. Innocence crawled across the floor. She overreached for a toy on the sofa, and rolled onto her back.

"Glasses, where are your glasses?" Rapz frantically patted down Paul. Unable to find them, he flung Paul down and shielded him with his body. Innocence screamed. Her cry was that of any ten-month-old baby that had slipped. The shock of it though, set off her mutation. She flooded the room with blinding light, whiting out every line, shadow, and colour. The glasses were a first defence. The initial light was less intense, and the glasses gave them time to close and cover their eyes.

Serenity took tiny steps toward her baby's cries. When she believed that she was close she felt across the floor. Once Innocence was in her mother's arms, she started to calm and dropped her wattage. "It is safe now, you may look."

Rapz lifted off Paul, and pulled him back up.

"You should wash up," Serenity said cheerfully as though nothing had happened. "Dinner will be ready soon."

"Yeah, wash up, sure." Paul placed his shaking hands on his knees. He hugged his third arm closer to his stomach. Despite repositioning, he still trembled. Rapz helped him up, and they awkwardly made their way up the stairs.

"What the hell was that? I thought there was a soundless explosion or a flash grenade."

Rapz pushed open the bathroom door and seated Paul on the edge of the bath where he could reach the basin. "That was Inny's light. It's got so much more intense."

"Lord alive, how often does she blind you?"

"When she gets frightened, so if she falls over or Serenity leaves the room for too long, or she has a bad dream. That one's not so bad, Serenity made us blackout eye-masks for sleeping in." Rapz started to laugh. "I think she's got to be the youngest person ever to get expelled from a nursery."

"They expelled her?"

"Temporarily, they want to include her, but have to put safety measures in place first. Serenity is gutted, she loved her job at the school, but they say it's not forever, and you know how Serenity sees the silver lining in everything."

Chapter 31: Prospect Heath

"I understand your concerns, but I can do this. This is the last piece of the puzzle, and you can't just send Mushroom-men, you need a human hand."

"Why must that human hand be yours, Jenna?" asked Adder. "What can you offer that myself, or James, or even Graham, cannot?"

"Compassion, humanity. You are brilliant, but you seriously lack people skills. James isn't much better in that respect..."

"Must be where she gets it from," mumbled Graham.

"... And Graham has mutated, his vines are visible. They could perceive his mutation as a threat." Jenna flashed her frustrated look around the room. "I can do this. We have Claire's co-operation for testing, and we have a huge selection of excreting mutants, thanks to Michael Brutus. Sadie Ratcher is the missing element." Jenna slammed her hand down on the map printout. Mallard Hill was circled in red.

"Chris, request, field work, in exchange, for his, Intel." James stuttered out the words, still maintaining his Mushroom-man cover.

"He's not going," Jenna snapped, "he could tip off the villagers. If Sadie won't come quietly, we will have to take her by force. I would prefer it if her people were unprepared for that."

"You will take bodyguards." Adder flipped through her list of personnel, and highlighted fifteen names. "You will need a large and skilled entourage to complete your mission." She handed Jenna the list.

"So, you're authorising this?" Jenna spoke with a cautious smile.

"I am. You shall leave tomorrow."

Jenna rushed Adder and flung her arms around her. "Thank you." Adder stared blankly, she did not engage in the hug. Then Jenna squealed and skipped off to make preparations.

"Why are you letting her go?" Graham tried to hold back his anger. "You were supposed to say no, you were supposed to tell her it's too dangerous."

"I have noted your objections, but she presented me with a logical argument."

"She has been your friend since childhood, your assistant for your entire career, how can you just send her to her death?"

"My affiliation with Jenna has no bearing on my decision. Jenna has proven that she can put people at ease and convince them to join our cause. She is the right person for this task."

Adder's response was so cold that it caused Graham's anger to heat. It took all of his mental restraint to stop him smashing everything in reach. James, having watched the discussion in silence, placed a hand on Graham's shoulder and led him out of the room. Graham resisted at first, but he had witnessed James argue with Adder before. She never rose to emotion or showed any herself. Screaming at her would be pointless.

"Talk to Jenna when you've calmed down," said James once they were out of earshot. "You may have more luck with her."

***

Graham's love for Jenna was unrequited, but that didn't stop it from being real. Over the last few months they had become closer. He thought he was getting somewhere, he thought she was developing feelings for him too. Now he stood in the car park, watching the Mushroom-men pack supplies into commandeered civilian cars, preparing to ferry her out of his life.

'No, I can't let this happen.' He turned away from the vehicles and rushed to her apartment. The door was open. "Jenna?"

"Back here," she yelled.

Graham rounded the corner and halted in the doorway to her bedroom. Jenna was inside throwing clothes into a bag. She held up two pairs of shoes. "Which should I take? Knee-high or ankle boots?"

"The ankle would probably — look, Jenna." Graham took the shoes from her, placed them on the bed, and held both her hands. "Please, don't go. We can do this without Sadie. Adder's close to the cure, you said so yourself."

"I'm coming home."

"You really see this place as home?"

"Of course, all my favourite people are here." Jenna pulled one hand free and cupped his cheek. "I'm coming back."

"You can't promise that."

Leaning in close, Jenna pressed her lips to his. Graham relaxed into their deepening kiss.

"Let me come with you."

Jenna pulled away. "I can't, you're needed here."

"You won't come back, you know that?"

"You have that little faith in me?"

"I don't want you to go."

"I'll miss you too, but I can do this. Don't you believe in me?" Smiling, she gently clasped his shoulder and squeezed.

Graham recalculated her chances with her entourage. "I would feel happier if you had a mutation to defend yourself with."

"What can I say," chuckled Jenna, "I'm a late bloomer." She held out her hand, and he took it. "Don't write me off, ok? I will be fine, great even, I will be victorious. Now, how about we get some lunch together?"

Her smile was contagious. Graham viewed his own with contempt and tried to stop his lips from curling.

Chapter 32: Riley

Morsel was flying low on purpose, goading Tib. The large dog kept stretching up on his hind legs and biting at the sky.

"Tib, could you like, not do that. You're embarrassing yourself. Morsel is laughing her tail feathers off at you."

The large dog grunted and trotted to Riley's side. That bird would land at some point then he'd be the one doing the laughing.

The grey seagull squawked course directions down to Riley, and though it was a long way to trek on foot, with Morsel's guidance, they found their way to the other side of the city with no unwanted encounters. The Ivanthor Manor was huge, as were its grounds. It crowned the landscape with magnificence and foreboding.

Riley let out a low drawn out whistle. "You're sure this is where Ethan is staying?"

***

Ethan sat at George's grave. Months had passed since the burial, but Ethan came out every day to talk to his absent friend.

"Caleb hit me again today. The bruises don't show under all this fur, but I feel them all the same. I want to leave, I do, but to where? And what about Claire and Brett? What happens to them when I'm gone? And if Brutus found me, I'd be beaten and forced back here." The most painful thing about his one-sided conversations was that if George had lived, if he were here to talk to now, Ethan wouldn't share these thoughts with him.

Brett often listened in from a distance, but he never spoke on it. He was in the same situation as Ethan. If it wasn't for Claire, then perhaps he would leave. When Claire turned Wailer, if that really was inevitable, he would go, and take Ethan with him.

Ethan rearranged the flowers on George's grave. Did George even like flowers? Ethan suspected not, but it was the customary gift to give to the dead. His head jerked from the grave towards a loud yip. The sun was bright but when he squinted, he saw a small white dog racing over the lawn in the distance. The call of a bird drew his attention to the sky. His eyes were dazzled by the sun. When he looked back the small white dog was seated and a large seagull circled it. Ethan got up from the ground and bounded after it on his knuckles. Now and then, the swooping bird would call and the dog would stop to let Ethan catch up.

Ethan jolted into a slower pace. In front of him was a tool shed, and guarding that shed, was the largest, meanest looking dog he had ever seen. The slightest growl would have rooted him to the spot in sheer terror, but the monstrous dog stayed silent. It nudged the shed door with its head and it opened a little. Part of Ethan wondered if this animal collusion was a ploy to make a meal of him. Curiosity dragged him past the dog and through the door into the cramped dark space. A human hand grabbed his and guided him to the ground.

"Once upon a time," said Riley, "there was this boy. He was cool, in that totally didn't know he was cool kinda way. He went to school and had friends and a loving home. Then his dad became a Wailer, and the boy became the son of a Collar, and because of that some of his friends weren't so friendly anymore. They picked on him, and he started to skip school. Then his dad was murdered, and the boy quit school altogether.

"After that, the world goes to shit and other survivors take the boy in. They're much older, and they don't see how cool the boy is. They're mean to him, they make him fight when he doesn't want to, and they put him in danger. At first the boy is scared, I mean who wouldn't be, right? But he becomes a good fighter, and he mutates into this super strong monkey thing. The boy can survive on his own now, but he still stays. Like, what's up with that?" Riley looked to Ethan for a response, but he sat dumbfounded, staring at her in the darkened shed. "Seriously, Ethan, why stay? I need to know."

Ethan turned his gaze to the floor. "There's this girl, Claire." Riley's heart sank. "She's like a sister to me, and she's been looking out for me."

"Well, she's doing a shit job," Riley snapped.

"She's pregnant with Brutus's baby and is as trapped as I am, more so even, Brutus won't let her do anything."

"Would she be worse off without you?"

"Yeah, she'd be lonely."

"Things won't get better for either of you if you stay. You leaving could kick her into leaving too."

"It will be better when we're on the island. It's Z-free, no more zombies or Wailers to hunt." He grabbed Riley's delicate hands between his large furry ones. "You should come too. The boat leaves tomorrow from Eggshell Crest, that's on the eastern shoreline. It's a massive cruise ship, and I'm sure there'd be room for you."

His voice was enthusiastic. She could tell that he wanted her to go with him. "Can you promise I'll never be forced to kill? That I won't have to bow down to that pig Brutus? Can you promise me my freedom?"

"No." Ethan's face fell. "I can't make any of those promises."

She nodded. "I'm sorry, but I can't promise we'll meet again." She leaned over and kissed his cheek. "Goodbye, Ethan."

Ethan sat trembling in her absence. The word 'wait' stuck in his throat more than once as he tried to voice it. Finally he found his feet and shouted after her. "WAIT." It was too late. Riley was a distant spec being carried away on the back of her monstrous hound. "Wait," he begged more softly.

Ethan let an hour slip by. He sat in the tool shed with so many thoughts crashing against one another. He acknowledged the soft steps crossing the grass to meet him, but found no will to move.

"Brutus is looking for you," Brett said. "We're all packed up. We need to head out soon." Brett sighed, grabbed Ethan under his arms, and pulled him to his feet. "You'll see her again."

"What would you know?" Ethan mumbled.

"She's heading east. Riley will make a try for the boat."

"You're lying to trick me."

"I don't have to trick you, I could just tell Caleb where you are and watch him bounce you back to the manor."

Ethan straightened with fear.

"So," said Brett, guiding his arm around the boy. "Does your girl know how to drive? Not sure she'll make it on foot."

They made their way back across the lawn.

"She was too young to drive a moped, but her parents were pretty liberal and the Authority never caught on because of how safe she rode."

"That won't cut it. She'll need a car if she's planning on bringing her dogs with her." They both stared at the empty grounds in the direction Riley had gone. "When we get back, you need to lie. I told Brutus that I sent you on an errand to the shed to buy you a little more time."

"The shed's empty."

"I know it is, the Ivanthors commissioned a larger shed closer to the main building years ago."

"Then what kind of errand did you say I was running?"

"Shh," Brett lowered his voice as they neared the manor. "We'll improvise."

Brutus stood at a back door, scowling at them.

Brett panicked. "Ethan fell asleep," he blurted.

"What!" Ethan cried. Brett jabbed him in the ribs. "Yes, sorry," said a distraught looking Ethan. "I fell asleep."

"We're all tired, Ethan, but we need to leave. I want to find a safe place in Eggshell Crest to bed down before nightfall." Ethan bowed his head. Brutus unfolded his arms and sighed. "Have you packed at least?" Ethan gave a speedy nod. "Then grab your things and go straight to the car, no napping on the way."

"The car?" Brett asked.

"Yeah, we filled the van with food from the store, so we'll be taking your car for passengers. Don't worry, I've filled the tank, checked the oil and water and all."

"Sounds like you've covered everything." Brett smiled and went to walk off.

"One more thing, Brett. Why did it take you so long to find him?"

"It would seem that I can't read sleeping minds, I had to look for him the old fashioned way."

"So you didn't meet up with the intruder on the lawn."

Brett paled. "What intruder?"

"We'll talk more on this later. Go grab your bag."

Chapter 33: Sadie

She could vocalise like a porn star if her lover's ego called for it, though the proximity of sleeping children often kept her elated screams silent.

They tumbled from the bed and Sadie pushed Luke on to his back. There was no physical way to bring their bodies closer. Sadie gripped him with the carnal ferocity they had enjoyed when their love was new.

She rounded his shoulder with her teeth, testing the sensitivity of his new socket where his wing joined familiar flesh. She felt the urge to bite — hard. Though she resisted, images of tearing flesh brought intensity to her climax.

Luke pulled away.

"What's wrong?" Sadie asked. "Why'd you stop?"

"That noise." He looked at her with trepidation. "You made a... sound."

Sadie had wailed.

Luke ran for the door and braced against it. There was no way he was the only one to hear it. Sure enough, their front door opened and feet hurtled up the stairs.

"Open up!" Cynlear was pushing from the other side.

"I'm not decent." Luke stretched out his leg and hooked his boxers with his foot.

"Your decency is forfeit, I heard a wail."

Sadie wrapped herself in the duvet. Luke had managed to heave his boxers up before Cynlear crashed through the door.

"There was no wail." Sadie scowled.

Cynlear glanced at Sadie and then pulled Luke out of the door, slamming it behind them.

"We have kids in bed," Luke snapped.

"Do you really think they're sleeping after that?"

"She was just enjoying herself."

"She shouldn't have been. I warned you about cohabiting with her. From now on, you two will need separate rooms."

"You can't dictate—"

"She is turning Wailer, when will you get that into your bird brain?"

"She is not turning Wailer."

"Her eyes are whitening."

"Just the ring around the pupil, most of it is still blue, it's not spreading."

"She is irritable and prone to mood swings."

"That's a symptom of being Sadie not a Wailer."

"She just wailed!"

"More like, she thoroughly enjoyed my cock."

The older woman's face flushed red. "If you think for one second that vulgarity—"

Sadie stopped listening in. It was pointless. What was she in denial for? She had not only wailed she had craved his flesh. How long would it be before she acted and took a bite? Maybe Cynlear was right on this one. Maybe she should limit her contact with Luke.

> *'I think we should run,' said the Brain. 'We can't risk turning Wailer and hurting the people we love.'*

'Are you kidding me?' groaned the Bitch. 'We are not turning Wailer, the Child tried and failed.'

'We just wailed.'

'SHE wailed, not us, it's two against one, and I don't know about you, but I'm not about to change my vote to pro-Wailer.'

The Brain sighed. 'You are that confident we can keep her repressed?'

'I am the embodiment of confidence.'

A guttural call came from the wrong section of Sadie's mind. The Bitch and Brain exchanged the same thought. 'The Child is no longer caged.'

Sadie felt that heavy hopelessness seeping back in. It twisted and lurched under her skin. Her vibrancy drained. Flopping on the mattress, weighted and defeated, she curled the duvet around her, not for the warmth, but for the swaddle. Her life as she knew it would be over soon. She would be Wailer and then they would execute her.

She sobbed into the covers and clasped them so tightly to her face they smothered her.

The arguing stopped and the front door slammed. Sadie's bedroom door swept open and then closed with a click. As she wept, Luke's warm hands dived under the covers. They caressed her hips and travelled up her sides, trying in vain to activate her known tickle spots.

"Come on, Sadie, stop hiding."

Luke tried to pry the duvet from her face. When he finally succeeded, he found a blanket of long mahogany hair covering it.

"Your hair is getting in the way again."

"It's trying to take over the world," Sadie mumbled.

"So you keep telling me, but I have yet to see any evidence of this."

He held her until they both fell asleep. In the early hours Sadie wriggled out of his grasp seeking out the cold wall and snuggling against it. Her gentle snores did not reflect the roar of her subconscious. The Wailer in her was fighting for dominance. She feared the *Child's* relentlessness would wear down the resistance. The *Brain* and the *Bitch* had an epic battle ahead of them.

***

Luke was gone when she awoke, but his side of the bed still held warmth. Sadie heard chatter downstairs. She slipped onto the floor and placed her ear on the carpet, listening in to a world she was no longer part of.

"Come on, Madam, if you don't eat you're breakfast you'll be hungry."

"Luke, do I have to go to school?" asked Kyan. "The class is so basic. I've already learnt everything they're doing."

"Yes, you have to go — stop putting cereal up your nose — this is their place, their rules, but only for another week or two — damn it, Madam, don't put it in your ear either. Mouth, food goes in your mouth."

"Inny gets to stay home. Bet if I shocked someone I wouldn't have to go."

"Inny can't control herself, Kyan, you can — where are you going, come and put your shoes on — besides, if you shocked someone they'd make you wear a rubber suit and gloves, and still send you to school."

The giggling grew louder as Madam raced up the stairs.

"Verity-Elise, come down here right now."

"I go see Mummy, Cat said I could."

"No, I'm sorry, sweetie, Mummy's sleeping. You can see her later." Luke reached for her hand. "Ride on my shoulders. I've put your shoes in my pocket."

"Cat come too?"

"Not to school, but he'll be right here waiting for you when you get home." There was a gentle thud and swish as the thrown cat teddy landed in Madam's hammock. "Kyan put your jacket on properly, arms in, it's not a cape."

Sadie's heart sank as she heard their footfalls trailing back down the stairs. The front door closed, and their voices faded.

Abruptly the door opened again and feet stamped up the stairs. Sadie dreaded the sound of those steps.

Cynlear stormed in and sat on a stool, her glare never wavered.

"Can't you bring a book or something? You constantly staring at me is unnerving."

"I am here to guard you, not read."

"Can I at least have a bath in peace?"

"You may draw the shower curtain but I will remain in the room."

It was only a smidgen of the privacy that Sadie craved, but she would take it.

The bath was hot and bubbly. Sadie sat back and stretched her legs. The backs of her knees stuck a little, it had been a while since she had washed. The water was heaven, but once the bubbles had burst, she was left with milky grey water. Tiny white flecks of dead skin danced and twirled on the water's surface.

'We can ask to change the water,' the Brain suggested.

'And be subjected to one of Cynlear's lectures about ungratefulness and wastefulness? No thanks, I'd rather stew in my own filth.'

A bath instead of a shower used to be part of her self-care routine when her depression was creeping in. Bath oils, scented candles, peace. Now all she had was fetid water and emptiness. It wasn't until she stepped out of the bath that she felt the weight of misery. On meagre rations she had lost weight, yet she felt as though sandbags were tied to her limbs.

Cynlear watched her dress then led her with a forceful grip back to her room. Sadie flicked her eyes to the right as she came out of the bathroom. The door to Madam's room stood open. She had done a good job clearing out the Wailer shrine and turning it into something pretty for her little girl. Cat's head and left paw drooped over the edge of Madam's hammock bed. Sadie imagined Madam rocking herself to sleep in it with Cat tucked under her chin. She shouldn't have to imagine. She should be able to see her child sleep.

Sadie slumped onto her bed and closed her eyes. Her dreams were the one place where Cynlear couldn't follow.

Chapter 34: Kronic and Tyde

"All clear," said Tyde.

Kronic passed through the hole and then bent the fence back how he had found it. He and Tyde paced quickly into the dense forest. Before long, they were concealed within the Eaves, far from the stifling village.

"This would be so much easier if Felicity was here," grumbled Kronic.

"Yes, because floating bags of food wouldn't be suspicious at all, would they?"

Kronic took Tyde's bag from him. He could have carried many bags, dangling them on his outstretched arms like strung up baubles, but that would have been suspicious, that would have drawn attention. Besides, they didn't have that much to transport.

The Odd Blockers had arrived at Mallard Hill with a van full of food, which Doven Spear had immediately confiscated and added to the village's collective supplies. The rations given out to civilians in Mallard Hill included much of their home-grown produce. This had made it difficult to save long life food for the boat.

They squelched and swerved their way through the dense undergrowth, the rains of spring had made the Eaves green and moist. Kronic stopped short of the jetty and handed the bags to Tyde. Tyde unlocked the boathouse. A tingle ran through him when he clapped eyes on Lola, it was like love at first sight every time he saw her. He tossed the bags onto her deck and climbed aboard.

"How close are we?" Kronic yelled from the shore. He wouldn't dare walk across the rickety jetty for certainty of its collapse.

"It's disappointing, not even close to what we need. We should be good for water, I understand your disgust, but I can make the sea water drinkable and we'll need the space for food." Tyde sighed and looked at the tiny pile. "We'll either have to take from the stores or scavenge further afield. We can't get what we need from siphoning off our own rations and Spear doesn't want us to go. The rebels are all coordinating through him. He thinks we're a liability."

"We already have to break Sadie out. We've got no fucking chance of busting into the stores as well."

"Then we need to keep up the pretence of trust, and go hunting for food."

"How much do we need?"

"Enough for four adults and two kids, the boat still has all the stuff you gave me for Cleaver."

"Five adults, Fliss is coming back."

Tyde thought about arguing, but stopped. "Right, five adults, I miscounted." The seas had been ready for them for a while. With the right supplies they could have left last week. At some point his friend would need to come to terms with the fact that Felicity Grange was not coming with them.

"I think you need to try out the dinghy again."

"I don't like it, last time I sank."

"The water is shallow near the edge."

"The mud will swallow me up."

"Kronic—"

"I trust your judgement, you say it will tow an elephant, I believe you, but you ain't getting me in it until I have to. Come on, we got an hour or two before they'll miss us. Let's keep walking along the river, see if we can find somewhere to raid for food."

Most of the zombies degraded over the winter months, and as a general rule the Wailers stuck to the larger towns and cities. The Mallard Hill patrols still filtered through the forest making sure nothing sinister stalked close to their home, but they rarely had a kill these days. A small patrol would be in another part of the Eaves. Luke was on patrol with them and would try to keep them away from the river.

"How about there?"

"Promising," said Tyde. The house was nestled inside of the trees, barely visible from the river's edge. "Looks lived in, not recently, but it's not dilapidated."

A lengthy dirt track led from the house, meandering through the Eaves for miles before merging with a named road. A light blue car sat in the drive, mulch from winter leaves clumped between the windscreen and wipers. Tyde skipped up the six steps, knocked, and placed his ear to the door. Nothing. He leant over the porch's rail and peered through his cupped hands in the window. The branches rocked in the window's reflection, but the room inside was still.

"No movement, but someone definitely lived here."

Kronic hesitated at the bottom of the steps.

"Come on buddy, this is a sturdy platform made from strong wood."

Kronic made his way up the few steps. They creaked and groaned under his weight, but the porch itself was more forgiving. He turned the handle. It stuck. He wrenched it further, forcing it into a new hole, and uncoupling the bolt. Inside smelt musty, but Tyde was right, this had been abandoned recently.

On the walls, small paintings travelled from room to room, all of them depicting parts of the forest. The Eaves were in bloom in the sitting-room paintings. The bloom theme continued in the floral patterns on the furniture and doilies. It was a well kempt home. A horseshoe of matching armchairs sat in the middle of the room with plenty of space to walk behind them. There were two bookcases and a small desk on the left wall, this set up mirrored the right. The position of the doors was the only thing to interrupt the symmetry. Kronic walked up to one desk and examined a large satchel sat upon it. Inside were premixed paints in airtight jars, a roll filled with brushes, and a clean palette.

"A real artist," Tyde said over his shoulder. "Painting life as it happens out in the wild, don't see many of them these days."

"Suppose not."

Were Sadie there, she could have told them that there was more than one artist in that house. The stylistic variance was subtle, but the canvases in the kitchen (despite being the same size and canvas material), were more vibrant, thicker in strokes. All that the men noticed as they entered the kitchen was the subject change.

"Who the fuck wants to look at that while they're chowing down?"

A fox stared out of some thick bracken, its blooded snout buried into the stomach of a hare. There was beauty in the rich colours and the way the light trickled through the fox's fur, though Kronic was right, it was an odd piece to find mounted above the dining table.

Clean cutlery and plates were stacked on the draining board. Kronic approached the fridge. Several documents were pinned to it with magnets. Some were invoices for canvas and lumber. A slip from the doctors in town showed that they had an appointment booked for Adder's immunisation last summer. Days on the calendar had been crossed off up until two months ago.

"Look here," said Tyde pointing at the annotated calendar. "Zombie sighting, grid three, written two days before he stopped counting days. Do you think it followed him home?"

Kronic glanced around at the kitchen paintings, all were of animals eating, but not all were carnivorous. "No, I reckon he went back to paint it."

The cupboards were well stocked. "Looks like he was prepared for a long winter."

"Living out here you'd have to be." Kronic looked at his and Tyde's rucksacks. "Not gonna cut it, I wanna load up as much as possible. One trip, then back to Mallard Hill." He pulled open doors. The first was a small washroom. Water was the theme of the canvases in here. Sadie could have told them that both artists shared the subject, one depicting water as part of the landscape, the other making close-up images, treating the surface and reflections as you would a portrait. Kronic noticed none of this. He glanced inside, closed the door, and opened the next.

The narrow door opened with a gentle tug. Tiny metal objects clinked as they fell to the floor. Steps led down, fading into the blackness.

"We don't need to go down there," said Tyde, grabbing the door and trying to close it.

"Don't tell me you're afraid of the dark?"

"We live in a zombie apocalypse, I would be a fool not to be."

"There could be food down there."

"We don't have enough bags to carry the food we've already found."

"So maybe there's a bag down there." Kronic mounted the top step. He groped the wall and flicked the switch out of habit. There was no electricity.

Tyde handed him a torch. "Have fun."

Kronic edged down the stone stairs, his torch put a spotlight on tools and benches, lengths of lumber, and rolls of canvas. Mitre saw, v nailer, and other tools specialised for frame making and canvas stretching were positioned on the long workbenches. Small pieces of metal jingled across the floor disturbed by Kronic's feet. He redirected the torch light. There were tens if not hundreds of staples on the floor. Staples, as a general rule, are sold in strips, so it was unlikely that so many individuals had fallen here. Someone had unloaded a staple gun.

Kronic had a flashback. *He was back in Greenshore, on the top landing with Tay, a nail gun in his hand.* He felt his trigger finger twitching and looked back down to the discarded staples.

In the darkness, he could hear her fumbling. Slow and dead. Kronic was a powerhouse, the groups muscle, and he had grown accustomed to his invincibility. She shuffled on the spot. It was odd there was no untoward odour, just the smell of wood and damp, if anything, the dead woman gave off a subtle smell of cherry blossoms.

When he laid the torch light on her, he could see her trying to wrench her upstretched hand out of a hole. Light spilled into the room through the hole once the hand was freed, but it was like no hand he had ever seen, it was a bouquet of lush green leaves. No longer content to soak up the sun, the dead mutant turned to face Kronic. Four fleshy petals dominated her face, stretching from the centre past her cheeks, forehead, and chin. Her nose and mouth had combined into three triangular folds, their points met in the middle. They folded back to reveal a pistil encircled by spines.

"Great, a flower zombie. What you gonna do, toothless? I ain't got hay fever." Kronic chuckled.

Her brightly coloured petals quivered. She neared him on root entwined feet. Kronic clenched his fist. One hit was all it would take. Suddenly, spines shot out of her face. One of them stuck Kronic in the neck. He plucked it out and lost his smile. "Tyde, I need you down here now, this flower bitch dosed me with something." His world was already blurring when he dropped to a knee.

Tyde charged to his friend's side. "No, you can't die on me, not over this." The flower zombie quivered her petals once more. Tyde raised his arm, filled it with air, and shot a salt bullet into her head.

"I didn't know you were packing."

"Yeah, always keep a round in the chamber. Where did the poison go in?" Kronic listlessly patted his neck, and Tyde jumped back as the big guy fell to his side. "This better work." Tyde upended his water bottle over the hole in his palm and drank it into his arm. Placing his palm over the hole, Tyde flushed the wound with water and then sucked it back out. "Buddy?" Tyde shook Kronic. "Come on." He sprayed the poison water mix on the other side of the room. Even though he had watered it down and expelled it, the hit of poison gave him a wave of dizziness. *'That's a good thing,'* he thought. *'Means I got some of it out of him.'*

Kronic groaned and sat up. "Mate, if that leaves a love-bite, me and you will have words."

"You feeling ok?"

"Not really, I just got my arse handed to me by a damn flower. Let's just find some bags and get out of here."

They retraced their steps back to the artist satchel and emptied it out.

"Not very spacious is it?"

"No," agreed Kronic. "Let's check upstairs."

More landscape pictures led up the stairs. On the landing wall were the only two portraits in the house, both self portraits. An impression of the old woman's face was built up in washes. Her greying partner had painted himself in colourful bold strokes, thick layers of paint and hard lines, sculpted into realism.

"An artist couple," said Tyde. "Living out their retirement here, so they could focus on their art."

"So where's Mr Artist?"

"Like you said, he probably went zombie painting and didn't make it back."

"Maybe." Kronic thought of all the staple rounds that had been fired down in the cellar workshop. He couldn't shake the memory of his last desperate moments with Tay.

Bathroom, more water canvases, spare bedroom, sleeping animals, master bedroom... "Holy shit!" Ceiling to floor, every inch, every surface, every piece of furniture, even the window was caked in paint. It was as though a pallet had exploded in here. "This is, I mean, fuck." Kronic hovered in the doorway. His brush with death had humbled him. He jumped as the painted figure peeled away from the wall. It scared him, for so long his weight had been his only threat.

"Kronic, make a move, either attack or retreat, don't just stand there."

The zombie mutant raised his hands, growing out of each knuckle was a brightly coloured flower. They wilted and greyed as he took the pigment from their petals into his fingers and mixed them with a secreted paste.

"Move."

Kronic flinched as a rainbow of colours squirted from the ends of the dead man's fingertips. Tyde leaned over his shoulder, pumped up his arm and shot out his last salt bullet. It missed. "I'm out, this one's on you."

Kronic wiped off some secretion from his cheek, rubbed it between his fingers and sniffed. "It's just paint."

"Yes it's just paint, but this one has teeth."

Kronic smacked the thing in the side of the head once, that was all it took to put it down, and yet he still felt vulnerable. Poison spikes from his wife were still embedded in the dead man's flesh. Her poison was deadly, and Kronic had been careless enough to take a dose. The rules of their world were changing again. He would have to live with a little more care.

Inside of the built-in-wardrobe he found two duffle bags and a wheeled suitcase. They filled these, along with their own bags, and the artist satchel, with all the dried and tinned food from the kitchen. Kronic carried the majority, and they made their way back to Lola.

"Will that be enough?" Kronic called once again from the shore.

"Yes, this should do."

***

"What have you two been up to?" Spear glared at them.

"Found some paint ball guns out there in the forest, we had a riot." Tyde lied so smoothly, he was accustomed to it, having spent his whole working life in the smuggling trade.

Tyde was only lightly splattered. Kronic wore the brunt of the zombie's paint. "You expect me to believe that you won?" scoffed Spear.

"Bit heavy handed is our Kronic, he bent his gun." Kronic said nothing, one liar was better than two. "Sorry we didn't sign out, it was an impromptu walk about."

"Been to see that boat of yours?" Spear had been probing Tyde for Lola's location for months.

"Yeah, not good news on that front, she sank, because of the bad weather, I guess. Won't stop us though, we're bound to find a seaworthy boat along the coast." Tyde layered the deception further, killing Spear's suspicions. "Say, you wouldn't have had anything to do with her sinking would you?"

"No, like you say, bad weather would be brutal on a boat left out there, uncared for."

"Jeez, don't rub it in. I'll find another boat but that won't stop me missing the one I lost." Tyde kept his would-be-captor ingratiated. "Can we get together soon? I'd like to talk about what supplies you can spare us, not a lot, but we brought a van full and we have helped out while we've been here, so something to tide us over would be due, don't you think?"

"Can it wait a few days? I will need to do an inventory and discuss it with the treasurer."

"Sure," said Tyde, knowing they would be long gone by then. "A few days would be fine, thank you."

***

Sadie feared that the freshest memories her children would have of their mother would be these infrequent supervised visits to this stuffy bedroom. Cynlear lurked nearby. Madam came in with her arms outstretched. Cynlear cleared her throat, but Madam ignored her and went in for a hug. Cynlear wrenched her off. "You know you're not allowed, now go stand in the corner." Kyan kept his distance, not wanting to even glance at his mum. They told him that her eyes had changed, but he wouldn't look at them. He wanted them to stay like his, to remember them as they had always been. His electrical discharge hummed quietly.

Kronic stood in the doorway waiting for his turn to talk to Sadie. Cynlear saw this as a good reason to cut the visitation short. "Don't forget to say goodbye, you may not see your mum again."

Sadie growled. That cruel woman may have written her off as a monster, but her children had lives ahead of them, lives that would be scarred by her insensitivity.

"Bye, Mum." Kyan still wouldn't look at her.

"Bye, Mummy, Cat say bye too. Love you."

"Love you too," Sadie croaked, desperate not to cry until after they'd left.

Cynlear glared at Kronic as she led the children away from their mother. He returned the glare and held it until she had passed him.

"How you doing, Sade?" Kronic snuck one last glance over his shoulder to ensure Cynlear's absence.

"Awful."

"Physically, can you run if you have to?"

"I'm not in the best shape of my life, but I exercise on the spot, it helps to pass the time."

"Sometime in the next twenty-four hours we're making a run for the boat. I can't be more specific than that, but there will be a massive distraction, so you'll know when it happens."

Sadie felt tears stinging. She gulped them back. He was offering her freedom, her children. "I'm ready."

"Wanna hear a story about some artists turned mutant-zombies?" Kronic grinned. "There's a lot of colour in it."

Sadie smiled weakly and sat forward.

Chapter 35: Prospect Heath

The mess hall was quarantined. Rows of beds ran through it, leaving only narrow walkways between them. It had just been a few Mushroom-men at first, ones converted from unruly mutants, but then civilians started to come down with it too. Their symptoms were extreme and fast progressing, leading to unconsciousness within hours of affliction.

A body, still warm, lay on the bed in front of James. He bowed his head, pinched the sheet, and pulled it up to cover the young girl's head. His eyes darted back to the corpse, which started to fizzle. The sheet fell from his grasp as he recoiled. At an alarming speed, the body blackened and hissed. An orange mist, not dissimilar to the mushroom spores, engulfed the girl. Before his eyes, flesh started to concave and fold in on itself until all that remained of the dead girl was a viscous stain.

Minutes passed with James slumped at the foot of the girl's bed. His heavy breaths were dampening the air between his mouth and his face mask. His ample mind, quietened by shock, started to flutter back to life. *'She was a spitter, an acid producing mutant, what if upon death the glands—'*

HISS.

In the next row, another succumbed to this ravaging illness. They too started to blacken and melt into nothing. James raced to the bed. The body was unrecognisable by the time he reached it. There was a chart at the end of the bed, he was unfamiliar with the name, but this man's mutation had produced slime, leaving a slick in his wake. *'His secretion was not acidic. This event is not localised to corrosive mutations.'*

Another body across the room began to fizzle.

***

"The other patients were already comatose when it happened, thank the Lord. To induce death is one thing, but to release a necrotizing fasciitis to dissolve the body? Well, that's another thing entirely, that sounds like an experiment to exterminate the dead gone wrong."

"An astute observation as always, James," Adder said. "I see that the spores' effects have worn off on you. I had theorised that you would overcome the mushrooms sooner." She was moving a little slower than normal, her eyes struggling to focus on the vials and slides.

"Is it contagious? I mean what are we even talking about here?"

"It will not affect a larger proportion of the populous than it already has." Loralias Adder rubbed her temples, warding off the growing pain behind her eyes.

"Only the secretors? I am not the only one to theorise that the cure would be naturally occurring within some form of secreting mutation. Do you expect me to believe it is a coincidence that every single secreting mutant just keeled over, died, and had their bodies dissolved?"

"Believe what you will, James."

"All of my samples are missing. Vanished. Gone. And what of the dead mutants Michael Brutus brought you? The spitter and the one with gas filled spiky balls growing out of its body. Where are they?"

"Burned. They were of no further use and a health risk."

"A health risk?" James spluttered. "You are the damn health risk. You had better have a cure for this. I cannot bear to watch another person dissolve before my eyes."

"They are dead prior to the flesh eating bug being activated. I must insist we continue this some other time, I fear I am developing a migraine."

James grabbed his daughter and thrust her against the wall. "These are people, Loralias, men, women, and children. They are dying and I can't even let their families in the room to say goodbye, I can't give them a body to bury. There will be panic, there will be a revolt. Where is your foresight? Where is your humanity?"

The vacant look on her face remained. James loosened his grip, feeling both ashamed and justified in his leap to aggression, then ashamed again for the justification. He left the room without further interaction.

Something dreadful clicked into place. If someone was trying to sabotage their work on the cure, the secretors weren't the only ones in danger. *'Claire missed her last check up.'* He raced to the computer suite. "Reese," James said. "Pull up the aerial footage of the Ivanthor Manor." The mushroom riddled IT tech did as instructed. Satellite footage of the Ivanthor Manor showed no heat signatures. "Damn it." Jenna needed to be warned. Sadie needed to be warned. His daughter was killing off any hope they had of making a cure.

James continued to run through Prospect Heath, up the twisting stairs, and along the top floor walkway. He turned the key and stepped in to greet the prisoner. The room behind the bars looked empty, but James knew better than that.

"I know you're in there." The room continued to appear empty. "Fine, just listen. We believed that secreting mutants may hold the key to the cure, now they're all dead or dying. A pregnant woman with a temporary immunity to Wailerism has vanished. She also holds potential links to the cure, and I know you are thinking why should I care? But there is one more element. I tested hairs found on Luke belonging to a woman named Sadie Ratcher, her DNA may have an insight into the cure. A woman called Jenna is on her way to Mallard Hill to collect Sadie, and as valiant as her intentions may be, the army of Mushroom-men that accompany her are programmed by Adder. They will follow Adder's orders and eliminate Sadie and anyone who dares to stand in their way."

They had kept her in that room for months, once they figured out that interrogating her didn't work, they had abandoned her. Her only contact was with the Mushroom-men who came in twice a day to push meal trays under the bars.

James unlocked the cell door and pulled it open. "Leave via the west stairwell." He tilted his head to the left. "There are no guards there, only the main entrance is manned."

Her scaly body flashed into view as she passed him. James started.

"That Jenna isn't as ignorant as you think. She has been stealing your research and is taking it to a new Authority faction, to work on the cure away from you and Adder. You won't see her again." Felicity reinstated her invisibility and drifted away unseen, away from James, away from her prison cell, and safely out of Prospect Heath.

Chapter 36: Jenna

The convoy of Mushroom-men had ditched the cars. Their numbers had grown since leaving Soarken. Jenna was a speck, plodding along in the centre, surrounded by the silent Mushroom-men who all marched in step.

Most people would have felt trapped, but Jenna grew accustomed to her place within the swarm. Intimidation was the quickest way to get Mallard Hill to surrender, and quick surrender was a necessity, she had a boat to catch. The next chapter of her life was within her grasp, she would leave Tave, most likely forever. Her thoughts wandered back to that last awkward hug with Loralias Adder. Jenna lingered holding her tightly. Adder had not returned the embrace, she stood there, arms limp at her side, waiting for it to be over. Adder was cold and logical, to the point of inhuman, but Jenna became very attached to her over the years. That last hug marked a severance that could not be undone.

The mud track meandered through the trees, and it was waterlogged in places. Jenna tried to sidestep the puddles, but the Mushroom-men boxed her in on all sides. It was warm where the sunbeams sieved through the trees, but mostly they walked in the shadows of the towering forest and her thick leafy eaves.

"We're close," Jenna said, consulting her electronic map. "But we must leave the track soon. It won't take us all the way."

The crowd grunted in acknowledgement. The birds chirped and flitted through the branches. Their calls grew as the sun began to dip behind the horizon. Night was drawing close. Jenna considered talking, reasoning, rationalising, bargaining for Sadie, but approaching in the dark with an army would allow for no such conversation. She would have to demand her prize and hope they gave in without a fight.

The trees were so densely packed that they didn't see the monumental wall of Mallard Hill until they were upon it. It was a towering mix of wood and metal sculpted into a solid mass of tree shapes. Colour from the setting sun trickled down the bronze and copper detailing.

"Wait back here," Jenna said to the army of automatons. Pacing forward, Fox and Berk ignored her request and stepped with her. As her personal protectors, they had no choice. They had been programmed to remain at her side.

It might not bode well to have the Mushroom-men on display, but before she had time to tweak their programming, a voice called from beyond the wall.

"Not a step further."

"My name is Jenna W—"

"We know who you are, we have been monitoring your communications. We also know why you're here."

"I just want Sadie. I don't need to come in, or see your numbers or capabilities. You can bring her to me here."

"Wait there."

Jenna sighed with relief.

A stern woman in her fifties appeared on Jenna's side of the wall. It was hard to tell where she emerged from as there were no visible breaks in the wall.

"I am Cynlear Spear, a senior officer of the Authority's military outpost here in Mallard Hill. My brother, Doven Spear, is the only officer on site who outranks me."

"Would it not be best for me to address the highest ranking officer?"

"He can hear what we have to say from where he is."

"OK," Jenna said hesitantly, she read something menacing in Cynlear's smirk. The older woman believed she had the upper hand. "I've come for Sadie. Preliminary testing shows she may have some genetic resistance to the Wailer gene, and we would like to take her back to our facility for full DNA sequencing and samples." Jenna added quickly, "She would be unharmed."

"That vile woman is a Wailer in waiting, no doubt in my mind of that. I'd have given her to you, had you not brought so much hostility to our home."

"But—" Jenna's protests were cut short, first by the clicking of Authority rifles and then the strange short war cry that the Mushroom-men gave in unison.

Jenna spun round. Her crowd had turned in all directions to face the Authority team which had flanked them through the forest. As she spun back round, she saw Cynlear retreating behind the wall. Cynlear turned with her drawn weapon and loosed a round at Jenna. One of her guards stepped forward and took the bullet in his arm. Authority weapons were locked with codes to stop civilian use, which meant that she readied her weapon before even speaking with Jenna. Diplomacy would not be an option here, but as the horde of Mushroom-men advanced, Jenna yelled at them to stop.

"Stand down," she screamed. "We come in peace." She said both to assuage her attackers and instruct her men. Screams tore through the air. Mushroom-men don't scream, they take their injuries silently and persist until they can no longer move. "I said stop," Jenna yelled once more. The screams in the forest stopped and the horde of spore controlled soldiers advanced. They scaled the wall.

Jenna surrendered with her hands in the air and dropped to her knees. "I come in peace, they're not listening to me. This is not my intention."

The code programmed into the spores overrode all verbal commands. Jenna continued to screech at her entourage. They strolled past her calmly and wordlessly, her presence ignored. A few stayed behind, as instructed by their programming, to protect Jenna.

"There are children in here, tell your monsters to stand down," Cynlear's gruff voice yelled.

"I can't, they're not listening," Jenna yelled back. "Their mission objective is to secure Sadie Ratcher, if you stay out of their way and lay your weapons down, they will not attack."

It started as a distant and indiscernible rhyme. Jenna picked out some words "... my crib, my home, fucked up orange clones, gonna unleash my tone, and protect my throne..." The words became louder, somehow growing in weight as well as volume. As this strange vocal climaxed, a massive sound wave crashed against the wall splintering and cracking it. Something knocked Jenna from her feet, it felt like a strong gust of wind. There was no doubt in her mind that the Mushroom-men who had already scaled the wall and reached the village would be downed if not killed. Her ears rang and her head swam.

Cynlear lifted Jenna to her feet, cuffed her hands, and led her through the battered wall into Mallard Hill. Angry faces glared at her. Luke's was the only one she recognised. "I tried to stop them," Jenna croaked hoping to appeal to Cynlear's absent good side.

"You still brought them with you," Cynlear snapped.

"I wanted to come alone. Dr Adder insisted on me bringing them."

"You'll tell us all about Dr Adder, Prospect Heath, and any other Authority stronghold you know about before the night is out."

Mallard Hill citizens and a few loitering Odd Blockers joined forces to restrain and transfer the dazed Mushroom-men into the cells of the Authority station.

"I count fifty-six of these fungus creatures," said Rapz.

"The cells are bursting at the seams," groaned Lieutenant Spear. "We should have shot more of them."

"I'm sorry about the wall," said Rapz.

"Don't be. Your sound wave did what we needed it to. We can repair the wall. You did good." Spear stopped his sister in the corridor. "Cynlear, I need you to lead the search party into the forest. Do a headcount first so we know how many of our guys are MIA. If you engage anymore of these fungus things, kill them. There's no more room in the cells." Cynlear nodded and walked away. "Rapz, please bring Jenna to me. I wish to have a chat with that little mouse."

Chapter 37: The Brutes

Would-be passengers crammed into the seafront houses and stores, all eagerly awaiting the cruise ship that would be their salvation. The Brutes sensed these survivors in their animalistic way. Brett brushed through hundreds of minds with a more comprehensive understanding than the Brutes' senses allowed. The hidden survivors all focused on the transport anchored on the horizon. Most were scared vulnerable souls, but they weren't stupid.

When the current occupants saw the troop of large, scarred apes traipsing up their path, they vacated their little sea-view sanctuary, sliding out of the back door. Brett sensed that they felt safer exposed in the open than in reach of his group. Sight alone had done that, they had no foreknowledge of Michael and his Brutes.

The house vacated for them was picturesque. It had a white picket fence with seashells glued on to it and a small front garden with tufts of green poking out of the white sand that had been blown onto it. Under the green window frames, sat blue plant pots filled with small flowering cacti. The type of place that belonged in image form, printed, and mass produced on postcards and tourist pamphlets.

It was an empty shell. A thing of external beauty preserved for appearances, but not lived in. The previous squatters had dragged in a few items of furniture. It was otherwise bare. The opulent Ivanthor Manor it was not, but the Brutes settled into it and claimed it for their own.

"What you got there," asked Brutus.

Ethan flinched, then uncurled his hands to show the group the scrunched up balaclava. "The Silver Dragon killed my dad. I found this in that block of flats that the mutants escaped from."

"Could be anyone's," said Brutus. "I bet there's a million of those floating around."

"I don't think so, the print looks custom made. I saw an art studio in that flat." Ethan gently rubbed his finger over the silver printed dragon. The paint was thicker in some places and when he looked closely, he could see a bubble of absence on the tail and a little colour bleed on one of the wings.

"What do it ma'er? Your dad were Wailer, ain't no blood debt owed for what the Dragon did." Caleb tried to snatch the balaclava from Ethan, but he hugged it tight and scooched back. "You fink we's murderers for what we done to George? You holdin' Brutus 'sponsible for that?"

"Back off, Caleb," snapped Joel. "You're twisting it. The boy's dad was killed before the Wailer regression. The Silver Dragon strung up the body, tagged it with the word *monster*, and took his mum's money. We treated George's body with respect, there's no reason to compare the two." Joel stretched out his hand and patted Ethan's arm. "Damn right the boy gets to hold a grudge."

***

'Crisis averted,' thought Brett listening in through Ethan. Caleb turned his blood lust in Brett's direction every time he intervened. He'd take a beating for the boy, but Caleb had

little restraint. Inside his twisted mind, he fantasised about killing both Brett and Ethan, he'd calculated he could get lighter repercussions for killing Brett. The mind reader kept his distance and made sure he never found himself alone with him.

He needed to get Ethan away from Caleb and Brutus. Riley was pivotal to this plan. Ethan liked her, she liked him, matchmaking shouldn't be that hard. He felt confident that between their two mutations they had a good chance of survival on their own. He sat alone downstairs. Volunteering for first watch? More like opting for some space. He shoved on some pink earmuffs he'd found discarded. They didn't fit over his head, so he put them on horizontally and let the band rest on his nose. He closed his eyes. With his senses dulled he could reach out into the world and search for Riley's voice among the many authors of thought.

It wasn't Riley that he found.

"I'm telling you this will be a problem. Michael freakin' Brutus is not just going to give us a free pass," said Shawn. Brett could feel the weight of Shawn's massive calcified fists as he slipped into his mind. *"Think of your boy, Dane, this ain't gonna end pretty and—"*

Dane thrust himself forward on his hind legs and pinned Shawn's shoulders to the wall with his front paws. *"Don't talk about my boy. Michael owes us. We were his goddam alibi. He'd have been rotting in Soarken's prison the day of the great Wailer regression, he'd have been in there when the station got burned to the ground. He got a shorter sentence because of us."*

Brutus had forbidden Brett to enter the minds of the guys they found at the church, but he was here now, so he figured the damage was already done.

"Alibis and parole don't mean shit anymore, Dane." Shawn *turned his head away. Dane's mouth was filled with jutted lacerating teeth. His smile full of knives was an edge away from Shawn's throat. "Brutus will make a move. He won't want to share power with you."*

Brett focused on Dane's words, 'He owes us,' and triggered a memory in Shawn.

He stood in a footpath subway. The walls were sprayed in graffiti, some of it came from a talented hand, most of it pertained to so and so's mum, and a number to contact for low cost sex. Only two out of the eight lights, integrated into the arched ceiling, worked.

Shawn felt red misted pleasure as he toe punted Joe Byrne's ribs for the fifth time. No, sixth time, he'd lost count. This lack of numbers brought even more glee as he kicked Joe once more. Cries of pain echoed through the tunnel.

"Please," Joe wheezed from his foetal position. "Stop."

"You still gonna tell the Authority where you got the drugs?"

"No, Shawn, I ain't gonna say nothing."

"What about Dane? You gonna grass on my boss?"

"No, I ain't saying nothing."

Shawn tossed an eight gram wrap at the bloodied heap. "Only a moron shops his own dealer."

This confused Brett. What did it have to do with Brutus?

The scene changed to another memory and Brett was whisked to Shawn's flat. *Shawn had washed Joe's blood off his boots and now sat on the couch with some polish, buffing them back to glory. The knock at the door knotted his gut.*

"Open up, Shawn, I need help."

Shawn cursed under his breath and dropped his boots.

Brutus barged passed him the second the door opened. "What happened tonight with Jonesing Joe? How bad did you do him over?"

"You barge into my home, accuse me of a crime—"

"I need to know how much time you'd get, or rather how much time I'd get? My record's clean so far."

Shawn looked at him with confusion. Michael Brutus was an acquaintance at best, until he showed up, Shawn didn't even know this guy had his address. Brutus had a nasty gash under his eye, chances were, it would be disfiguring.

"Don't fuck with me, Shawn. I lost it with Nicole tonight. Now either I go down for your assault on Joe, or I go down for something worse. So how much time am I getting?"

Shawn snapped out of the memory dragging Brett's consciousness with him into the present.

"He owes us," Dane repeated.

"The way Michael sees it, we owe him."

Dane went silent for a moment. His eyes fell on his son curled up in an armchair, sleeping through their exchange. "Then we take him out before he makes a move. We'll get him on the boat, his friends too, and toss the bodies overboard when no one's looking."

***

The gash he had seen in Shawn's memory was the shooting star-shaped scar that Brutus wore now. It was so embedded in his features it would have been strange to see him without it. Brett opened his eyes to find that scar and the grinning monkey face it belonged to, inches from his own.

"See anything good?" Brutus gnashed his still smiling teeth.

Brett pulled the earmuffs off of his face. He had a vague impression in his memory banks that when a chimpanzee smiles, it's bearing its teeth in aggression. "Just scanning through the brain waves of the neighbourhood," Brett said calmly.

"Smart." Brutus sat back and relaxed. "Anyone we should be concerned about."

"Mostly a bunch of scared nobodies." Brett thought about what he'd just seen. Brutus was a monster and had been before the zombies and Wailers showed up. But Dane and Shawn were the group's most immediate threat.

"Mostly?"

"I found Dane and Shawn," Brett said.

"What did they say? What did you see?" Brutus stiffened into an aggressive posture once more.

"I just got the sense of them. You told me not to read them."

"Where are they?"

"I don't know."

"Try looking through them now." Brutus hastily added, "One time permission."

Brett closed his eyes for effect but kept his mind inside of his own body. "They are in a room, in a house. There are no discerning features that would give me an exact location."

"Ok, good job, I will send Caleb down for a shift. You go get some sleep."

***

It was three am when Leighton took his turn on watch. Brutus was happy to be relieved and headed up the stairs. The rest of the Brutes lay on the floor in one room, he peeked around the doorframe. He was satisfied that they were all sleeping and headed into the next room where Claire slept alone. Brutus spooned Claire under the covers and cupped her stomach with his hands. The fluttering of tiny feet vibrated through her bump.

"Claire?"

She groaned and wriggled but did not wake. Brutus kissed her jaw just below her ear and dragged his lips down her neck. At the same time he moved his hand down to the elastic of her joggers and pulled them down.

This time she woke. "What are you doing?" she said groggily.

"It's been long enough, Claire, I've been patient."

"But the baby—"

"Will be fine." He held her tighter as she resisted. His palms were flesh, but the wrists were furry. His touch had an unnatural sensation and Claire recoiled. Her attraction towards him fled when he shed his human form. This was the real reason she had held him off all these months.

He hoisted her trousers down further, pushed his erection against her, and smothered her whimpers under his hand.

"This is happening. Just relax."

Chapter 38: Prospect Heath

See the wound, stitch the break in my heart
Frame the knife in my back, call it art
Let it weep, let it fester, gather flies
Watch me drown in a narrative of lies

"Loralias, we need to talk." James stilled his breath and held his ear to the door. He heard no movement inside the lab. He tried the handle again. It was definitely locked, so he pounded on the door. "Damn it, Loralias, you don't have to like me, but you need to listen to me."

Saxon skulked nearby, a shock of white-blond hair sat on top of his seven ft summit and orange mushrooms sprouted out of his neck. Today his mushrooms looked wilted, with a greying edge that was spreading inwards.

"Saxon, break down the door."

The Mushroom-man paused for a moment. For the first time in five months he was questioning an order instead of immediately following it. Self thought wavered and vanished. With a grunt, Saxon took his massive boot to the lab door and bust it open. The door settled on its bottom corner and teetered on crooked hinges.

The lights were off and all the blinds were drawn. Loralias Adder lay on the floor. A small towel covered her eyes, held in place by the ear defenders she wore.

"Loralias." James shook her. Her pulse thumped through her wrists and her chest rose and fell with breaths, but he could not rouse her. James thought the worst. Was she about to dissolve and blacken before his eyes as all the people in quarantine had? There was no discolouration of her skin, no temperature registered through touch, and a beat slow and steady pulsed. All of this contradicted the illness seen in the secretors, but he could not wake her, and felt that something was very wrong.

"James? James? Are you in here?" Graham's voice drew closer, along with the opening and closing of doors. "There you are." Graham flicked the light switch and frowned at its unresponsiveness. "Something is up with the Mushroom-men. All their mushrooms are dying. I went down to the storerooms to look for the jars of spores, maybe they need a top up or something. Jenna told me where they were kept ages ago, I mean, I wasn't always listening, sometimes I was too busy looking—" his hands groped imaginary breasts in front of his own chest "—deeply into her eyes, but I can't find them."

"Saxon, have, head pain." The enormous man slunk to the ground and cradled his head.

"Right, just like that, that's how they all are," said Graham pointing with far too much enthusiasm at Saxon. "Ugh, what's that smell?" A subtle stench came from the fridge. Graham opened it. The samples inside sagged and oozed and the inner light remained off. "Why would she turn off the fridge?" Noticing Adder for the first time, Graham ran to her other side and tried to help wake her. Saxon continued to groan in the corner.

"She turned off everything to kill the electrical hum."

"And the light, it's so dark in here." Graham flipped up the circuit breaker. The room flooded with light and Saxon let out a booming scream proportionate to his size. Graham flicked the breaker off and carefully made his way back to James as his eyes readjusted to the dark.

"She was complaining of a headache the last time I saw her." James removed the towel and ear defenders from his daughter's head. He clasped Adder's wrist tightly. His irrational subconscious feared her pulse would stop beating if he stopped monitoring it. "I didn't think it was serious."

"What? A headache?" Graham looked at Saxon rocking back and forth in the dark. "Like the Mushroom-men?"

"No, not like the Mush—" The word caught in his throat as a possibility dawned on him. "No, surely not." James stripped off Adders lab jacket and rolled her on to her side.

"What are you doing?"

James put his hand under Adder's collar and starting from her neck he felt along her spine. He found exactly what he hoped not to. Something broke in him that moment. "I should have known. Damn it, I should have seen."

"Known what? What is going on?"

James ignored Graham, pulled his hand away from her back, and grabbed some scissors. He cut a line down the back of Adder's shirt. "This whole time." His voice was beginning to crack and whine. "Every second I spent with her." He separated the fabric revealing Dr Loralias Adder's Mushroom riddled spine.

Graham crumpled to the floor and flopped his head into his hands. "But it would take years," he whispered. "To make a Mushroom-man that can pass for human, that can form thoughts and sentences while keeping to their handler's agenda."

"How do you know that?" James snapped.

"Dr Adder told Jenna that, when she asked about the Mushroom's stop-start speech."

"You heard this conversation?"

"Well no, Jenna told me about it."

"Leave us," James's voice finally broke into sobs. "Please, just go."

"I'll give the Mushroom-men pain meds," Graham said mostly to himself, as he edged out of the room.

James lifted Adder off the floor onto his lap, and held his daughter for the first time. Her breathing was shallow and her pupils unresponsive. She was not responsible for the atrocities made in her name. He had always hoped for her innocence, but somehow that seemed redundant in this moment. He had never known her, never met his daughter, he had only interacted with this facsimile. Her cold and abrasive persona was down to programming, a more diverse personality would have been too complex to maintain via the spores. His daughter was a pawn of the mushroom spores and had been since before he had met her. James wept over her comatose body.

***

"You would need to insert spores directly into the brain stem and instruct them to rewrite personality, and habitual responses, basic instinct even would need to be bypassed. There would need to be frequent updates with spores to keep the subject complicit."

Graham played Jenna's voice over and over in his head, trying to remember everything she had said about the more complex Mushroom-men. *'Directly into the brain stem, that explains the mushrooms being localised to the spinal cord. Frequent updates with spores?'* As Graham thought these words, he got a flurry of flashbacks. All were of Jenna touching Adder, grabbing her shoulder, hugging her without reciprocation. "Hugging or interfacing? The spore mutant is female," Graham said aloud. *'No, Jenna isn't like that. This is some unknown person, someone lurking in the shadows or hiding in plain sight as one of the Mushroom-men.'*

The spore interlink with Adder could have happened behind closed doors, but the fact he'd paused for thought brought Graham to Jenna's door.

'I'm here to put this nonsense out of my head. To prove her innocence, should James have the same thought.'

Jenna's vacant apartment was unlocked. Graham stood in the doorway for the longest time. Her scent lingered inside. It filled Graham's nostrils and caused his pining heart to ache.

"She didn't do this," he said, and took a tentative step over the threshold.

Chapter 39: Mallard Hill

Lieutenant Doven Spear sat opposite Jenna. He removed her restraints and watched her rub her wrists.

"Can I get you a drink? Tea, coffee?"

"Water please."

Spear nodded. He walked to the door, whispered to Rapz who was standing just outside, and then returned to his seat.

"I really did come here to talk," Jenna said meekly. "I didn't mean for any of this."

"Soldiers died tonight Miss West, because you brought so many of these *things* to our home." Spear sat on his desk rather than behind it. He glared down at her, trying to make her feel meeker still. Jenna slunk a little deeper into her chair and stared at the floor.

"I'm sorry."

Spear answered a rap on the door, and placed Jenna's water down on his desk in front of her.

"Thank you." Jenna lifted the glass and awkwardly tipped splashes of water past her lips.

"Don't thank me yet, you have a lot of explaining to do. For a start, how did you get so many of those fungus creatures? Some are men, some are Wailers, that fellow with snake bodies for legs is a mutant, and yet they are all under your control."

"They were infected with mushroom spores, we code the spores with programmes that force them to behave a certain way and act out our instructions."

"We tracked you via satellite. Your numbers are eight times that of when you left Soarken. Where did they all come from?"

Jenna took a large gulp of her water, then she placed her glass back on the coaster, brushing Spear's leg as she did. She raised her hands. Hidden in plain sight for decades, Jenna revealed her true nature with a smile. "I made them." Bright orange spores poured out of her open finger slits and penetrated Spears airway. He gasped and clawed at his collar. "You caused the deaths here today, not me. The Mushroom-men are programmed to ignore my verbal commands if they conflict with my safety. You put me at risk," hissed Jenna. "Now you will join their ranks."

The mushroom riddled Spear now stood obediently and waited for Jenna's orders.

"New mission objectives. We will release your mushroom brethren and convert anyone who stands between us and Sadie." Jenna smiled. "Starting with that vocal friend of yours who's just outside the door."

A mutant like Rapz could be useful.

***

"We'll never get a better distraction," said Luke.

"We just need to get Sadie and the kids, right? Did you ask Serenity, Paul, and Rapz again?" said Tyde. He was panting as they raced up the hill.

"I did, they're staying."

Mallard Hill villagers loitered in the street all gossiping and speculating on the failed attack. "Did you hear?" One woman said to another. "They killed our guys in the woods, and Digger is missing. I reckon that he died too, but reanimated and walked off. I don't envy the patrol that finds him and has to put him down."

"Don't be daft," said the other woman. "Digger never had an injection, he couldn't be a zombie."

Luke heard them digress to mumbled conspiracy theories about Adder contaminating their water supply. He didn't care about that, but he felt a twinge of loss with Digger gone. He had helped Luke to glide, trained him to be more manoeuvrable, he wouldn't be as comfortable in this winged body had it not been for Digger.

The ground rumbled as Kronic ran up to join them. "Did you see them? They looked like those documentary ants that got raped by shrooms."

"Yeah," said Luke through gritted teeth. "I saw them. They're the bodyguards of Prospect Heath." Luke felt an old surge of anger. They had kidnapped him, experimented on him, and the only way he had escaped was through breaking the neck of a scientist called James. That death stained his conscience and never would have happened if not for Adder and her mushroom mutants.

"What the hell is that?" said Tyde.

It took them a moment to interpret it. Rapz's lyrics were hardly recognisable through his stop start speech, but the build up was working just the same. "Submission, position, not all, stars, glisten, they listen."

"Who is he fighting, can you see?" Luke tried in vain to find Rapz in the gathering crowd in the distance.

Before either of them could respond, the sound wave tore through the streets, blowing people over like skittles.

"Us," Luke wheezed from having the wind knocked out of him. "He's fighting us."

Kronic stood firm. The sound wave had no effect on him, which was why he was the one to go out in the woods to practise with Rapz. He helped Luke and Tyde up off of their backs.

"I'm not sure what that orange cloud is, but I think we need to move," said Tyde. They ran to the nearest house and shut the door.

The villagers remained floor bound, and though they tried to get back on their feet, the cloud of spores soon engulfed them. When the Mallard Hill residents rose, they were no longer themselves. They were Mushroom-men, and they all had one goal.

"Where do you suppose they're heading?" whispered Tyde as they ferried past their hiding spot.

"They're after Sadie," said Luke. He bashed the wall with the butt of his fist.

"How can we even fight them, they're people, right?" said Tyde.

"Some are," said Kronic still watching the crowd pass the house. "Others are white eyed. And we don't know if we can change any of them back from what they are now."

***

Sadie looked out in horror at the madness marching under the street lamps. Cynlear had left her locked in that dingy bedroom and not returned. If Sadie looked hard enough, she would see her among the many others encrusted with bright orange fungus.

From the next room came a squeaky infant scream. "Madam, is that you?"

"Mummy, I no like the things outside. Cat scared."

"Where's Kyan, is he with you?"

"I'm here," he called from the other side of the door. "I'm trying to reach the lock but it's too high."

"Is no one else with you?" Sadie could hear them now, a quarry of grunts, and slapping feet.

"They left us alone."

Sadie sank her head against the door. Her babies were so close, but she couldn't protect them from what was coming. A surge of conviction from the *Bitch* replaced the brief stab of helplessness. "Step back, both of you go into Kyan's room," Sadie called out.

The doors were cheaply made, and to her credit Sadie had been working out every day in the small space under Cynlear's watch. She screamed as she repeatedly kicked through the door, releasing pent up anger. Her shoe broke through the doors centre, the hole wasn't big enough to climb through, but it made the once flat surface more malleable. She pried the edge away from the frame, bending and ripping her nails as she did. "Mum!" The handle latch came loose, the lock on the top held firm, and Sadie wrenched a tepee shaped hole between the door and the frame. Her skin scuffed, prickled and even tore as she squeezed through.

"MUM!" Kyan screamed it this time.

The permanently unlocked front door stood open. They were already inside. "Madam, I need you to cling to the ceiling above Kyan's bed and stay there. Kyan, I need you on the bed electrifying the metal frame." The hum that came from him signalled that he was ready to vent.

"What if Madam slips? I'll burn her again."

"Madmam no slip," scorned the cross-armed toddler, diverting back to her third person speech. "I best climber." She tucked Cat up inside of her top and allowed the tiny suckers to grip his faux fur. With some reluctance from Kyan, the children did as their mum told them.

Sadie stood at the top of the stairs. In that moment the *Bitch's* rage was all consuming, she would take on the world and enjoy the carnage. Two controlling forces caused the adrenaline that rushed through her. The *Bitch* made Sadie feel invincible with rage, and the *Broken Child* with her Wailer needs, added a cannibalistic twist to her blood lust.

The Mushroom-men breached the threshold, but an odd distortion in the air reached Sadie first.

"What are you going to do, Sadie?" snapped a coarse and familiar voice. "Moan at them? Get up in the loft!" Felicity Grange stood before her for a moment before shimmering back out of view.

Sadie looked at her scaly armoured skin and concluded that the meat underneath would be bitter. The *Broken Child* was getting a foothold. She wanted to bite, she wanted to tear, she had no forethought other than destruction.

Invisible arms hoisted her into a foot-lift. "I mean it, Sadie, get in the damn loft." The *Brain* took enough of the reins to guide the adrenaline surged Sadie to safety. She didn't slide the hatch over all the way, leaving a crack to view from, and kept herself tightly coiled, panting and drooling, ready to pounce from above.

Felicity set and lay a taser net on the landing and stood back. It was an invaluable piece of Authority kit used against the dead during Felicity's service as an Infection Control agent. She set it to pulse and taped down the trigger. *'Kronic will come,'* Felicity told herself. *'The others will come.'* As the horde of mushroom automatons surrounded the house, bursting their last bubble of personal space, she wondered if their coming would have any real merit.

Chapter 40: Prospect Heath

"Here you are," James groaned, entering Jenna's living room. "I've been looking everywhere for you. I thought you were going to give those poor sods a shot? Their screams are wretched. Graham? Can you hear me?" Paper crumpled under his feet, small avalanches of it had slid from the sofas. Graham sat in the centre of it all, looking like a bewildered hatchling in an oversized nest.

"She sends her apologies," Graham croaked. "And a cure." He held up a small wedge of paper.

"Who sends apologies? And a cure for what? Wailerism, mutation?"

"Jenna." Her name passed Graham's lips as a whisper. "She's our mushroom mutant, and she's synthesised a cure for the effect of her spores." He paused, adding almost as an afterthought, "synthesised from your blood."

James leaned over the mess, feeling a new sense of preciousness to the scattered paper around his feet. He took the wedge from Graham. The formula for counteracting the spores was exquisite; a testament to true genius, penned in Jenna's neat and delicate handwriting.

He stared at it, reading it over and over to the point where he could have recited some sections from memory. "This would have taken me months."

"Who's to say it didn't take her months, she has been working on it longer than us."

James looked at the flood of intellect laying about the room. "We could get lost in all this, and no doubt we will, but for now we must give pain relief to those who need it." James placed the papers down and offered his hand to Graham. "Come on, Graham, I need you."

Graham took his hand and rose to his feet. "She's not who I thought she was," he said sullenly.

"No she's not." James kept hold of Graham's sleeve, half afraid the man would stand idly if left unguided.

"What about the forest village? Can we warn them?"

"I sent Felicity Grange after them yesterday, not after Jenna, but the secreting mutants had been slaughtered and Claire is missing, I feared for Sadie Ratcher's safety."

"Will Felicity be enough?"

"Perhaps, she should be, if they have skilled fighters." There was no conviction in James's voice. "Forewarning is the best I could offer them."

The spring sun was warming. Dotted here and there on the distant streets, trees were filling with blossom. Bird song would fill the air if not for the anguished screams of the Mushroom-men drowning them out.

"Pain meds first," said James handing over half of his syringes and morphine vials. "Then we'll synthesise Jenna's cure and test it."

Graham juggled the medicine from hand to hand before stashing the vials up his sleeve and cupping the syringe packets.

James rolled his eyes. "Graham, you're in a lab jacket, use your pockets." Graham looked a little embarrassed as he pocketed them. His mind still swam with disbelief. James attempted to refocus him. "You start on the top floor, I'll start on the first, and we'll meet in the middle."

Graham nodded, grateful to have the easier start. The Mushroom-men on the top floor were Wailers. They didn't speak, but were as compliant as any mushroom afflicted human. Locked in their cages, they would stick an arm through the bars, and take the injection. Job done. James would have to track free roaming Mushroom-men down in the staff quarters, some of them mutants. It could become complicated to get to them, especially if they turned off the lighting and blacked out the windows as Adder had.

James left Graham at the stairwell. He made a detour to his daughter's lab and gave the anguished giant a shot. Saxon eased his screams, his pupils dilated, and he curled up on the floor.

"Loralias." James tried to wake Adder again. When he failed, he gave her a shot, just in case she regained consciousness and still suffered pain. The giant he passed on his way out breathed steadily, Saxon even cooed a little in his new found relief.

Then James hurtled down the stairs to the staff quarters. He ignored the screams coming from the levels he passed. Working systematically reduced their chances of missing someone.

James went room by room following the screams. The Mushroom-men didn't have the cognitive capacity to find the fuses and disable electricity in their rooms.

A fridge leaned on the opposite worktop in this apartment, its plug yanked from the socket. Glass littered the floor from smashed light bulbs. Someone cried out. They had attacked any appliance that made a hum or produced light, but from the sounds of it, they hadn't dulled their headache.

Glass crunched under James's feet. So many to treat, but he had to consider his safety as he stepped through debris. He heard her in the back room. The wardrobe had been tipped over, clothes and belongings scattered. He picked up an Authority shirt and saw the name A. Reese stitched on the pocket. James felt a chill between his shoulder blades and cringed.

Adrienne Reese was the Authority officer who attacked him before the mushroom spores domesticated her. She hated him for his involvement in project Re-gen all those years ago, and promised to have a hand in his demise. Now she writhed somewhere in this room. James sighed and continued his search. The cries came from under the bed. James lifted the bed-sheet, inadvertently spilling light into Reese's sanctuary.

Without warning she lunged at him. James threw himself back taking the sheet with him. He threw it over Reese as she came at him and wrestled the woman to the ground long enough to jab her with a pre-prepared syringe. As she calmed, she twitched and spoke a few stunted words. "Re-gen, project Re-gen, ruination of, mankind." Her words, verbalised from her own thoughts, something impossible under mushroom control.

There were wider implications for James if the Mushroom-men gained cognition, a cell with a view and no chance of parole, but for now he had a self-imposed duty to quell their screams.

He went through the rest of that floor much the same way, listening for the screams and hunting out the hidden man or woman, under beds and in cupboards. Unlike Reese, he found them debilitated rather than aggressive.

The last one was hard to find, its moans were the hoarse rasps of a dying man. He wandered all around the flat trying to find the quiet noise. He found him in the kitchen.

"Oh, you stupid, stupid creature," James said. He hoisted the man out of the fridge and rubbed him with a blanket, before wrapping him in it. Blue lips framed the man's chattering teeth. "I put money on you being hypothermic." James chastised the Mushroom-man like a child. The man moaned and wilted.

***

Graham envied James. His patients were caged and compliant, but those white eyes sent creeps inching and wriggling through his flesh. Several cages stood empty. Graham tried to remember how many of Jenna's entourage had been Wailer. It was hard to say. Maybe they were all accounted for, or they could be loose and waiting for him. Trying to push his fears aside, Graham persevered. The routine became rhythmic.

"Come to the bars, present arm," he said. The mushroom Wailer complied. Graham injected the painkiller and moved on to the next cell.

Standing at the central cage Graham reached for the door with a whimper. Both stairwells were an equal distance from him in this spot. With a deep sigh he walked in.

His feet scuffed on the tiles as he shuffled to the next set of screams. The child was curled up at the foot of the far wall, clawing at his scalp. His bed (the only furnishing in the cell) was upended against the window, but it did little to dim the overpowering spring sun.

"Come here, little one," Graham said kneeling by the cell door. "Give me your arm and the pain will stop." The child didn't even acknowledge him.

'Something's behind me.' Graham shot a look over his shoulder to the open door. There was nothing there. He tried to shake free of his fear, he had after all already dosed half of this section, but a chill persisted on his skin and his instincts begged him to run.

The child was still a Mushroom-man, perhaps it would respond better to an order. "Come here. Present your arm." The child remained where it was.

'Behind me!' Graham spun round, only to once again confront an empty doorway. The feeling of being watched wouldn't shift.

The needle pierced the seal, and he pulled a small dose into the syringe. "I'm coming in." The master key on his chain would open any cell — except for James's — but he didn't need it. He pushed the bars, and the door clicked open. The boy was still curled and trying to burrow in to his head with his nails, to dig the pain out of his skull. Graham pulled the child's arm straight. "Sharp scratch, then no pain."

The boy's mushrooms had greyed and shrivelled more than the others he'd seen. In fact that chill on his skin grew brittle as he realised that many of the mushrooms had flaked and fallen off. "All, erm, all done," Graham said shakily.

He stayed crouched and backed towards the cell door. The child had yet to look at him. Graham continued to back out. His head snapped round once more towards the doorway. This time it was darkened.

The screaming had stopped, not just from the boy, a wide spread dimming of anguish silenced the whole floor. *'How can the Wailers recover while the humans fight their mushrooms still?'* Graham's eyes darted back around the cell. The boy had vanished, there was only one logical place that he could be, but it wasn't until the upended bed fell upon him that Graham realised where that was. The child wailed. Graham cursed his conservative dose, wishing he had drugged the child into a stupor. They came at Graham, a swarm funnelling through the open doorway.

The distance of those stairwells meant nothing. He wouldn't even make it to the door. They didn't pause. Quickly finding exposed skin on his arms and legs, they bit into him. Graham was the one to scream now, a deep guttural, gargled scream of both shearing pain and hopelessness. *'This is how I die, oh Lord of all, this is how I die.'* His inner monologue whimpered but his mouth did nothing but scream. It was cruel of them not to make a killing blow.

The vines up Graham's sleeves coiled and tightened around his wrist, cutting off circulation. On the opposite side they slithered down his trouser leg and formed a tourniquet there too.

Two of the Wailers knelt at his side, sharing the meat of his hand. Graham watched them gnaw and tear flesh from bone. Within no time at all, they were snapping back his naked finger bones to reach the meat of his palm. Their greedy mouths filled up with his flesh. His hand was in tatters, no digits remained, and others feasted on his legs.

He had the means to dull the pain, to end it all should he draw a large enough dose of morphine, but they pinned him. One on each leg, two at his hand — a generous description of the appendage at this point — and the boy gnawed on his shoulder. He tried to wriggle and twist and fight back. Every move he made, they countered and subdued.

He had screamed his loudest, now he couldn't scream at all, his throat was raw and his voice lost. The urine he'd voided stung his wounds but did not deter the frenzied Wailers. *'This is it.'* The blood loss made him weak and shock had overwritten most of the pain. *'Any second now will be my last.'*

His vines were untouched, no blood pumped through those. Tightly coiled they protected some of his arm. He couldn't tell you what made him lasso the first, if there had been thought behind it, it wasn't a conscious one. His vine grabbed the Wailer, wrenched it from him, and thrust it through the door. Other than the tourniquets, they all uncoiled. His vines had strength, power, and they herded the devils back. Still on the floor barely conscious Graham watched the green blur of another vine uncurling and whipping out. It caught a Wailer by the neck and dragged it out.

Other vines were lashing those already ousted to keep them at bay. A woman Wailer still ate his hand, grinding his palm between her teeth shredding it down to the butt. Vines had thrown her friends from the cell, undeterred, she continued to eat him.

How dare she? He was dying, bleeding out, and she carried on stealing his flesh so brazenly. A vine whipped out again, this time when it caught the woman around the neck it squeezed. The only reason he flung the thing instead of killing it, was his waning strength.

With his last conscious act, Graham hooked the key in one of his vines and with great dexterity locked himself inside of the cell. The Wailers shook the bars and sprayed saliva into the cell with their over enthused wails.

Though he lost consciousness, his mutation continued to aid him. Leaves sprouted around his injuries and matted to them as bandages. Their secretions coagulated the blood, numbed the area, and cleaned it of contaminates. Graham lay there, in a bed of his own blood, barely breathing, while his would-be-murderers tried to force the door.

Chapter 41: Mallard Hill

One of the three houses assigned to the Odd Blockers shone brightly in the night, acting as a beacon from a distance and an eye blinding deterrent up close. The light that poured out of Innocence was a physical response to the gathering crowd outside. Her mother had on an eye-mask sewn from dense scrap fabrics. At its core was leather, cotton covered the outside to improve comfort.

Serenity held Innocence in the crook of one arm, groped for the arm of the sofa with the other, and lowered into it. She could tell that light had not abated by the dim glow that made it through the bulky eye-mask.

Innocence was growing well and had already taken her first steps. In just over a month she would have her first birthday. Serenity's babe was weighty in her arms as she rocked her back and forth.

"The Lord of our lives shines his light through all of us. That light may appear dimmer in some more than others, but he loves us as equals. The Lord weeps for our pain and laughs with us in our joy." Serenity strummed her fingers through Innocence's coarse curls. Serenity's unwavering faith brought her strength. That faith also gave her peace as an unknown force pushed its way into the blinding light.

"It's ok," said a calming voice. "My name is Jenna, I mean you no harm." Jenna's entourage waited outside of the house.

"I cannot make her stop," Serenity replied. "You must allow her shines to run their course."

"Then we shall speak with our eyes screwed tight." Jenna raised her fingers and poured a mass of spores into the air. Serenity couldn't dim the baby's light, but with a little reprogramming, Jenna could. Innocence tried to catch the strange orange specs that only she saw in the light of her creation, but her mother's bubble of protection repelled them. When they came within that protection they died and greyed leaving a circle of dust around Serenity and Innocence.

It was one of those rare moments where Jenna's cool facade almost slipped. She sensed her failure through the dying specs. Her spores were infallible, perhaps deadly to plant mutants. Her spores should penetrate any mind. This was a certainty until now. By the time Innocence had stopped glowing, all the spores had drifted and settled. Only a trained eye would notice their presence.

Jenna's warm smile had returned. "So the bad news is that the village isn't safe anymore. The good news is that I have somewhere safe to take you and your baby."

"What of my friends?"

"They will be taken care of. My priority is to get you and your baby to safety."

Serenity stood without further protest. "Then let the Lord guide us in journeys new."

As Serenity stepped out into the cul-de-sac, she was unnerved by the strange orange welts that infested the faces around her. Jenna rested her arm over Serenity's shoulder. "This is all going to be fine."

Serenity looked over at Sadie's house, saw lots of movement, and heard the sounds of battle coming from within.

The darkness of night did not black out the eeriness of those glassy stares around her. The Mushroom-men queued up to get into Sadie's. Their deadpan faces looked past Serenity, yet they moved to make a path as she neared them. The mushroom Wailers gave her a wider berth still, responding to Serenity's mutation on a biological level, which superseded their programming.

"Are those men contagious?"

"No, they are enhanced, an army for good. They will clear the village of threats and lead the civilians to safety."

Serenity thought on this. She could hear no wails, see no risen dead, but if the village was under attack those walls would be their undoing. Jenna smiled at her again, and Serenity was grateful for her aid.

A yell came from the surrounded house. Sadie was stubborn and defiant. She would fight to her last breath. Serenity prayed for her friend to see sense and allow Jenna's people to rescue her.

Still guiding Serenity with an arm curled over her shoulder, Jenna loosed a few spores behind her back and watched them grey and die. She grimaced out of view, then squeezed Serenity's shoulder. Jenna was used to repressing her true feelings, but it was rare for her to feel this level of rage. Her spores were not infallible, she was not infallible. Serenity brought into question Jenna's own mortality.

Jenna left with the snake-like creature Roger Smiles and a man named Kenneth, and marched Serenity far from Mallard Hill.

***

Paul rolled off of his hospital bed. No easy feat in his current condition. His weighty extra arms and legs distorted his centre of gravity, pulled at his skin, and put pressure on his vital organs. But what choice did he have?

They planned to amputate multiple limbs, a temporary (and what would need to be a recurring) solution, in order to save his life. That wouldn't be happening now.

Lashale, his squeamish nurse, had gone to the window desperate not to be left out of the latest gossip. The Mushroom-men saw her. She squealed and rushed out of the clinic, not even bothering to apologise to Paul. The fate of an oddity was less important than her own, he supposed.

Paul dragged himself under the bed. Footsteps marched through the door. They were searching. Not haphazardly like a human would, they did not check by most likely places of concealment. They went from one potential hiding spot to the next in order of proximity. It was this thoroughness that made certain every resident of Mallard Hill was found and converted.

"Ahh!" Paul screamed in pain as they dragged him out. One Mushroom-man held a jar of Jenna's spores in front of him, but he did not twist the lid.

"He, too, damaged," stuttered one Mushroom-man.

"He too, broken," agreed the second.

So they left him there. Paul, who could barely move with his many extra limbs, was the only free thinking man not trying to leave the village. Come the morning, he would have inherited Mallard Hill by default.

Chapter 42: The Brutes

Brett woke up to the inhuman squeals of what sounded like an injured animal.

"Look a' me like at, will ya? Ya little shit."

Caleb batted Ethan back and forth between his massive hands. Ethan yelped with every hit. Brett lunged at Caleb and clawed at his fur, and Caleb swung round catching Brett in the mouth. His lip instantly fattened, and he tasted blood.

Leighton jumped in and restrained Caleb as Brutus appeared in the doorway.

"He's high on testosterone," snarled Leighton. The troop was more sensitive to the stink than Brett. To him they just smelt like animals.

"It's more than that. I've had enough experience with addicts to know when someone's jonesing," said Brutus. The words *Jonesing Joe* sprung into Brett's mind, and reminded him once more of Brutus's life before the Wailer Regression.

"Where's Joel?" asked Brutus.

"He's down on guard duty," said Leighton.

"Take him with you to the van. I want an inventory done on our medical supplies."

"S'all gone," Caleb whimpered. "Uppers, downers, anyfing that'd get me high."

Brutus put power behind his hook. Caleb's jaw crunched and blood splattered on the wall behind him. "We can't get that shit on an island. It's irreplaceable!" Brutus heaved Caleb up against the wall. The scrawny ape whimpered and lowered his eyes. "Brett, can you reach anyone on the boat? Get us a departure time?"

It stretched Brett's capabilities. His head started to throb long before he found the minds on the boat. "They haven't heard from Jenna yet. They are delaying for the time being, but still plan on leaving today." His nose trickled blood, a side effect of the mental strain. When he first tested his ability, the headaches and bleeds were commonplace, but he'd had no symptoms in months.

"Fine. Leighton, take Joel and find pharmacies, hospitals, clinics, hell steal from survivors for all I care. Just get our med supply back up." Brutus snarled at Caleb, drawing back his muzzle and brandishing his teeth. "I'll stay here and help our *friend* detox."

***

Brett was certain that not all the noises coming from the other room came from withdrawal. He felt no sympathy for Caleb. That guy might benefit from a hiding.

Ethan curled in a corner nursing his bruised arms, and Claire slept on the bed Brutus had raped her on the previous night.

Brett stretched, his back pushed into the wall, and his legs stretched out along the carpet. A few gentle clicks ran along his spine. He probed his swollen lip with his tongue and then stared up at the ceiling. *"I lost it with Nicole."* The words sprang into his head. Brett knew he should have remained bored and kept his mind to himself, but he wanted to find out who Nicole was, so he closed his eyes, reached out into the next room, and entered Brutus's mind.

The memories he saw of Nicole were like snapshots at first. She smiled, then cried, wore her hair up and then down. Blonde and petite like Claire, Nicole was beautiful and Brett got the sense she knew this, that she could be a little vain and conceited. She had a strong sense of self and any passion she had, she stoked with fire. Brutus had tried to tame her, but she was strong of spirit. This triggered the memory that Brett searched for.

"You think you're so special. The Authority wouldn't even take you on," Nicole said.

"I'm in the reserves," Brutus yelled.

"The reserves," Nicole laughed. *"That just means if they ever need cannon fodder your name will be top of the list."*

Brett felt Brutus's anger rising as he watched Nicole through his eyes. *"You spiteful bitch, after everything I've done for you."*

"Done for me? This is my place. I'm the one supporting you, and maybe I don't want to do that anymore." Nicole stretched out her hand and admired the giant star shaped gem on her middle finger. It was a present from her dad and a constant reminder to Brutus that he couldn't afford her. Any jewel he bought her would be pitiful by its side. *"I want you gone by the time I get back."*

She opened the front door, but Brutus slammed it shut. He grabbed her wrist. She jerked round and punched him in the eye. That giant star scraped across his eye socket and embedded just under his tear duct, permanently branding him. It was so un-

expected, that someone so small could muster that much power, and that she would dare to strike him at all. They both stood in shock. Nicole mimed the word, "Sorry." She shook with fear and coiled in on herself like a wilting flower. Submission was her only hope. Brett suspected that part of her realised what would happen next.

Brutus grabbed a handful of her hair and dragged her through the flat. He took her into the bathroom and loosed her hair. As she tried to stand, he punched her to the ground.

"If you're man enough to throw a punch," he yelled. "Then you're man enough to fucking take one."

Her face was swelling already, she couldn't go out looking like that, he'd get into trouble, but she kept trying to crawl past him. He booted her chin and sent her flying back into the room. She bit clean through the tip of her tongue and wailed at the sight of her severed flesh on the floor. This was bad, but her screaming made it worse. Brutus grabbed her arm and twisted it.

"You need to be quiet, Nicole, you need to shut up." The bone in her arm cracked. The euphoria he felt at the sound of the break and the gentle vibrations the snap sent into his hands, elated Brutus and made Brett queasy. Brett wanted to leave now, but he couldn't, he was stuck watching this horrific assault through Brutus's eyes. *Brutus picked up her other arm and snapped that too. Nicole's screams now enhanced his delight. He screamed at her to be quiet, only as an excuse to inflict more pain on her.*

He left the room. In a box under the kitchen sink was Brutus's small selection of tools. His fingers danced over the screw-

drivers and pliers, but it was the claw hammer they curled around.

Nicole lay on her back dragging herself forward by her feet alone. Her tattered arms lay across her chest.

"Where the fuck do you think you're going?" Brutus said this with a smile. All of Nicole's progress was undone as he pushed her with his foot, sliding her back into the room. He still grinned when he brought the hammer down on her kneecap.

Brett tried once more to leave the memory. Watching it all through Brutus's head he felt his thrill, his sensual release. Michael Brutus was getting off on this. Brett couldn't reconcile this in his own head. He sympathised with the victim. Where were her rescuers? Had no one heard her screams?

As Brutus knelt all his weight on Nicole's chest, Brett begged for this to be the moment, for this fragile broken thing to be released from her misery. Brutus's knees dug into her chest, and he cupped his hands on her chin forcing his weight on her lower jaw. Was it the crunching of ribs or the popping of her jaw that finally let her rest? Both had given Brutus that extra rush, but when she fell unconscious, his high began to dip, and he lowered enough to ask rational things of himself.

He wanted to get away with this. It was a silly fight, a blip, it had turned so suddenly. He shouldn't lose his whole life over a momentary lapse. Brett virulently argued the contrary, but his thoughts had no sway in the memory of another.

Michael Brutus showered. He stepped over Nicole to reach the towel rack. He dried himself, dressed, wrapped Nicole up in a sheet, grabbed his keys, and unlocked his van as he stepped out of the front door. The bundle in his arms may have looked like a sleeping child being carried to a passerby. Brutus fastened her into the passenger seat, looked to make sure that no one was around, and then returned to the apartment.

Brett got a sense from the fading light that this might be the same time that Shawn was kicking seven shades out of Joe Byrne. *Brutus cleaned every speck of evidence from the bathroom and dumped the blooded cleaning materials in Nicole's footwell. His own spray of blood remained on the wall. He couldn't undo Nicole's punch. That ring of hers had left a distinctive mark on him.*

He had a smooth drive through the city. The traffic lights were all on his side and the roads were quieter than usual for this time of night. Michael Brutus began to feel that the universe was on his side.

The polluted river was quiet. Brutus carried Nicole once more like a bundled child out of the van. He rolled her out of the sheet to the water's edge and then kicked her in. She landed face down in the sludgy water.

Some lingering survival instinct bucked Nicole's shoulders, shunting her head back into the air. Her battered body convulsed like that for a while, but she couldn't take a sharp enough breath before her face dipped back into the shallows. Brutus watched until she grew still. He hadn't minded the wait. Once she had been still for long enough, he walked back to his van and drove to the other side of Soarken.

The Moorland estate was in disrepair, the place where the lost and the poor festered. He knew it well. Brutus pulled into an area of garages surrounded by flats on three sides. He found an empty one and parked up. No one would question it. Dodgy vehicles appeared and disappeared all the time on the Moorland estate. He took the bag of evidence and dumped it in a communal bin. Then he took out his Authority radio and scanned through their channels.

Joe Byrne had taken a beating nearby. If Joe took a kicking, Brutus bet it was Shawn Mayer who wore the shoes. He decided to pay Shawn a visit.

Finally, Brett retreated into his own mind. As he opened his eyes, he found Michael Brutus's staring right back at him. He looked away quickly.

Brutus gripped Brett's shoulders and shook him. "Brett, it's me, you were screaming. What the hell is going on?"

"I must have dozed off," Brett panted. He didn't dare make eye contact with Brutus while the memory was so fresh. "I had a bad dream."

Brutus eyed him suspiciously. "Oh yeah, what about?"

'Can he sense when I'm inside of his head?' "The ship went down." Brett wrestled with the image of Nicole's convulsing body as her lungs filled with water. His voice lowered to a whisper. "We all drowned."

Brutus patted Brett's shoulder. "You're safe. No one's going to drown." He walked over to Claire and kissed her forehead. She stayed asleep. "Let me know if that ship docks," Brutus said to Brett as he turned to leave the room. "I want to be at the front of the queue."

Bile curdled in Brett's stomach as he watched Claire sleep. The resemblance was too striking to ignore. Michael Brutus had a type, and he had a temper.

Chapter 43: Prospect Heath

James revelled in the silence. He wiped a bead of sweat from his brow. Giving pain meds to all the Mushroom-men had been taxing, and it was only a stopgap. Their mushrooms would continue to harm them without treatment. Jenna left them with the cure and, if her calculations were right, it would be simple enough to synthesise. He walked down to Jenna's quarters to retrieve her notes.

"Graham? Graham?" James searched the flat but found no sign of his friend. "Huh, he must have gone straight to the lab," he muttered to himself. He picked up the notes and decided to send Graham back down here to gather the rest of Jenna's papers later.

In the lab, Loralias Adder lay unchanged on the floor. Saxon had seated himself on a stool with his head on folded arms, resting on the workbench.

"Hello, Saxon."

He grunted in recognition at James's greeting.

"Has Graham been in here yet?"

Saxon grunted again.

"I'll take that as a no."

James rolled up his sleeve, tightened the rubber tubing tourniquet with his teeth, and placed a needle into his vein. Once he'd released the tubing, the blood sped into the vial. "I'll be the pin cushion and, you, my oversized friend can be the guinea pig."

Saxon grunted again.

James sighed. "The conversation is always scintillating with you, Saxon." He placed the first vial of blood into a centrifuge and prepared to draw another. His regenerative abilities replenished his blood almost as quickly as he drew it. "There," James said triumphantly when he filled the last slot in the centrifuge. The whirring sound was hypnotic, but it wasn't the only noise. Wails and screams called out from the floor above.

"Graham," James gasped.

Saxon stood. He was as alert as he could be under the morphine dose.

"We must get to him before—" The rest of that sentence caught in James's throat.

They slinked in through the doorway, their predatory eyes focused on James. A familiar fear bubbled up in him, one where he was eaten alive, healed, and then eaten again—perpetually.

James picked up the nearest stool and swung it. Its metal legs were almost as long as the tall workbench. The reach kept the wailers in front at bay, but it didn't take long for two to flank him.

"Keep back," he yelled, twirling his stool around like a rotor blade. A Wailer caught the metal legs and jolted James back into another Wailer. The breath warming his neck smelt of blood. James flailed, throwing his arms around. Their wide white eyes dilated as they closed in. James looked around for help. *'Where the hell is Graham?'* James thought. The beasts drew closer, blood from their victims splattered and smeared on them. *'Where the hell is my friend?'* They wrenched his legs from under him and he hit the floor with a sickening crack.

James blinked away the blood. His body shook, his head pulsed and his vision faded in and out. He craned his head to look beyond the frenzied Wailers already claiming his flesh. Adder still lay where he had left her, untouched. A smile graced his lips. With a lolling head he turned towards something in his peripheral view. The last thing James saw before he lost consciousness was a flash of white-blond hair exiting the lab.

***

Chris was shaking. He held Lara tightly. *'To keep her calm,'* he told himself. She wriggled and snarled in his grasp. There had been screaming, howls of anguish from the aggrieved Mushroom-men, but it was the newly found silence that marked Lara's unrest. Chris shushed her and covered her stitch scarred mouth.

People talked in the passageway outside of their flat, mumbling at first but growing in urgency, other survivors, civilians assigned quarters on this floor.

"But what about us? No one has come, we tried… but got no reply."

"The intercoms have always been shit, you can't rely on…"

"… my Carol? In fact, have any of you been allowed into quarantine?"

These were parts of conversation, the snippets heard by Chris. They stood right outside of his door. Lara thrashed at the sound of them. The instant his hand slipped from her mouth, she let out a wail.

Someone shrieked.

"Calm down, it's just that wierdo and his pet Wailer," a man said from beyond the door.

"That proper shit me up," gasped someone else. The nervous laughter that followed stopped dead as Lara's wail was answered in kind.

"They're coming from both ends."

"Run, fucking run!"

"How the hell are they so fast?"

Their shouts drew away from Chris's flat only to be herded back towards it. Lara wanted nothing more than to be part of the fray and reverted into a frenzied state. Chris shut her in the bedroom and latched the door. He jumped as she threw herself against it, as he backed up towards the front door, banging erupted from there too.

"Let me in. Please!"

Chris ducked onto the floor.

"Please, I have a kid," the man shouted. "I have a fucking kid, let me in!"

Chris sat between the two pounding doors and put his hands over his ears.

"Damn you, you can't be hurt. Wailers won't attack you, that's what they say!"

It was an untested theory. Chris had only interacted with Lara since his mutation developed. The child in question began to cry. Chris pushed his hands down harder until his ears throbbed.

"You can't have him, he's not fucking food!"

The next noise was chilling. A child's scream pierced and dimmed to nothing in a singular note.

"I'm coming," Chris said spurred to action by the lack of need for it. He stood and pressed his eye to the spy-hole in the door. The thing that looked back at him wasn't human. Its blood-stained face drew in closer until a single Wailer eye filled the glass. Lara smashed against the bedroom door.

"You can't have her, she's mine, I saved her," said Chris. The white eye staring back through the peephole blinked. "She's not like you, they will cure her." As he said this, a part of him wondered if there was anyone left alive out there who could make a cure. "She will be cured," he whimpered, "because of me."

The Wailer backed off, but still faced the door. Others lined up beside the first and waited. Chris watched them with curiosity. The six-year-old Wailer who had tricked Graham — known as Oscar before his affliction — approached. All the afflicted children were bright, but Oscar was also unusual. Sadie had gained hope for a cure when she cared for Oscar at Future Smiles collar care home, because of the obsessive-compulsive traits he kept, in spite of his Wailerism. Some part of his human self had shone through, despite his condition.

Oscar approached the door. Knock, knock. Pause. Knock, knock. Pause. This pattern continued. On and on went Oscar's knocking.

Lara thumped the bedroom door, clumsily at first. She palm heeled and back slapped the door, but after some practice, she found her knock and tapped out the same rhythm as Oscar.

Chris opened the bedroom and let Lara out. She walked up to the front door and knocked in unison with Oscar once more. Chris groaned and pushed his thumbs into his temples, dragging them up towards his hairline. "Just stop. Enough, stop knocking."

The knocking stopped, not just Lara's, Oscar stopped too. Chris inhaled and held a shocked gasp for some time. He tried to wipe away sweat from his upper lip, but his hands were just as clammy. "Knock," he said, shakily releasing his gasped breath. Lara knocked, then Oscar, and then others joined in, until all the Wailers within range of his voice were knocking on a door or wall. "Stop." Instantly the knocking ceased.

Tears streamed down his face. This was it. In this moment he had found his origin story. This was where the great and mighty Chris was made — no, it was where greatness was forged.

Chris opened the door and stepped among the Wailers who, because of his mutation, knew him as kin. The concrete walkway was solid beneath his feet, but his legs still felt like jelly underneath him. The Wailers parted. He held onto the wall and looked over the drop. Below, two bodies were sprawled in the car park — a man and a child. The piercing cry that dimmed, the sound of their fall, replayed in his mind. "If they'd waited," he said to himself, "just a few seconds more and I would have let them in." He erased his cowardice from his mind and replaced it with a scenario where he desperately tried to unlatch the door.

Chapter 44: Mallard Hill

Sticks and stones may break my bones
But just try and get them near me
I'm tough as nails and slick as ice
You bitches best start fearin'

Sweat dripped from Sadie's brow onto the oblivious mob below the loft hatch. Her breaths quickened at the promise of warm flesh. The Mushroom-men streamed up the stairs, under the open loft hatch, and into the bedrooms. Kyan's electricity flowed through the metal bed-frame. Madam clung out of harm's reach on the ceiling above.

The *Broken Wailer Child* in Sadie flitted between two emotional extremes. She was ravenous at the sight of the Mushroom-men born from humans or mutants, and felt like kin to the Wailer-mushrooms. Both were being electrocuted. The *Bitch* and *Brain* were little more than background noise in her mind.

Another mushroom riddled Wailer hit the deck, and Sadie directed her rage at its attacker. Her son. The thought of killing Kyan to save the Wailers was enough for the *Bitch* to tear back control.

> *'You expect me to stay put?' screamed the Bitch. 'Can you not feel my rage? Can you not sense our body writhing, hyperventilating, twitching? I need to release this!'*

'Where exactly? On whom?' asked the Brain. 'The Mushroom fiends would destroy us. Kyan is keeping his sister safe. They no longer approach the bed. And I'm not sure how she is doing it, but now and then I see a body drop, and Felicity is the only logical explanation for that. We must wait here.'

'To what end? Kyan will deplete his reserves and Madam can't hold on forever. At some point the children will be in danger and I can't help them from up here.'

'Help them? We're unarmed!' Logic and passion were facing the same dilemma, and neither had all the answers. 'We stay,' said the Brain. The Bitch shot her a scathing look. 'Just listen. We watch, and if Kyan and Madam's situation worsens, we will distract the Mushroom things, throw things at them, scream, whatever it takes to make us their target.'

Rage streamed from Sadie's eyes. The mass of uniformed and orderly bodies pushed their way up the stairs. She closed her watery eyes, drawing away from the sound of shuffling, from creaky floorboards, and the hum of electrical charge. Her attention refocused on an unintelligible rumble coming from outside. It built in volume. Much louder than normal human capabilities, yet it still had the quality of a human voice. There were words, odd, nonsensical words, stuttered in time to the growing thrum.

The sound-wave impacted the house and violently shook it. Many of the Mushroom-men fell, and so did Sadie — right through the hatch into the mob below.

***

"Oh, like that is it? Well come on then, I ain't got all fucking day." Kronic stood firm. All around him mushroom riddled puppets tried to bring him down. "Just like play fighting with a toddler," he said, laying his restrained hits on each approaching foe. A fraction of his available force went into each tap. Kronic knocked out another, and another. He barely noticed the hits they landed on him. Most of the Mushroom-men had turned away from the house and focused on Kronic. He continued to stand his ground, not even fighting back now they were backing away from the house.

Then it started, an indiscernible rumble, a mash of human words that lacked the vocalist's true talent.

"Come on, Rapz," Kronic whispered with a grin. "Lets me and you play some dominos."

***

Though streetlamps lined even the dirt track roads in Mallard Hill, the garden around the back of Luke's house was pitch black. It should have been comforting to know that they were so well concealed, but something deep and primal prickled through Luke's skin.

Tyde was fine with the dark. There were no streetlights on the open sea. It was Cleaver wrestling with him on the lead that frustrated him.

"Cleaver," Tyde hissed. "Calm down."

Luke knelt and tousled Cleaver's ears. "You're all right, girl." She sat with her eyes half closed and nuzzled into Luke's hand.

It was coming. The growing noise threaded a string of pain from ear to ear. They crouched low to the wall. Luke wrapped one of his wings around Cleaver and held her close.

They fared better this time when the wave hit. The lower centre of gravity and distance from the wave's focal point helped. They recovered their footing and made their way into the kitchen through the back door.

"Should we be bringing her with us?" Luke asked. Cleaver jumped up, trying to go beyond the lead's reach.

"We're going straight to the boat from here. Kronic would never leave without her." Tyde tilted his head and put his finger to his lips. They crept into the living room. Above them, Mushroom-men were finding their feet, bumping, and scuffling. Then they heard a scream.

"Sadie!" Luke lurched forward and smacked into an invisible wall. His leg twisted from underneath him and he crashed to the ground. A shimmering weight mounted him and clasped his mouth shut. Cleaver didn't bark at the intruder. In fact, she started to wag her tail.

"You need to be quiet," a voice hissed from the darkness.

Luke's mouth was released and the weight that had pinned his torso and wings, lifted. "Felicity? Is that you?"

Luke squinted in vain; the ex-Authority officer was perfectly camouflaged. There was a blur and a hand once again rested on his mouth.

Past their open doorway the Mushroom-men marched — a procession of orange with a single splash of Mahogany — right out of the front door into the streetlamp bathed cul-de-sac.

Felicity materialised in front of Luke, grabbed his face and pointed it toward the door. "You can't run after her," she whispered. "The kids are still upstairs. We need a plan, not haste." Tyde huddled in close to hear her. Cleaver licked her feet. "How good is your swooping? Have you learnt how to use these things yet?" Felicity pulled out the flap of his wing as though she was measuring a length of fabric.

Luke snatched it back. "I've got a long way to go, but I've been practicing."

"Here's what we do," she whispered and glanced over her shoulder. The Mushroom-men were still trickling past. "We wait until they're all out, then we go upstairs."

***

Sadie tried to see through her hair. She was bobbing upside-down, her head knocking against the beast that had her slung over its shoulder. They were quiet. Freakishly quiet. The ones marching from her house stepped in tune. Dull thuds of the same beat.

"Come on then, you bastards!" Sadie heard Kronic's call cut through the night, but the mushroom fiends were no longer answering his challenge. They were forming a circle around her.

Sadie slipped from her kidnapper's shoulder, rolled to the floor, and scrambled around on her hands and knees. All around legs blocked her path. Shakily, she raised her head. She was surrounded.

Spear stepped out from the circle. His mushrooms, engorged orange welts, hung over the collar of his Authority uniform. They circled his black eyes and infested his black rooted hair. He took a warrant card from his pocket and scanned Sadie's face. The screen lit up with a positive identification and he unholstered his pistol. Still registered to his fingerprint, the safety slid, and a round cocked. Spear levelled the gun with Sadie's head. She scooped in a breath and let it trickle back out as a growl.

Kronic's tiptoes took his enormous weight for a second before dropping him back down. He couldn't see Sadie over the mass of Mushroom infested heads, but he saw Spear, and he saw the gun. "Oi, fuck-face." Kronic picked up a rock and tossed it a few times to feel the weight of it. He drew his arm back and flung it through the crowd with a force that ripped through flesh and sinew, and an aim that was greatly lacking.

The rock zipped past Spear. He paused. Two injured Mushroom-men crawled forward. Spear looked at them. One had taken the rock through the neck, the other to the gut. "Too, badly, damaged," Spear stuttered. He shot them both and pointed his gun back at Sadie.

Drool streamed from her mouth and mania lit up her eyes. Had Jenna programmed him to factor in facial expressions, he may have predicted the bite that tore through his trousers, and split the flesh of his shin. Warm blood soaked through his clothing and pooled around Sadie's mouth. The taste spurred her on. Her jaw tightened and teeth gnashed. Spear lined up his shot with the top of Sadie's head.

Kronic picked up a handful of stones and gravel and drew back his arm. The projectiles cut through the crowd and blood pebble-dashed the ground. Not a single Mushroomman made a noise in response to their injuries, but Sadie's scream was loud and clear. The projectile rubble had pierced her leg and shoulder.

"Shit." Kronic started to push his way to the centre of the circle.

Something cast a shadow as it glided under the streetlights. Luke soared down from the house. He couldn't grab Sadie and clear the crowd with this limited momentum, but he could take out the target with the gun. He caught Spear with his tail, forcing him off his feet, and then hurtled into the crowd, knocking down anyone within his wingspan.

There was no longer an organised circle. The mushroom spores were overcoming an *If Error, Then,* clause in their programming. Between Kronic sweeping them down and Luke's messy landing, they needed to assess their hive capability and individual injuries before resuming.

They picked themselves up and looked around. A small blood pool lay on the floor where Sadie had been, but she was no longer there. They started to march toward her house. For good measure, two splinter groups split off to search the other houses.

"Tyde," Kronic shouted. "They're coming back!" He rushed to Luke and helped him to his feet.

"Where's Sadie?" Luke asked.

"Ran back in the house. She's probably trying to get to the kids." Kronic turned back towards the house. "Tyde!" he shouted again.

"They already left," said Luke. All around them the Mushroom-men stayed focussed on finding Sadie, ignoring Kronic and Luke.

Kyan and his group had made it to the woods. A bolt of electricity shot up into the air like a flare gun.

"They might be safe," said Luke, "but we still need to get to Sadie."

Kronic put his fingers to his lips and pointed at the blood pool. There were trails leading off. A stream of blood had followed Spear's path, but smaller droplets went in another direction, away from the street, towards the wall, towards the woods.

"Sadie's not in the house," Kronic whispered. "She's smart. She'll head to the boat."

"But she's been locked up." Luke stared at the blood. He wanted to follow her trail, but they couldn't risk the Mushroom-men following it too. "She's never been to the boat. How will she find it?"

Chapter 45: The Brutes

"This isn't good." Leighton paced, dragging his knuckles over his scalp. Joel was trying to appear calm, but his leg kept twitching. "This isn't good," Leighton repeated. "This many people gathered in one place. It's a trap. The Authority's afraid of mutants. This boat thing is bullshit. They're just gathering us up to wipe us out."

"Brett," said Brutus, "Time for another look."

Brett slouched against the wall. He still had dried blood under his nose from the last time they called upon him.

"It's not fair, Michael. Who knows how much damage you're causing asking him to reach out that far," said Claire.

"No, it's fine." Brett sat up as best he could. He closed his eyes and sent his mind out, leaving behind the house and the beach, as he touched a mind on the boat

"What did you see?" Brutus growled and grabbed him by the shoulders.

Brett convulsed in his grip. Blood trickled from his nose and ears and a pink tear left his unfocused eyes.

"Damn it, Michael, can't you see he's in trouble." Claire grabbed hold of Brutus and tried to pry him off her friend. His heavy, fur covered paw swung back and clocked Claire in the face. She stumbled back, whimpering and pressed her fingertips to her swelling cheek.

Ethan jolted, a knee-jerk reaction, which he instantly regretted.

Brutus bounded on his knuckles over to the teenager. "Do you have something to say to me, boy?" Brutus puffed out his chest and drew his muzzle back, revealing his large teeth.

"No," Ethan said, trying to curl up small. Before him lay his only friends, both of them were bloody and submissive. "No, Sir."

Brutus raised his hands once more, but Brett's gasped words drew his attention. "They're worried too."

"What do you mean, who are?" asked Brutus.

"The people manning the ship want to leave too. They are waiting on that Jenna lady, but she's running late."

A wail rang out, jumping from monster to monster until a multi-voiced shriek surrounded the whole beach town.

"Well, that was inevitable," sighed Joel. "Surprised they didn't show up sooner."

Brutus pulled Caleb up from the floor. He was shivering, his fur drenched with sweat. "You ready for a scrap?" asked Brutus. Caleb's bloodshot eyes bulged, making his wide grin — crooked, from his jaw injury — look even more maniacal. "Good. We're moving out. Claire, Ethan, pick Brett up off the floor."

One of Brett's arms was slung over Claire's shoulder, but it was Ethan who shifted Brett's weight down the stairs, and out through the picket-fenced garden onto the beach.

With every twinge and spike of pain in her abdomen, Claire's hand moved to cradle her small bump. She didn't want to draw attention to it. Composure, that's what she needed. She had read that a mother's stress might damage the baby. Swelling spread out from her cheekbone and under her eye, causing a squint. She didn't focus on that either, because that would hurt the baby. It would then be her fault if something happened to it, and for that she couldn't forgive herself. Worse, Brutus would never forgive her.

Dawn wasn't that far away, a fact that did little to help them now. The wind of the sea blew fiercely against them. It was hard to hear anything else. Panicked people fled in all directions, being herded towards the bitterly cold sea.

"The pier!" Brutus's arm gesture did more to guide them than his words.

Other unlikely survivors of the apocalypse were forming the same plan. Bustling shapes moved in the night, lit up by the moon and its reflection off the sea. Dane had a distinctive profile though, a lion shaped body, lizard skinned, with a snout a little shorter than a crocodile's, but still rammed with teeth. Shawn was distinctive too, especially when he ran. His giant calcified fists swung out in unison. When they landed on the ground, they propelled him forward. Brutus spotted them at a distance, and once he had, he kept them in view.

Dane slowed at the edge of the pier, he engaged his son in a bizarre crooked hug, and then sent him on alone.

Those with more offensive mutations lingered at the entrance to the pier. They meant to fight and defend those who couldn't. Dane and Shawn took their place beside them.

Brutus smiled. He made Claire and Brett go on without him. With reluctance, he allowed Ethan to go with them too. Claire really was struggling and Brett showed no signs of coming back round.

With the vulnerable cowering behind, the strongest stood on the pier's edge; a defensive wall of muscle and mutated wonder.

Terrified squeals escaped those running along the sand. It was hard to make out in the darkness who was friend and who was foe.

"Hold the line," Dane ordered. People naturally rallied behind him, it wasn't just his size, he had a commanding presence, an aura that demanded respect. "We must keep these Wailer bastards back." He shot a fierce look at Michael Brutus who had positioned his group in the forefront.

"Brutes," yelled Brutus. "Disperse!" On his command Joel, Leighton, and Caleb tore off into the crowd. Bits of dismembered Wailers hurtled through the air.

No matter how hard Dane fought, he kept one eye on Michael Brutus. If there was an opportunity here and now to take him out, he would. Therein lay his downfall. Dane was so preoccupied with Brutus, that he didn't see Caleb coming.

Caleb jumped on Dane's back, holding on with his muscular hand-like feet he took Dane's snout in both hands. He put all of his strength into the pull. Dane bucked and squirmed as Caleb pulled his mouth past its limit. There was a crack as it snapped back. Caleb grabbed his whole head this time and twisted until he heard a loud click.

It was high tide. Caleb didn't have to drag the body far down the pier before the water underneath got deep. He pulled him up, flopped him over the rails, and then let him drop.

Two onlookers approached Caleb. "He's a hero, 'im died to save you lot." They didn't catch much of what Caleb said, but the words *hero* and *died* got through loud enough to make them bow their heads. One man even patted Caleb's back as he passed. Caleb turned away and grinned from ear to ear.

***

"The ship is coming," Brett tried to say. His incoherent mumble was lost in the bustling crowd. Even Claire, who cradled Brett's head in her lap, missed his words.

Light flooded onto the pier, and a voice cut through the wind and the crashing waves. **"This is the Authority,"** said the woman with a megaphone. **"I am a sergeant aboard the Voyager Serene. We will ferry you to the ship via lifeboats. Please do not push. Everyone will get their turn, if you are calm and cooperative. If your behaviour endangers us, we will return to the ship and leave without you."**

"She means it." Brett's mumbles were once again lost. Slipping from thought stream to thought stream, he was having trouble staying in his own mind. He needed a quiet mind to retreat and refocus. He found it flailing in the waves — a mutant zombie with a mouth full of teeth and a lion shaped body, covered in lizard skin. Brett lingered there in the quiet, with no thoughts to contend with but his own.

Chapter 46: Prospect Heath

Saxon observed the splashes of red in the abstract. The self awareness — slipping past the spores programming — swam in a morphine haze. He saw James lying on the floor. The scientist's chest cavity was being emptied by the Wailers that sat around him. The white-haired giant stumbled out of the lab into the chaos. His mushrooms had wilted and greyed, yet a lingering kinship existed between him and the Wailers. They passed by him covered in gore. Too drugged up to feel fear, Saxon stumbled on. He went up the stairs to the Wailer holdings.

Graham wasn't hard to find. The two Wailers outside of his cage were calling and thrashing around. They flinched at the sight of Saxon, confused by the comradery they felt. They snapped at the air in front of him. Saxon advanced, and they stepped aside. When he pulled out a key, they began throwing themselves around.

Saxon squeezed through the door, without letting them inside, and locked it. His foot knocked against a vine. The key curled at its end tinkled on the floor. Saxon was careful to step over it as he neared the man matted with leaves. A pulse beat in Graham's neck. Saxon gently reeled in the vines and coiled them on Graham's chest.

The Wailers jumped up and down rattling the bars.

"He too damaged," said Saxon. "He too broken." The Wailers cocked their heads. A fleeting recognition of those words resonated with them. Cradling Graham in his arms,

Saxon opened the cell door. "In," he ordered. The Wailers sneered at him. They let him pass, but would not take commands from him.

Saxon took the journey down the stairs and back to the lab unchallenged. The Wailers that attacked James had already left. Saxon laid Graham on a workbench. Blood and an oozing healing sap matted the leaves that covered his wounds. A little colour returned to Graham's cheeks.

Inside this room lay a mutilated body, a comatose woman, and a man that was a matted mess of leaves and blood. On some deep level, Saxon knew that these three were humanity's best hope. He locked these precious assets inside the lab when he left.

The mushroom wilted Authority lined up outside of their apartments. They were a sorry lot, with different levels of cognitive awareness, and in various states of undress.

"Attention," Saxon called. Most of them were unsure of the meaning of the word, others were too drugged up to stand without the aid of the wall. "Any you, mission ready?" His speech wasn't perfect, the spores still lingered, festering and rotting within him.

"Me." Adrienne Reese stepped forward. She was in full Authority uniform, a personal weapon already strapped to her thigh, although shoelaces had proved too much for her.

"Others?" Saxon called. Mervin Hatter stood forward, followed by Delilah and Field. "Everyone other, go bed," Saxon ordered.

"What do, Boss?" Reese asked.

Saxon grunted at the wails coming from above. "Infested, we go catch."

***

Chris had all the Wailers doing star-jumps. Except for Lara, whenever he gave a command he excluded her. In a world run by Wailers, he was their king, he could rule them all, make them do anything. This wasn't the life he had wanted, or one he had planned for, but it seemed like an apt consolation.

"Stop jumping and stand still." He'd heard something, boots, coming up the stairs. "Do not attack," he ordered, this time he opted Lara into his command.

When he saw them he realised what he'd been missing; an audience to bear witness to his greatness and lavish him with praise.

"Don't panic," Chris yelled with a smile. "I have them under control." *'A cape,'* he thought. *'And a leotard. Eye-mask? No, I want them to know it's me.'*

Saxon turned the corner. Reese walked behind with two chained Wailers pulling on their restraints.

"Stop struggling, walk nicely," Chris yelled.

The Wailers stopped.

"You control Wailers?" Saxon asked.

"It's my super power," Chris said proudly. "I mean mutation."

"Like mushrooms?" Saxon glared.

"Oh no, nothing like that," said Chris. "It only works on Wailers." He looked back at the Wailers behind him. "Follow me, single file." He grinned at Saxon. "So, where do you want them?"

"You take cells. Lock up. Field, show you where."

"I go too," said Reese.

"No," said Saxon. "We need med pack. Help fix good guys."

When Reese and Saxon arrived in the lab, Reese became confused. "Not good guy." She pointed to James's remains. "Monster."

"Need him," Saxon said, pointing to the cocoon of leaves that held Graham together. Then he pointed at the regenerating body of James. "Need him too."

"No need him," snapped Reese. She spat on the pulp which had been James's chest.

"Need his blood, need both their smarts."

"No," Reese growled.

"We are dying," Saxon shouted. "Mushrooms kill us, if they not help."

Reese glowered. "He live, until we cured."

Saxon frowned at her. "He live, until I say."

Chapter 47: The Forest of Eaves

The gaps in the damaged wall were hard to find in her frenzied state. Sadie groped along it at first; then her touch became less tentative. A flash in the sky lit up the wall, dazzling her eyes and obliterating her night vision. She pounded the wall with her fists and growled. Eventually, she found a gap and clambered through.

The Forest of Eaves was something else at night. The tangled branches, now thick with leaves, blotted out the moon and the stars. It was like walking through an unearthly large cave. There were calls, owls and other nocturnal creatures greeting the night, but there were other sounds too, groans and creaks, and the shuffling of leaves.

Sadie stumbled on, clutching her bloody shoulder. Every noise filled her with dread, every step away from the shelter and familiarity of the village sent shivers through her skin. The wound to her ankle was minor, but still tender enough to force a limp. She grunted and plodded on.

"Huuauun."

Sadie froze. It was wheezing. She followed its stumbling path with her ears through the darkness, feeling no kinship to it. *'One of the dead things,'* she thought. At least it made itself known. Any of the rustles around her could mark a stealthier foe.

The zombie gave out another low moan. It was further away now. Sadie strained her ears until she heard nothing but the ominous animal calls and scuffling in the undergrowth.

Rooted to the spot, Sadie's head flicked from one side to the other seeing nothing but blackness.

"Kraaaw!"

A wail in the distance — answered in kind by many voices. Sadie jerked her head in their direction and started to march towards them.

'She's not thinking clearly,' said the Brain.

'Yeah, but she's thinking loudly.' The Bitch scowled. 'We'll be drowned out again if she keeps this up.'

There was comfort in that call. It triggered a longing in the *Broken Child*. Sadie didn't know where the boat was anyway. She could wander aimlessly, or move with purpose. Against the advice of the *Bitch* and *Brain,* Sadie changed direction.

***

"What the hell was that?" asked Luke as they forced their way through the perimeter wall.

"Come on, Luke. We made enough noise," Kronic said. "Did you think they wouldn't come?"

"There have been so few on patrol. I figured they were dying out."

Kronic shrugged. "Zombies, maybe, but the Wailers outnumber us. The forest is a big place, easy for us to stay lost in. We just gave a bunch of hungry mouths our location."

Luke tucked in his wings to streamline his way through the trees. "Sadie's running towards those hungry mouths."

"Look, mate, we ain't gonna find Sadie. Forest this big? No chance. Trust her to find us." Kronic turned away from the Wails. He didn't know how to feel at the prospect of the village being overrun with Wailers. He had friends there, well, they had been friends before the mushrooms came. But he was grateful that the route to the boat sounded clear.

The ground was dry, so Kronic didn't have to worry about his weight pressing him into the ground. The crisp undergrowth crunched and snapped beneath his feet.

Luke was reluctant to follow. He kept pausing to listen to the Wailers.

"There's a difference," Kronic said, "between Wailer calls. One's like they're making now are just keeping the group connected, if they had prey they would be angrier and more of them. They haven't found Sadie."

"I'm sure she headed that way."

"She can hear them as well as we can. She'll come towards the boat to get away from them."

An image flashed in Luke's mind of the white rings in Sadie's eyes, he heard the wail she had let out during their last intimate embrace, and his gut, the thing he had learnt to rely on during his work for Guy, screamed that she was with them.

The sky illuminated. Pinpricks of blinding light made it through the dense eaves. "We best get a move on," said Kronic. "If we don't get to those morons first, someone else will."

"The Wailers don't seem interested in the light," said Luke.

"No they don't, but if I was looking for Sadie and came up empty, I'd look for her kids."

The Mushroom-men. Luke had almost forgotten about them.

***

"Jeez, kid, are you trying to get us caught?" asked Tyde. "Lay off the fireworks."

"But Mum—" Kyan started

"Your mum — uh — how do I get this thing off of me? She can walk, right?" Madam's hands were suctioned onto Tyde's forehead, which wouldn't be so bad if her legs were on his shoulders and not swinging behind his back. "Your mum will find her way, but if you keep lighting up the night, everything else will find its way here too." Tyde tried in vain to grab Madam's dangling feet and take some of the weight from his head. He even contemplated shooting a water-blast into the little girl's face. There was a reason Tyde had no children of his own.

"Verity-Elise," Felicity commanded in her Authority tone. No one noticed her materialise, they all shared her gift of invisibility in the darkened forest. "Get down."

Madam did as Felicity said, only to get knocked down, and tongue washed by Cleaver. "Madmam no like. Madmam no like." Cleaver nuzzled under Madam's top. The toddler's squeals turned to desperate cries. "No! My Cat, my Cat, give him back!"

Felicity grabbed hold of Cleavers collar and the stuffed toy the dog had clenched between her teeth. "Drop it!"

Cleaver let go of Cat and slunk behind Tyde's legs. "It's like running a circus," Felicity sighed. "Right, listen up. I scouted ahead to the boat. It is presently clear. I suggest we leave now. I am authorising the use of torches, as I believe the benefits outweigh the risks." She bent down, picked up Madam and placed her on her hip. "Move out."

"But Mum," Kyan protested.

"For goodness sake," Felicity snapped, "it's like the flats all over again. I have told Sadie to meet us at the boat, not in the middle of the woods, the boat. Are we going to have an electrical outburst like last time, or can you control yourself?"

Kyan said nothing.

"Good, off we go."

Tyde turned on a torch and pulled Cleaver forward on her lead. Kyan scowled in the darkness and drew strings of electricity between his fingers and his thumb. He maintained the electrical flow and used it as his own personal torch.

"Nice, kid," Tyde said.

"I've been practicing." Kyan smiled.

***

Drool dribbled down Sadie's chin. She limped through the forest, her eyes glazed, her sense of reason drowned out. The wound on her ankle, from Kronic's rubble toss, was getting worse. She was blinded to the pain, dragging her blooded wound through bracken and thorns, encrusting it with dirt.

They were close. She heard more than their calls now, she could hear their bodies pushing through the woods.

A leg flung up from the ground, tripping her up. Muscular arms clamped her tight and a large hand covered her mouth.

"Sadie, it's me," a voice rasped in her ear.

The meaty hand was warm. His life pulsed so close to her mouth. There was a wound, a bad one. She smelt the blood, but also the sweetness of ripening infection.

"Sadie, it's me." The injured man repeated his laboured words through strained breaths. "It's Digger."

Sadie tried to wriggle free, but Digger held her to his chest. "There are Wailers out there, lots of them." He loosened his grip and handed her his infrared thermal imaging headgear.

Sadie put it on and stared into the night. There they were, so close and so bright, much brighter than the woodland creatures that were now visible to her. She looked down at her arms — the Wailers were much brighter than her.

'We told you,' screamed the Bitch. 'We're not like them.'

"Sadie," Digger whispered. "I need your help. I need medical treatment, but I can't get there on my own. We need to get to the village before the Wailers do."

"No," said Sadie. "The village is lost. We need to get to the boat."

"The village is humanity's last stand. It can't be lost." He tried to stand, but crumpled back against the tree that supported him.

"The villagers are all mushrooms. All infected." Sadie looked down at her arms through the thermal vision once more. Part of her was still disappointed that she didn't glow as brightly as the Wailers. "We are all that's left of humanity, and we have to throw our hats in with the mutants, if we are to survive."

Digger stayed silent for a long time. "It's my home," he said weakly. "They're not blood, but they're family."

"You're not a one-man-army, Digger, and you're injured. If saving them is your fight, you won't win it today." On some level she was talking to herself. To the bitter *Child* who wanted to drag her human meat into the Wailer horde. "Not today."

"So where's this boat? Spear had us hunt for it, then he said it sank, I never saw it though. To be honest, I didn't look that hard. Never felt right about us trying to keep you here."

"I don't know." Sadie lifted her head and scanned the forest. The Wailer troop had passed. "On the river somewhere, hidden in a boathouse."

"That doesn't narrow it down much." Digger winced as Sadie helped him to his feet.

"Kronic told me a story, about two artists. Both mutants, both deceased. He ran into them while raiding their home for supplies. I think the boat was near there."

"Mr and Mrs Stellar. Nice enough people, retirees, lived alone, painted in the forest. If the boat is near there, we have a rough direction at least." Sadie went to pass him the headgear. "Ignore it and use your ears," Digger said. "That thing makes the Wailers flash up, but the dead are invisible through it."

They limped through the forest, supporting one another, with only two good legs between them.

Chapter 48: Prospect Heath

James felt a bed underneath him and tried to figure out where he was. *'Trauma,'* he thought. *'Massive trauma.'* When the Authority first imprisoned him, they had run a whole range of experiments on him to test the limits of his ability. It had been many years since that last happened, but the shock of having over forty percent of his body regenerated was still familiar enough for him to form an understanding. Looking over through blurred vision, he made out a figure on the bed opposite his.

"The world has gone to shit, fuck your rank," screeched Reese. "This man is a mass murderer, worse than that, he has practically wiped out our entire species."

"Fuck rank? By that logic..." The large man squared up to her "... you're not Authority material and have no right to speak here." Saxon looked over at the two bedbound figures. "I saw everything under the mushroom's control, being a bodyguard for the labs. This man is humanity's best hope. This man cares about a cure."

"You don't know what you're talking about. This man helped to make the damn Wailer gene. They paid him to make zombies."

"This man gave me painkillers, he gave you painkillers, he gave his blood to cure us."

"Enough!" Graham glared at Saxon and Reese.

DECAYING DAYS: EVOLVE

James jolted a little in the bed at the sound of his voice. James's last thought before the world went black was of his friend.

"This is a room for patients," Graham continued. "If you want to sound off, you can find somewhere else." The platinum haired giant shot him a scathing look. "Please," Graham said with less assertion, "if you wouldn't mind."

"If there are any other Mushroom-men found, your help with them will take priority," said Saxon. Graham nodded and the two officers left.

Graham took a syringe and a vial over to James's bedside. "I made the cure for the mushrooms from your blood. It worked, but I need more blood for the centrifuge." James held out his arm. "It's like they were talking about two different people," said Graham.

"Hmm," said James absently.

"The you that's here now, the you that wants to find a cure, and then there's the maniac who invented the stuff that destroyed the world. They say you hurt people, that you—"

"Wait. Invented the stuff? I played my part, like anyone on the team — and hurt people?"

"When you were known as Tobias Davidson, you went mad and killed most of your team. You tried to kill Anika West, the woman who was pregnant with your daughter."

"I have never been known by that name. Yes, Anika was pregnant, but not with my child. I had Loralias before I worked for project Re-gen, Adder is my wife's maiden name. Who on earth told you I was Davidson?"

Graham thought back to his first days in Prospect Heath, excitedly gossiping about the war criminal imprisoned in their midst. "Jenna," Graham said quietly. "Jenna told me you were Dr Davidson, and Loralias was your estranged lovechild, conceived while you made monsters in an underground lab."

"And you befriended me?" James chuckled. "Wait, what happened to your hand?"

Graham tucked his stump behind his back. "Turns out, that I can heal well too, but I can't regenerate." He looked into the distance, his eyes slipping out of focus. "I'll get by just fine without it, my vines are more dexterous than I realised." He stood to walk out.

"Wait, Loralias, is she?" James asked a partial question, but Graham understood his meaning.

"Over there." Graham nodded to the figure in the other bed. "She hasn't woken up yet."

James looked longingly at his daughter. When he turned to ask Graham another question, he found him gone.

***

"What is all of this commotion about?" Saxon said, striding up to the cured Authority officers.

"You tell him," said Field with a grunt.

"Fine." Hatter sighed. "I was on guard duty when Jenna gave instructions to some of the other mushrooms, the ones she took with her. She told them that once they completed their mission, they needed to come back here to Prospect Heath, and destroy what's left of us."

Saxon smiled. Finally something he was good at. "Look lively boys and girls. We need to prepare for war."

***

Chris walked around Prospect Heath, with Lara on his arm. The civilians were uncomfortable with this at first, but he kept her under control. He was no longer a prisoner, and considering his ability, it was only a matter of time before they included him in all the most vital meetings.

Chris followed the sound of a pressure hose and looked over the barrier. In the car park, the last remnants of the fallen man and child were being washed away.

'Such a shame, if they had only taken the help I offered, they'd be alive. People will listen to me now. They will accept my help, for I am their hero.'

Chapter 49: Riley

"Like, for real," groaned Riley. "I mean for real. Are you seeing this crap?" The beach was swarming with Wailers. "How the hell am I supposed to sneak through that?" Riley watched Morsel take to the sky.

Entrée, the sleek bird of prey, sat on the shoulder pad that Riley had fashioned for him. "What do you mean you're leaving? Entrée, what the hell? Yes, the boat will have mice. You're afraid of water?" Riley paused and listened to the bird's clicks and squeaky throat grumbles. "So, your just gonna leave me?"

Riley glanced over at Terror. With his head between his legs, he was deep into a ball clean, and it was unlikely that he would let up soon.

"Show off," Tib, the neutered giant, growled.

"You're leaving me with them?" hissed Riley.

Entrée pulled some strands of Riley's hair through his beak and nuzzled into her cheek, then the bird of prey flew off Riley's shoulder into the night.

"I'm gonna miss you, feather-face."

Morsel returned. At least the sea bird wouldn't abandon her.

"Hypothermia? I don't even know what that word means — a cold, you're worried I'm going to catch a cold. News check, bird-brain, I'm worried that I will get ripped apart by a pack of hungry Wailers." Riley spun around, searching the sky. "Entrée? He's gone. Did you know he wasn't coming with us? Of course you did." Riley sighed. "Ok, I need a wetsuit. Are you guys good at swimming?"

"Oh, no," said Terror, "I don't do swimming. Never learnt to paddle on three legs."

"Strongest swimmer at the park, I can retrieve a stick from river, sea, or pond," said Tib. He squared his shoulders, tilted his head up, and glanced down snidely at Terror. "Shame you won't be able to come with us."

Riley ignored the continuing rivalry between them. "I'm not bad at it, not gold medallist or anything, but if this is our only option." Riley looked along the beachfront shops. "There, the scuba place, see? That should have what we need."

The scuba shop was far enough away from the Wailer gathering not to draw attention. Unlike every other beachfront store, this one hadn't been broken into. She would have to force her way in.

"What do you think, do I like, wrap my elbow and slam it into the glass? Do these shops have power? I'm not gonna like trip an alarm or something, right?"

Neither dog was equipped with the knowledge to answer her questions.

"Fine," she groaned. "Why couldn't they sell food or something useful, you know, so people would rob them?"

The glass was single paned and broke after a few of Riley's best strikes. She reached through, and finding the latch, she twisted it and opened the door. The glass crunched under her worn designer trainers.

"If I find a wetsuit, can you guys check for some kind of waterproof bag? Or maybe airtight containers?" said Riley.

Terror's tiny mouth stretched wide into a yawn. "What's my motivation?"

"Dude, all the food I have for you is in this bag. If it gets wet, you go hungry."

Tib started to growl, his hackles stood right up. It was a fearsome sight. He pounced past Riley. His feet skidded, making a clattering scratching noise, until they found traction on the tiled floor.

Preserved against the elements, in the locked shop, the zombie was still stable enough to stumble forward. Tib jumped up and knocked it down.

"Ew, Tib, don't put that in your mouth!" Riley recoiled.

Tib thrust it down again. This time its head smacked hard onto the floor. It didn't get up.

"Did you know that was in here?" Riley asked Terror.

The little dog was giving one of his fluffy ears a good scratch.

"You were asking him to find a bag," Tib growled. "Did you really think that tiny brain could hold more than one thought at once?"

Riley shook her head and found a good fitting wetsuit to change into. She sat on a bench away from the broken glass to put it on. Her trainers slipped back over her pink ankle socks. Instead of tucking the laces in the sides, she did them up tight enough to feel the pulse of her circulation.

Then, she transferred the contents of her bag into a new backpack, one which claimed to be waterproof. A cardboard label hung from a plastic loop, threaded through the zip. The man modelling the bag on the label was wading in chest high water with a waterfall crashing down on him.

"Come on." Riley scraped away the glass to make a path for them to walk on. She felt guilty for not doing that on entry.

Once they stepped outside of the darkened shop, it became clear that something had changed. Spotlights stretched over the sea and onto the pier.

Morsel flew down and perched on Riley's outstretched arm. "They're leaving? How? Crap, we need to get to the sea and swim to the pier without being eaten, but we need to do it quick."

Riley took the pack off her back and placed Terror in the top. She pulled the ripcord most of the way, so that just his head poked out. The shop next door sold bikes and camping gear. People had broken in for the camping stuff. Riley took a bike. There was enough of a hill to get up speed before the wheels slowed in the sand.

Terror whimpered on her back, Tib kept pace — taking giant bounds he could easily outrun the bike — and Morsel circled above.

Riley's legs ached. She pounded the pedals hard. When she could run quicker than the bike would travel on the beach, she leapt from it and started to run. The water was up to her chest before she registered how cold it was and let out a squeal. Riley saw the pier looked emptier than it had before she went into the shop. The window of opportunity for rescue was closing, and that spurred her on.

Waves slapped her around. If it wasn't for Morsel's cries from above, she would have been too disoriented to find the pier. Tib wasn't lying when he said he could swim. The Great Dane crossed Rottweiler, cut through the waves, tearing forward on muscle and determination. They had entered the surf some way off, now the pier was close.

A large shadow bobbed towards her. The flotsam had no momentum of its own — until it saw her. A spotlight glanced over her, but didn't linger. A flash of the monster was all she needed. It was large and misshapen. Its crocodile like snout was unhinged, the top half of its head flapped about with far too much ease. Riley took comfort, knowing that zombies can't swim, but inside of this damaged head was a confused mind, which recognised Riley, and he badly wanted to greet her. Brett knew how to swim, and though he had never done more than observe before, his desire to see Riley was influencing his mindless host. No longer just scanning through the radio waves, Brett was transmitting.

"Holy rolly polly! Is that thing coming for us? I am seeing this, right?"

Tib answered her in growl. He swam to her, put his head under her arm and strengthened her paddle. "Wait," gasped Riley in between face slaps of water. "The pier." Gasp. "Is that way."

"We're going to the people with the lights," barked Tib.

The people with the lights, he was trying for the rescue boats. Riley thought on this. *'Will they take a dog aboard with so many survivors desperate to get off the pier?'*

"Can you make the big boat?" asked Riley.

"Easy," Tib boasted.

Riley kept an arm over Tib. She paddled with her free arm and kicked her legs. The waves grew quieter as they ventured further from shore and the screams of desperation dimmed. There was this no-man's-land somewhere between the pier and the cruise ship. It was vast and all consuming. The dark waters raised and lowered them and they paddled harder. Terror yelped in the bag. He mouthed at Riley's head and came close to biting her whenever the water splashed in his face.

The boat was close now, a towering form sitting in the sea. The rising sun painted the sky behind it pink and purple. Wisps of golden clouds sat on the horizon with the Voyager Serene silhouetted against it.

When she reached the ship, a new problem arose. She could see no ladders or ropes to climb, just a smooth metal hull.

"Hello!" Riley yelled.

The sound of the lapping waves seemed louder now, like they were conspiring to drown her out. The repurposed cruise ship was huge, and she was insignificant by its side.

"You're too quiet," said Tib.

"Thanks for pointing out the obvious," Riley said through chattering teeth. Treading water wasn't as warming as swimming.

Tib began to bark. He had a mighty bark befitting a breed of his size; it bounced off of the boat and echoed across the sea.

"Who's down there," Captain Maylor shouted through his cupped hands.

"Riley, I swam from the shore, we like, request sanctuary, and a towel."

Captain Maylor leaned over the barrier. "Is that a seal swimming next to you?"

"It's my dog," yelled Riley.

"I don't think having a dog on board is a good idea."

"I totally promise to feed him and clean up after him." Terror gave a yip from her pack. "The small one, too."

Maylor took out a spyglass to get a better look at them. "The little one maybe, but that big one looks dangerous."

"Tib is not dangerous. Look, you know how some people developed weird abilities? Mine is the ability to communicate. Watch this. Tib, bark twice." Tib barked. Riley's teeth continued to chatter and Terror shivered uncontrollably. "We're freezing here, are you gonna let us up, or what."

"If you come aboard, you have to find a way to be useful," Maylor said. He tied a small life raft to a winch.

"Dude, I will mop the decks, make people walk the plank, just let me up."

The small raft plopped into the sea on Riley's right. She swam over and helped Tib in, before flopping in beside him. The crew winched the raft up. Maylor was waiting at the top to help her out.

"You can really speak to the dogs?" Maylor asked, giving Tib a wary glare. A torrent of wet dog smelling rain splattered around him as he shook off the sea water.

"Sure can," chimed Riley. Terror nipped her hand as she pulled him out of the bag. "Ow, Terror, don't do that."

"No," Terror growled, "*You* don't do that. I'm not luggage, nor am I a rat to drown."

Maylor watched the exchange. Riley was speaking in growls and yips, and the dog responded in kind. "Can you make them crap straight over the railing into the sea?" he asked.

Riley translated Maylor's request.

"I'll happily take a crap in that stupid hat he's wearing," Tib growled.

"I might teach them to use the toilet. It'd be less messy," said Riley.

"The first of the rescue boats are coming back," a crewman yelled.

"Excuse me," said Maylor. "I need to help with this."

They had set winches up, all along the starboard side. More of the small rafts that Riley had come up in were being launched overboard. Groups of six were brought up and unloaded, then the rafts were sent back down for more. Once the rescue boats were empty, they sped back towards the pier to gather more.

The whole atmosphere had changed. The refugees were screaming, crying. Crewmen in Authority uniform rushed around, trying to help, responding to requests for warmth and food and first aid. One woman was screaming for her lost child, and everyone just walked past her.

"Why are they ignoring her?" asked Riley. She watched for a while longer. One woman told her to calm down, but no one offered her comfort or solutions. Riley pushed through the crowd.

"Are you ok?" She reached out and held the trembling woman's hand.

"My son, he's six. We were separated on the pier. Everyone jostled for the boats. They pulled us this way and that. I keep asking for him, but no one understands."

"That's freakin' awful, man. I'll have a word, look after Terror, he likes a scratch behind the ear."

Riley found Captain Maylor in the crowd and wordlessly dragged him back to the woman.

"This Lady, sorry what was your name? Denemya, huh, that's an odd one, anyway Denemya has lost her little boy and no one is helping her. I want you to do something."

"You speak Conclese?" said Maylor.

"I got an F in my last oral, so what do you think?" said Riley. "So, she last saw him on the pier and I don't even wanna guess how many of your people just walked past her. Some random offered her a towel. She doesn't need a towel, she's lost her kid."

"Do me a favour, Riley, ask her for her son's name."

"Why don't you do it? She's sat right there."

"Humour me." Maylor smiled.

"Uh, fine. Denemya, what is your son called?" asked Riley.

"He's called Fleriyka. Flerk for short. I've been calling for him, but he's not answering," Denemya said.

"Right, but there's a lot of noisy people here. Maylor, what do you think?"

"Honestly," said Maylor, "other than *Maylor, what do you think,* I didn't understand a damn word."

"The kid answers to Flerk, she's been calling for him, but it's too noisy. How did you not get that?"

"Riley, this woman is speaking fluent Conclese. It would seem that your talent is not limited to animals."

Riley took a moment to absorb this. "But I'm terrible at Conclese. I flunked every exam, no ear for language, my teachers all said."

Maylor shrugged. "I don't know what to tell you, Riley, you're speaking it now." He held out his hand to Denemya. "Tell her we will go to the observation deck. We can use the megaphone to call for him, and if he's not here yet, we will have the best view from there as the rescue boats bring in more survivors."

Riley relayed this information to Denemya, and she thanked her profusely.

"You're coming too," said Maylor. "My multilingual officers are manning the rescue boats."

"Can my dogs come?"

"Yes." Maylor grinned. "Looks like we've found a way for you to be useful, without you making people walk the plank."

"While I'm in your good books, how do you feel about having a large seabird aboard?" Riley held out her padded arm and Morsel landed on it. She stuck out her tail, splattered the deck, and then ruffled her feathers.

Maylor sighed. "Two dogs, one bird, nothing else?"

"No, that's it."

"Fine, but you're responsible for cleaning up after that one too."

***

"That's my baby, praise the Lord of all, that's my baby." Tears of joy streamed down Denemya's face.

Flerk hadn't been on the second rescue trip, or the third. Riley had comforted the distraught woman when they said the fourth trip would be the last.

There he was, a tiny figure sat among the fierce fighting mutants that had held back the Wailer force. Riley ran with Denemya to the starboard side where the last survivors were being hauled aboard.

Riley watched the last boat being winched up. Her tummy fluttered at the sight of Ethan, but something about the scene stopped her from running to him. A young woman, Claire, Ethan had called her, stepped off the boat. She had a small round bump under her t-shirt, and a swelling on her face that had blackened her cheek and her eye. Ethan's bruising was severe enough that you could see it through his fur. They took a man Riley had never seen before off the boat by stretcher. Blood pooled under his nose and ears. His lip was swollen in a way that stopped his mouth from closing properly.

The man's words sent slithers of ice down Riley's spine as they carried him past her. "Riley," Brett mumbled. "I saw Riley in the surf with a dog at her side. She swam away from me."

Four burly Brutes stepped onboard last. Riley felt such unease. The weaker and smaller in their group were injured, the strongest looked unmarked.

Ethan cast his eyes down when he saw Riley. He didn't raise his head again in all the time she watched him, but he did put his hand in his pocket. Delving deep, past the Silver Dragon's balaclava, he felt for the bit of tapestry that Morsel had dropped for him, and rubbed it between his fingers.

Chapter 50: Lola

"What happened to the others," Sadie asked.

"Most of them were quiet from the start," said Digger. "Some of them, injured like me, made noise to begin with, but they fell silent, pretty quick."

Sadie tried not to over analyse all the times the ground beneath her feet had felt like something other than dirt or root.

"Should we..." Sadie's stomach lurched "... check them? Just in case someone else survived."

Digger shook his head. "No need. Why do you think I had the thermal imaging to hand?"

Sadie tried to process that horror of watching your friends, your colleagues, grow cold. The *Broken Child* used the thermal imaging reference to force her disappointment into Sadie's thoughts. If she had glowed hotter, or even if she had never seen, she would have been with a Wailer group by now.

Sadie pushed the *Child's* thoughts away. She had an urge to check, to see the warm outweighing the *Child's* selfish desire for the hot. She slipped the headgear on and looked back.

"Digger," she whispered.

"Yes, Sadie?"

"The forest behind us is lit up. Bright figures are advancing slowly."

"Shit. Are you sure?" Digger lowered his voice to match Sadie's whisper. "Can you see what they're doing?"

Sadie could do better than that, with the *Wailer Child's* insight. "They're flanking us, holding back and listening for now, trying to see if we might lead them to a larger group."

Digger looked down at his sliced leg, not that he could see it in the dark. It was only now that he noticed Sadie had a limp too. Running wasn't an option.

"Lord of all, it's not even like I can say we're close. I can get us to the river near the Stellar's house, but we need time to search for the boat."

They heard something in the distance; a growing thrum. The earth began to vibrate.

"Is that—?" Digger gasped.

"Yeah, it's Rapz," said Sadie. "Don't get too excited, he's not on our team anymore."

Digger had seen Rapz in action. The wave was about to hit. He grabbed Sadie and flung them both to the ground. The sound wave sped through the forest with the force of a percussive wind. Trees bent to its will, it hurled forest floor debris, and knocked the stalking Wailers down.

Sadie was quick to get up and drag Digger from the floor. They staggered on, each trying to put as little strain on their injuries as possible. The Wailers were not their only pursuers.

***

Torches lit up the jetty by the boathouse. The odd, "Shh," and, "Will you be quiet!" interspersed their constant mumbling. Luke smiled. They'd made it.

"Wait," gasped Kronic, "is that?"

"Oh, shit yeah," said Luke. "I completely forgot to mention. Felicity's back."

Kronic powered towards her.

"Stay off the jetty! Keep off the jetty!" Tyde yelled too late.

Kronic's foot went through the first slat. "Ah, fuck."

"I'm surrounded by idiots," Felicity moaned. She walked over to Kronic and grabbing his ankle with both hands, helped to guide his foot back through the hole.

"I knew you would come back." He tried to tone down his smile, but it stuck. It looked odd on a face that was usually so sullen. If there was a moment to be had between them, it was lost to Cleaver, who bounded to Kronic with her lead dragging behind her.

"Mum," said Kyan. "Where is she?" The air crackled around him.

"She's coming," said Luke. "I believe it." And he did, his gut had shifted, Sadie was alive and heading towards them.

In the distance Rapz's sound wave hit, it was far enough away that the Odd Blockers only felt a breeze.

"They're after Mum!" The air around Kyan crackled louder and tiny sparks fizzled in the air.

"Look," said Tyde, "we need to get Lola out of the shed and everyone on board. That will not be an easy task for you, big boy." Kronic raised an eyebrow at him. "Kyan, we're not abandoning your mum, she's heading here. We need the boat ready for when she arrives. How about you light up the night? Show her where to run."

***

"Run towards the light!" said Digger.

They couldn't run, but shuffled quickly. Wails erupted behind them, and a strange in unison war cry of the Mushroommen.

"I think they're fighting each other," said Sadie.

"Good for us if they are." Digger wheezed and cringed. The pain in his leg was becoming unbearable.

"Kyan keeps sending up flares. What do you think it means?"

"That they're getting impatient," said Digger. "At least we know where the boat is though." He was trying, he really was, but more and more of his momentum became reliant on Sadie.

A Wailer man lunged at the pair, hurtling Sadie to the ground. "Run!" Sadie screamed. "Get to the boat. Get help." Digger was capable of no such thing, but he did try to move.

The Wailer drew in close. His breath stank of carrion. But when his eyes met Sadie's, he paused. He put his face to her neck and drank in her scent. When he reached her eye level again, his aggression had gone. He sensed a kinship too. Sadie smiled.

The bullet tore through the Wailer's head — temple to temple. The light in those white eyes instantly darkened. "No," Sadie whimpered. She rolled as he fell toward her.

Lifting her head from the dirt Sadie saw Digger, with his Authority issued gun raised. Another bullet sped past Sadie. It clocked the Wailer behind her in its third eye. Sadie's blood lust resurfaced. "Move!" Digger yelled. Sadie scrambled to her feet and started after him.

Digger forced himself to run on his bum-leg. Shooting pains threatened to collapse him, but he kept going — and Sadie kept coming for him.

She was hyper focused. Drool started to collect in the corners of her mouth. The Wailers called behind her. Her brethren were following her in this hunt. The gap between them closed. Digger was almost within her grasp. A curled tree root hooked Sadie's toes and slipped her foot out of its shoe. She fumbled, grabbed the lost shoe, shoved it in her waistband, and resumed her sprint after Digger.

"Sadie, we're close, keep up," Digger yelled. He got a grunt in response.

The forest opened up into the short clearing of the river bank. Lola was lit up on the river. Digger had little left to give by the time he reached the jetty.

Sadie closed the gap. She collided with Digger with so much force, it threw him into the river. Sadie was a split second from following her prey into the water, when something crashed into her. Feet hooked her under the arms and she glided over the river. She looked up. Huge wings rode the updraft long enough to land them on Lola's deck.

The sight of Luke wasn't enough to snap her out of it.

"Warm blood. Devour. Devour," mumbled the Broken Wailer Child

"Mummy! Madmam miss you."
"Mum, your here!"

"Cat miss you too."

"Not our babies!" the Bitch screamed. "NEVER our babies." Her rage forced the Wailer side to recede.

"Mummy missed you too," said Sadie, pulling them both into a hug. She mimed, "Thank you," to Luke, and he blew her a kiss.

"I got a live one over here," Kronic called.

Kronic's strong hands scooped Digger out of the water. "Welcome to my dinghy."

Digger coughed up the wretched river water. "What is this?" Digger prodded and flicked the strange cup like float they were seated in.

"That would be polymer, the same stuff you lot use to retread your patrol car wheels. We couldn't risk me putting a hole in Lola."

"How did you—"

"Tyde, jack-of-all-trades," said Kronic. "You let him in to just about every building you've got, fixing things, building things, plumbing things, didn't ya? Big mistake, light fingered is our Tyde."

"Should've known," laughed Digger. "So, where are we going?"

"You are going onto Lola. They've got med supplies, might stop you bleeding everywhere."

Tyde winched the dinghy closer to the boat where Felicity helped Digger onboard.

"Hey, Digger," said Kronic. "I'm glad you made it. Come visit me anytime." Kronic could just make out Felicity in the dawning sun. "You too, Fliss, don't be a stranger." She raised an eyebrow at him, and then gave all her attention to her patient.

They were all relieved to be sailing away, but Sadie's emotions were mixed. She kissed the top of Madam's head and held her close. Her eyes focused on the sun kissed Eaves. There was a longing in her sparked a new with every distant Wailer call. It wasn't just her emotions that were split — it was her sense of belonging.

Great news!

If you liked this book and want more, you won't have long to wait. The Decaying Days trilogy is complete, and the next book is in the final polishing stages before release.

Please join Rachael Boucker's newsletter list to receive email updates on upcoming releases.

https://rachaelboucker.com/signup

Lightning Source UK Ltd.
Milton Keynes UK
UKHW011453221020
372042UK00001B/31